By Kris Tualla:

A Woman of Choice

A Prince of Norway

A Matter of Principle

Loving the Norseman

Loving the Knight

A Discreet Gentleman of Discovery

A Discreet Gentleman of Matrimony

A Discreet Gentleman of Consequence

LEAVING NORWAY

FINDING SOVEREIGNTY

*****

A PRIMER FOR
BEGINNING AUTHORS

BECOMING AN
AUTHORPRENEUR

FINDING SOVEREIGNTY

Kris Tualla

Finding Sovereignty is a work of fiction. Names, characters, places and incidents are products of the author's imagination or are used fictitiously and are not to be construed as real. Any resemblance to actual events, locales, organizations, or persons, living or dead, is entirely coincidental.

Published in the United States of America.

© 2012 by Kris Tualla

ISBN-13: 978-1480159419
ISBN-10: 1480159417

*This book is dedicated to the characters
who tell me about their lives.*

*They make me laugh,
and make me cry.*

And make me fall in love all over again.

PART ONE:
FINDING

CHAPTER ONE

Reid Hansen tried to open his eyes but something was holding them closed. He lifted his arm to remove the obstacle. Warm fingers and a soft palm stopped him.

"Let it be." The voice was soothing and female.

His hand was placed on his chest. The stranger's hand rested on top of it.

Reid's head throbbed with his pulse and his right leg ached. When he flexed his calf, a slice of searing pain slid up his thigh. Whatever happened to him, at least he still had a leg.

He searched his mind for an explanation, for the last thing he remembered. He knew he was in Philadelphia. He marched here with the New Jersey regiment as they headed south toward Williamsburg.

Reid stayed behind as an emissary to General Rochambeau and the French army, who were expected to arrive in Philadelphia the next day. He was directed to an encampment of Pennsylvania soldiers stationed in the city and housed at the docks on the Delaware River. He planned to spend the night with them.

He recalled being surprised to find a modest stockpile of munitions; Charleville muskets, several kegs of gun powder and a canon strapped to a huge caisson and aimed toward the river.

Something happened to me there.

The incident pranced around the edge of his thoughts but

wouldn't be reined in.

"Am I blind?" he blurted.

After a pause the voice replied, "No, the doctor doesn't think so."

Pauses generally did not portend good news. "My head hurts."

His unseen attendant turned his hand over and stroked his palm. It felt good. "You were concussed rather severely. Do you remember?"

No. "My leg?"

"A shard of metal. It left a deep gash, but a clean one. The metal was so hot that it cauterized the wound and you didn't bleed. Of course—" she turned his hand over and began to massage his wrist, "—once the doctor pulled it out, you bled. But he stitched up the gash and you should heal well."

He still didn't know about his eyes. He lifted his other hand slowly so he wouldn't be stopped again and laid his fingertips on the bandage.

She answered his tactile question. "The doctor put a salve on your eyes and he wants you to keep them covered for another couple of days."

Another couple of days. "How long have I been here?"

"This is the third day since they brought you in." She moved her massage to his other hand.

Reid had no idea why she did that, but her soft warmth and sure touch relaxed him. As long as her hand was on him, the burgeoning panic—caused by his blinded state and threatening to undo him at any moment—was kept somewhat at bay. He needed to keep talking to distract his tumbling thoughts from dragging him down into hysteria.

"Where am I?"

"My home. My parents have a large manor and we offered the lower parlor as an infirmary for American officers."

"What's your name?"

Another pause. "Call me Nurse."

"Do you know my name?"

"No."

He couldn't smile effectively with half of his face bandaged but he offered his free hand, holding it in the direction of her voice. "Reidar Magnus Hansen, Captain of the Massachusetts Militia."

She gave it a small shake. "You are Norwegian, are you not?"

That observation surprised Reid out of his self-focused contemplation. "American born, but of Norwegian parents. Why do you ask that?"

Reid thought he detected a smothered chuckle.

"Because you are speaking in Norse."

The soldier's jaw fell open. "*Jeg er?* I mean—I am? *Skitt*. Shit!" He waved the hand she wasn't holding. "I beg your pardon, miss. Apologies for my language."

Kirsten Sven laughed at that. "You are forgiven, Captain."

Captain Hansen stilled. "Wait—you understood me. And you answered in Norse."

"As incredible as it sounds, I am American born of Norwegian parents as well," she confessed. "And while I would love to sit with you longer, I do have others which require my attention."

She was amazed at how clearly she saw his mood change in the shift of his mouth. She wondered what his eyes looked like and how expressive they might be.

"Of course. I understand." He pulled his hand from hers and clasped them over his chest. "I'll just be waiting here, on this cot, if you need to find me."

The man had a sense of humor, that much was sure.

Kirsten stood and walked through the otherwise empty parlor of the Sven home. She needed to get away from Captain Hansen and assess this odd twist of events. Finding servants at every turn, she lifted her skirt and hurried up the stairs to the private rooms.

"Kirsten?" Her mother's voice snared her and Kirsten halted, caught in its tether.

She clenched her fists and drew a calming breath. "Yes, *mamma?*"

"Is anything amiss?"

Kirsten walked to her mother's doorway. "Not at all. In fact, I have very interesting information about the injured soldier."

"Oh?" Marit Sven looked up from her correspondence. Her pale blonde hair had nearly completed its transition to white, but her eyes were as dark blue as always. "Is he awake finally?"

"He is," Kirsten answered without entering. "And it turns out, he's of Norwegian descent."

Her mother looked surprised. "He is? How did you find this out?"

Kirsten shook out her skirt. "When he awoke, he was speaking Norse."

"Hm. How odd," Marit said as she turned back to her letters. "Where are you off to?"

Kirsten took a step back. "I only wanted to lie down a bit before supper."

Her mother gave a look over her shoulder. "You have been sitting too long with that soldier, haven't you?"

"It's not that. I didn't sleep well last night. The thunder woke me and I couldn't get back to sleep," she lied.

Marit nodded. "I'll be sure to rouse you in time to prepare for supper. We are having guests."

Kirsten gave her mother a compliant grin. "Thank you, *mamma*."

She turned and walked to her room, careful not to draw any more attention. She closed the door and flopped on her back on the bed.

Kirsten wasn't given to lying as a rule, but she had told two fabrications in the last five minutes.

The first was to the officer lying in the room below. In truth, he was the only injured soldier in the house, a fact he was certain to discover in short order now that he was awake. The explosion which injured him had claimed the life of five foot soldiers. Two other officers caught in the debacle weren't hurt as severely as he and didn't require lying-in.

Captain Hansen was unconscious when they carried him to her home, and only today had said anything coherent.

And in Norse. Kirsten smiled. That was quite a surprise.

Unlike what she told her mother, she had been spending all of her free hours beside the injured man. Something about him tugged at her—and not, she told herself, because he was the only distraction from the boredom of life in a country long at war. He seemed interesting.

He was quite tall to begin with. Kirsten had to set crates at the end of his cot for his feet to rest on. His thick, straight hair hovered between blond and light brown, with sun-streaks of polished brass glinting in her lamp's light. Untied, it hung just below his shoulders. On his first night here she carefully brushed out the tangles and detritus of the explosion, and then plaited it out of the way.

When he spoke today, his voice was deep and smooth, like a far-off storm on a heavy summer night. She loved hearing her parents' native language tripping off his tongue, and wondered if he had ever been to Norway.

I'll ask him when we speak next.

Kirsten turned over and applied herself to her nap. The soldier hovered in her thoughts and she wondered if she would dream of him.

She truly couldn't wait to see his eyes.

Reid listened to the sounds of the household, evaluating what actions were taking place. Any diversion from the throbbing in his head and thigh was highly welcomed. Because he could do nothing but lie on this negligibly comfortable cot, the beat of his pulse as it surged past his injuries kept pulling his attention. He was afraid it might soon make him crazy. Plus the fear he might be blinded.

Don't think about that.

When he listened, Reid heard the muffled sound of china plates being set on a cloth-covered table. The zing of silver utensils rubbing together accompanied the settings, as did the snap of linen napkins. He wondered if the formality was commonplace, or if the family was expecting guests.

He also listened for signs of other injured men, supposedly ensconced nearby. He heard nothing but silence and the tick of a clock. He couldn't smell dirty uniforms, other than his own long-familiar aroma, nor could he detect the stench of fleshly injuries. No breathing, no shifting on cots, no low conversation.

His solitude wasn't a surprise, though. Philadelphia hadn't seen any battle for years, and most of the active warfare had moved south into Virginia and the Carolinas. Reid was glad that the family still took him in, as apparently he had been hit fairly hard.

By the explosion.

There had been an explosion. On the dock. Something set off

the powder.

Reid sighed and shifted his weight on the cot trying to lessen his pain. That was all he could remember. He needed another track for his musings before he let this lack of memory deepen his frustration even further.

Why would his nurse claim to have others to attend to when clearly he was the only man there? And why wouldn't she tell him her name?

Perhaps she was young and had been instructed to keep her distance from the soldiers who received comfort there. It was possible she was told to stay away completely and was disobeying parental orders.

No, that didn't feel right.

Her touch on his hands bespoke someone with experience at nursing. Philadelphia was attacked five years earlier, so she may have been treating officers for half a decade. She might be older than he; a spinster in her thirties.

Reid concentrated on taking deep and regular breaths to assuage the pounding in his head. He felt for the bandage around his thigh and discovered that his trouser leg was cut away. He began a physical inventory of his condition.

Shirt. No jacket. No boots. Small clothes. Half his pants.

Head hit, hard. Eyes—burned? Thigh gashed. No other injuries.

Hair brushed and plaited.

Reid smiled. *Thank you, nurse.*

The exhaustive aftermath of his injuries, combined with the recollection of her soothing voice, slowly lulled him back to sleep.

Kirsten changed into a dinner gown with her maid's help, waited with feigned patience while her hair was done up, and then tiptoed barefooted past her parent's bedroom to avoid detection. She hurried down the stairs and into the parlor where her lone patient was housed.

Captain Hansen was sitting up.

He turned toward her when she stopped in the doorway. "Nurse?"

"How did you know I was here?" she asked, padding across the carpet.

"I heard the swishing of your gown," he answered. "And I smelled your odd perfume, if you will forgive me for saying that."

Kirsten sat on the chair she had left next to his cot. "I forgive you. My mother calls it odd, as well. She says cloves are too masculine for a lady and will turn suitors away."

His lips twitched. "Is it working?"

A decidedly unladylike laugh burst from her. Kirsten clapped a hand over her mouth and looked toward the door. No one was in sight.

"Your sense of humor is going to get me into trouble," she accused and began to work her feet into her slippers.

"You are not married, then," he ventured.

Captain Hansen was leading her into awkward territory and she needed to divert him. "I am not. Are you?"

The query bordered on outright rudeness; as soon as it was out of her mouth, Kirsten wanted to pull it back. However the soldier didn't seem to be put off by her direct question, which was a relief.

"No. I have been at war these last eight years," he replied.

"Eight? This is seventeen-eighty-one. Have you forgotten your arithmetic?" she teased, still fiddling with her shoes.

"Boston was under siege long before the Declaration was made in seventy-six. Would you like some tea? We have a harbor full," he teased back.

"Oh. Yes. I—I was out of the country for some time and forgot." Kirsten felt her face flush and was glad he couldn't see her. She sat up straight and changed the conversation once more. "Have you ever been to Norway?"

The captain tilted his head. "Am I still confused by the influence of my injuries, or are you changing subjects again?"

Her defensive hackles rose. "I'm only making polite conversation."

"By demanding to know if I am married?" Hansen chuckled. "Be careful, Nurse. I *like* cloves."

Kirsten's jaw fell open.

Hansen's hand shot toward her and landed on her arm. His fingers closed above her elbow. "I apologize for that! It was far ruder of me to point out your bluntness, than it was for you to be blunt in the first place."

"Well, yes, I—"

"You see," he interrupted. "I find that without being able to see your face, I cannot judge your mood. Please forgive me and attribute these grievous social failures to my recent troubles, I beg of you."

Captain Hansen was certainly the most unusual man she had ever conversed with. That wasn't necessarily a bad thing. Flocks of bland suitors, past and present, flew through her awareness chased by this odd bird.

"Kirsten," she murmured.

The lips beneath the bandage curled upward. "Call me Reid."

CHAPTER TWO

"**K**irsten? Darling? What are you doing in here?" The woman's endearment couldn't hide the irritation that colored her tone. She was obviously displeased with his nurse.

It was interesting how not being able to see made other aspects so clear.

Reid let go of Kirsten's arm as she moved to stand, bemused by his own forward behavior toward her. As much as he couldn't see her, he felt like she couldn't see him. He needed to remember that she absolutely could, and not step too far over any acceptable lines.

"*Mamma*, come meet Captain Reidar Hansen," Kirsten said.

More swishing fabric approached him. He held out his hand. "Pardon me for not standing. I would if I could."

A gloved hand landed in his. He pressed it to his lips. "Are you the one I must thank for the aid I am receiving?"

"My husband and I are honored to be of assistance to those brave souls fighting King George's oppression," she deflected. "*Jeg stoler du føler deg bedre?*" I trust you are feeling better?

Reid frowned; was this some sort of test?

"*Egentlig føler jeg forferdelig.*" Actually, I feel horrible, he began. "*Hodet mitt er pounding, min lår er bankende, og jeg kan ikke se noe med disse bandasjer på.*" My head is pounding, my thigh is throbbing, and I can't see anything with these bandages on.

"But I sincerely appreciate your enquiry, my lady. Thank you," he finished in English.

Silence resounded from the second skirt. He relinquished her hand.

"You should lie back down," Kirsten chided. "Have you had your supper?"

"I was given coffee and biscuits just after the clock chimed five," he said. "Was that my supper?"

As if to object, his belly rumbled in a most conspicuous manner. The aromas from the family's coming meal had set his mouth to watering an hour ago, and he prayed there was more substantial sustenance heading in his direction.

"Of course not!" Kirsten declared. He imagined a glare from daughter to mother. "I'll have one of the valets assist you."

"Thank you, again, for your kindness," he offered. "Might I ask another indulgence?"

"What is that?" the mother—whose name was not yet mentioned—asked crisply.

Reid gave an apologetic shrug. "I am not in any condition for polite company. Would it be possible to bathe and procure clean clothes from my pack?"

"We don't have your pack," Kirsten said softly. "It must have been lost in the fire."

There was a fire?

"You may borrow one of my husband's shirts while yours is laundered," the older voice conceded.

"And trousers? Mine have been destroyed, I'm afraid." He had to ask, fairly certain that prancing about in only a shirt with his privates banging about would not go over well.

"Yes. I'll have the valet see to *all* of your requests." The fabric swished away. "Come along, Kirsten. Our guests should arrive at any moment."

An ungloved hand squeezed his before all footsteps left the room. The warm scent of cloves, however, remained behind.

✳ ✳ ✳

Kirsten counted to ten—twice—before she addressed her mother. "Why were you so short with him?" she whispered loudly as they entered the formal drawing room.

Marit Christiansen sank into a chair and considered her daughter somberly. "I can see your interest in him, Kirsten. This is not an appropriate connection, as you are well aware."

Kirsten groaned and took a seat facing her mother. "You sent me to Norway when the Declaration was signed, where I spent three years in the questionable safety of your family without making an appropriate connection. It's time to give up the idea, *Mamma*."

"I cannot. You have a responsibility as my daughter," her mother reminded her.

Kirsten shook her head. "You ask too much."

Marit waved her hand around the luxuriously appointed room. "And you have gained far too much to be so cavalier about your heritage."

Kirsten bit her lips together, quelling the rebellion which bubbled too close to the surface. She accepted a glass of wine from one of their liveried servants and took a calming sip before attempting to speak again. The cannonball she was about to launch was a big one.

"I'm already twenty-six, *Mamma*. And I have decided not to marry. Ever."

Marit stared at her daughter. "Don't tease. It's in bad form."

Kirsten shook her head. She could barely summon the courage to look her mother in the eye. "I'm not teasing. The remaining prospects are boys barely shaving, or men too decrepit to fight."

Her mother's smile resembled a cat leaping after a cockatoo. "Then I expect tonight's events will give you renewed hope."

Kirsten glared at her mother, incredulous at the woman's persistence. "Is this another suitor you have dug up? Is that who our guest is?"

"And his father. He is a very successful lawyer—and of Danish descent," her mother chirped.

"He? Or his father?" Kirsten grumbled. "Or are both men available? Perhaps we could share."

A jolt of remembered pain shook her core; her jest was extremely ill-considered. She gulped the remainder of her wine.

"Watch yourself *datter*," her mother warned.

Kirsten stood and crossed to her mother's chair. She fell to her knees and clasped her mother's hand. "Please, *Mamma*. Don't do this to me. I don't wish to marry anyone."

Marit's expression was kind but firm. "You are the only living child your father and I were blessed with. If you don't marry and have children of your own, then all that I have will be lost to us."

Kirsten wanted to say she didn't care, yet she knew how deeply that statement would hurt her mother. She held her words in check, though their silence made them no less true.

"Try to enjoy our dinner. You may be pleasantly surprised," Marit urged.

Kirsten gave her a weak smile, abandoning the battle for tonight. "Yes, *Mamma*."

Henrik Sven strode into the room. His graying hair was powdered and tied back, and he was neatly dressed in dark green silk. He shot a surprised look at Kirsten on the floor.

"Get up, girl! I saw the carriage coming up the drive!" he enthused. He clapped his hands together. "I'm glad they are on time. I'm starving!"

✳ ✳ ✳

"Good evening, sir. My name is Horace and I'll be assisting you with your toilette," a middle-aged voice finally said, following a prolonged rustle of unrecognizable activity.

"Thank you, Horace," Reid said in its direction. "I am at quite a disadvantage as you can see. Because, of course, I can't."

"Yes, sir." Reid detected the smile in the valet's tone. "I have placed a screen for your privacy between your bed and the door. There is a small stool for you to rest on as you wash, and oiled cloth beneath it to protect the carpet from water. Shall I help you off the cot?"

"Yes, please." Reid swung his feet to the ground, wincing when his right leg bent. "I can't stand on this leg as yet," he said indicating the bandage.

"If you can stand on the one good leg, I have brought a footman, George, to assist you. Lean on him, he's quite sturdy," Horace instructed.

After some highly unaccustomed awkwardness on his part, Reid managed to gain his feet. Or rather, his foot. Horace began to undress him while George faithfully kept him upright and balanced. Once he was stripped to his bare skin, Reid lowered himself to the stool with George's guidance. Another set of footsteps carried away his clothes. How many men were required to make him presentable, he wondered.

"Would you like a shave?" Horace asked.

That sounded like heaven. "I would very much like a shave," Reid answered.

He tilted his chin upward and submitted to the soothing routine. Hot towel. Lathered soap. A razor sliding over his skin. The scratchy sound of bristles being harvested. Horace lifted the bottom edge of Reid's bandage and scraped away the beard trapped beneath. Another hot towel appeared when he finished.

Reid wiped his cheeks and jaw clean and handed the cooled towel to a grasping hand. He ran his fingers over his smooth skin. He was starting to feel human again. Horace splashed water nearby and placed a dripping cloth in Reid's hand.

"Wash yourself freely, sir, and remember the carpet is protected," he said. "The water is by your right hand and George, behind you, has the soap."

Reid felt for the bucket. He used the cloth to wet his skin and then held out his palm for the soap. Bit by bit he washed himself, top to bottom and parts tucked between. Though he tried to keep his movements corralled, the disorientation of his blinded state grew stronger the more he moved. He began to feel a little nauseous. Perhaps his dinner would cure him.

"Towel?" he asked.

Dry linens were draped over his shoulder. Reid scrubbed his skin dry, eager to regain his cot. The swish of fabric and the patting of his mattress told him that George was remaking his pallet. Clean sheets were a lot to hope for, but Reid thought himself an optimist. *Usually*.

"I have a shirt for you," Horace said. "Allow me?"

Reid held up his arms and Horace dropped the garment over his head.

"Small clothes." The valet pressed the undergarment into Reid's hand.

Reid managed to get it on, though his right thigh burned its protest when his leg was forced to bend again.

"And breeches. I thought they would be more comfortable than trousers. Let me assist you." Horace slid the legs of the shorter pants over Reid's feet.

He and George helped Reid to stand, Reid pulled the breeches to his hips, and Horace fastened the flies. Reid grew lightheaded; the effort of standing after sitting unsupported for an extended amount of activity had drained him.

"Easy, sir," Horace warned. "Let's get you back to bed, shall we?"

Relief flushed Reid's frame once he stretched out on the cot. The sheets were clean and smelled like an outdoor breeze. The pillows were nicely fluffed. His main concern, however, was food.

"I'm hungry," he croaked.

"Yes, sir," Horace replied. "George is going to clean up your bath and I'll send in your tray immediately after."

Reid sighed his contentment. Being clean and wearing clean clothes were luxuries he so seldom enjoyed as a soldier. "Thank you, Horace. And thank you, George."

"You're welcome, sir," they answered in tandem.

✷ ✷ ✷

Kirsten smiled politely at Halvor Nilsen across the dinner table. She had to admit that this son of a lawyer—for it was indeed the father who was successful—had no visible faults at first meeting. He was easy to look at, trim and well groomed, and about six feet tall to Captain Hansen's six-and-a-half or thereabouts.

Stop it.

"I'm sorry, Mister Nilsen, what did you ask me?" she asked when she realized he was staring at her expectantly.

"Please, call me Halvor," he said with a smile. "I asked what sort of activities occupy your time."

"My daughter is active in service to the community," Marit answered before Kirsten could speak. "She has a tender heart when it comes to the less fortunate among us."

"A Christian attitude is very important in those of higher rank," *Pappa* Nilsen approved.

Halvor returned his regard to Kirsten. "What sort of service, Miss Sven?"

"In actuality, Haldor—"

"Halvor," he corrected.

Kirsten gave him a small nod. "I am currently acting as nurse for an injured soldier."

Halvor's brows lifted in surprise. "How, uh... noble. Where is this soldier being cared for?"

"In the parlor." Kirsten sliced her roasted beef.

"Here in the house?" Mister Nilsen blurted.

"We began the practice back in seventy-seven, when Philadelphia was attacked," Henrik explained. "We gave over the parlor for the treatment and recuperation of wounded American officers."

"The numbers have dwindled as the fighting has moved to other areas," Marit added. "And Kirsten was in Denmark and Norway for most of that time."

Halvor appeared relieved. "How long were you in Denmark?"

Kirsten held up one finger in a silent request for a moment's grace as she chewed her meat. Halvor waited, unmoving. She swallowed and took a sip of wine before she spoke.

"I was sent there in 1776 after the Declaration was signed."

Halvor relaxed as the conversation seemed less precarious. "And how did you find it there?"

Kirsten rested her hands in her lap. "To be honest, Hallvard—"

"Halvor," he corrected again. The color in his cheeks heightened.

"I was very homesick for Pennsylvania." She gave a little shrug. "I am an American in my heart, it would seem."

"She did return earlier than we had hoped," Henrik said. He laid a hand over Kirsten's. "Though I confess, in spite of the dangerous climate here I was quite happy to see my daughter's face across my breakfast table once more."

Kirsten leaned toward Halvor. "I had been gone three years. That was quite enough for me."

"And yet you are currently housing an injured officer?" Nilsen pressed.

Kirsten saw her mother's irritation at the man's persistence displayed in the set of her mouth.

"There was an unfortunate explosion. The man was carried to our home out of habit." Marit indicated the decanter with a flourish. "Would you care for more wine?"

Nilsen nodded. "Yes, thank you. It's a lovely vintage."

A servant stepped forward to pour.

"Would you care for more wine as well, Hallfred?" Kirsten

offered.

"Hal-*vor*," he growled.

"The captain is on the path to recovery," Henrik informed their guests. "Soon he'll be back to fighting those damned British, I assure you."

"And I intend to do all that I can to ease the poor man's suffering and speed his recovery, I promise you that." Kirsten lifted her wine glass. "I give you American soldiers and their officers."

A frown flickered over her mother's brow. The unacceptability of Kirsten offering the salute deepened a crease in Marit's forehead, one Kirsten recognized as of her making. Glasses clinked, and wine was sipped even so.

"I assume you are adequately chaperoned in your service to the man," Nilsen posited. "A family of such high standing as yours would certainly hold to propriety."

"The door to the parlor remains open, if that's what you are asking," Kirsten stated. She gave him an innocent look and forked a bite of beans.

Halvor frowned. "You are alone with the man?"

Kirsten covered her mouth with her hand and laughed. "He's quite harmless in his current situation, I assure you. I've spent hours by his side, so I know."

"I'm not certain that I approve," Halvor declared, looking like he was about to detonate.

Marit's mouth opened and closed. She glared at Kirsten and huffed air out her nose like an angry horse. She looked to her husband but Henrik was no help; he only stared at Kirsten as if she had grown a second nose.

Kirsten gave everyone at the table the sweetest, most naïve smile she could conjure. Her gaze landed on Halvor and rested there. He smiled cautiously in return.

"Do you like cloves, Halvdan?"

The man's fist hit the table hard, rattling silverware on the china and splashing wine in the goblets.

"HAL-*VOR!*"

CHAPTER THREE

Reid was laughing so hard he was in danger of wetting himself. He curled on his side while carefully keeping his right leg straight, and struggled to not make any sounds. The dining room was close enough to the parlor that Reid could hear the dinner conversation, and he found Kirsten's sabotage of her mother's obvious matchmaking unspeakably comical.

"Hal-VOR!" he wheezed quietly. "Å *min Gud!*"

His eyes watered with his hilarity, but the bandages kept him from being able to wipe them. If he was honest, though the tears stung a bit, they felt good.

After George had cleaned up the mess of his bath, a maid named Elsa helped Reid eat his supper—a situation which was more than a mite humiliating. Reid was far too hungry, however, to risk losing any of his food or soil his clean shirt through blind pride, so he allowed the girl to feed him the very palatable stew. At least he was able to hold his own mug of ale.

Even sightless he could get that particular liquid to his mouth.

The earlier knock on the front door drew his attention away from his meal. Reid heard several polite and unmistakably male voices. The voices moved away, and remained unintelligible through the rest of Reid's meal. But while Elsa was clearing away his dishes, the dinner group moved to the dining room.

Reid settled back onto his cot, then, for an evening of shameless eavesdropping under the assumption that he would be at the table if he was of sufficient health. Everyone speaking was polite and none of the discussion concerned subjects with any weight. Reid found himself dozing off, lulled by the monotonous conversation, his soothing bath, and a full belly.

But when Kirsten called Halvor by the wrong name—repeatedly—he began to snicker. Obviously she was doing it intentionally; the lady was clearly intelligent enough to remember a name. The more variations she found, the more Reid chuckled. And when the man lost his composure, Reid lost his as well, though in an entirely different way.

"George!" he called out.

Reid needed a chamber pot and he needed it now. He still laughed and he heard the mirth in his own tone. "George? Can you give me a hand?"

"Reid?" Kirsten inquired from inside the parlor. "Is something amiss?"

"You can't help me with this one, Nurse," Reid warned, though he still laughed. "Will you summon George?"

"Of course," she replied. Reid heard the pique in her tone.

"Yes, sir?" George asked. Reid heard his footsteps approach.

"Chamber pot?" Reid croaked.

"Yes sir." The sound of the screen being dragged on the carpet preceded George's grip on Reid arm.

Reid sat up, turned, and set his feet on the ground. He unfastened his flies. George guided his hands to the edges of the crockery receptacle. Reid relieved himself into the pot.

"Ah, thank you, George," Reid said.

"I'll empty the pot and place it under your cot, sir," he replied, handing Reid a wet cloth.

He wiped his hands and held out the cloth. "Thank you again."

Reid fastened his breeches and laid back down. Soon the scramble of footsteps on a hard surface—stone? marble?—proclaimed the end of the social portion of the evening. Mumbled appreciation for the invitation and the hosts' hospitality echoed in the entry. If Reid was a betting man, he would wager on fireworks exploding any moment, and wondered if he would be lucky enough to hear the blast. Anything to break the monotony of his weakened condition.

"I beg you, don't say anything," Kirsten beseeched. Her voice faded as she continued. "I know that was mean of me, but I want you to please stop trying to marry me off."

"If you continue to behave in such a contrary manner, I don't believe that will be a problem," her mother snapped. "Do you understand how humiliating that was for your father and I?"

The voices dissolved into wisps and the meager display ended.

Reid rolled on his side.

He wondered why Kirsten was opposed to marriage. Perhaps because the prospects were slim, considering that the able men in this country had been at war with England for so many years. America's population was a slapdash conglomeration of immigrants from Europe. Did her parents hope for her to marry a Dane or a Norseman? That might be the real reason she was sent overseas, not to escape the officially declared war.

There are damn few of us *here* to choose from, he mused.

Kirsten was obviously a willful woman. Reid didn't know her age, but judging by her speech he now thought she was probably in her twenties. He assumed she was reasonably attractive, but until the bandages were removed he couldn't know for certain.

He prayed that when the bandages were removed that he *would* be able to know. The prospect of being blind worried him mightily; he had no idea how he would manage if that proved to be his fate. At this point, he planned to rejoin an army regiment and continue his career, but a sightless soldier was a useless soldier.

This was a path of consideration that was certain to take him nowhere good. Reid heaved a deep sigh, turned to his other side, and tried to bore himself to sleep.

☆ ☆ ☆

Kirsten opened her bedroom door slowly. She left her chamber and snuck past her parents' room, assured by her father's sonorous rumbles and her mother's soft counterpoint that they both slept soundly. She descended the carpeted staircase in the dark, her way lit only by thin slices of moonlight through the windows.

This wasn't a challenge. Kirsten was born in this huge house and could find her way flawlessly with her eyes closed. She tried that sometimes to amuse herself.

Single children did not have ready playmates.

She knew where she was heading, but hadn't actually

acknowledged her destination. She felt a bit like a moth flying toward a flame. The dangers lurking in the firelight compelled her to approach nonetheless.

This evening when she heard him call out for George, she hurried to the parlor afraid that something had happened. She wasn't prepared for his transformation. Clean and shaved, his full lips proved soft and expressive. A strong jaw dominated the bottom half of his face. His hair was still plaited, though it was coming loose. Her father's shirt was a bit too small and the fabric hugged his chest. The snug breeches rode low on his hips and were nearly indecent.

Kirsten's heart thumped very disconcertingly at the sight. And at its recollection.

Enough.

When she reached the open parlor door, she stopped and listened. Reid's breathing was steady. In the dim light she could see that he was lying on his back, and wondered why he didn't snore.

"Kirsten?" he whispered.

The soft sibilant sound sent lightning through her frame. For a moment she thought to flee. Or remain still and silent until he fell asleep. But if she did either, she had to wonder why she came to his door in the first place.

"Did I wake you?" she whispered back, knowing that she had not.

"No, I can't sleep." He sat up and swung his feet to the floor, his right leg held straighter than his left. "I'm glad for the company."

Kirsten stepped closer. She had no slippers on and wore only her nightgown. Her hair was loose, hanging freely over her shoulders. If anyone in the household caught her in this man's presence in such a state of dishabille, the scandal would ruin her.

Well that's a thought.

But Reid's eyes were bandaged. He couldn't see her lacy cotton gown, her carelessly wanton hair, or her bare feet. As far as he knew, she was wrapped up like a sausage.

"Did you hear me, or smell me?" she asked, taking her seat beside his cot.

He huffed a quiet chuckle. "Both. I hoped I wasn't imagining it."

"What's keeping you awake?" she asked, intentionally directing the conversation away from her own restless state. "Are you in much pain?"

Reid faced her. The thick white bandage over his eyes made him eerily odd-looking in the darkened room. "The pain is there, yes. But it seems that I have been sleeping quite a lot of late. I cannot convince my mind or my body to continue at this point."

"I'd offer you a book," Kirsten teased. "But then I'd have to stay up and read it to you."

Reid smiled at her jest. "The clock struck twice not long ago. What has destroyed your slumber?"

What indeed. "I behaved badly this evening. My situation weighs on me," she confessed.

"What situation is that?" he asked gently.

Kirsten hummed a sad sigh. "My parents want me to marry, and they keep parading me in front of men they find suitable."

Reid spread his hands. "That's not an unusual practice. Why does it distress you so?"

"Let me ask you a question," she deflected. "Why is it so important for a woman to marry?"

Reid tilted his head. "So she's taken care of, I suppose."

"Then it's a financial arrangement," she observed.

"Most often," he conceded. "Marriage hopes for an heir to assure the passage of wealth, lands and titles. In exchange, the woman's needs are seen to for her lifetime."

"Under perfect circumstances," Kirsten amended.

His shoulders lifted and fell. "Yes, under perfect circumstances."

She leaned closer to him and lowered her voice. "You can't see this yet," she began.

Reid's chin lifted when she said *yet*, as if to recoil from the opposite possibility. Kirsten caught her breath, then continued.

"This house is enormous. My parents are very wealthy." For a beat she wondered if she was revealing too much. And yet her point could not be made unless she finished. "And I am an only child."

"Ah. I see," Reid murmured.

"I will never need to worry about money for the rest of my life."

That statement was most definitely too revealing. Kirsten

leaned back away from him, as if by doing so she could pull back the words. Something about talking to this stranger, who couldn't see her, made her feel safer than she probably should.

She was sitting here nearly naked, after all. That wasn't wise.

Reid was quiet. Kirsten girded herself for his next words, expecting the man's response to be in some way either cajoling or chastising.

"Tell me about Norway."

For a moment she didn't understand his request. "What?"

"I heard you say you were sent to Denmark and Norway in 1776," he said. "I've never been there. What's it like?"

Kirsten's mind scrambled past the responses she expected from him; through the pain where his question dragged her; and toward a carefully crafted answer.

"You heard me?" she stalled.

His lips twisted in contrition. "I could hear the dinner conversation from here."

Kirsten gasped at the newest split in their conversation. Her cheeks were set afire. "Oh! I'm so embarrassed!"

Reid put up a hand as if to stop her. "Don't be. I haven't laughed that hard in—well—I cannot recall how long."

She was tossed off-balance yet again. She had never met a man so completely confounding. "My rude behavior made you laugh. I don't know how to respond to that."

Reid began to snigger. "Every time you called him a different name, I laughed harder. That's why I called for George. I was afraid I might wet myself."

Judging by the sudden twist of Reid's head, he had just divulged more than *he* intended. "Forgive me, Kirsten. That was quite crass."

She gave him a smile he couldn't see and laid her hand over his. "Whether for good or bad, it would seem we bring out the honesty in each other."

"It's because we cannot look each other in the eye, I think," he theorized. "To me you are only a spice-scented apparition with a warm touch and delightful voice. It's easy to be bluntly honest under those circumstances."

That was another shocking consideration. "You don't know what I look like…"

He sobered. "I do not. I can't even judge your age."

"I'm twenty-six," she stated before she had time to think better of it.

"And I'm thirty-one," he replied. "I have been at war since just before I turned twenty-three."

"Were you educated?" she asked, suddenly curious to know more about the man.

"Harvard. I studied engineering and architecture like my father. He went to Oxford."

Another surprise. "In England?"

Reid's chin lifted again. "Is there another one?"

"No, I—I don't believe so," she stammered, feeling another blush blooming and glad he couldn't see it.

"That was before he came to America. He came here to build things," Reid explained. "As for myself, King George's repeated abuses in Massachusetts redirected my path."

"What will you do after the war is over?" she asked softly.

"If I'm not blind?" he qualified in a sardonic tone.

She shook her head, another useless response like the smile. "You won't be. The doctor was quite confident."

Reid heaved a sigh which Kirsten recognized as resolve. "I don't know what I'll do. Some days I feel like we'll be fighting forever."

For some reason she ached to raise his hopes. "Might you work with your father?" she suggested.

He shook his head, a useful response in her case. "I think I'll leave that to one of my brothers. I've lost interest."

"How many brothers do you have?" she probed.

"Three. And three sisters. All younger than me," he answered with a grin. "My father made good use of his training—he was always expanding the house."

Understanding dawned as bright as a summer day. "Did any of you make it to Norway?"

"No. My mother said she offered to take me when I refused to be born, but six more children and the war changed that."

Kirsten slapped her forehead at his continuing stream of odd statements. "You refused to be born? What does that mean?"

Reid laughed. "Apparently she was trying to push me out, but until she promised to teach me Norse, and perhaps take me to

Norway, I wouldn't budge."

Kirsten was fascinated. "And when she did?"

"I practically jumped out, or so she claims. *Som du vet, holdt hun en av sine løfter!*" As you know, she kept one of her promises!

"Reid Hansen, you are certainly one of the most unexpected men I have ever met," she declared. "I cannot imagine what you will say next."

"Tell me about Norway," he repeated. "I really want to know."

CHAPTER FOUR

He heard the creak of her chair as Kirsten shifted in her seat. "It's beautiful. Spectacular. Unlike anyplace I have seen on this continent," she responded after a pause.

Reid marked her hesitation and wondered what she wasn't saying. "Describe it so I can see it," he prompted.

"Well... First of all, the coastline is very jagged with outcroppings of rocks and inlets everywhere," she said slowly.

"Those are the fjords?" he asked.

"Oh no, the fjords are wide as ten rivers or more and go inland for miles. They are unimaginably deep, and fill the valleys between huge mountains which are so steep they go nearly straight up."

She shifted in her seat again. Reid could hear the wonder in her voice.

"The water in the fjords can be as smooth as glass, and reflect the peaks so the sight is doubly beautiful."

Reid smiled. "Did you see any glaciers?"

"Oh, yes. Many. They are very rugged and surprisingly blue in color. In fact, the water in the rivers which flow from them is blue like a winter sky and very dense. You cannot see through it."

"I've never seen water that color," Reid said. "It sounds beautiful, but it's so hard to imagine."

"My—no. Nev—never mind," Kirsten stammered.

"Tell me," Reid urged.

"I shouldn't have said anything," she demurred.

Reid gave an exaggerated sigh. "Have we not become friends?

Perhaps I misunderstood your intentions," he said with a one-shoulder shrug and turned his face away.

"Don't say that. That isn't fair," she chided. "I would like to think we are friends."

"Then tell me," he challenged, facing her again.

She gave an exaggerated sigh which mimicked his perfectly. "When the bandages come off, you will see my eyes. I was told they are the same color as the glacier water."

Reid gave a long, slow nod. "Now I will recognize you when I finally see you."

Kirsten scoffed. "I am so relieved, since my voice and my scent would never have led you to that recognition."

Reid laughed softly. "Tell me what Christiania is like."

Her chair creaked again as she repositioned herself. "Most notably there is a large medieval fortress, called Akershus Festning, built on top of a cliff which overlooks the innermost point of that fjord," she began.

Reid nodded. "I have been told it has protected the city for nearly eight-hundred years."

"Then you know that the port is just below it?" she asked.

"That's what my parents said." Reid laid back on the cot, his strength still not recovered. "How big is the city?"

Kirsten seemed to be thinking about her answer. "Eight or nine thousand, I believe."

"Philadelphia has about thirty thousand," Reid observed, surprised by the comparison. He always assumed Christiania was larger. "So a third of the size at best."

"That sounds right," Kirsten concurred.

"What are the people like?"

There came another noticeable pause. "I spent my time in the company of my mother's family. My mother's brother has residences in both Christiania in Norway and København in Denmark."

"He must be wealthy as well," Reid responded. It wasn't a question.

Kirsten's answers went from effusive to cryptic in that one moment. "Yes. He is."

Reid cocked his head. "You don't like him."

"Not very much, no."

"And the rest of the family?" he fished.

"We didn't get along."

"But you were there for three years, even so."

"I stayed as long as I could stand it. Then I came home." She shifted her weight again. "I'm afraid I'm getting sleepy."

Reid heard nothing of sleep in her tone. It was obvious to him that she wanted to avoid telling him anything more about her elusive uncle and cousins. While he wondered what secrets she kept, they were not any of his business. He was going to leave her as soon as he was sufficiently recovered and rejoin the Continental Army.

That realization poked him in a very uncomfortable way.

"I won't keep you if you need to go," he said.

She didn't get off the chair.

"The doctor should be visiting tomorrow to check on your recuperation," she said after a space of silence.

"I hope he is pleased with what he finds," Reid commented. "Will he look at my eyes, do you think?"

Her voice held a bit of question. "I expect so."

He rolled his head on the pillow. "It's very disorienting, not being able to see."

"I can only imagine," she whispered.

Reid held out his hand. Kirsten laid her palm in his. He pulled her hand to his lips and gave it a lingering kiss. "Thank you for visiting me tonight. Your nursing skills are exemplary."

"You're welcome, Captain Hansen." She retrieved her hand and stood. "I do hope you are able to sleep now."

"My wish for you as well."

He listened for her footsteps as she padded across the carpet and ascended the wooden stairs. Her bedroom door quietly clicked. The ticking clock in the corner chimed three times.

September 7, 1781

Doctor Jackson Haralson introduced himself to Reid, then moved right into the reason for his visit without further pleasantries. *He must be a very busy man.*

"How is your head?"

Reid sat sideways on his cot, having finished breakfast only a quarter hour earlier. "It still hurts. Though less than yesterday when I first became aware of my surroundings."

"Good. Take off your breeches, will you? I want to examine your leg."

Horace had thankfully remained in the room after escorting the doctor in and closing the parlor door. He now came to Reid's aid, pulling off the breeches as Reid lay back on the cot. The doctor cut through the bandage on Reid's right thigh and peeled it away.

"Hm. Yes. Good."

"Doctor?" Reid prompted.

"No infection. Healing as expected. I'll take the stitches out in another week." Reid heard the hollow sounds of rummaging in a leather satchel. "In the meantime, keep the leg straight. If you tear the wound open, you run the risk of infection and will likely lose the limb."

"I understand." This man did not believe in sugar-coating his words, that much was clear.

I'll be here another week. Reid wasn't certain how he felt about that, but there wasn't anything to be done. He did enjoy having two legs, after all.

"Can I walk on it before then?" he asked.

"As long as you don't bend it. I recommend a cane." The doctor applied himself to re-bandaging Reid's thigh without any further comment.

"Close the drapes, will you?" he asked when he finished. "I want to look at his eyes and the daylight will be too bright for him."

Reid's pulse surged. This was the moment he both hoped for and dreaded. He listened as Horace pulled the heavy fabric over the windows, and wondered how he would react if he saw nothing when his eyes were freed from their constriction.

Doctor Haralson cut away the bandages as he had done on Reid's leg. "Don't open your eyes until I tell you to," he instructed.

Reid said nothing and tried to calm his pounding heart.

The bandages floated away.

"The bruising is still rather severe," Haralson stated as if there was a roomful of witnesses. Perhaps there was, Reid realized. "The swelling is notable, but I've seen worse."

Reid clenched his jaw to keep from shouting his question.

"Go ahead and open your eyes, but slowly."

Reid fluttered his eyes open, unsticking them from a crust of salve and dried tears. He squinted—the dim light in the room hurt. His eyes stung. He couldn't keep them open.

"Can you see?" Haralson demanded.

"I see light," Reid answered and tried to force his eyes to stay open. "I see shadows."

"Can you see this?"

A blurred jagged shape wiggled in front of him. "A hand?" he guessed.

"Good. Close your eyes." More rummaging in the satchel. "I'm going to apply the salve again and put the bandage back on. We'll leave everything in place for three more days before I remove it."

A cool swipe of some gelatinous substance soothed his stinging eyes.

"You'll stay in the dark for a day after that. Gradually move into light over the next couple days."

Gauze rested on his eyelids.

"You should procure a pair of smoked eyeglasses and wear them when you are out of doors for a week or two after that, until all of the discomfort is gone."

Reid's head was lifted. A strip of cloth was wound around his head, holding the gauze in place. As much as he hated being blinded, the bandage was physically comforting.

"I'll be able to see normally again?" he asked when the wrapping was finished.

"I can't promise you anything," Haralson deflected. "But from what I've seen here today I don't believe you've lost much of your vision."

Relief flowed through Reid's veins. "Thank you, doctor."

"I'll check your eyes yet again when I return to remove the stitches."

The satchel snapped shut. Drapes were pulled over their rods. The parlor door opened.

★ ★ ★

Kirsten jumped back from the door, embarrassed to be caught eavesdropping. She had her ear pressed to the portal practically from the moment Horace pushed it closed. She heard everything.

"Doctor Haralson!" she exclaimed. She gave him what she hoped was a disarming smile and offered him his hat. "How is our soldier faring?"

"As well as can be expected under the circumstances." The doctor took his hat from her hand and moved toward the door.

"Haralson!" her father's voice boomed from the staircase as he descended. "Are you rushing off?"

The doctor bobbed a quick nod. "I'm afraid so, Sven. I've lots of patients waiting."

"And our Captain?"

Haralson grabbed the doorknob. "Should be right as rain in a couple of weeks."

Henrik glanced at his daughter. "That long, eh?"

Kirsten moved her smile to her father. "He has to wear the bandages over his eyes for three more days. Doctor Haralson will come back in a week to take the stitches out of his leg. In the meantime, he can walk with a cane as long as he keeps the leg straight."

Haralson cleared his throat.

Knowing she was caught, Kirsten's head swiveled to meet the doctor's eyes. They twinkled with amusement.

"Don't forget to purchase the smoked eyeglasses," he quipped.

Kirsten's face flushed. "Yes, Doctor."

He clapped his tricorn hat on his head. "I'll see you in three days." He disappeared out the door.

Henrik stood in front of his daughter. "You do make a good nurse, I must confess."

"Thank you, *Pappa*." She went up on her toes to kiss his cheek.

He considered her with a somber gaze. "Guard your heart, Kirsten. He'll be gone in a fortnight."

She gaped at her father. "I don't—I mean—why would you say that?"

Henrik pulled her into his embrace and rested his chin on her head. "You have a very strong will, daughter, and you have sent away every suitable prospect your mother and I have found for you. I don't want you to set your sights on a man you cannot have."

Her father's voice vibrated from his chest to hers. Tears stung her eyes.

"*Pappa*, please don't worry about me. I have no intention of falling for the captain," she murmured. *Or any man. Ever.*

"I cannot help but worry over you," he replied. "You are my daughter. My only child. I long to see you safe and happy."

Safe was a Norwegian ship that had sailed far, far away never to return; but she couldn't tell him that. Her parents believed they had done the best for her. She wouldn't break their hearts with the truth.

Kirsten tilted her head back and looked at her father. "Let me live my life as I choose to. That would make me happiest of all."

Reid smiled when he heard Kirsten repeat all the explicit instructions from Doctor Haralson. He knew that if anyone else was in the room besides Horace, it wouldn't be her. Or any woman, for that matter. The only explanation, then, was that she was listening outside the parlor door.

Just as he expected her to.

She was a pistol, this woman—for at twenty-six years of age she was far from being a girl. Reid liked that. After spending eight years in the nearly exclusive company of men, he had developed some fairly rough edges and he knew it. He had managed to drive off some prospects of his own when he forgot to be gentle in his manners.

For reasons he had not yet discerned, Kirsten wished to remain independent. Reid found that comforting. If he was to remain in this house and under her care for the next two weeks, he didn't want to have to dance around an inconvenient romance in the process. Or worse, the assumption of a romance.

Kirsten's declaration of disinterest had set them both free from social convention. He would continue to be blunt with her, and he expected the same treatment in return. After all, that is how their burgeoning friendship had begun, and he saw no reason to make a change now. Such a thing could only muddy the waters between them.

Waters.

Blue like a winter sky.

Reid sighed. He couldn't wait to see her eyes.

CHAPTER FIVE

September 8, 1781

"I want to walk this afternoon," Reid announced.

Kirsten looked at him, surprised. "You'll need a cane."

"Or a strong stick," he qualified. "Might there be one around here?"

"I'll send George in search," she promised. "Finish your luncheon."

An antique cane was found in the attic amongst random items her parents brought when they moved from Norway. Black lacquer with a curved brass handle, it was a little too short for Reid.

"I'll make do," he insisted. "I need to get off this cot and into some fresh air before I lose my sanity."

"Wait! I have an idea!" Kirsten yelped. She ran off in search of the tallest brass candlestick she could find on short notice, leaving Reid to fend for himself.

Returning to the parlor, she jammed the tip of the cane where a candle would go. It stuck. And it added half a foot to the length of the cane.

"How is that?" she asked when he pushed himself to stand on one leg.

Reid leaned on the cane. "That's perfect. How did you do it?"

"Take my arm," she said, ignoring his question. "I'll lead you."

Reid complied. He limped across the parlor carpet without comment. But when the brass foot of his cane hit the marble floor of the manor's entry, the resounding metallic clang brought him up short.

"What am I leaning on?" he demanded.

Kirsten smothered a giggle. "A candlestick."

Reid's jaw fell, hung slack for a moment, and then snapped shut. He bounced a brief nod. "Lead on."

Pleased that he approved of her makeshift solution, Kirsten found herself beaming. It was a simple thing, really. The cane needed to be longer, the tip was about the size of a candle, the problem was solved—until a cane of the right length could be made or purchased.

Purchased, she decided. A man like Captain Hansen deserved the dignity of a proper accessory.

"We'll go out the front door and down the steps," she explained.

"I trust you to lead me," he replied.

Another wash of pleasure followed his words.

Kirsten led Reid to the steps and steadied him as he worked his way down. He winced when he put weight on his injured leg, but he was careful not to bend it. Once they stood on the drive, under the protective portico, Reid stopped.

He leaned his head back and drew several deep breaths. "Lord, that smells good," he moaned.

Kirsten wrinkled her nose. "I smell manure."

"So do I—and it's glorious!" he declared.

Kirsten laughed. "Perhaps your sanity is already in jeopardy."

He wagged a finger in her direction. "You are the one that has me prancing about on a candlestick foot. Poor, blind cripple that I am!"

She laughed again. "I'll send George today for an appropriate appendage. Do you want to go back indoors until then?"

"*Helvete* no!" he barked.

Kirsten rested his hand on her shoulder. "Then let us continue."

She walked slowly, knowing he would tire easily after spending nearly a week in bed. Reid hobbled along beside her. Step, shuffle. Step, shuffle. The pair strolled in amicable silence, bathed in autumn sunshine with a soft breeze hinting of the chill to come in weeks ahead.

"What is war like?" she asked after a while.

Reid pressed his lips together. He stopped walking. "Why do

you ask?"

"I don't know," she answered honestly. "I suppose I want to know what your life has been like."

Reid faced the ground. "Most of the time, it's damned boring. Waiting and marching, marching and waiting. Between battles, we track our enemy and try to engage them when it's to our advantage."

"I never thought of it like that," Kirsten admitted.

Reid leaned on the cane. "Food is never plentiful, unless we have time to hunt. Or fish. But those times are rare. Soldiers often go hungry."

She recognized his need to rest so she changed the direction of her query. "Are you a good shot?"

One side of his mouth curled. "I am."

"You like to hunt, then?"

"I love to hunt. When I was younger, I would go into the woods for a couple days and bring home enough game to feed my family for a month. We sold the pelts as well," he said. "We don't farm, other than my mother's vegetable garden, some chickens, and a couple milk cows. My father has his own architecture firm and that keeps him very busy."

Kirsten considered the land surrounding them. "We have several hundred acres here, and tenants who farm it for us."

Reid nodded his understanding. "Like back home."

"That is not my home!" she snapped. "I am an American."

Reid put up a defensive palm. "I meant nothing by it, Kirsten. I'm sorry."

Humiliation at her apparently unwarranted outburst heated her skin, chest to scalp. "No, I'm sorry, Reid. After insisting I be defined that way for three long years, I'm too quick to jump now that I'm back."

"You have been back for two years, have you not?" he pressed.

Kirsten grabbed his hand and placed it firmly on her shoulder. "Let's head toward the house. You shouldn't overexert yourself on this first outing."

Reid followed her again. This silence was not so amicable. She had been rude and she knew it. Kirsten bit her lips together and willed herself not to succumb to tears over such a small infraction.

"We're dirty all the time."

She frowned. "What?"

"Soldiers," he murmured. "We seldom get to bathe. We wear our clothes until they practically fall off us, and then have to purchase new garments wherever we can find them."

"Oh." Kirsten knew he had forgiven her, but that only made her more likely to cry.

"Sometimes..."

She looked back at him and walked on in silence. Judging by the lines on the sides of his mouth whatever followed that introduction was not going to be easy to say.

"Well, many times, to be honest," he took another run at it. "We'll take clothes off those in our regiment who fall."

Kirsten made herself keep walking, though her gut's response was to stop and stare at him in horror. She never considered a soldier's condition would be so desperate that they would steal clothing off corpses. *Out of necessity.*

"You—you must have had a hard time finding—clothes to fit you," she managed.

He snorted. "Tall boots hide short trouser hems quite effectively. Besides, fashion falls far behind when compared with freezing to death in some obscure valley."

Kirsten didn't know what to say to that. He was right, of course. And the dead men didn't need the clothes any longer. She found it gruesome, nonetheless.

After several minutes of sober silence, Kirsten asked the question she wanted to ask every soldier who came through their parlor hospital but had never worked up the courage. She only did so now because this soldier couldn't see her.

"What is it like to kill a man?"

Reid sucked a breath through his teeth. "That depends on how you do it..."

She did stop walking this time.

Reid smacked into her back. "Ouch! *Skitt!*"

Kirsten whirled to face him. Reid had dropped his cane and held the sides of his right thigh while wobbling on his left leg. His mouth was twisted in a grimace that silently screamed his pain.

"I'm so sorry!" Kirsten cried. She squatted and retrieved the cane. "Oh, Reid! I'm so very sorry!"

She rested one hand on his shoulder, partly to steady him and partly so he would know where she was. She leaned the handle of the cane against his wrist.

"I'm sorry, Reid," she said again.

He lifted his chin. "My fault. I didn't see you stop."

A sob burst from Kirsten's chest before she could contain it. For reasons she couldn't name she began to cry. A shoulder-shaking, blubbering, bawling mess of a cry. She hadn't cried this hard since that night in Akershus.

"Kirsten?" Reid ventured. "What is it?"

"I don't know," she gulped. "I c-can't s-stop."

"I'll be fine," he assured her.

Kirsten pulled her hand away from him to wipe her dripping cheeks.

Reid swung his arm in an arc in front of him and hit her shoulder. He grabbed it and pulled her close, pressing her to his chest. He wrapped her in long, strong arms, and held her tight. For a moment she felt secure. Safe.

And then she remembered her singular situation and pushed him away.

"We should go back." She turned around and waited for him to take hold of her shoulder.

"Kirsten."

"No, Reid," she said firmly. "We need to go back."

His hand brushed up her back until it reached her shoulder. Hot and heavy, it felt like an anchor pushing her down. She stepped forward, her back stiff with resolution. She didn't say another word to Reid, other than to warn him of obstacles in his path, until they were at the house.

"Have I offended you in some way, Miss Sven?" he asked once they reached the parlor.

"No," she whispered. "Of course not."

"Then, what may I ask—"

She put a finger against his lips. "Please don't worry yourself. I'll check on you later."

Kirsten turned toward the stairs and looked up.

Her mother stared down at her, unsmiling.

✫ ✫ ✫

What the hell.

Reid fumbled his way to his cot. He set the cane within easy reach and stretched out on the mattress. His thigh ached, though he didn't believe the collision with Kirsten's arse had done any new damage. But his head was pounding again.

His earlier intuition that something happened to her in Norway solidified in his mind. He also made up his mind to ignore that intuition.

In two days the bandages would come off his eyes. In five days, the stitches would be out of his leg. Soon after that, he would be on his way.

A crush of depression sat solidly on his chest.

Kirsten's questions reminded him of what he was returning to. Battles fought with limited ammunition, side by side with fourteen-year-old farm boys and forty-year-old shopkeepers, most of whom would end up dead in an unnamed forest or a trampled wheat field. Dirty clothes, thin jackets and boots that leaked. And another winter was visible over the horizon of the calendar.

All this effort to take down a uniformed enemy; one provisioned, trained and skilled in warfare. It was a miracle the Continental Army had lasted these five long and brutal years since the declaration, considering the pounding they received in the year before Congress pulled its collective head out of its ass and signed the damned thing.

Thank you, John Adams. You made Massachusetts proud.

Patriotism aside, the war with England was an effort he could not give up on now. The United States of America had been born, and Reidar Hansen was determined not to let the infant die. If he did, then the previous eight years of his life—and all the sacrifices he both suffered and chose—would be wasted. The crush of that depression would kill him.

The end was near. It had to be. He only needed to survive the coming months.

Reid tried to relax. His walk was tiring, though not for the physical exertion alone. He would be a fool to become too connected to Kirsten. There was no point in following a path which he had neither the time nor intent to fully explore.

He pulled a deep breath. A nap before supper struck him as a good idea.

✸ ✸ ✸

"Have you told him?" Marit asked.

Kirsten sat in her mother's study and sipped tea behind closed doors. "Told him what?" she asked innocently, though more than one secret jumped to the front of her mind.

Her mother shot her an irritated look. "Don't play games, Kirsten. You know what I'm talking about."

Kirsten shook her head. She did indeed know what her mother meant. "There is no reason to do so. He'll be gone soon of his own volition."

Marit's attempt at a compassionate expression was as upsetting as it was misplaced. "I saw the way you looked at him."

"You are wrong, *Mamma*," Kirsten insisted.

"Am I? He's a compelling man. Even I noticed," Marit admitted.

"I already told you, I have no intention of marrying. Even when a tall, Norwegian army officer is deposited at my own feet, in my own parlor," Kirsten declaimed.

"What about his feelings?" Marit pressed. "You know that injured men often become enamored with their nurses."

"He is not enamored with me, *Mamma*," she objected.

"Are you certain?"

Kirsten flipped her wrist at her mother. "He is merely bored with lying around and wants a diversion. I don't blame him—do you?"

"No," Marit conceded.

"I'm bored as well, *Mamma*. Having someone interesting to talk to brightens my day. But there is nothing more to come of it." She sipped her tea, and stared intently at the pattern in the carpet. Her mother's interrogation prompted emotions best left buried.

Marit was silent for a minute and Kirsten believed her mother's chastisement might be finished. She was wrong.

"If I believe that either his affections for you, or yours for him, grow to an unacceptable level, then I will take matters into my own hands."

Kirsten rolled her eyes, unable to restrain her irritation. "When will you *ever* trust the things I say? Stop treating me as if I cannot control my life!"

She set her empty teacup down with more force than the delicate china could withstand. The handle snapped off.

"Kirsten!" Marit exclaimed angrily. "Now look what you have done!"

Kirsten jumped to her feet, the broken cup clenched in her hand. She felt like a canon ball about to be loosed in the room. "Nothing beyond a brief friendship is going to occur between Captain Hansen and me. Not one thing. How can I make you understand that?"

"Give me that before you cut yourself." Marit took the broken china from her daughter. "All I'm saying is that Captain Hansen is not a suitable choice for your husband."

"I know that. You have already made it quite clear," Kirsten declared. "Why do you keep harping at me?"

Marit pinned her with the intent gaze of a mother protecting her only offspring. "If the time comes, I want you to understand. That's all."

"Trust me, I do understand." Kirsten strode toward the door. She hesitated, her hand resting on the handle. She drew a deep breath and spoke over her shoulder. "Thank you for the tea, *Mamma*. I'm sorry about the cup."

CHAPTER SIX

September 9, 1781

Reid waited all morning for Kirsten, but she didn't appear. He listened for her voice, but that too was missing from the house. An hour after the midday meal, he rang a little brass bell to summon assistance—a helpful addition to his accommodations after he was forced to shout George's name during the dinner party.

"Yes, sir?" It was Horace who answered the call.

"I was hoping to exercise again today, but Miss Sven appears to be otherwise engaged," Reid explained. "Is there someone who might accompany me and act as my guide?"

"I shall send George with you, Captain. He enjoys your company and would be happy to assist you."

Reid smiled. "Thank you, Horace."

"I understand your blindfolds come off tomorrow?"

"That is my expectation," Reid replied. "So I should be able to see my own way after this."

"We are all glad to watch your recovery, sir."

Reid dipped a nod. "Thank you again."

George arrived several minutes later. Reid grabbed his cane and stood. George snickered.

"I understand Miss Sven used a candlestick to lengthen my appendage," Reid said with a grin. "Are you embarrassed to be seen with me?"

"No, sir. It's funny-looking is all," George said cheerily. "But I expect it works just fine."

Reid extended his hand. "I'll hold your shoulder and follow you. Warn me if we encounter any obstacles, such as stair steps."

George placed his shoulder under Reid's hand. "I will, sir. Are you ready? It's a right fine day out."

"Lead on."

Once again, Reid stopped and breathed in the aromas of the land. "Tell me what I'll see tomorrow, George. When I stand here."

"Well... the fields are all around us," he began tentatively. "But they've been harvested."

"What did they grow?"

"Wheat. Barley. Corn. Hay for the winter." George paused. "There's cows in the fields now, eatin' what's left."

Reid chuckled. "Yes, I smell them."

George twisted his body if the pull on Reid's shoulder was a trusted indicator. "Out back are the chickens."

"And one happy rooster. I've heard him in the mornings."

George turned back to Reid. "Yes, sir. He's happy alright. And meaner'n a son-of-a-bitch!"

Reid laughed. "Protecting his harem, no doubt. Let's walk shall we?"

"Any particular direction?"

"Take me where I can walk without tripping."

George began to move. "We'll walk to the end of the drive. That's flat."

Reid followed along, stretching his good leg and testing the injured one. He moved more easily than yesterday and was glad to mark the improvement. Once they left the shade of the portico, the afternoon sun warmed his head and shoulders. His headaches were abating, dimmed to a dull pressure just behind his crown.

I'm feeling quite human, he realized. Except for not recalling the actual explosion Reid would have to say he was on an encouraging road.

And speaking of roads, they had been walking further than he expected. "How long is this drive?" he asked George.

"It's not a quarter of a mile," he answered. "But it's close."

Reid halted. George stepped out from under his hand, but quickly moved back in place.

"Are you tired?" he asked, concern defining his tone.

Reid shook his head. "How many acres does Sven own?"

"One thousand, two hundred and eighty-five," came George's very precise response.

"How far are we from the city?"

"Oh, you can see them buildings from the upper rooms," George assured him. "We are only a mile from the dock where you were hurt."

Reid struggled to map out what he remembered of Philadelphia from the first day he arrived. "Which direction are we from the city?"

"North mostly, and a little west."

Reid nodded and gave George's shoulder a little shove. George understood and started walking again.

"I didn't have much time to explore when I arrived," Reid said. "I was waiting for the French to come so I could send them after the New Jersey regiment."

"Oh they came through, alright," George said. "And they went on their way. I guess someone else told them."

"Did they?" he mused. He knew the French were less interested in helping the Americans than they were in hindering the English whenever in the world that particular opportunity arose.

Something about that thought pinged in his mind.

When he arrived at the dock to search for the Pennsylvania regiment's quarters, he remembered interrupting a conversation. Two men, talking about stopping the French army's progress. Or did they say, *hoping the French army progressed?* The elusive snippet wasn't clear. Thinking about it made his head hurt.

"Will you be rejoining the New Jersey regiment, sir?" George asked.

"I suppose so," Reid answered. "Unless I can find a regiment from Massachusetts."

George made a clucking sound. "I hope this war gets over with. And that we win it, of course."

"No colony has ever broken away from its parent. We've already made history by attempting to," Reid observed.

"England can't make us stay with them. Can they?"

Reid blew an exasperated breath. "They are certainly trying."

"We've reached the end of the drive. Now we'll go back." George led Reid in a tight half circle. "And here comes the carriage. Miss Sven must be returning."

✯ ✯ ✯

Kirsten saw Reid and George from the carriage window.

The sight was quite comical, she had to admit. The tall captain, his eyes covered with a thick white wrapping, wore a too-short shirt which barely reached his hips and tight breeches with a hem which hovered above his military boots.

With one hand he gripped the shoulder of her much shorter, though better dressed, servant. Extending from his other hand was the black-lacquered brass-handled cane; an elegant accessory until one's eye followed it down to the wide bottomed brass candlestick which was jammed on its tip like a round metallic snowshoe. Only then did she remember she should have bought him a cane.

As the carriage rolled into the drive and past the pair of men, George touched his forehead in salute. Reid didn't acknowledge the vehicle's passage.

A stab of guilt told Kirsten why.

Though he could refer to his blindness as an excuse, Kirsten assumed George would have warned Reid that a carriage was approaching, and then led him to stand aside and make room. It would also have been natural for George to comment on who was in the carriage.

After her emotional outburst yesterday, Kirsten avoided Reid. She took her supper in her room, claiming a headache after arguing with her mother. This morning she slipped out without eating breakfast, choosing to have her first meal of the day in town while she waited for her errand to be completed.

As much as she wished to think of other things, the fact that her errand was on behalf of Captain Hansen naturally kept him the forefront of her mind all day.

Kirsten opened her little leather satchel and took out the linen-swathed bundle that embodied her assigned task. She unwrapped the spectacles for Captain Hansen and held them up to the carriage window. The flat lenses were made of gray-tinted glass intended to block light, and they appeared to do an adequate job.

The task did require the better part of her morning as she searched for someone who would fabricate such a thing. She was about to give up when, in a desperate attempt to find someone creative who worked with glass and metal, she entered a jeweler's shop.

The jeweler was from Scotland, and as she explained what she needed he grew quite excited, claiming to know exactly what to do.

"I have a countryman who makes such things. You go on and have tea, lass, and come back in two hours," he said, rubbing his hands gleefully.

She did as he bid, and when she returned he laid the spectacles in her hand. They were perfect. Kirsten wrapped them back in the cloth and placed them in her satchel.

Now she only needed to summon the nerve to give them to him.

The clock chimed three times, its soft melody a jarring cacophony in Kirsten's sleepless ears. Though the attempt would no doubt be fruitless, she knew she had to speak with Reid once more—alone—before the doctor removed the bandages from his eyes. So for the second time in four nights, she snuck downstairs to the parlor.

His door was closed, now that he was awake and mending well enough that his nighttime needs were not an issue to be dealt with. Kirsten rested her forehead against the panel and listened to the snoring on the other side.

I'll ease the door open. If he doesn't awaken, I'll leave.

The click of the latch echoed through the entryway and seemed loud as a pistol. She paused, then eased the door open, hoping equally to wake him and not disturb him.

The snoring marched on, its rhythm unbroken.

Kirsten pushed the door shut until only the slightest crack remained. To the casual night wanderer it would appear closed. Yet in her conscience she knew that she and the captain were not actually closeted. It was a fine point, but an important one.

She crossed the room not trying to be quiet, though bare feet on carpet made scant sound. Once she stood beside his pallet she struggled with what to do next.

The wooden chair had been moved to another part of the room. Should she search for it and carry it to Reid's bedside? Or perhaps she should sit on the floor. The cot was too narrow for her to sit beside the slumbering soldier, but that was too intimate a choice for her to make in any case.

She settled for pulling a cushion off the settee and placed it beside Reid's bed. When she knelt on it and rested her head on the edge of his mattress, she was comfortable enough to fall asleep.

Kirsten scolded herself not to do such a thing. She wasn't certain why she was compelled to be here in the first place, but being discovered in this room, asleep in her nightclothes, would make any other disaster she could imagine look like an idyllic picnic by comparison.

Reid's snores halted. He adjusted his position, turning on his side toward her, and resettled. He sighed in his sleep and his breathing returned to its calming pace.

Kirsten wished the night wouldn't have to end. She had been acquainted with Reid for such a short time that she was amazed at how safe she felt in his presence. Certainly he had dark secrets she knew nothing about; all men did. But his secrets were still buried in the fact he was a stranger. All she knew of the injured man were his limitations.

That might be the key, she realized. She hadn't yet seen his strength. The strength he clearly possessed and could use to hurt her.

She gasped when his hand landed softly on her head.

"Why are you here?" he whispered.

"I don't know," she answered honestly.

"You couldn't sleep." It wasn't a question.

"No."

They were silent for a while. Reid's fingers began a soft massage on Kirsten's scalp and she leaned into his hand.

"I'm sorry about yesterday," she offered.

"The day you cried, or the day I didn't see you?" he asked.

It was a fair question. In the middle of the night days don't have sharp boundaries.

"Both, I suppose," she admitted.

Reid's massage moved to the back of her neck. "Why did you cry, Kirsten?"

"Because I hurt you." Yet she had no idea why she cried so hard.

"Hm." He began to knead a knot she didn't know was there. "And why are you sorry about not seeing me?"

"I—well I thought that you expected me to spend time with

you," she ventured. "And I left without saying anything. And then I didn't check in on you afterwards..."

"You were embarrassed and avoided me." His hand on her neck was warm and soothing all the while his words defined her humiliation. "I understand. Though in truth, I am the one who should be embarrassed."

"You?" she squeaked. She re-lowered her voice to a whisper. "Why you?"

"I was the one standing by the road, holding another man's shoulder and wearing a tight shirt, short breeches with my knees on display over my boots, a mask that makes me look like an effeminate pirate, and out walking with a candlestick stuck on the end of a cane!"

Kirsten began to laugh, holding her hand over her mouth to stifle the sound. Reid began to wheeze huffs of mirth. He had described the vision to perfection. The absolutely memorable-until-she-died and hilarious vision.

"I must have been a sight," he managed between exhalations. "I'm sorry you had to see that."

And then she knew. The reason she needed to talk to Reid tonight. It was so stunningly clear that she didn't know how she nearly missed it. Her laughter died.

"I just realized why I felt compelled to come to you tonight," she murmured.

Reid's chuckles faded. "Tell me," he urged gently.

"Your bandages come off tomorrow. You are going to see me for the first time."

She couldn't see his mouth in the dark, but she thought he smiled. "I must confess, I am curious."

"It will change everything," she whispered.

Reid hesitated. "Why?"

"I am always judged by how I look, as all women are," she began.

The neck massage resumed. "Go on. I'm listening."

"It seems that men won't take the time to examine what sort of mind, or heart, or character awaits behind any unsettling façade," she explained.

"Are you claiming that no one has truly known you?" he asked, his disbelief evident. "In all of your twenty-six years?"

"It's true, Reid. Remember our honesty? I wouldn't lie to you, especially not now." Tears thickened her throat. "Not when it's so important for you to understand."

His hand stilled. "What do you want me to understand, Kirsten?"

"That as long as you couldn't see me, then for once in my life how I look didn't matter. All you knew was *me*." She sniffed and ran her hand under her nose. "Tomorrow, the woman you think I am disappears the moment your blinders are gone."

Reid was quiet for a long time.

"I'd like to believe I'm not so petty as that," he said.

Kirsten clambered to her feet, her grief threatening to swamp her. She needed to return to the safety of her chamber and her bed before it took control. She leaned over and felt for Reid's face. She laid a hand along each side of his jaw. And then she kissed him.

His lips were soft and warm. They pulled at hers as if trying to keep the kiss from ending. She wanted to kiss him forever, to stop time at that moment, and live in their shared darkness untouched by the harsh reality of day. But she could not.

Kirsten pulled her mouth from his. "I guess we'll find out tomorrow, won't we?"

She hurried away before he could say anything else.

CHAPTER SEVEN

September 10, 1781

Reid was nervous. There was no skirting around that fact.

He already knew he wasn't completely blind, but he didn't know how much his vision had been damaged by the explosion. When Doctor Haralson took the bandages off this time, they would stay off. And his life would simply begin again, in whatever state he found himself.

What's taking the man so blasted long?

Reid had been washed and waiting since breakfast. Now lunch was a memory. If the doctor didn't arrive soon, Reid was going to rip the damn bandages off by himself.

Kirsten sat with him for a while, but she was so fidgety that her presence was not helpful. Neither of them mentioned the kiss, but of course they wouldn't. There was nothing to be said about it.

Reid understood that she was saying goodbye in a way. He had wondered all along what she looked like, but didn't think it proper to ask. He held on to his optimistic belief that, in due time, he would be able to see her for himself.

Now he hoped his reaction at seeing her would be the sort of reaction she hoped for, whatever that was. He enjoyed her company, and their midnight chats were interesting to say the least. He truly didn't want to disappoint her or hurt her in any way, though her words had made him wary.

As if his composure wasn't already a wreck.

But that kiss...

He could still feel the shock of her lips against his. He kissed her in return, wanting her to know that he appreciated the gesture.

Appreciated? Hell, he thoroughly enjoyed it.

Sadly, Kirsten would be one more wartime loss he must bear. He would be gone in a fortnight or sooner; there was no chance to explore what might blossom between him and his enigmatic nurse. The one who spoke Norse.

A knock on the front door shot through his chest, zinging in all directions like a powder burn.

He sat stiff and straight on the edge of his cot, his left knee bouncing his impatience. He heard Doctor Haralson's voice, and Kirsten's muffled reply.

Come on.

"There you are, Captain." Reid heard the hollow sound of the leather case dropped on a table. "How are you feeling today?"

"Headaches are just about gone. I've been walking with a cane. My thigh is tender, but not overly so," he answered.

"Is there any bleeding or discharge seeping through the bandage?" Haralson asked as he rummaged in the case.

"Not that I can feel," Reid replied. "I can't see it, you realize."

"What? Oh! Of course. Let's have a look, shall we?"

"I'll be outside," Kirsten stated. "Let me know when I can return, will you?"

The door latch clicked.

Reid began to unfasten his breeches. He stood to shove them down past his thighs. And he waited.

"Uh, huh. Excellent," the doctor observed. "No signs of putrefication coming through." He prodded Reid's thigh. "Does that hurt?"

"Yes. A little," he admitted.

"I'm satisfied. You can pull your breeches back up."

Reid did as he was bid. He heard movement on the carpet and the door opened.

"Please pull the drapes closed," Haralson instructed. Reid assumed he addressed Kirsten, though she had not yet spoken. He sat down on the cot.

Once the sound of rings on rods ceased, Reid braced himself for the unveiling. His heart thundered in his ears. A film of sweat prickled over his skin.

"Let's see what we see," Haralson quipped.

The cold steel of scissors slithered up Reid's temple, pressing in rhythm as the doctor cut through the bandage.

"Don't open your eyes yet," he warned as he removed the wrapping. "I want to watch your pupils."

Reid bounced a tiny nod. His eyes remained closed.

"Go ahead, then," Haralson said after a couple eternities passed.

Reid tried to blink his eyes open.

"Hold on! Close your eyes," the doctor laid a hand on his arm to stop his efforts. "Warm water and a cloth, please."

"Yes, Doctor," Kirsten said. Her footsteps picked up sound when she left the carpeted parlor.

More eternities lumbered by before she returned.

"Wash his eyes," Haralson said.

Reid heard the sound of water splashing nearby. Kirsten—he assumed it was her—grabbed his chin to steady his head and began to swab away the salve and dried tears crusted there. He could feel her fingers tremble when her grasp loosened and she rinsed the cloth. She was almost as nervous as he was, though for entirely different reasons.

"I'm finished," she said after her third round.

Shuffling indicated the two were repositioning themselves.

"Try again," Haralson urged.

Reid swallowed, though his mouth was dry as a dead tree. He lifted his eyelids.

"Look at me," the doctor ordered.

Reid did so. It turned out that Doctor Haralson had an intelligent brow and sharp features, all draped in skin which reflected at least thirty years of medical service. The vision was blurry, but Reid could see him better than the last time, when all he could do was identify the man's hand.

"Your pupils are reacting. Can you see me?"

"Yes."

"Clearly?"

Reid gave his head a little shake. "It's foggy."

Haralson nodded. "Some of that is the salve. It may take a full day for your tears to wash it all out."

"Do my eyes look bad?" He refrained from saying *good* and sounding overly confident.

"I don't recommend a mirror just yet." The doctor coughed a chuckle. "The bruising is almost gone, but there is still some swelling."

"But my actual eyes?" Reid pressed.

Haralson was disconcertingly close, leaning his head this way and that as he examined Reid's eyes. "Bloodshot. But the cornea is clear. That's the most important part."

Reid needed to hear the news in plain talk. "So I'll be able to see normally?"

"That would be my expectation."

Apparently that was the best he was going to hear.

"Did you procure the smoked spectacles?" The doctor addressed Kirsten without turning around.

"Yes, Doctor. I was actually able to buy some with tinted glass, not only smoked," she answered.

He turned around at that. "Were you? Let me know where. That's a valuable resource."

"The Scottish jeweler on Market and Seventh," she replied. "I spent most of yesterday searching the city, and he made them for me in a couple of hours."

"Excellent. Thank you." Haralson resumed his close and intense staring. "Does the light in here hurt your eyes?"

"No. But it seems bright." Reid still couldn't see Kirsten. Obviously, she had placed herself behind Doctor Haralson on purpose.

The doctor nodded. "Light will bother you until your eyes are fully healed, perhaps longer."

"Will that pass?" Reid asked. His marksmanship relied on his vision being sharp in all forms of light.

"It should." The man straightened. A feminine figure shifted out of Reid's sight. "Remember this: if it hurts, don't do it."

"Yes, sir," Reid acquiesced.

Haralson began to repack his case. "I'll be back in three days to take the stitches out of your leg. In the meantime, don't overdo the walking."

"Yes, sir," Reid repeated.

Haralson turned to his left. "Miss Sven, do you have the spectacles?"

"Here, sir."

The doctor accepted an object and turned toward Reid, offering it to him. Reid took the spectacles from Haralson and unfolded the curved side pieces. He slipped them over his ears and rested the frame holding the glass on his nose. The room darkened noticeably.

He looked at the doctor.

"Comfortable?"

Reid shrugged. "I suppose so."

"Good. Miss Sven, will you see me out?"

The woman whirled and scurried out of the parlor. Haralson followed.

Reid took that opportunity to investigate his surroundings unobserved. The furnishings were elegant and expensive. The walls were covered in painted silk from the floor to the high plastered ceilings. If he could trust his judgment in the dark and with the spectacles on, the predominant color was a deep rose or burgundy. The carpet, which was protected during his bath for good reason, sported a richly detailed pattern with fleurs-de-lis in the corners and Tudor roses in the center. Blues, greens, and burgundies predominated.

Kirsten was telling the truth when she said her family was wealthy.

Of course she was. *Honesty, remember?*

Reid knew his honesty might be tested when Kirsten returned. If she returned. Surely she wouldn't be so cowardly as to *not* return. If she tried, he would hunt her down and find her. The house couldn't be that big, no matter how rich they were.

A shadow dimmed the light in the doorway.

Reid stood slowly and faced the door. "Kirsten."

"Yes," she answered.

"Are my eyes so bruised?" he asked.

She took a step closer. "The bruises are healing, so they're at the yellow and green stage."

"And the swelling?" he continued.

Another step. "I don't know what you looked like before so it's hard to tell."

Reid's shoulders slumped. "I must look like a monster."

Two steps. "No, Reid! Not at all!"

He blew a frustrated sigh. "Can you even tell what color my eyes are?"

Two more steps. "Take off the eyeglasses."

He did. When he looked at her the light from the doorway surrounded her and made him squint. She remained cloaked in backlight and shadow.

"Gray," she said. "With dark blue around the outer edge."

"Not the color of glacier waters," he said with a crooked smile. He held out a hand. "Come close so I can see you."

Kirsten faced the floor and walked toward him as if condemned to the gallows. She laid her hand lightly in his. He pulled her around to the side so that the light from the hall would illuminate her face. He slid a knuckle under her chin and tipped her face upward, though her eyes remained downcast.

Reid's pulse surged.

Her skin was like porcelain, clear and smooth. Her cheeks were pink like the most delicate of spring roses. Her lips were a shade darker; he already knew how they tasted. Kirsten's features were classically Nordic. Broad brow, high cheekbones, wide set eyes. Her thick blonde hair was tied back and braided.

"Kirsten, you are—"

He didn't finish the sentence because her eyes flicked up to his and stole his voice.

Light, clear, blue. Not like his mother's pale eyes which resembled aquamarine gemstones. Kirsten's held more color. To see such intensity in such a pastel shade was unusual. Hell, he'd never seen anything like them before.

"What, Reid?" she whispered. "What am I?"

"You're—"

Reid stopped, suddenly aware of what her words in the deep dark of last night meant. He sat down hard on the cot and worked the glasses back over his eyes. He was stalling for time. He knew it. He hoped she didn't.

"My eyes are stinging, I'm sorry," he said. "I have to put these back on."

Kirsten didn't seem to know what to do.

"Will you stay and talk?" Reid asked as he settled the spectacles on his nose.

She clasped her hands in front of her waist, twisting her fingers until even he could see her knuckles whiten. "I'm not sure."

He looked up at her through the armor of the tinted glass and threw the first thing at her that came to his mind; anything to stay away from the subject of her remarkable beauty.

"Now that I can see, might I join your family for supper?"

"I, um..."

"As an officer of the Continental Army, I do have the social rank for such an invitation," he chided.

"Yes, but..."

"Are you afraid I cannot hold up my end of the conversation?" he prodded. "If so, I'll be quite offended. I have to be honest."

Her expression shifted then, from confusion to irritation.

"I shall consult my father and let you know," she said coldly. She whirled and stalked from the room.

Reid flopped back on the cot. His sudden and startling realization stopped him from saying the wrong thing—barely. And oddly, the wrong thing was simply *you are beautiful*.

In the middle of the night, when Kirsten told him she was always judged by her looks, he naturally thought she meant she was unattractive. That didn't worry him. They had been thrown together by his unfortunate circumstance, and her continued declarations that she would never marry placed a natural barrier between them.

As it turned out, she wasn't unattractive. She was stunningly beautiful. For the first time in his life, Reid understood how beauty could be a problem.

At his moment of realization, he refrained from telling her what all of her suitors must have said to her. Assuming it was a compliment, they would have extolled the virtues of her perfect physiognomy without—so she claimed—ever getting to know the woman beneath the flawless skin and startling eyes.

Reid had begun to become acquainted with that fascinating woman. He liked her. A lot.

That didn't change the fact that he had grown into a soldier by trade. America's war for independence had interrupted his life and tens of thousands like him. Until the war ended, he resigned, or was killed in battle, Reid didn't foresee any changes in his immediate future.

To complicate matters, though he had only seen this parlor thus far, it was obvious he could never hope to meet Kirsten's economic expectations if he ever chose to court her. His wife, if he ever found one, would have a simple existence wherever he could manage to provide a home for her and their children.

And at this moment, that was precisely nowhere.

Whatever Reid did in his remaining days in Philadelphia, he couldn't mention Kirsten's beauty. He needed to continue to speak with her as he had from the first moment he became aware after the explosion. He must treat her as a friend and nothing more. Be more interested in her conversation than her appearance.

Above all else, he mustn't let his lonely heart be swayed into considering any sort of future with her.

CHAPTER EIGHT

Kirsten stomped to her father's study, angrier than she had any right to be, or any ready explanation for. She didn't know what she expected from Reid when he saw her for the first time, but she expected more than nothing.

Henrik looked up when she knocked on his open study door. He smiled when he saw her, but his smile faded in the force of the exasperation she felt wafting from her entire frame.

He set his pen in the inkpot. "What is it, Kirsten?"

She strode into the room and plopped into a chair. "Doctor Haralson was here."

Her father's face brightened. "And how is the captain?"

"He can see." A prick of conscience led her to add, "I am happy to report."

"Wonderful," Henrik replied, clearly relieved. "And his leg?"

"The doctor will be back in three days to remove the stitches."

Henrik nodded his approval. "So what has you put in such a thunderous state, *Datter*?" he probed.

Kirsten sat forward in her chair. "He asked if he might join us for his suppers, now that he is no longer blinded."

Her father had the audacity to grin. Broadly. "What a splendid idea!"

She blinked at him. "Are you serious?"

"I am, of course," Henrik replied. "I am quite interested in hearing about his experiences and his opinions concerning this war."

Kirsten's features twisted with disgust. "Do you believe stories of battle to be appropriate dinner conversation?"

Her father chuckled. "Not the gory details, no. But strategies, outcomes, and plans. Yes."

She sighed. It would appear Reid was going to be the focal point of her evening meals for the next week or so. She wondered how many times she could claim to be indisposed and eat in her room without raising her parents' concern.

"If you truly feel he may join us, I'll tell him," she conceded.

"Who may join us?" Marit asked.

Kirsten turned to look at her mother, struck suddenly by how beautiful the woman was. Kirsten had always taken that fact for granted until half an hour ago. Now she looked at her mother with fresh eyes and wondered if she, too, had been misjudged all of her life. Perhaps that was one of the reasons her mother left Norway.

"Kirsten has just reported the happy news that Captain Hansen's eyes are healing. The man has retained his sight," Henrik explained. "We are going to have him grace our supper table for the remainder of his stay."

"He is an officer." Marit admitted. Her evaluative gaze slid to Kirsten. "Might you have an objection?"

Backed into a corner with no understanding as to why she felt that way, Kirsten had nothing to say but, "No, *Mamma*."

Her mother nodded. "I'll let the kitchen know."

Kirsten stood and affected a smile she hoped was convincing. "I'll tell the captain. Then I believe I'll catch up on my correspondences."

She gave her mother a kiss on the cheek as she left her father's study. She walked slowly across the entry, breathing deeply to slow her overly-excited heart, and went to tell Reid he would be joining them for supper.

✯ ✯ ✯

Reid wore the tinted glasses to supper. Even so, his healing eyes watered in the candlelight. He apologized and used his linen napkin to blot the tears.

"Nonsense!" Henrik stated over his soup. "We are all greatly relieved that you are mending so well."

"Thank you, sir. I do have another concern, if I might?" Reid ventured.

"Of course. What can I do for you?" Henrik asked.

Reid shifted in his chair, embarrassed by the need to bring up his particular situation. And yet it was, indeed, necessary. He avoided looking at Kirsten, even so. Her opinion of him was the one he wished most to preserve.

"I don't remember the explosion," he began. "But obviously I was carried here without my belongings. The suggestion was made that they burned in a fire."

Henrik's expression shifted from curiosity to understanding. "You have need for clothes. Not my ill-fitting garments."

"Well, yes. And weapons, I'm afraid. I'm not much good to the army without either one," Reid admitted.

"Is there anything else?" Henrik pressed.

Reid's face felt like it was set on fire. "No. But I don't have any money. I am owed quite a bit of past compensation from the army, although I don't know when to expect payment."

"How much past?" Kirsten asked.

Reid looked at her through the tinted glass; the grayed lenses provided a modicum of social protection as well. "Two years."

Henrik leaned forward, his expression incredulous. "You have not been paid for your labors for two years?"

He returned his gaze to his host. "No, sir."

"How do you survive?" Marit asked.

Reid saw Kirsten wince and knew she remembered his revelation about scavenging from dead soldiers. "It's a challenge," was all he said.

Henrik slapped his palm on the table. "This is not acceptable. That an officer of the Continental Army should be forced to beg for his supplies like an indigent pauper."

"What will you do?" Kirsten asked her father, her eyes wide. Her beautiful glacier-water-blue eyes.

Stop it.

"What any upstanding American should do, I believe," he stated. "I'll summon my tailor tomorrow and have Captain Hansen completely outfitted."

"I shall only need the one uniform," Reid demurred.

"Nonsense. You'll take what I provide," Henrik objected. "The subject is closed."

Reid looked at Kirsten, trying to judge her reaction. Was she proud of her father's generosity, or might she feel Reid had somehow manipulated the situation?

"Thank you, sir," he responded. "But I must make you aware that your benevolence may clothe more than one soldier."

One side of Henrik's mouth curved. "Well played, Captain."

Reid grinned. "I followed your lead, sir."

Silent servants cleared their bowls and set down small plates of pickled vegetables.

"You said you went to Harvard," Kirsten stated out of nowhere.

All eyes jumped to him.

"Did you finish?" Marit asked.

"I did, yes. I studied architecture and engineering like my father," he answered, wondering at the sudden shift.

"Tell us about your family," Marit urged.

Reid saw Kirsten's satisfied smile. It occurred to him that perhaps she understood his embarrassment at being forced to ask for help. Having him talk about his education and his family might be her way of giving him a chance to prove himself better than a beggar. If that was so, Reid's already high opinion of her ratcheted up another notch.

"My parents emigrated from Norway in 1749. They met and were married on the ship, and I was born in Boston after an appropriate passage of time," he began.

"Where in Norway?" Henrik asked.

"My mother was raised in Christiania, but my father's family has lived in Arendal since the Viking age," Reid explained.

"You are the firstborn?" Marit confirmed.

"I am."

"Have you left any siblings behind?" she probed.

Reid faced her. "Three brothers, two of which are also serving in the Continental Army. The youngest remained behind to help my father and mother. My three sisters are all married."

Marit continued her interrogation. "Did your brothers attend Harvard as well?"

"The one after me began his education there, but left to fight the English." Reid sipped the German wine that accompanied the soup and vegetables. It was excellent, as was every other detail in this elegant house.

"The war was necessary, I do believe that," Kirsten observed quietly. "But the cost is high, and in so many ways."

Servants served the main course of the meal while Reid waited in silence. His white wine was replaced with a French Bordeaux. Again, it was excellent—and the perfect accompaniment to the roasted beef.

"You set a beautiful table, Mistress Sven," he complimented and turned to Henrik. "And your taste in wine is exemplary, sir."

"Do you possess an educated palate?" Henrik asked, his interest clear.

Reid gave a small shrug. "My palate is not as educated as my mind, I confess. And both have suffered from the lack of uplifting stimulation for many years. That said, I do recognize a good vintage when I taste one."

Kirsten beamed at him. Obviously he was playing his undefined part well.

Marit tilted her head as she cut her meat. "What will you do once the war ends, Captain?"

What indeed. His future was a hazy area which he hadn't seen clearly for years.

"That will depend on which side wins," he opined. "And what sentence is imposed on the losers."

Henrik coughed a harsh laugh. "We'll beat the English. And their crazy king. Why, he's a—"

"Henrik!" Marit snapped. "You forget yourself."

The man managed to look outraged and chastised at the same time. Kirsten's eyes were round as the candlestick on the end of Reid's cane. Reid couldn't believe they were all still cautious about criticizing King George, in spite of Henrik's claim the man was as good as done.

"I do believe we will win as well," Reid assured them.

Henrik lifted the decanter and refilled Reid's wineglass, and then his own. "Sooner better than later, I pray."

"What will you do, Reid?" Kirsten asked. Judging by her expression, she was sincerely concerned. "When you finish soldiering, that is."

"I have no idea," he admitted. "I have stopped making plans. Each time I thought we were winning the war and began to, a new battle erupted and set us back. It seems to be bad luck."

Her head tipped to one side. "Do you hope to have a family someday?"

Reid saw Marit's head jerk just the smallest bit. He imagined he knew what she thought of Kirsten's question. Even if he wanted to persuade Kirsten to accept him someday, his prospects could never match her expectations. Her mother needn't worry.

He looked directly into Kirsten's eyes as best he could through his healing fog and dark glasses.

"Every man hopes in his heart to found his own dynasty, does he not? To reign as sovereign over his own lands and family." He paused and closed his eyes, giving them a moment's respite. "I'm no different from any man in that regard."

"Will you accomplish it, do you believe?" Her query was soft, almost wistful.

The weight of her question pressed down on his shoulders. With each passing year, that likelihood became less and less probable.

Sometimes he felt as if their entire country had been cursed to live in a purgatory of war and struggle only because they had the unified nerve to stand up against a tyrant.

Reid opened his eyes and blotted the tears he could blame on his recuperation. "I'm already thirty-one years old. And because of the circumstances of my Bostonian birth a quarter century before this fight erupted, I am worse than penniless."

He sighed and looked at Kirsten again. "I honestly don't know if I ever will."

"This conversation has become rather maudlin," Henrik declared. He lifted his wineglass. "I give you Captain Reid Hansen of the Continental Army. You, sir, are a hero in my family's eyes and we thank you from the depths of our hearts for your continued sacrifices on our behalf."

Reid felt himself blush and he allowed a shy smile as he lifted his own glass. "Thank you."

Henrik drained his glass and set it on the table. "Ready for dessert?"

★ ★ ★

Reid was amazed how much having his sight back improved the way he felt.

His headaches had disappeared. The sporadic nausea caused by the disorientation of unexpected movement was gone. He was no longer at the mercy of others for his basic needs, including the need to do something as simple as taking a walk.

When dinner was finished, Reid took the liberty of walking out of doors. Because it was dark, with only a waxing moon for light, he didn't need his protective glasses.

He still relied on the cane-and-candlestick contraption to keep from overusing his right leg, but even that appendage was strengthening. *Thank God.*

He strolled to the end of the drive, not trusting his sight to lead him well enough in the dark to venture off the known path. He turned when he reached the end and walked back toward the house.

He could see it ahead of him, its size and scope now apparent. The portico in front was supported on tall white pillars. Every window was lit, as if some huge event was happening inside. The mansion—for in truth, that is what is was—glowed like a rich man's jack-o-lantern.

Reid smiled at his impromptu mental description. *I'll have to remember that and use it again.*

As he approached, he saw a light-colored dress standing on the porch in front of the door. It began to sway and move toward him.

"I was worried about you getting lost," Kirsten scolded when she drew close.

"So was I," he chuckled. "That's why I stayed on the drive."

She swung one hand toward the house. "Are you going inside?"

He shook his head. "Not yet. The weather is refreshing and I've been trapped indoors for so many days."

She looked up at him. "In that case, would you mind company?"

"Not at all." He offered her his arm. "I'm being polite. You still must chart our course."

Kirsten wordlessly hooked her arm through his and led them away from the manor. They walked for several minutes without speaking.

"May I ask you a question?" she said when they were at a safe distance from the house.

"If I said no, would that stop you?" he teased.

She yanked on his arm. "Be nice."

"My apologies," he offered. "What is the question?"

She hesitated and cleared her throat before releasing her words. "Do I look anything like you thought I would?"

Reid knew this was a subject which could explode in his face, and experiencing one explosion was enough for this season. He took a gamble, praying he wouldn't lose.

"No," he began slowly. "I thought you'd be pretty."

Kirsten pulled his arm, stopping his progress and spinning him to face her. "What?"

Even through his blurred vision, Reid could see her indignation. He spread his hands and leaned his face closer to hers. "What do you expect me to say, Kirsten?"

She appeared baffled. "I expect you to tell me the truth."

Reid wagged his head in strong denial of her words. "If I had told you the truth this afternoon, all you would have heard is one more man judging you by the way you look."

Her mouth gaped. "How can you—"

"Stop!" he commanded. "Not another word."

Her mouth snapped shut. Her brow lowered and her eyes narrowed. Her lips pressed into a tight line. He wondered if anyone else ever ordered her about in such a way.

"We became acquainted when I could not see you. You said our friendship would change once I saw you. Why? Because you are stunningly beautiful. Am I correct so far? Nod if you agree," he barked.

Her brow lifted when he acknowledged her beauty. She jerked a small, silent nod.

"I don't care that you are the most attractive woman I have ever laid eyes on. I knew this"—he pointed at her heart—"before I saw this." His finger traced a quick circle in front of her face.

She looked stricken. "Reid—"

"I am not finished," he growled.

"I'm sorry," she whispered.

"There is one thing you need to know about me. Are you listening?"

Another tiny nod. Her eyes were pinned to his. Her chest rose and fell with her breath, pressing the swells of her bosom against the restraint of her gown.

He leaned over to whisper in her ear, knowing that there were times when a quiet tone could shriek louder than a banshee's wail.

"The next time you kiss me, you had better mean it."

CHAPTER NINE

Kirsten gasped. She would have slapped him if he hadn't already moved out of her reach.

"How dare you?" she yelped at his back.

"I'm just being honest," he tossed over his shoulder as he climbed the steps to the front door. He paused at the top and turned to face her. He gave an awkward bow which had an unexpectedly courtly flavor due to the necessity of keeping his right leg straight. "Sleep well, my friend."

She watched him hobble into the house, shocked to her core, unable to move.

Reid Hansen confounded her at every turn. Every conversation she had with the man started with one subject and somehow ended up in an entirely different place. She never anticipated his changes in direction and those changes kept her off balance. Reid seemed to think in such a unique way that he made mental connections she didn't foresee, nor was she prepared for.

Kirsten had been raised to act certain ways in certain situations. Her training was formal and precise—and utterly necessary when she was in Norway and Denmark. Here in Philadelphia she seldom met her match when it came to courtly manners, however, so she was accustomed to leading the conversation around subjects that interested her. In fact, she was quite skilled at it.

Those skills were useless with Captain Hansen. He had his own subjects of interest and unabashedly led the conversation down those paths. The fact that he was blunt, almost to the point of rudeness, made her pristine manners useless. She either had to meet his challenge or not converse with him at all.

That was not a pleasant prospect either.

Kirsten began to circle the portico, unable to remain still any longer as Reid's forceful words echoed in her mind. His claim—if he had told her the truth this afternoon, she would have assumed he was judging her—rang uncomfortably true. When he avoided the subject, she thought he was being intentionally contrary. Now she understood he was merely dodging the musket ball she had aimed squarely at his head.

And yet, when she pressed him tonight for an answer, he gave her the dressing down her attitude deserved but her status had always protected her from. He actually shouted at her. No one ever shouted at her. Her sense of outrage bubbled up again until the truth bashed it back down where it belonged. The captain didn't know who she really was.

Another realization elbowed its way into the forefront of her thoughts. Buried in that dressing down were the words she thought he would say, but not at all in the way she thought he would say them.

Our friendship would change because you are stunningly beautiful...

I don't care that you are the most attractive woman I have ever laid eyes on...

The more she paced in circles around the portico the more she understood. He wanted her to know he noticed. No, more than noticed; appreciated. He did find her beautiful after all. But Reid grasped her point in the dark intimacy of his makeshift bedroom well enough to know he could not say those things to her outright. If he had, she would have dismissed him as just another man blinded by what he saw.

Kirsten stopped as if she had walked into a stone wall. In truth, she felt as if she had. Her pulse pounded as the ramifications of her understanding flushed through her frame and set every last nerve on alert.

Reid Hansen did not want her to see him as just another man.

And he acted in such a way to assure that she would not.

When Reid was blinded by his bandages, Kirsten discovered a sense of freedom which she had never felt with any other man, ever.

His restraint somehow removed hers. She was able to be her true self in his presence and drop the strictures of her position.

Their conversations were honest ones, never the sort she might have with a suitor begging for her favor. When Reid was blind, he saw her. Now that he could see again, he wanted her to know that.

Kirsten's hands began to shake. When she burst into those humiliating tears the other day for no apparent reason, Reid pulled her into his embrace and held her there. For the first time in years she felt safe in a man's arms. While she should find that a comforting thought, she did not. Even if Reid was not a soldier about to march back to war and out of her life, she could never marry him.

She shook out her hands and began to walk toward the front door. He challenged her not to kiss him again unless she meant it. Kirsten needed to give that some thought. Perhaps before he left she would do so, if only to claim one last reminder of how happy her life might have been.

September 11, 1781

Reid stood in his private parlor room while the tailor measured the length and breadth of his frame and wondered once more what in the good name of all that was Holy prompted him to challenge Kirsten to kiss him again.

That thought pestered him all night. He even dreamt she kissed him, but in the convoluted manner of dreams she did so in the most public of places and inappropriate of times. He awoke confused and irritated.

He had to remind himself that she hadn't actually committed the act, so his irritation couldn't be directed at her. In fact, he probably owed her an apology for chastising her yester eve. She was a genteel woman, not a soldier. He should not have barked orders at her like she was some wet-behind-the-ears farm boy.

There remained his challenge to her, however, spoken without forethought. Was that what he truly desired; that the independent, intelligent, unpredictable—and yes, beautiful—Kirsten Sven would kiss him again with intent? If she did so, he would need to respond.

Reid was fairly certain that, this gift of clothing aside, her parents would not be pleased to have their daughter courted by an apparent pauper even if he was a captain in the army. They had higher aspirations for her, even if she had dug in her heels against fulfilling them.

That was not a battle he wished to engage in. Kirsten's conflict was not his. Better to hold back and remain safely entrenched out of range.

The tailor's hand slid up the inside of Reid's thigh and startled him back into the room.

"Spread your legs a bit will you?" the man asked. "I need to measure your inseams."

Reid complied, a little embarrassed by the man's unanticipated intimacy. The only other people who ever sewed his clothes were his mother and sisters. When they measured him there, he held the tape in place. For a tailor to do so was obviously expected, as evinced by the man's businesslike air. He moved the tape quickly from one leg to the other, then wrote the numbers down on his list. Still, Reid had been caught off guard and that always made him uncomfortable.

"Now, Captain, let's look at materials." The tailor unrolled several selections of woven wool and linsey-woolsey. "I recommend the linsey-woolsey for your regular uniform as it's a bit hardier."

Reid agreed. Though not as elegant a fabric, he was less concerned about that than the idea this might be his last chance to procure a uniform that actually fit him. He would need it to survive as long as possible.

"I agree. I'll take the gray." Reid pointed at a sample that matched most of the tree barks he encountered. Moving unseen in forests was an important consideration. "Be certain to add yellow stripes on the sleeves."

"Yellow for a captain. Of course. And the trousers? Perhaps something darker." Reid was presented with charcoal gray and dark brown options.

"Brown." Mud was always a concern.

"Very good, sir." The tailor made the appropriate notes. "For your dress uniform, however, I recommend going with the wool. Do you want the same colors?"

Reid frowned. "My dress uniform?"

The tailor looked up from his paper. "Mister Sven said I was to outfit you for both battle and social occasions."

That was unexpectedly generous. Reid glanced at the fabrics and picked the first color he saw. "The dark blue."

The man looked back at his paper and resumed writing. "And the trousers?"

"Gray, I suppose."

"Excellent," the man replied without looking up.

An intuition niggled at Reid's mind. "What else did Mister Sven order?"

The tailor straightened. "Three linen shirts, three sets of small clothes, and four pair of stockings, two of those wool."

Reid sat down hard on his cot. "That much? How will I carry it all?"

The tailor grinned. "In the new pack my brother-in-law is making."

"And my weapons?" Reid prompted, another suspicion making itself known.

The grin widened. "My father has the best selection of Pennsylvania long rifles left in Philadelphia. Yours will be delivered later today."

Reid glanced at his boots, standing by his cot. "At least I still have my own boots."

The tailor's gaze followed his. "Oh, dear."

"They are a little worn," Reid admitted.

The other man's brow wrinkled. "A little?"

He reached into his satchel and pulled out a sheet of paper and a stick of charcoal. He marched over to the boots, plopped them on the paper one at a time and traced their soles.

"Black, I assume," he said as he worked.

Reid chuckled. "Don't tell me—your uncle is a cobbler."

"Cousin, actually." The tailor looked up and winked. "Uncle Seth retired last year."

"Did Mister Sven account for the boots?" Reid asked warily. "Because I have no money to pay for them."

The boots were back in their spot and the man straightened. "He said to procure whatever else you needed that he hadn't thought of."

Reid was honestly stunned by Henrik's generosity. "I don't know what to say…"

"The same thing I did," the tailor quipped as he gathered all of his paraphernalia and dumped it in his satchel. "I do thank you, sir, most sincerely!"

★ ★ ★

Kirsten waited until the tailor had been gone for a quarter hour so she wouldn't appear too eager to see Reid. When she knocked on his open door he looked up from his book. He wasn't wearing his spectacles and she noticed that a little of the swelling around his eyes had receded.

"You found the library, I see," she said as she strolled into the room. "Can you read well enough in this light?"

"It seems bright to me," he replied with a rueful grin. "But I'm not complaining."

Kirsten sat in one of the upholstered chairs near the settee where Reid lounged. He closed the book and laid it in his lap.

"I owe you an apology," he began.

"No, that's why I'm here," She objected. "I owe you one."

Reid's gaze was pensive. "Go on."

"You could have objected longer," she said, partly in jest.

He laughed. "My turn is coming. But I was always taught to let ladies go first."

He made a salient point. Kirsten drew a deep breath. "I am afraid I did put you in an untenable position."

Reid waited, his expression unchanged.

"After I told you that people judged me by my looks, I was offended when you didn't say I was pretty," she admitted. Her cheeks flamed her embarrassment and she silently blessed the room's dim light. "And yet, you were right when you called me to task."

When she paused he asked. "How so?"

He was not making this easy on her. "If you had said I was attractive, then I would have been just as offended. There was no answer you could have given which I could have accepted."

"Do I receive credit for realizing that before I blurted out my answer?" Reid asked.

Was that a twinkle in his eye? Kirsten wondered. Or perhaps they were simply watering again.

"Yes," she conceded. "You do."

Reid dipped his head and gave her a soft smile. "Apology accepted, Miss Sven. All is forgiven."

"Thank you, Captain Hansen," she responded. "Your turn."

Reid straightened on the settee and set the book on a side table. He leaned toward her, resting an elbow on his one bent knee.

"Kirsten, I apologize for raising my voice to you. You are a woman gently born and you should never be spoken to in such a manner," he began.

Kirsten stared into his eyes as he spoke. Their gray centers and blue rims were so unique that she couldn't look away.

"Furthermore, I purposely buried my compliments in such a way that they didn't sound like compliments at all," he confessed.

"I heard them," she interrupted. "That was when I realized what I had done."

"I'd like to correct that failing," he continued.

Kirsten shook her head. "There is no need. I don't need to hear—"

"Yes. You do." His retort was almost a command. Almost.

"Reid…"

"Just listen, will you?" he pressed. "Might you do a poor, injured, and unimportant soldier this small favor?"

Kirsten smiled at that. "You are incorrigible."

"So I have been told."

She flipped her wrist dismissively. "Go ahead then. If you must."

Reid resettled his stance on the settee and flexed his arms, as if preparing for some physical event. "Are you ready?"

Kirsten nodded. Curiosity shoved aside her lingering embarrassment and plopped down next to her in the chair. She honestly wondered what sort of recitation was about to take place.

"First of all, you are a kind and generous woman. I know this because you were at my side when I first became aware after being injured. Your touch and your voice calmed me when I thought I might be blinded."

"Thank you," she murmured.

"Secondly, I heard your—how shall I describe it?—intentional dissuasion of the suitor your parents put on display that first night."

Kirsten's embarrassment returned and knocked curiosity to the floor. "That was—"

"Funny," he interrupted. "And clever. And you made a point which, if I'm not mistaken, you had tried to make before?"

She nodded. "My mother refuses to believe me."

Reid put held up his palm. "Third, you visited me in the night. Under the cover of darkness and bandages, you showed me what was in your heart. I saw the real Kirsten."

Kirsten glanced at the open parlor door.

"No one is there," Reid assured her. "I wouldn't have said it aloud if someone was."

She turned back to face him.

"Last of all, my bandages were removed and I saw your visage. And you are, indeed, the singularly most beautiful woman I have ever come across," he admitted. "I have to be honest with you. I don't know how else to be."

"Thank you," she whispered.

If she was the honest one, she would say that his complimenting her beauty now was so unimportant after hearing his other declarations. Staring into his bloodshot, bruised, and beautiful eyes, however, had silenced her voice.

"I have one more thing to add." He shifted forward in his seat. "I already believed you were a truly beautiful woman. Seeing how you look didn't change my estimation."

Kirsten's gaze dropped to his lips. The urge to kiss him overwhelmed and terrified her. She froze, unsure of what to do.

"Not unless you mean it," he murmured.

Her eyes shot up to meet his, intense and pinned on hers. For a pace, she didn't even breathe.

"I have to go," she rasped.

She stood and walked from the room, fighting the urge to flee.

CHAPTER TEN

September 13, 1781

Reid assumed the resounding knock on the manor's front door would be Doctor Haralson coming to remove the stitches in his leg. He was surprised by the envelope brought to him in the doctor's stead. It was addressed simply to R.H.

He looked up at Horace. "Who brought this?"

"A rather non-descript soldier wearing brown," the valet replied.

"Horseback or on foot?" Reid pressed.

Horace's brow furrowed. "I didn't see a horse."

Reid pushed himself up from an upholstered bench in the library, his heavy book falling to the ground with a loud, flat-sided crack. He step-hopped to the entry and yanked the front door open. Between the portico's pillars he could see all the way down the drive.

No one was there.

Skitt.

"Is anything amiss, sir?" Horace asked from just behind his right shoulder.

Reid shook his head, still staring down the drive as if he could make the mystery messenger reappear by sheer will. "No," he grunted.

Reid closed the front door, resisting the urge to slam it, and hobbled past a worried Horace into his parlor.

"Would you care for tea?" the valet offered. "Perhaps a

biscuit?"

"Yes, thank you," Reid answered without looking up. He broke the seal on the note and unfolded the thick paper.

Just received word you were injured, not killed. When you are able, come directly to the farm. More was discovered regarding the target and the marksman.

     102

Reid refolded the paper. He walked to the fireplace and tossed it into the small flame. The paper flared briefly before crumbling into ash. He stared at the remainders of the message and knew for certain that the explosion was no accident.

He just needed to remember what happened.

"Was that the doctor?" Kirsten asked from the parlor's doorway.

Reid turned and smiled at her. "No. I had hoped so as well."

She clasped her hands behind her and returned his smile. "Would you care to take a walk while we wait?"

"Horace is bringing tea and biscuits," Reid said as he limped toward her. "Will you join me? We can walk afterward if Haralson still has not arrived."

"Yes, that would be lovely," she replied.

Reid reached the parlor door and offered his arm. "Let's have our refreshments in the drawing room. I spend enough time in here."

Kirsten hooked her arm through his, offering him support in his lameness.

Reid hoped that once the stitches were removed he might be able to test the limits of his leg. The message in the note cleared away the cloud of denial he had rested in these last ten days and the time for him to return to his duties was nigh. Once his clothing and weapon arrived, he would leave the Sven household. And Kirsten.

He settled into a chair and considered his hostess. She had made her views regarding marriage quite clear to him. Even so, her actions toward him spoke of more than friendship, and he wondered if she was reconsidering her position. Though he had nothing to offer her at the moment, he might in the future. By the time he went on his way, he needed to decide whether to open that door, or leave it closed and walk away with no strings trailing behind.

"What are you pondering so somberly?" she asked.

"I have a war to return to," he answered. "That isn't a pleasant consideration."

Her expression cooled. "No. It is not."

A servant girl carried in the tray of tea and biscuits. Neither Kirsten nor Reid spoke as she poured their cups and set out plates.

"Will there be anything else?" she asked.

"No, thank you," Kirsten replied.

The girl curtsied and left.

"I shall be quite bored when you leave, you realize," Kirsten said.

Reid gave her a crooked grin. "Perhaps I should write to my superiors and ask their leave to remain here and entertain you on a daily basis."

She huffed a little chuckle. "You are not *that* much fun."

He clapped a hand over his heart. "You wound so deeply with your words. Alas, I am cast back into the cauldron of conflict," he teased.

Kirsten flashed him half-a-smile and blew on the liquid in her cup. She took a sip of her tea. Reid bit into a sugared biscuit.

She considered him over her steaming cup. "After the war you hope to get land of your own."

He nodded. "I do."

"Do you know how you will manage that?" she probed.

He shook his head. "I do not."

Her brow twitched. "To reign as sovereign over your lands and family—wasn't that what you said?"

Reid made a dismissive gesture with the biscuit still in his hand. "Expansive dinner conversation is not to be used as testimony against anyone."

Kirsten sighed and stared at nothing. "Sovereignty is not an easy burden, just the same," she said after a pace.

"And I don't expect to run a country. Only a few hundred acres with a servant or two," he countered. "Where is this grave humor coming from?"

She blinked her turquoise eyes back to his as if she had forgotten he was there. "Don't mind me. I was reading a book about

Denmark."

Reid laughed. "Was it Hamlet? No wonder you are so maudlin."

Kirsten smiled, appearing relieved for some unexplained reason. "And without you to walk me out every afternoon and enliven my dinner conversation each evening, how will my spirits be lifted?"

"I'm certain you will adjust to the loss," he quipped with a grin. "After all, I'm not *that* much fun."

☆ ☆ ☆

Kirsten nearly choked on her tea. After much coughing and resultant back-slapping, she squinted up at Captain Hansen through watering eyes.

"Are you trying to kill me?"

"I'm so sorry!" Reid declared, looking quite contrite. "Are you recovered?"

"If you stop beating me to death I might have a chance," she squeaked.

Reid dropped back into his chair, his expression still etched with concern. "You said once that my sense of humor was going to get you in trouble."

"I was jesting, you idiot!" she rasped between intermittent coughs and reluctant giggles.

The door knocker drew her attention.

"Shall I ask the doctor to see you first?" Reid asked.

"That's not necessary." Kirsten took a long gulp of her cooled tea. "I am fine."

Horace appeared at the drawing room door. "Doctor Haralson has arrived."

Kirsten set her cup down, careful to not break off this one's handle, and stood. "Show him to the parlor, Horace. We shall join him presently."

Horace gave a small bow. "Yes, Miss."

Kirsten steadied Reid as he hobbled across the entry. She helped him into the parlor, wondering if she might be allowed to stay.

"Thank you, my dear," the doctor said gently as he gestured

toward the door. "I'll call you back in when we have finished."

Kirsten flashed a gracious smile, and then positioned herself outside the closed portal with her ear smashed flat against it. The men's words were muffled, but she caught most of them. There was a pause while Reid removed his breeches. Kirsten bit her lips and tried not to imagine what the captain might look like disrobed.

"Good. Very good," Doctor Haralson said, followed by the sounds of rummaging in a case. "This will probably be a bit uncomfortable, and the wound might bleed."

Reid didn't say anything intelligible in reply.

The next several minutes passed in silence. Kirsten blew her impatience out loose lips.

"There we are. How does it feel?"

"Sore. But not intolerable, by any means," Reid answered.

"I'm going to wrap it again to give the wound support as it heals. You can begin to bend your leg now. But if you feel the gash pulling, you must stop immediately or you might reopen it."

Reid must have nodded his response.

"Headaches?"

"Gone."

"How are your eyes?"

"Improving."

"Are you still wearing the spectacles?"

"I do when I go out of doors."

"Mm-hmm."

More rummaging in the case.

"Doctor, may I ask you a question?"

The rummaging stopped. "Of course."

"I don't remember the explosion, nor do I recall what happened just before it…"

Kirsten held her breath, shocked by Reid's words.

"That's not unusual. And it's nothing to be worried about."

There was a pause. "Will I ever remember?"

"I can't answer that." This time the doctor paused. "Is there a reason you need to remember?"

"There might be."

That's interesting. I wonder what could the reason be?

The rummaging continued. "In that case I wish you luck. There isn't anything further I can do."

"Thank you, Doctor."

"It has been my honor, Captain."

Kirsten backed away from the door. As soon as the latch clicked she walked past as if the timing was mere coincidence. She spun to face the opening portal.

"Doctor Haralson! Are you finished?" she enquired cheerily.

"We are," he said turning toward the front door. "And I am glad to report that Captain Hansen is well on the road to recovery."

"That is such good news," she gushed.

Haralson rested his hand on the door handle. "He should be able to return to his regiment in another week."

"That long?" Reid's voice spilled over her shoulder.

She was thinking *that soon?* Based on their conversation before the doctor arrived, she didn't expect Reid to sound so eager.

"Stay off horses for two weeks," the doctor ordered. "And God speed."

Kirsten turned to Reid as she closed the door behind the departing physician. "Do you have a horse?"

"No," he replied.

"So you walk everywhere you go?" That seemed inefficient. And slow.

Reid shrugged. "Now you know why the war drags on."

She stepped closer. "How does your leg feel?"

Reid bent his knee into a right angle. "Bending it this far doesn't hurt. That's an improvement."

Kirsten wagged a finger at him. "You know what Doctor Haralson said. If you feel the gash pulling, you must stop immediately or you might reopen it."

"I heard him." Reid flashed an incredulous grin. "But how did you?"

✫ ✫ ✫

Reid watched with amusement as Kirsten's cheeks turned an amazing shade of deep rose. The color was stunning next to her eyes. He debated whether to let her squirm or offer her dispensation.

Dispensation won out.

"Because if our roles were reversed," he offered. "There is a very good chance that I would have been listening outside the door."

"You are incorrigible," she huffed.

"As are you, so it would seem." He winked and swept a hand toward the door. "Are we still taking our walk?"

Kirsten wavered. "I thought your leg was sore."

"It's the sort of sore that exercise would be good for, I think." He glanced out one of the two tall windows flanking the carved wooden door. The sun was currently hidden by clouds, though an abundance of blue sky was still visible. "Do you need a wrap?"

"No, I'll be fine." She tucked her hand in the crook of his arm. "Let's go before the weather turns.

Reid donned his tinted glasses before he led Kirsten down the steps, the first time he did so without using his funny-looking cane. It felt good to be relying on his own strength. He set off on their accustomed stroll down the long drive. Clouds scudded overhead, alternately allowing and withholding the warmth of the sun in their spirited game of chase.

"Since you know I was listening at the door—and were rude enough to tell me so," Kirsten began.

"Oh no," Reid objected. "You revealed that indiscretion yourself, if you will recall. Keep your facts straight, darling."

Kirsten blew huff of irritation. "The details are unimportant. But there is something I wanted to ask you about."

"Go on," Reid urged.

"I heard you say you can't remember the explosion, nor what happened right before it." She looked up at him. "While I can understand that must be disconcerting, why else do you want to remember?"

Reid walked in silence and considered how to answer her. "Because... it's possible that the explosion was not an accident."

"You mean you were attacked?" she clarified.

"I mean," he said slowly. "That it's possible that someone meant to do harm to someone else."

She shook her head. "That's a rather esoteric answer, isn't it?"

Reid stopped walking and looked down at her. "If there was a reason for the explosion, then my being able to remember is critical to discovering that reason."

"Is that your responsibility?" she pressed.

Reid hesitated before admitting the truth. "Yes."

Her eyes widened. "Why?"

"Because that is one of the reasons I was sent here."

Her brow furrowed delicately. "You were sent here in case there was an attack? Or because you knew there would be one?"

Reid struggled with how much to tell her. It wasn't likely she would ever have a conversation with anyone to whom this information might be of interest, but one never knew.

"We had reason to believe something might happen," he allowed. "Please don't ask me any more."

He watched her decide whether or not to be offended by that request, and was amazed at how her emotions played so openly over her features. This woman could never be a spy. Her thoughts were displayed as clearly as if they were written in ink across her forehead. At least, they were to him.

"Because if I tell you any more," he cajoled, trying to make her laugh, "then I would have to kill you in order to keep our secrets."

Kirsten screwed up her mouth and stuck her tongue at him. He laughed, glad to see her playfulness.

"Walk me back to the house?" she beseeched. "I'm starting to get cold."

CHAPTER ELEVEN

Reid stood in the parlor and stared at the wrapped bundles lined up on his cot. His new wardrobe had, apparently, arrived. On the floor, resting against the crate which extended his pallet, was a sturdy leather pack, generous in size, and designed to be worn on a sling that went over his shoulder and across his chest. The pack had two buckled pouches on the outside, so he would have easy access to whatever he found useful to store there. Next to the pack was a pair of tall, black boots.

His rifle had arrived days ago, and came with oil and a box of bullets. Reid had taken the weapon outside to practice shooting and was very pleased with both the accuracy and distance which the Pennsylvania rifle was capable of. The desire to return to his duties began niggling at him that very day.

Standing in his adopted chamber now, he flexed his right thigh. There remained some stiffness and soreness, but he assured himself of daily improvement. Now that his uniforms had arrived, he should make plans to leave.

Reid began opening the bundles. He shut the door of the parlor, stripped off the shirt and breeches which had been his only attire for the last week and a half, and began to try on the new garments. As he did so, he folded the items and stacked them on the cot in a way which made sense for stowing them in the leather pack.

The fit was excellent, down to the smallclothes. The linen shirts were roomy, but not excessively so. The daily uniform of linsey-woolsey was solidly constructed and should last him years. When he unwrapped the dress uniform, however, he sucked a slow breath of appreciation.

The dark blue wool was finely woven and deceptively soft. His yellow captain's stripe circled the left sleeve—a solution Reid preferred over General Washington's suggestion of a captain's cockade on his hat. Mostly because he seldom wore a hat; he found them to be a hindrance. Other than the stripe and a touch of red piping here and there, the jacket was simple and finely tailored. Reid slipped it on. It fit perfectly.

Next came the gray woolen trousers. Though he would tuck the trousers of either uniform inside his boots when he was in battle, both pair were long enough to be left outside the boots on more formal occasions without making him look like an adolescent pup whose mother couldn't sew fast enough for his spurting growth.

Reid smiled at the clearly remembered, and accurate, illustration of his youth.

He swiped his palm across his chin, rasping his whiskers, and decided to thank Henrik by putting himself on display tonight. He would shave, bathe, and wear the formal uniform to dinner. Tonight he would show them the man who had been hidden and hobbled by his injuries.

Reid removed the formal garments and laid them out on his cot before searching out Horace.

"I'll need a shave and a proper bath," Reid told the valet once he ran the man to ground. "My new uniform has arrived and I want to make a proper show of my thanks."

Horace looked as though he had been handed a plate of Christmas sweets. "Yes, sir! I should be happy to oblige. Follow me, will you?"

Reid followed Horace to an alcove off the kitchen. Along the way, the valet ordered the tin tub and hot water to be set up in the space. He directed Reid to sit in the simple yet sturdy wooden chair waiting there.

"I'll shave you first, while we await the bath," he explained.

Reid took his seat and gave himself over to Horace's skilled ministrations. The hot towels to soften his skin and beard, the richly whipped-up soap lather, the rasping scrape as his stubble was removed row by row. Horace had an experienced hand and didn't nick him even once. The man possessed a rare skill indeed.

Another hot towel wiped away the remainder of the soap. Reid always missed this luxury when he was in the field. He promised himself yet again that he would treat himself whenever the opportunity arose. If he had any money to pay the barber, that was.

"Would you like me to cut your hair, sir?" Horace asked, the razor still in his hand.

"I need it long enough to tie out of the way," Reid explained. "In battle I cannot have hair in my eyes."

Horace set the razor down, untied Reid's hair, and combed it out with his fingers. "I could trim it a good three or four inches and it would still have adequate length," he suggested.

"Why not?" Reid acquiesced, chuckling. "I should take advantage of your services while I have the chance. Lord knows when I'll find myself in such luxury again!"

The valet smiled, obviously pleased that his suggestion was taken. He procured a proper comb and worked the tangles out of Reid's hair before trimming it just as he said.

When Horace was finished, Reid ran his fingers through his hair. It hung just to his shoulders—a much easier length to maintain.

"That's perfect, Horace," he complimented. "Thank you."

"My pleasure, sir. Will you need help with your bath?" The steaming tub was now ready and waiting in the alcove.

"I believe I can manage," Reid answered.

"Very good." Horace placed a folded privacy screen across the opening to the small space. "Here is the soap. I'll bring your towels. Take as much time as you need."

"Thank you."

Once he was sheltered, Reid again stripped off the borrowed shirt and breeches, as well as the bandage around his thigh. The gash was healing, though it left a dark pink trail about half an inch wide and six inches long through the dark blond forest on his leg.

He stepped into the tub of hot water and eased himself into another luxury he seldom experienced. For several minutes, he closed his eyes and merely enjoyed the heat. It soaked into his thigh and eased the ache. Reid didn't move until the water began to cool.

Dunking his head under the water, he scrubbed his scalp clean. Then he soaped and scrubbed his other important parts. Having finished his pleasure, and done his duty, he stood in the tub and began to dry himself off.

Kirsten waited for Reid to join them for dinner, her impatience playing out in the tap of her slipper under the table and the bounce of her fork on top of it.

After their walk today, Reid had disappeared. His door was shut. He neither joined her for tea in the drawing room, nor met her in the library to read together, as had become their habit in the shortening afternoons.

The worst part was how much she missed him; this was not a good development. Reid was only a temporary diversion. Kirsten knew he would be leaving soon, probably in a few days at most. She hated to think about what her life would return to after the captain's presence was removed. She had grown accustomed to his easy presence and his undemanding friendship.

A movement in the corner of her vision pulled her from her reverie.

She looked toward the doorway intending to chide Reid for being as late as he was. The vision in the opening silenced her. Captain Hansen was so transformed that astonishment robbed her ability to breathe, much less speak.

The uniform's jacket hugged his broad shoulders and narrow waist. The gray trousers were snug against his thighs and dropped straight to the arch of his polished black boots. Newly shaven, his strong jaw was once again quite noticeable. His blond hair was clean, combed and neatly trimmed to a length which only brushed his shoulders.

He stood straight and tall, his scalp less than half a foot from the top of the door jamb. When his eyes met Kirsten's, the blue of the jacket made them appear the most amazing color; at this moment they were more blue than gray.

"Good evening. I apologize for my tardiness," he said in a voice that was somehow deeper and richer than she noticed before. "My toilette took longer than I anticipated."

Henrik jumped up and crossed the room, his hand extended. "My God, sir, you do look the part of an officer now!" he enthused.

Reid pumped her father's hand. "Thanks to your generosity."

He shifted his regard to Marit. "And to your gracious hospitality, Madame Sven. I would not be so well recovered without it."

"We were honored to be of help," Marit replied softly.

Kirsten noticed Marit's use of the past tense. She dragged her eyes away from Reid to consider her mother.

Marit's gaze shifted from the captain's to her daughter's. Kirsten saw the warning there. What was her mother thinking existed between Kirsten and the captain? She narrowed her eyes in defiance.

"Come sit, Reid." Kirsten's irritation had released her voice. She turned back to face him and smiled. "Your unveiling has been quite successful and we are all duly impressed."

Reid bowed from the neck before striding to his seat. Once in place he grinned at her so brightly that she nearly burst into tears.

Kirsten never imagined the possibility of becoming so connected to a stranger in only two weeks, that his imminent departure might reduce her to hysteria. She faced her soup and spooned the liquid into her mouth without really tasting it. Conversation colored the air around her as her father and Reid chatted amicably about where he would be going and what he would be doing when he arrived there.

Perhaps it was best that he left. Her unwavering objections to marriage remained solidly in place, and his continued presence in her home could only bring that situation to an ugly conclusion. Kirsten was certain of that.

At least, she believed that she was.

She looked up at Reid again.

His gaze moved to hers.

The intensity with which he regarded her conveyed both his respect for her, and his kind affections toward her. She felt the impact of both surge through her veins. She realized she was smiling at him only after he smiled back.

Her mother cleared her throat. "Coffee, Captain?"

He looked away. The spell was broken. As broken as Kirsten was.

And every bit as irreparable.

✳ ✳ ✳

Reid hoped the knock at his parlor door might be Kirsten. She was so withdrawn through most of dinner that he wanted to speak with her and discern what might have occurred to put her mood off, yet she hurried away from the dining room before he could say anything.

He did not expect to see Marit Sven facing him. Luckily, he was still wearing his jacket, though it was unbuttoned.

"Might I have a word with you, Captain?" she asked.

Reid began to fasten the brass buttons. "Of course, Madame Sven."

She turned and spoke to him over her shoulder. "Follow me. We'll speak in my husband's study."

Reid obeyed, his curiosity rudely shoving him forward. Once in the room, Marit closed the door and indicated the two upholstered chairs in front of the banked fire. The nights were beginning to chill and low fires now burned in several of the manor's lower rooms.

"After you, ma'am," he said politely. Whatever was on her mind, he didn't want his lack of manners to become part of her concern.

Marit sank wordlessly into one of the chairs. Reid sat in the other, his back straight.

"I have something to tell you, Captain. It's about my daughter. Something I don't believe that you know," she stated with confidence.

"Is she ill?" Reid asked the first thing that popped in his mind.

Marit waved a heavily ringed hand. "Oh, no. It's nothing like that. Kirsten is in the best of health, both in mind and body."

"I am relieved to hear that," he said truthfully.

She flashed a mirthless smile. "It's about who she is."

Reid waited. There was nothing to say to such a statement, and Marit was clearly enjoying his bemusement.

"To be more correct, I suppose, it's about who I am. And my father," she corrected. This time she waited.

"Who is your father?" Reid asked, realizing that this could be a very long conversation if he did not.

Her regal tone suited her words, "King Christian the Sixth of Norway and Denmark."

Reid fell back in his chair. Whatever he anticipated she might say, this was definitely not on the table. *Helvete*, it wasn't even in the room. Or the building.

"You are the daughter of the king?" he asked needing to be certain he heard correctly. "You are *Prinsesse* Marit?"

This smile was self-satisfied. "I am."

"That means—" he began.

She interrupted and finished the thought for him. "That means that Kirsten is the granddaughter of one king, and niece to my older brother Frederick, the current King of Denmark and Norway. Yes."

Reid sat in stunned silence, trying to reconcile the woman he knew with his assumptions about royalty in general. The two images were as incongruent as a truth and a lie, leaving him to wonder which was which.

"So you see, Captain, any flirtations which may have passed between the two of you cannot be followed through on. Obviously." Marit's soft, firm voice reflected her authority and clarified exactly what this interview was about.

Reid wanted to challenge her. He wanted to declare Kirsten a woman of legal age and with her own quick mind, capable of choosing for herself. He wanted to ask Marit what she could possibly do if Kirsten chose him over her mother's objection.

But he didn't.

Because Reid knew he was not in a position to take on any wife, much less a royal one. He was an impoverished soldier, dressed up in charity, and without a scrap of land to call his own.

The war had rendered him useless as a provider, and unless something happened to change that, he would be a bad choice for anyone's husband. That reality crushed his objections under the hard heel of his newly gifted boots.

"I understand," he conceded.

"I'm so glad that you are wise enough not to argue with me," Marit replied, her tone now kind. "And whatever you may think, I am truly very sorry."

Reid nodded. His next decision was so easy, he didn't even need to think about it. "I'll be gone before she rises on the morrow."

September 19, 1781

The sun still slept behind a bank of clouds as Reid walked away from the Sven household. He, however, had not slept at all.

Every one of his attempts to write Kirsten an appropriate goodbye note had proven futile. Page after page of his words had died as ash in the fire while he struggled over what to say to her.

He thought to say how much she meant to him, how much he enjoyed her company and cherished their friendship. However, even if those feelings were reciprocated as he believed them to be, nothing could ever come of them. So there remained no helpful reason to declare them.

Yet to dash off a quick and casual message with no personal touch would be just as dishonest. Painful for him to write, and dismissive for her to read.

He thought about confessing the conversation with her mother.

Though Marit hadn't said so, Reid was as certain as he could be that Kirsten knew nothing about it. Furthermore, if she wanted him to know about her royal status, Kirsten would have told him herself. Breaking her mother's confidence would only serve to cause more strife between the woman and her headstrong daughter, and Reid had no desire to bring that about, if only for poor Henrik's sake.

He did write a quick note to Henrik, thanking the man again for his provisions. He dated it the day before and slipped it under another paper on the man's desk, hoping everyone in the house would believe it to be written before their last supper together.

When the clock in his parlor room chimed four times that morning, Reid dressed in his battle uniform. He folded the dress clothes and the rest of his meager possessions into the leather pack, and slung it over his shoulder. Rifle in hand, he paused in the kitchen to pack some food. He departed out the kitchen door in the event someone might hear the front door open and close.

As the clouds over Philadelphia were lightened from behind by the reluctant sun, Reid turned south at the end of the long drive. He did not look back.

PART TWO:
CHALLENGING

CHAPTER TWELVE

February 12, 1782
Philadelphia

Kirsten would recognize him anywhere. It was the shock of seeing him here, five months later, which stilled her tongue. He stared across the ballroom with such thunderous intensity that if she could reach him, she would have slapped him for his impudence.

He moved toward her slowly, deliberately, through the crowd. His storm-gray eyes fixed on hers and, though she knew she should, she couldn't look away. The posh assemblage parted in his path, pushed back by both the authority of his impressive stature and his officer's uniform—which now strained a bit to contain his broad shoulders.

It was the same dark blue jacket he wore the last time he sat across from her at dinner; the last time she saw him before he snuck away from her home without a parting word.

Kirsten's emotions roiled as violently as a ship in a tempest. Flashes of joy at seeing Reid again were doused by waves of fury at his betrayal. Constrained by social mores, all she could do was stand rock still and attempt to contain the trembling caused by her surging pulse and pounding heart.

With a jolt she noticed he was still limping. Not so much as anyone else would mark it but she knew about his wound. That little touch of human weakness shot steel into her backbone.

When he reached her he smiled softly, as if he feared her reaction. He bowed a little from the waist. "It's nice to see you again, Your Highness."

So he knows.

The multiple ramifications of his greeting were far too numerous to consider now. Kirsten lifted her chin and did her best to smile at him in return.

"Mister Hansen."

He touched the second scrap of yellow stitched to his sleeve. "Colonel."

Her eyes followed his hand. "You were a Captain last we met, as I recall."

"It would seem that being nearly killed, and yet sufficiently recovering, warranted a promotion." Reid dipped his head and lowered his voice. "And last we met, you were a princess."

She felt her face heating. "Yes," she whispered. "We don't mention that."

His eyes grew cold. "I am well aware."

"We cannot have this discussion now," she warned, afraid of what he would say.

He glanced around the curious crowd and took her elbow. "No we cannot. But we can dance."

Kirsten couldn't object without creating a spectacle. She allowed Reid to escort her into position for the minuet and wondered if his leg would hinder his ability.

As the music began, Reid moved in perfect time. Step, together. Step, step, step, together. For being so tall, the man was surprisingly light on his feet. Either his injured thigh didn't cause a problem, or he was a master at ignoring the pain.

Kirsten felt the weight of eighty pairs of curious eyes as she danced with Cap—*Colonel* Hansen. Several of her spurned suitors were in the crowd and for a brief moment she hoped they saw the superior assets of this particular partner. Perhaps they would leave her alone if they believed Reid was courting her.

That might prove one positive outcome to his unexpected reappearance. She couldn't imagine a second.

As they danced, Kirsten considered Reid with an evaluative eye. His eyes were clear with all traces of swelling and bruising obviously long gone. The ring of blue around his gray irises still fascinated her, and as his mood seemed to lighten it became more noticeable.

His face was somehow different. His clean jaw was still strong, his even features still planed and sculpted. But he looked older. Tired, perhaps.

Five months ago his movements still evinced the caution of recent injury. Now, in spite of the fluidity of the dance, his powerful body radiated danger.

Her heart thumped painfully. If he was handsome before, he was heartbreaking now.

Thankfully, the minuet ended.

"I'm thirsty," she stated.

Reid followed her to the refreshments where he procured two tall, thin glasses of champagne. He handed her one.

"Thank you," she murmured.

Before she could take a sip, Reid grasped her elbow and led her from the ballroom to an attached solarium. Kirsten intended to protest, but his strong grip pulled her curiosity along with him. Beyond the glass walls, oil lamps poured silky yellow light over a snow-covered garden, illuminating the delicate brown bones of dead foliage poking defiantly from their icy shroud.

Kirsten perched on a wooden bench before her knees might give way.

Reid sat ramrod straight beside her, a warrior even now.

"Why are you here?" she blurted, unwilling to dance around her thoughts.

If she offended him and he left her alone, that wouldn't be an altogether bad outcome. Though based on their interactions months ago, she didn't believe he would take offense now when he had not before.

"To testify in the trial concerning the explosion," he replied before sipping his wine.

Of all the reasons she thought he might come back, that wasn't a possibility she ever considered. "When is the trial?"

He lowered his glass and met her gaze. "It began yesterday."

"How long have you been back in Philadelphia?" she asked before wisdom screamed at her not to appear over-eager.

"Four days."

"How long will you remain?" She bit her tongue. Over-eager was clearly winning.

Reid's eyes narrowed. "A month at most, I think."

Kirsten nodded and pressed her glass to her lips. She needed to stop talking before she asked him way too much.

"May I visit you?" His tone gave away nothing of his motives.

"Why?" she needed to ask.

His gaze dropped to the floor. "I behaved badly. I'd like to make amends."

Kirsten hesitated, unsure.

Reid looked up at her again. "I intend to visit your father. I didn't want to do so without your knowledge. But I would like to spend some time with you as well."

A pang of disappointment deflated her. She didn't know what she wanted from Reid, but coming as a second thought to her father was not it.

"I suppose so," she conceded. "When?"

"I can send a note tomorrow, and come the day after that," he suggested.

She frowned a little. "What about the trial?"

"It's moving slowly," was all he offered.

Kirsten drained her champagne glass and stood. Getting far away from Reid suddenly became her utmost desire. She handed him her empty glass and asked one last question, hoping the answer meant his stay in her city would be brief.

"How does your testimony help if you don't remember the explosion?"

Reid stood as well, holding one tall glass in each large hand. He blinked his regard to the cut crystal, glinting in the dim yellow light. His voice was so low, she almost couldn't hear it.

"I remembered."

✸ ✸ ✸

Reid walked a roundabout path through the frozen streets of Philadelphia as he returned to the modest hotel where the army had him ensconced. He hoped the chilled air would cool his blood, but he was not having much success with that goal.

He would have been a fool to think he could come to Philadelphia and not seek out Kirsten Sven. After only three days in the city he decided to attend tonight's charity ball knowing there was a good chance she would be there. And if she wasn't, he planned to go to her home. The suggestion that he wanted to see her father was a flash of momentary brilliance, hopefully putting her off his true intent.

Princess Kirsten was a brightly burning flame. He was the hapless moth, attracted to her dangerous glow and fully aware that flying too close would destroy him. And yet after five full months away, he still dreamt about her. Sometimes he was even asleep when he did so.

There was no hope for it; Reidar Magnus Hansen was deeply smitten and he knew it.

He huffed the same sort of sardonic laugh which he did every time he faced that truth. He had to be a lunatic to believe anything could come of his affections.

Kirsten's uncle is the King of Denmark and Norway, he repeated his internal litany, desperately hoping that someday it would change how he felt. *She is never going to settle for a penniless soldier.*

And yet, here he was.

Reid approached the hotel, his boots crunching on the frozen slush of a hundred footsteps. He saw the figure leaning against a building across the street and gripped the pistol strapped at his waist. A man in his position could never be too prepared.

The stranger crossed the street, obviously not attempting to hide his approach. He raised both hands to show his intent was peaceful. Reid pulled his hidden pistol from its case. The man halted.

"Two-three-o?" he asked when Reid was about ten feet away.

"Yes," Reid responded cautiously. "You?"

"One-o-seven. Did you receive my note?"

"Put your hands down," Reid instructed. He relaxed his grip on his pistol. "I did. Is there more?"

The man reached one hand into his coat and pulled out a folded and sealed parchment. "The French are grateful," he said as he handed it to Reid.

Reid chuckled. "If gratitude appeared in the form of gold or silver, I would be grateful in return."

"Wouldn't we all?" his cohort laughed. "Have a good evening."

"You as well," Reid replied.

The men parted ways without another word. Reid walked around the block to assure he was not being followed. He stepped into a pub and used one of his few coins to buy a mug of ale. Only then did he return to the hotel.

Kirsten couldn't sleep, not that any surprise could be found in that reaction. She stood in her nightgown, woolen wrap, and woolen slippers at the door of the parlor which once housed the enigmatic Captain Reid—now known in her thoughts as the infuriating Colonel Hansen. Why she was here tonight, after months of resisting the urge to make this midnight visitation, she refused to consider.

All she would admit was that the man was intolerable, and his impudent dismissal of her was unacceptable.

Kirsten strolled across the room and collapsed on the settee, tucking herself into the warmth of her wrap. She was in a very precarious position with the soldier and she knew it.

Of all the men she had ever known in her life, he was the one that interested her the most. That was the problem. So many immovable obstacles stood between the two of them that to bash herself against those barriers would serve no purpose.

When she came downstairs that morning so many months ago, and discovered the servants returning the parlor to its normal state with all traces of the captain removed, her first thought was that he was recovered enough to manage the steps and was moved upstairs. She soon learned the truth.

He was gone.

She pressed her mother and all of the servants, insisting there must be a note left behind somewhere which expressed his farewells. Kirsten combed through the rooms herself, even going so far as to flip through all of his favorite books in the library in search of a missive. Her insistent ranting was to no avail. The only note found was to her father, thanking him for the hospitality and clothing.

Kirsten retreated to her bedroom, locked the door, and sobbed. She took her meals in her room for two days before her mother barged in, nearly damaging her door in the process.

"What did you expect?" she asked her grieving daughter. "He's just a common soldier from a common family."

"He was more than that, *Mamma*," Kirsten objected.

"Yes. He was smart," Marit added. "Smart enough to gauge his surroundings and understand that he could never be an appropriate husband for you."

"But why did he leave without saying goodbye?" Kirsten asked, risking several perilous possibilities.

Marit sat on the edge of Kirsten's bed and tucked a loose strand of hair behind her daughter's ear. "What could he have said, *Datter?* What would have satisfied you?"

That simple question haunted her, unanswered, ever since.

Kirsten never asked her mother if she had followed through on her threat to tell him about their family because she didn't really want to know.

On the one hand, she saw the revelation as another betrayal by her meddling mother. On the other, the truth provided an easy escape.

Either way, Reid somehow found out about her royal status. Now she felt guilty for not telling him herself.

A stack of folded garments against the wall pulled her attention. Every endeavor into which Kirsten had thrown her energies since Reid's departure was somehow connected to the man.

The ladies who met here twice a week to sew clothing for the Continental soldiers was the first group she organized. Once she told them about the men being forced to take clothes off the dead in order to survive, she had abundant volunteers. Now she needed to find out how to get the supplies to the men who needed them

Reid should be able to help her with that, she realized. She would ask him when he came to visit.

Tonight's charity ball was another of her efforts. The cash profits would go into an account meant to pay soldiers' families their owed salaries immediately if the soldier was either killed or badly injured. While she hadn't yet found a way to administer it, the fund was growing nicely.

Kirsten sighed.

I'll ask Reid about that as well.

After their interview on the day after tomorrow Kirsten would need to judge for herself what action to take next as far as her friendship with Reid was concerned. If Reid persisted in his visits, then for once in her adult life Kirsten might actually lean on her mother's ideas about suitable matches and use that to push him away from any thoughts of a future together.

A shiver shook through her, prompted by the chill in the room. She stood and stretched, hoping that sleep would no longer elude her grasp. Before she tiptoed back to her room, she stopped and looked out the tall windows toward the dim lights of the city.

Snow was beginning to fall.

CHAPTER THIRTEEN

February 14, 1782

Reid walked up the long drive to the Sven's house. He decided not to waste his scant coins for a carriage when he only needed to walk about a mile and a half in snow that barely reached his mid-calf. Besides, the sun was shining and he had his tinted glasses for protection against the glare that occasionally bothered him.

He stomped the snow off his boots once he reached the clean-swept porch. The door opened before he knocked on it.

"Horace!" Reid grinned. "It's good to see you again. Why are you answering the door?"

The valet returned his smile. "I'm afraid the butler is indisposed, so I am filling in."

Reid removed his spectacles and stepped into the house. The richness of the furnishings hit him like a club to the chest; he had conveniently forgotten how wealthy the daughter of a king was. Once again standing in the understated elegance of the Sven home, he wondered if his feelings toward Kirsten should be forgotten. No more permanent than his footsteps in the snow.

He glanced down at his feet. His snow-caked boots were creating little puddles on the marble floor.

"I'm sorry, Horace," he said.

Horace shrugged. "It's the bane of winter, I'm afraid. May I take your cloak?"

Reid swung the heavy cloak from his shoulders—a second-hand garment he was gifted with when he was promoted—and handed it to the man.

"Tea?" the valet asked.

"Yes, thank you." Reid followed him to the drawing room before Horace turned around. "I'll let Master Henrik know you are here. It is good to see you again, sir, and in such fine health."

Reid strolled around the room remembering the vase on the sidebar and the paintings on the wall, each bit of sophistication sending another dart into his confidence.

"Colonel Hansen!" Henrik called out his greeting.

Reid spun to face his host. "Mister Sven!"

The men clasped hands. Henrik winked, "Now that we've done with the formalities, what say we descend to informalities?"

"Much less cumbersome, I do agree," Reid said with a smile.

The tea arrived, carried by a maid Reid didn't remember.

"Sit, Hansen." Henrik waved at a chair. "Tell me what's been happening with you since you left the bosom of our care."

He obliged. "The war carries on, though winter weather does slow it a bit," Reid began.

"Are we winning?" Henrik asked.

"I believe so, sir," Reid answered truthfully.

Henrik helped himself to a thick slice of cake. "What brings you back to Philadelphia?"

"I have been asked to testify about the explosion which nearly claimed my life." Reid blew on his tea to cool it.

"It wasn't an accident, then," Henrik probed.

Reid shook his head. "No."

Henrik leaned forward. "Can you say any more?"

Reid shook his head again. "Sorry. No."

Henrik leaned back again. "I suspected as much. Will you catch the culprit?"

There was no point in skirting that issue. "He's already caught. Now we only have to prove what he did."

"Excellent." Henrik sipped his tea, made a face, set it down, and gave Reid a conspiratorial look. "Would you care for a bit of brandy in your tea?"

Reid laughed. "Well, I did walk here in the snow."

Henrik's expression shifted toward surprise. "You walked here?"

Reid shrugged. "After marching across the country for days on end, this was merely a stroll through a rose garden."

Henrik stood and retrieved a bottle of dark amber liquid. "When you leave, I'll send you in my carriage."

Reid was about to object when a twinge shot through his thigh. "I appreciate your continued generosity, Henrik," he said instead.

Henrik poured a generous splash of brandy into Reid's tea and then his own. He set the bottle on the table between them.

"In case you want more tea," he said with a wink.

Reid lifted his delicate china cup in a silent toast before drinking the fortified liquid.

"So." Henrik leaned back in his chair and brushed a crumb from his waistcoat. "To what do I owe the honor of your most welcomed visit?"

Reid opened his mouth to give the answer he meant to give all along before a sharp realization widened the metaphorical club-wound to his chest.

Ever since the front door opened, Reid had been watching, listening, and yes, sniffing for Kirsten. He wondered if she was in the house. Or if she knew he was there. He already knew she still smelled like cloves. Every nerve in his body was on high alert, searching for traces of her presence. That sudden understanding knocked his original purpose to the ground and stomped on it, chest wound be damned.

"I would like to formally court Kirsten and have come to ask your blessing," he declared.

Henrik quirked a brow. "I'm not certain…"

"I know she's royalty," Reid attacked the first objection.

"Let's do start there," Henrik responded. "My family is very highly placed in the court. Even so, the expectations which accompany a royal marriage were more onerous than I anticipated."

"Is that why you emigrated?" Reid asked.

Henrik considered his fingernails. "To be honest, yes. In a large part."

"I respectfully suggest that those expectations will lessen over time and generations," Reid posited. "What is your next objection?"

Henrik pinned him with a probing stare. "Why Kirsten?"

Reid chuckled. "That, sir, is a very good question."

"I hope you have a very good answer," Henrik warned.

Reid settled into his seat and took another gulp of his brandied tea. He set the china cup on the table so he wouldn't drop it. He leaned forward and met Henrik's eyes.

"Kirsten is the most interesting woman I have ever met. She has a fine, quick mind, a unique sense of humor, and a strong, independent will. I find all of those qualities attractive."

"And you discovered this in only two weeks?" Henrik pressed.

Reid spread his hands. "You would be amazed how much you can see when you are blind."

Henrik pulled a breath and considered Reid through narrowed eyes. "How long will you be in Philadelphia?"

There was part of his problem. Once the trial was completed, Reid would be at loose ends.

"The trial will last another three weeks, I imagine. After that, I'm not certain of my plans," he said honestly.

"What are your options?" Henrik demanded.

"I can stay in the army." Reid indicated his right leg. "Or I can leave because of residual limitations from my injury. Then I'm free to go anywhere I wish."

"How will you support yourself if you do?"

Henrik was asking the hard yet important questions. Reid had taken himself by surprise with his startling request, so his course was not yet planned out. His mind raced down different paths, sprinting in search of an acceptable answer.

"I have hopes for my back pay," he began. "Then I suppose I'll go to Boston and see my family. I can look for work there."

"Would you stay in Philadelphia?"

Reid shrugged. "I could."

Henrik paused his inquisition, poured a little more brandy into his tea, and held the bottle toward Reid. He accepted. Afterward, Henrik set the bottle down and sipped from his cup.

"Kirsten is beautiful and wealthy," he accused.

Reid chuckled again. "Believe me when I say that there are a dozen or more beautiful and wealthy women in every city I've visited. And most of them have more pliable temperaments than your daughter. If that was my goal, I could reach it more easily than courting a princess."

Henrik did smile a little at that. He waved a hand around the room. "Kirsten is accustomed to a certain level of luxury, you are aware of that."

Reid nodded. "I am. And in truth, it's a level I cannot hope for."

"Would you expect to live here?"

"In this house?" Reid frowned. "No. Thank you, but no. I expect to provide for my wife in my own home."

Henrik's brows flew toward his thinning hair. "Do you think Kirsten would agree?"

Reid shrugged. "Obviously I have not asked her."

"That could be a problem," Henrik pointed out.

"There are countless potential problems, Henrik," Reid admitted. "But until Kirsten and I talk seriously about them, it does no good to imagine the answers."

Henrik's expression grew pensive. "I have a great deal of respect for you, Colonel. You are clearly a man of upstanding character and high intelligence."

Reid's face warmed. "Thank you."

"Your current financial bind is not of your own making, as you have chosen to fight so many years for this country's independence," Henrik continued. "I laud you heartily for that."

Reid was certain he saw an objection lingering at the end of the man's commendations. "Thank you again," he said, waiting for the words he still anticipated.

"It's important you understand that what I'm about to say is not a judgment of your fitness as a man in general, nor a husband specifically. I am truly impressed with your sincere and determined personality."

Henrik was evidently building up to something big. His features sobered. Reid forced his body to relax, assuming what was coming, and readying his response.

"Yet in the face of all that, the unfortunate truth remains. My daughter is a royal princess of Denmark and Norway. The responsibilities which are incumbent with her birth cannot be ignored."

"In light of that, are you are refusing to give me permission to court Kirsten?" Reid wanted to clarify what, exactly, he would be objecting to.

"Well, it's not the courting so much," Henrik deferred. "It's that the hoped-for marriage would be impossible. So why begin the process, you see?"

Reid adjusted his impromptu battle plan. "What if she refuses me?"

Henrik frowned. "Excuse me?"

"Look at it from this angle, Henrik. What if I court her and she decides we are not suited?" Reid offered. "Or perhaps I'll decide that same thing, after spending more time with her."

The man's mouth flapped open and closed. It was apparent the father never thought anyone would refuse his daughter. Reid's salvo had knocked Henrik off balance. He pressed his advantage with a blast of cruel truth.

"I have to be honest with you, sir. My request for your blessing was a formality which I engaged in because I have so much respect for you," he said.

"Thank you," Henrik responded with noticeable caution.

"But I will reach thirty-two years of age next month. Kirsten will turn twenty-seven later this year."

Henrik's eyes widened. Reid believed the man saw the point coming and wondered if Henrik might launch a counter-attack. Reid moved quickly.

"We are both mature adults. Our time is shortening. And if I decide to take Kirsten as my wife, her answer is the only one I will accept."

"You would court her without my permission?" Henrik exclaimed.

Reid thought it best to withhold his declaration that he would *marry* her without the father's permission if it came to that. Henrik didn't seem to believe that it would. Reid wasn't so certain.

"Yes," he said simply.

"What if I forbid it?"

"You won't."

"Why not?"

Reid smiled softly. "*Fordi du elsker din datter. Du vil at hun skal være lykkelig.*" Because you love your daughter. You want her to be happy.

Henrik's surprise shifted to recollection. "I forgot you speak Norse."

Reid didn't hesitate, but shot another ball. "Furthermore, you see the possibility of her happiness dimming with every dinner party you subject her to."

Henrik blinked. "You heard."

"I did." Reid smiled. "The parlor door was open."

The older man's face ruddied. "This path can only end in disaster, Reid. Mark my words. Kirsten will never turn her back on her heritage."

Reid bobbed a respectful nod. "I am willing to take that risk, rather than spend the rest of my life wondering what would have happened if I had not walked away."

Henrik opened the brandy bottle and refreshed both of their cups. "I may need to revise my opinion of you, Hansen. Now you sound like a fool."

"Do you love Marit?" Reid queried.

The bottle twitched. "I do."

"Was your courtship without trials?"

Henrik's recollection played across his face as a soft grin. "No."

Reid leaned forward. "Was it worth it?"

Henrik sighed, recapped the brandy bottle, and set it on the table. He lifted his cup and met Reid's gaze, all traces of the smile gone.

"I have no hope for you. But I won't try to stop you. And I won't feel guilty when your hopes explode in your face."

Reid laid a hand over his heart. "And I won't blame you if it does, Henrik. Thank you."

Henrik shook his head. "This has got to be the oddest conversation I have ever had."

Reid laughed. "For me as well."

Henrik looked askance at him. "You never courted before?"

"Not as an adult. I don't count adolescent infatuations," Reid replied.

"Your inexperience with women might put you at a disadvantage here, son," Henrik chortled.

Reid wagged a finger at his host. "I never claimed inexperience, mind you."

Henrik laughed aloud at that.

"What's so funny?"

The bottom dropped out of Reid's assurance the moment he heard Kirsten's voice. All his bravado about wooing a princess fled. He turned to face her and wondered what Henrik would say.

"I've just had the most unusual conversation with Colonel Hansen," he began.

"Oh?" Kirsten's eyes shifted to Reid's. Curiosity made them glow. "About what?"

"Tell her, Reid," Henrik urged.

Reid stood. "I have asked your father for permission to court you."

Kirsten recoiled. "What did you say, *Pappa?*"

"I said no, of course," he answered. Even with his back turned, Reid could detect Henrik's mirth. He smiled as well.

Kirsten appeared equal parts relieved and confused. "Why are you both smiling?"

"Because I said I would court you anyway," Reid stated. "And I shall."

"And I told him he is a fool," Henrik added. "And then we drank a toast."

Kirsten's incredulous regard bounced from man to man. "How much have you two been drinking?"

"Less than you might imagine," Reid assured her. He stepped forward, took her hand, and kissed the back of it. The aroma of cloves grounded him. He straightened and gazed into her eyes.

"Do you have time to talk, or should I come back tomorrow?" he murmured.

"I—I have time now," she stuttered.

Henrik rose to his feet as well. "I'll leave you two the drawing room. Don't forget to order the carriage before you leave, Hansen."

CHAPTER FOURTEEN

Kirsten kissed her father's cheek as he walked past her. She still wasn't certain what had transpired between the two men, but she was determined not to allow Reid to leave until she was. A maid came to collect the tea tray and Kirsten asked for fresh tea. She needed something to do with her hands if what she heard thus far was to be trusted.

"Have a seat, Princess," Reid said gently.

She shot him a look. "Do you mock me?"

He wagged his head. "No. I only want to show the correct respect."

"Then call me Kirsten. Or Miss Sven."

She crossed to the settee and sat in the middle of it so he wouldn't try to join her there. Her heartbeat had fluttered disturbingly when she heard Reid's voice in the drawing room. Seeing him once more in her home was unsettling to say the least.

Reid reclaimed the chair he was sitting in when she entered the room. His gray eyes rested on hers; apparently he was waiting for her to speak first. She could either do so, or stare back at him. The man was contrary enough not to take that hint, however, and Kirsten didn't wish to spend the rest of her day in a contest of wills.

She opened with, "What did you and my father talk about?"

Reid shrugged. "How the war is progressing, the trial, what my plans are for after the war."

She rolled her eyes. "What did you discuss concerning me?"

"Oh. That." Reid gave her a little grin. "I asked for his blessing to court you."

Kirsten's shoulders fell. "Oh, Reid. Why would you do such a thing?"

Their conversation halted while the maid set out the fresh tea tray. Kirsten's fingers trembled as she poured her tea, shaken by her pounding pulse. Reid's declaration provoked such violently warring factions in her emotions that she couldn't properly sort them out.

She leaned back on the settee and risked another look into his eyes. "Tell me, Reid. I don't understand."

"I asked your father because I hold such respect for the man," he said.

"That's not what I mean and you know it," she declared. "Why do you want to court me?"

Reid leaned his elbows on his knees. "Because you interest me. You have from the moment I became aware of you. I haven't been able to forget you."

"Then why didn't you say goodbye?" she asked of a sudden.

He leaned back again, as if shoved away by her question. "I didn't know what to say."

"That's ridiculous, Reid, and you know it!" Kirsten snapped. "You were just a coward!"

Reid shook his head. "Again, Princess, you are angry at *me* for not saying the very words which would anger *you*."

"Don't call me that," she growled.

He threw his hands up. "A simple 'goodbye and thank you' would have denigrated our friendship. You would have been offended, would you not?"

Kirsten folded her arms in front of her chest, hating to think he was right. "Go on."

"And if I told you about my conversation with your mother about your royal status, you would have been furious with her. True again?" he demanded.

"She told you that night? The night before you left?" Kirsten thought that might be the case, but to hear Reid confirm it now pained her anew.

"She did," he confessed.

Kirsten hated to think of the row she and her mother would have had if she had been certain five months ago of her mother's interference. It mattered not that the information was correct; it was the telling of it behind her back which she objected to.

Reid understood that, and he protected her by protecting her mother. Again, he was right.

"Wasn't there anything else you could have said?" she probed.

Reid shook his head. "If I had declared how much you had come to mean to me, Kirsten, then what? You made it clear we had no future together and to leave that door open would have been futile."

"And yet, here you sit," she challenged.

His expression transformed and Kirsten abruptly saw the man, not the soldier. The man whose path in the last eight years had stolen away all the plans and aspirations of his youth. A man with little hope.

"Yes. Here I sit." His voice was so low she almost didn't hear it. He stared at her, his expression somber. "Why didn't you tell me yourself?"

Her brow lifted. "About my family?"

"I thought I knew the real Kirsten Sven, the one you hid from all those unlucky suitors." He sighed heavily. "It seems I was wrong."

The unguarded pain in his eyes sent shards of guilt through her heart. "I didn't hide it from you with any sort of purpose," she offered. "It just didn't seem important under the circumstances."

"What circumstances?" he asked. "Friendship?"

"That's not fair, Reid," she retorted. Her eyes stung and she quickly rubbed away the threat of tears.

"Perhaps. Perhaps not." He shifted in his chair again, his features brightening a little. "Nothing will be gained by debating what was. The question to consider is, what is next?"

Kirsten felt she was on surer ground now. "What did my father say when you asked for his blessing?"

"He said no," Reid stated casually as if the word meant nothing.

She tilted her head, puzzled. "So why are you asking me what is next?"

Reid did grin then. "Because, as I said, I told him I was going to court you anyway."

"What if I don't want you to?" she yelped.

He shrugged. "Then we'll remain friends. You are my only social acquaintance in Philadelphia, Princess. I do hope you'll take pity on me and not force me to remain on my own, day after day and night after night in my lonely hotel, while the trial drags on interminably, with no diverting company to share my meals, nor stirring conversation to keep my mind alert and my spirits elevated."

Kirsten frowned. "That's the longest sentence I ever heard you say. And don't call me Princess!"

"It's a term of endearment. I like it," he replied.

"Well I don't!" she snipped.

"You haven't answered my question."

As usual, she was confused by his twists. "What question?"

Reid leaned forward. "Will you spend time with your friend while he languishes in Philadelphia?"

"How long will you be here?" she deflected.

"Three weeks. Or less." He lifted one shoulder. "Not too cumbersome a request, I wouldn't think."

"Fine. We'll spend time together." The pile of clothing in the parlor leapt to her mind. "I actually do have a couple of things I could use your help with."

Reid clapped his hands together. "There! You see? You are already being rewarded for your gracious acts, Nurse."

"Can you not call me by my name?" Kirsten huffed.

"I like endearments," he objected, his eyes twinkling. "I always use them with my closest friends."

"What other close friends do you torture thusly?" she demanded.

"None." He chuckled, obviously enjoying his own joke. "You are the first, Svennie."

"Oh good Lord!" she cried.

Reid gave her an innocent smile. "What is it you need my help with?"

Kirsten clenched her fists and counted to ten. She knew he was teasing her purposefully and she didn't want to lose this test of wills. "I started a sewing circle," she managed. "Well two, actually."

"I'm afraid my stitching isn't quite even," he demurred.

A laugh burst from her. She couldn't contain it. The image of Reid's large, rough hands holding a delicate needle was too incongruous for her composure.

Reid laughed as well. "How do your sewing circles need my help?"

Kirsten stood and shook out her skirt. "Come, let me show you."

Reid jumped to his feet. "I am your servant, Miss Sven."

She slid a suspicious glance in his direction but didn't comment on this formal but thankfully inoffensive choice of title. He walked beside her into the parlor that was his erstwhile home without saying anything else. Once there, she indicated the piles of new clothing.

Reid's brow wrinkled. "What is this?"

"We have been making clothes for soldiers," she explained, finding herself unexpectedly shy in the presence of her handiwork.

"You have?" Reid was clearly surprised. He squatted in front of the stack of shirts and began to rifle through them.

"After you told me about where you and the other men were forced to procure additional garments... Well, I made that circumstance known. And the women were eager to help," she explained.

Reid looked up at her over his shoulder. "This is incredible. You have no idea how much these will be appreciated."

Kirsten's cheeks warmed with the compliment. "The only problem is that I don't know where to send them."

Reid moved to the pile of trousers. "That would be my part of the plan, I assume."

"Yes."

Reid stood. "I'll make enquiries immediately. We should be able to send these on their way next week."

Kirsten smiled so wide her cheeks hurt. "Thank you."

"No. Thank *you*, Stitchy," he replied.

She punched him in the belly. Hard.

"Make that Sargent Stitchy," he coughed. "Where did you learn to hit like that?"

"When I am sufficiently provoked, I fight back," she proclaimed while shushing unwanted memories of another battle. "Did I hurt you?"

He shook his head. "Caught me off guard is all."

"I'm sorry." She stuck a finger in his face. "But you deserved it."

"Perhaps. Perhaps not," he said again, but this time he smiled. "You said you needed help with something else?"

"Were you aware of the charity my ball was for?" she asked.

"Your ball?" He looked awestruck. "That was your handiwork?"

Kirsten lifted her chin. "It was, indeed. And it wasn't the first."

Reid's brows drew together. "If I recall, it was to benefit wives of soldiers?"

"The Society to Benefit Wives and Families of the Injured and Fallen," she corrected. "The monies raised are to ensure that those affected by the loss of husband or father receive the back pay owed to that soldier."

Reid stepped backward and lowered into a chair. "How much money have you raised?"

"Thousands," she said honestly. "But I don't know where to send that either."

He shook his head slowly, though his eyes never left hers. "I am duly impressed."

She felt her blush return, climbing up from her chest. "Your particular circumstances made me aware of the needs."

"And you took action," he observed. "You are to be commended."

Her cheeks flamed. "Thank you. Can you help?"

"Of course. I am honored to be able to." His gaze grew vacant. "I believe I know exactly the person to contact."

Kirsten felt the burden float off her shoulders. It was an easy thing to rally support. She hadn't anticipated the distribution end of her schemes. "I am so thankful for your help, Reid."

He regarded her again. The impish twinkle had returned, making her wary. "Anything for you, Mary Charity."

Kirsten let out a long groan and sank into a chair. "Oh, how might I make you stop?"

Reid shrugged. "I'm still searching for the right endearment."

"Why any endearment at all?" she objected. "You have to understand that my position has not changed."

Reid looked at her with such tenderness that her heart gave her ribs a kick of protest. "Which position is that?"

"Marriage," she said bluntly.

"You are still opposed?"

"Until my dying day," she affirmed.

He leaned toward her. "That only means that while I was absent from you in body—though clearly not in spirit—no other man of worth has crossed your path."

She blinked. "What do you mean, not in spirit?"

"Look at what you have done since I left, Kirsten." He pointed at the clothes. "You organized two groups of women to sew clothes for soldiers because I had nothing to wear."

"That doesn't mean—"

"And," he interrupted, "you are raising money for the families because I haven't been paid in over two years."

"This isn't about you!" she protested—despite the sudden and shocking realization that, in actuality, it was. Her actions kept Reid in the forefront of her mind. She felt a close kinship with him as she worked on behalf of other soldiers in his same situation.

"Perhaps. Perhaps not."

"Stop saying that!" she barked.

"*Has* another man of worth crossed your path?" he queried.

"No!" She frowned at the implication. "Do you call yourself a man of worth, then?"

Reid looked quite confident. "Yes. I do."

"But you have no money or prospects," she pointed out. Her words might be cruel but at least they were honest.

He pinned her gaze with the gray steel of his. "I am worthy, nonetheless."

Kirsten's breath caught. "Reid. Don't."

"Don't what?"

"Don't court me. It will only end badly. I promise you that." The sting of tears returned and she rubbed her eyes again. "I'm getting tired," she deflected.

Reid waited until she looked at him again before he spoke. "Your father offered his carriage to drive me back to my hotel. Would you call for it?"

Her gaze fell to his right leg. "You walked here?"

As if pulled by her consideration, his palm dropped to his wounded thigh. "I did."

She pulled her regard back to his eyes. "You still have a limp."

"The muscle pulls. I don't expect it to get better," he admitted.

"Does it hurt?"

He gave a one-shoulder shrug. "Not enough to mark."

"Yet you may remain in the army, even so?" she probed.

"I may leave the army after the trial is over if I choose to do so."

"Will you?" she asked.

He gave a slow blink. "I haven't decided yet."

She stuffed her misgiving under a mental rock and, in spite of the flock of them, asked, "What will affect your decision?"

"Money, undoubtedly," he began. "Without the funds I'm owed I'll be hard-pressed to begin a productive civilian life."

"Perhaps that consideration will be put to rest now," she offered.

He nodded. "Thanks to your charitable efforts."

Kirsten rose to her feet and rang for the carriage. She waited with Reid in stilted silence until George came to fetch the colonel. She walked him to the door, having no idea what else to say.

Reid swung his cloak over his shoulders and paused in the open door. Cold air turned his breath into ephemeral ghosts as he leaned over and kissed her cheek.

"I'll be in touch very soon, *Prinsesse*," he whispered in her ear. The warmth of his words sent shivers down her spine.

As she watched him descend the steps and pull himself into the carriage she realized that perhaps princess wasn't such a bad endearment after all.

CHAPTER FIFTEEN

February 15, 1782

"State your name and rank."

"Reidar Magnus Hansen of Boston, Massachusetts, a Colonel in the Continental Army," Reid complied.

"Tell us when you arrived in Philadelphia and your reason for coming here."

Reid nodded at the line of five gentlemen seated on the raised dais in front of him.

"I accompanied the New Jersey Regiment to Philadelphia and arrived on September second of last year," he began. "That regiment planned to move on the next morning, but I was staying behind to meet with General Rochambeau, who was expected to arrive in Philadelphia the next day."

"Did he?" one of the men asked.

"I cannot say," Reid answered. "I was prevented from meeting with the French because I was injured in the explosion."

The man who asked the question looked down and shuffled some papers. "Of course. Here you are."

"How badly were you hurt?" another man asked.

"I was temporarily blinded, half-a-foot of searing metal was shot into my right thigh, and I was severely concussed," he replied.

"Back to the French," the paper-shuffler asked. "Do you know why they were coming to Philadelphia?"

Reid nodded again. "They expected to restock their provisions before heading south."

"Food?" the second man asked.

"And their arsenal. Weapons, gunpowder, shot," Reid clarified.

The first man glanced back at his papers. "Did they?"

Reid threw him an incredulous look. "Do you have any idea what happened here?"

The man glared at him. "Were they able to restock before the explosion?"

"No, sir," Reid growled. "The explosion happened before they arrived. I believe that was the point."

"The point of your statement?" a third man asked.

"No!" Reid barked. "The point of the explosion!"

The second man hit the tabletop with a gavel, sending a shot-like report around the walls. "Everyone calm down!" he ordered.

Reid chewed his tongue.

Second Man pointed the gavel at Reid. "Is it your contention that the explosion was not an accident?"

"Yes, sir."

"And are you saying the explosion was set off to prevent the French from restocking?"

Reid blew his relief out rounded lips. Someone here was paying attention. "Yes, sir."

"And do you have proof of this?"

"I am here to testify about what I knew before I arrived, and what I saw that night." He paused. "Where do you want to begin?"

The five men glanced at each other. Paper-shuffle-man turned back toward Reid.

"Tell us your story," he instructed. "We'll stop you if we have any questions."

Reid nodded and made himself as comfortable as he could in the hard chair. This could be a long afternoon.

★ ★ ★

Kirsten stepped back from her handiwork. The note she received from Reid at midday instructed her to make individual packets of the garments, matching the pieces. *In other words*, he wrote, *imagine the man who will wear that shirt, those trousers and smallclothes, and these socks, and match the sizes.*

She huffed. Obviously.

Once she had all of the clothes sorted she would have two of the maids tie the bundles and label them tall, short, or average. The leftover garments would be the seeds for the next crop. She was looking forward to her next gathering of ladies so she could tell them the good news that their efforts were finally headed to where they were intended.

Now she counted her packets. Fifty-nine. Too bad that the last shirt was so huge and the last two pair of trousers so slim, or she could have constructed an even sixty packets.

"Oh, well. I'm out of socks anyway," she said aloud.

"You've done a very good thing here," Marit responded as she walked into the room. "How many soldiers will benefit?"

Kirsten spun to face her mother. "Fifty-nine."

Marit looked at the few scattered garments left over and chuckled. "I see what you meant. Sixty would be nice and neat."

"Does *Pappa* have any clothes we could add to the last bundle?" Kirsten asked.

Her mother nodded. "I'm certain we can come up with something."

"I'm to take these on the morrow to the hall where Reid's trial is being held," Kirsten said. "Apparently there are some highly placed officers in attendance and they will see the clothes distributed."

Marit glanced at her. "So you want the extra clothes this afternoon."

Kirsten gave a cajoling smile. "If it's not too much trouble."

"Ah, you are my daughter," Marit sighed and patted Kirsten's shoulder affectionately. "It's no trouble at all."

Marit turned away but Kirsten stopped her. "*Mamma*, wait."

She hadn't thought to bring the subject up, but it felt like a boulder plunked down between the two of them, disrupting the flow of her life. She needed to talk about it.

Marit turned to face her again. With her blue eyes and fading blonde hair her mother was still a beautiful woman. Kirsten saw her own future in those aristocratic features.

"Why did you tell him?" Kirsten whispered.

Marit pulled a deep breath. "So now you know. Did he tell you?"

Kirsten nodded, not trusting her voice.

"It was for the best, *Datter*. I saw the way you looked at him that last night—and he at you."

"But—oh, I don't know," Kirsten sputtered.

Marit led Kirsten to the settee and moved a stack of clothes to the carpet so they could sit. Kirsten let her mother take charge, wishing with all of her being that she could be a young girl again with an entire world of possibilities ahead of her. Marit sat facing Kirsten and gripped both of her hands.

"Even if he was of an acceptable family line, you never could have been happy with him," she said. "It would have been fun and exciting to start, but his poverty would soon grate on you—and your wealth would be a constant thorn in his side."

"I'm not planning to marry anyone, *Mamma*, Reid Hansen included," Kirsten declared for what felt like the thousandth time. "Why couldn't you allow us to remain friends?"

Marit gave her daughter a look which clearly called her a fool. "*He* cannot allow you to remain friends, Kirsten. Isn't that obvious now?"

"He knows I won't marry him. I've told him that," Kirsten explained. "All he wants is a friend to pass the time with him while he is in Philadelphia."

"And you believe him?" Marit asked. Her voice was kinder than her words.

"He must believe *me*," she retorted. "And so must you."

"The heart is not so easily commanded," her mother warned.

"It's not my heart that is in control. It's—" Kirsten pulled back hard on her internal brake handle. She almost said too much.

Marit's demeanor changed; she stiffened and her eyes narrowed as if afraid of what she might see. "It's what?"

Kirsten tamped down her regret and restated her resolve. "It's my decision. And I shall not be swayed."

Marit rose to her feet. Her sharp gaze probed Kirsten's. "I do wish you would be honest with me, Kirsten."

Kirsten felt the floor shift under her; this was dangerous ground. "About what, *Mamma*? What do you believe me to be hiding?"

Marit pulled a resigned sigh and looked away. "I'll get the clothes." She left the parlor without glancing back.

Kirsten slumped on the settee, her pulse thrumming. Even if her mother suspected the truth, Kirsten would never admit it. She could never hurt her parents so deeply.

Her gaze traveled over the chaos of fifty-nine neatly stacked bundles, knowing without a doubt that her life embodied those two very mismatched afterthoughts.

★ ★ ★

"I received word that there was a British sympathizer who had recently joined the Pennsylvania regiment," Reid said. "I was sent to ferret the man out. Unfortunately, I only preceded the French contingent by just one day, which didn't give me much time."

"What did the French have to do with it?" Paper-shuffler asked.

"They were stopping for provisions. A British sympathizer would not want them to succeed," Reid explained the obvious. "He would do something to ensure that they did not."

"Something like blow up the munitions," posited Second Man.

"Exactly," Reid agreed.

"Did you figure out who he was?" Second Man asked.

"I had my suspicions. I listened to the men's conversations that evening, and then followed a man who called himself Jack Smith. He claimed to be going to the privy. Only he didn't go to the privy, he went to the warehouse," Reid narrated. "He went inside and didn't reappear for several minutes. When he did, he pissed into the river before walking back to the barracks."

"Where were you?" the third man asked. Two of his inquisitors hadn't said a word yet.

"I was hidden behind a stack of crates about fifty yards from the warehouse."

"What happened next?"

"I approached the warehouse trying to discern if anything was amiss. There was a group of five soldiers playing cards around the corner of the building and I asked if they noticed anything. They said they had not." Reid began to sweat at the recollection.

"I understand they were killed in the blast," Paper-shuffler offered.

"So I was told."

"Did you know them?"

"No." He pulled several deep breaths.

"Go on."

"I was walking away from the warehouse when I heard an odd hissing sound. I turned around and moved closer—I was about forty yards away—when the building blew up." His heart pounded as if he was hit again.

"Colonel?" The voice sounded far away.

Reid began to unbutton his uniform's jacket. "Water. Please."

A glass was shoved into his hand. Reid gulped the cold liquid and held the empty container out for more. The hastily refilled glass overflowed, sloshing water on the cuff of his jacket. He didn't care; he felt as if he was on fire. He swallowed the second helping in one pull.

"Shall we take a moment?" someone asked.

Reid bent forward so his head was between his knees. He concentrated on slowing his breathing, inhaling through his nose and blowing out through his mouth.

His body cooled in increments. His pulse slowed. His head cleared.

He was safe.

There was no new blast.

He was in one piece.

"I apologize," he croaked as he sat up. "I haven't spoken about that night since it happened."

"Understandable," Second Man said.

"Are you recovered? May we continue?" Paper-shuffler sounded put-out.

Reid wanted to put him out—outside with a bloodied nose. Instead he stared the annoying man down and waited to be asked a question. Paper-shuffler fidgeted under Reid's unwavering visual assault.

"You—you said he called himself Jack Smith?" he stammered.

"Yes." *Ask me another question, jackass.*

"Is that his real name?"

"No." *Keep going.*

"Do you know his real name?"

"No." *Confused?*

Paper man threw up his hands in exasperation. "Then how do you know it's not Jack Smith?"

Reid folded his arms over his chest. "Because I know."

"You expect us to accept that as your answer?" Second Man queried.

Reid shifted his regard. "I was told what the sympathizer looked like, and that he uses a variety of names."

Second Man frowned. "How do we know we have the right man in chains?"

Reid held his gaze. "The man you have locked up right now for committing this crime is the man I saw entering the warehouse that night. I'll swear to it, no matter what name he is going by."

"I have a question." These were the first words this man had said throughout the entire afternoon.

Reid considered the man sitting at the far end of the dais. "Yes, sir?"

"You said you were sent, and you were told." One brow lifted. "Are you a spy?"

Reid laughed out loud. "I assure you, I am loyal to the United States of America, and have spent the last eight-and-a-half years of my life doing everything I was capable of to ensure her independence."

"That doesn't answer the question," he pressed. "Are you a spy? One of those Culpers?"

Reid frowned. "What's a Culper?"

"Come now, Colonel. Even I have heard of them," Paper man sneered.

Reid slid his gaze back to the pompous ignoramus. "Tell me about them."

The man grunted his impatience but was apparently unable to resist the chance to lord his knowledge over Reid. "Major Tallmadge organized them under the orders of General Washington almost five years ago. They use numbers instead of names so if someone gets caught they can't be made to reveal the others' identities."

"Fascinating," Reid said.

"Are you saying you are not a Culper spy?" Second Man clarified.

Reid looked at every man on the dais in turn. "Gentlemen you cannot be serious. If I was, I would deny it. I am not, and I still deny it. Do you have any more legitimate questions for me?"

After a pause, the five men huddled together, mumbling.

Reid waited, glad he had a few more minutes for his legs to stop tingling before he needed to walk out of the room. His composure was shaky after his unexpected reaction to talking about the blast. He just needed a little time to regroup.

"That's all for today, Colonel," the third man spoke for everyone. "Please be sure to remain in the city until our investigation is concluded."

Reid dipped his chin. "Of course."

"Uh... You are dismissed, Colonel."

"Thank you."

Reid pushed himself to stand and took inventory of his limbs. All seemed present and accounted for. Plus his head was firmly attached.

March.

He turned and walked out of the hall, keenly aware of his limp.

CHAPTER SIXTEEN

Kirsten's carriage was parked outside the hall. As Reid strode toward it, careful not to slip on the icy path, the door clicked open.

"I brought the packets of clothing," Kirsten said without preamble.

Reid could see the tied bundles filling her carriage. "I'll unload them. Then I'll buy you dinner."

She made a face at him. "You cannot afford to buy me dinner."

He flashed a lopsided grin. "I didn't say what sort of dinner."

Kirsten laughed and the sound of it renewed his strength. "I'll help you unload them, and then I'll buy *you* dinner."

Reid reached the carriage door. "That's not right," he objected.

She grabbed the front of his coat and gave it a shake. "We are friends. It's perfectly acceptable for me to buy my friend dinner if I wish to."

He laid his bare hand over her gloved one. "I don't want you to see me only as one of your charity cases."

Her expression sobered. "I don't, Reid. I see the man you are."

Before he thought better of it, he leaned in and kissed her on the mouth, stealthy and quick.

"Thank you, *Prinsesse*," he said. He reached beyond her and grabbed armfuls of the tied and labeled bundles. He spun around and began the treacherous path back toward the building.

She didn't slap him. She didn't scold him.

And she didn't tell him not to call her princess.

Three good things.

Once inside, Reid set the packets on a side table and went in search of the army clerk, assistant to the major who promised to disperse the clothing. He found the man in a small office, working over a book of ledgers. A brief explanation set everything to rights and Reid went back outside for another armload.

Kirsten was on the path, her arms full. She took small steps, wobbling now and again but still upright. Reid hurried toward her as fast as he could without tumbling to the ground himself.

"Let me have those," he said as he reached for the bundles.

Kirsten handed them over and turned back toward the carriage.

"Be careful, it's slippery," Reid warned.

"You aren't having trouble," she shot over her shoulder.

"My boots are big and rough," he pointed out. "Those delicate calfskin things you are wearing don't have the same traction."

She waved a hand backward. "I'm fine."

Reid shook his head and carried the second armload of bundles into the hall. Her stubborn will was one thing he would have to grow accustomed to if his suit to win her was successful. Kirsten needed a strong man who could pull in her reins when necessary, and yet was strong enough to give her freedom she was right.

The transference of clothing packets went well on the first three passes. The winter afternoon was dimming quickly and the air grew sharp with ice crystals. Reid wanted to finish and get on their way. The clear sky didn't indicate snow, but it did portend a very cold night. The walkway glittered with fresh frost. He returned for what he hoped was the final pile.

"This is the last of them," Kirsten called out cheerily. "It's a good thing because I'm starving!"

Reid reached her in four long strides and caught her around the middle just as her hands flew up and scattered the bundles like a flock of startled birds. He managed to keep them both upright, ignoring the painful pull in his right thigh.

Kirsten's arms flailed in a futile search for balance before they wrapped around him. Her open mouth and wide eyes declared her discomposure before her exhaled holler, "Whoo!" made it past her tongue.

Reid froze, assuring himself that all of their combined movement was halted. He looked down at Kirsten. Her cheeks were deep red either from the cold or her embarrassment—or both. The contrast with her light blue eyes was so striking, Reid couldn't look away.

"I'll collect the packets," he said in a voice much softer than he meant it to be. "You go back to the carriage and wait for me."

"Yes." She still stared up at him.

Reid forced his limbs to loosen their grip. Kirsten pulled her arms away from his shoulders as he slowly let go of her.

"Be careful. The frost is thickening without the sun," he chided.

She flashed a tremulous smile and gave a tiny nod.

Reid spun around and applied himself to retrieving the flung bundles. He didn't look toward the carriage because he didn't want Kirsten to think he was being overly solicitous. In reality, he only wanted to look at her again. But he knew now was not the time.

Once the packets were corralled in his arms, Reid walked into the hall to deliver them. He was glad this was the last batch because his belly had been grumbling for food for the last two hours.

Kirsten sat in the carriage and waited for Reid, her feet tucked next to the small iron burner. Heat emanated from the radiant coal inside and chased some of the chill from the enclosure.

She was so embarrassed that she nearly fell. She knew better than to rush; she was born and raised in this climate, for heaven's sake. Nearly half of her life had been spent in winter weather.

She became careless because she was hungry. And in truth, because she was so looking forward to dining with Reid. Her opportunities to enjoy his company were finite and she wanted to make the most of them. It was unfortunate that she would be distracted by the strong and solid feel of his arms around her, assuring her safety.

And then there was the kiss.

That damned kiss. Kirsten wanted to ask him why he did it, even though she knew. In spite of her warning him away from such notions, Reid was clearly stubborn enough to try to woo her. He refused to understand that she meant what she said.

"And he'll be the one hurt in the end," she murmured, her eyes on the red glow at her feet. "I cannot let myself feel guilty when he is."

The carriage door opened and Reid pulled himself inside. He sat on the opposite bench and grinned at her. His cheeks were ruddy and his eyes bright.

"The major was very pleased with the generous bounty. He said he'll be sending you a note on the morrow."

"Is he the same man who will handle the funds for the soldiers' families?" she asked, choosing to ignore the annoying nickname. The fight wasn't worth the energy for only a few weeks' company.

"No, that man is not in Philadelphia," Reid explained. "I have sent him a letter asking him to come. He should arrive before I leave."

That was a disconcerting thought. "What if he doesn't?"

"We will adjust if that happens," Reid deferred rather enigmatically. "The current question involves our destination for dinner."

Kirsten had given that quite a lot of thought since she first stated that she would be paying for their shared meal. She considered going to an establishment she was familiar with, yet not so elegant a choice that Reid would feel uncomfortable.

"I am deciding between the King's Arms on Race Street and the Archer Hotel on Arch Street," she said. "Do you know either of them?"

Reid's mouth twisted. "I have a natural aversion to anything with the designation of *king*."

Kirsten laughed. "The Archer Hotel, it is."

She tapped on the carriage roof and informed her driver of their destination. During the short drive to the hotel, she was quiet. For the first time since she met Reid, she couldn't think of what to say. He sat silent as well, watching her with a pleasant expression that somehow set her nerves on edge.

When the carriage stopped moving, Reid opened the door and hopped out without waiting for her driver. He helped her down, closed the carriage door, and tucked her hand in the crook of his arm.

As they walked into the lobby, and were subsequently escorted to the dining room, Kirsten was keenly aware of the magnitude of the soldier whose arm she held. His ramrod straight bearing and colonel's colors drew every eye—the women with blatant interest and the men with evaluative envy. Whether they wanted to be him, or be with her, was unclear.

Either way, Kirsten knew they made a striking couple. She wished for time to slow down so she could savor the experience before Reid left her life permanently.

Reid removed her hand from his arm and held her chair for her. She smiled her thanks and sat. He took the seat on her right and opened his menu.

"What do you recommend?" he asked as he glanced over the offerings.

"I usually let the chef decide," she answered. "I'm always surprised and never disappointed."

Reid closed his menu and set it aside before facing her. "I shall do the same."

"You look so handsome in your uniform," she said.

He dipped his chin. "Your father has an excellent tailor."

Kirsten thought he misunderstood her compliment and was about to correct him, when a glint in his eye told that her that he had not. Reid had intentionally deflected her words so they didn't insinuate any personal interest. In doing so, he challenged her avowed indifference where he was concerned.

"Nicely played," she murmured.

He smiled, and turned his attention to the wine steward. After a moment of discussion, he ordered two bottles of wine, one white and one red.

"Because we don't know what we will be eating," he explained. "We should be prepared."

"Of course," Kirsten agreed.

Her rugged soldier was proving to be a polished gentleman. She found she was less surprised about that than logic would have her be.

"I must tell you, Kirsten, you are quite the heroine of the day," he said as he laid his napkin in his lap. "The major's eyes got bigger and bigger with each armload of clothes I carried in. I was actually afraid they might fall out of his head."

Pleasure at his words suffused her core. "And I must tell you, Reid, that I enjoy this project very much."

"So you will continue?" he asked.

"Oh yes!" she exclaimed. "And I'll continue to raise funds as well."

Reid touched his bladed hand to his forehead. "I salute you for your work. You have no true understanding of the impact you will have."

Kirsten knew she was blushing; Reid always seemed to bring out that response in her. "I have to be honest—for the first time since returning home from Norway I feel like I have purpose. I feel like I truly do have value as a person."

The wine steward returned with their wine and offered both bottles.

"We'll begin with the white," Reid instructed before Kirsten could speak up. He shifted his gaze to her. "I have a feeling we'll see cheese or fish before any beef or lamb. Do you agree?"

"Yes," she replied happily. "You are probably correct."

They waited in silence while the wine was poured, then Reid lifted his glass. "To you, Kirsten Sven. And to your valuable purposes."

She grinned broadly, unable not to. She touched her glass to his and added, "And to the soldier who opened my eyes while his were still closed."

Reid made an appreciative face. "Excellent analogy. I am quite impressed."

"Oh, drink your wine," she giggled.

Reid swirled his glass, held it to the light, and sniffed its contents before he deigned to let the golden liquid pass his lips. His expression had grown pensive. The man clearly had something of a serious nature on his mind.

"I like it. Do you?" Kirsten asked, hoping to lift his mood.

He nodded as he stared at the crystal goblet. "Yes. I do as well."

She set her glass on the table. It made a soft thud on the finely woven white cloth. "What sour subject has suddenly grabbed your thoughts?" she pressed.

His gray eyes lifted to meet hers and his features radiated kindness. "What happened to you?"

Shock skated up her spine and narrowed her vision. Lightning flashes of violence and pain threatened to swamp her.

"Nothing."

She lifted her wine glass, pressed hard between fingers gone white, and took a long, slow sip. How did he know? No one knew. She needed a moment to pound her memories back down into place, hidden away where they belonged.

"I wish I could say the same," he said.

"What?" Her eyes jumped back to his.

Reid sipped his wine as well before he answered her.

"I have seen way too much death." He spun his goblet on the tabletop, rolling the stem between his thumb and forefinger.

"Oh," she whispered.

He stared at the glittering cut glass. The liquid inside swirled intoxicatingly. "In the last eight and a half years I have slept far more nights on the hard ground than in any bed. I have eaten game half raw because it wasn't safe to keep a fire burning. I have spent a week smelling like my companions' blood."

"Reid…" she murmured and laid a hand over his.

His voice was low. "I have shot countless men. If they were lucky, I killed them cleanly."

"Stop," she said.

He looked at her. "No. You need to hear this."

She shook her head. "I don't."

Reid laid his other hand over hers, holding her securely in place and covered in warmth. "I'm going to be thirty-two next month. I have no money. I have no home to call my own. I have nothing."

"No! You have your intellect. And your education," she objected.

He exhaled. "Don't you understand that every single one of my youthful aspirations has been beaten to a bloody pulp and left for dead in some distant frozen field?"

Kirsten's throat thickened. Tears prickled her eyelids. "I'm so sorry, Reid. I can't imagine all that you have lived through."

The arrival of their soup interrupted the dismal exchange.

"No, I'm the one who is sorry, Kirsten," he offered. "This isn't the most desirable of dinner conversations."

She lifted her soupspoon and gazed into his dark blue-gray eyes. "Let's discuss something else, shall we?"

He gave her a resolute smile. "Yes. Let's do."

"Can you talk about the trial?" she asked before spooning the creamy yellow liquid into her mouth. "Oh—this is delicious!"

"I agree. Is that curry?" he asked, clearly trying to lighten the mood.

She reached for her wine to counteract the spice. "I believe so."

"Yes, I can talk about parts of the trial," he gave a delayed answer to her question. He chuckled. "Would you believe I was asked if I am a spy?"

Kirsten blinked. "Are you?"

He shook his head. "I'll tell you the same thing I told them: if I was, I would deny it. And I'm not, so I will deny it."

"So you are," she said. "How fascinating."

Reid gave her an incredulous look. "You, *Prinsesse*, are fascinating," he countered. "It will require the rest of my life to figure out how you think."

She wagged her finger at him. "Stop courting me."

Reid grinned. "I make no promises. Finish your soup, now."

The rest of the meal passed in good-humored conversation. It seemed that no matter what subject Kirsten tossed out, Reid had something to say about it. They talked until their server pointed out that the clock had struck eleven and they were the only people left in the room.

Reid pulled out her chair and helped her with her wrap. He rested his hand in the small of her back and escorted her to her waiting carriage.

"Where is your hotel?" she asked.

He waved a hand. "It's not far. I'll walk."

"Don't be so stubborn," she chastised. "I know your leg gives you trouble and it's very cold out tonight."

Reid stepped close. He lowered his face and tipped hers up to meet it. He stared into her eyes. Kirsten's lips parted. He was going to kiss her. She was not going to object.

"Not tonight," he whispered. "I'll be fine to walk."

He turned to go. Her breath left her in a whoosh of unexpected disappointment.

"You cannot give up, Reid," she called after him. "You have the rest of your life ahead of you."

He turned and pinned her with his gaze. Even in the dim light their steely gray held her without mercy.

"So do you, *Prinsesse*. Goodnight."

CHAPTER SEVENTEEN

February 19, 1782

Kirsten hadn't heard from Reid for three excruciating days. One week of the three she expected to spend with him was gone and she felt as if time was melting away as irrevocably as the last Pennsylvania snowstorm. She didn't understand her sense of urgency and she didn't intend to try. Furthermore, she staunchly refused to think about Reid's parting words and what they might mean.

But she wanted the kiss.

Just because there was no future between her and Reid didn't mean she couldn't enjoy a few kisses with the man. Kisses were sweet. Romantic. A reminder of her own youthful aspirations. She imagined that Reid's kisses would be thoroughly agreeable and she hoped for the chance to find out.

Her impatience was relieved by a note that was delivered right after breakfast.

K ~

My contact arrived last night. Please come to the Heinrich Hotel at your earliest convenience and we will arrange for the disbursement of the funds you have raised.

With grateful affection,
R

Kristen's heart leapt quite unhelpfully when she read the casual declaration of Reid's feelings. She realized with a jolt that she needed to tread carefully—or she might well end up being the one who was hurt.

She rang for the carriage and went to tell her mother where she was headed. She found Marit in the solarium.

"I'm going to meet with Colonel Hansen regarding the funds I have raised, *Mamma*," she said. "His contact has arrived and I imagine we'll be going to the bank."

Her mother looked up from her book. "Do you expect to be gone long?"

Kirsten nodded, secretly hoping to spend the afternoon with Reid. "I have some other things I'd like to do while I'm out. I might not be back until evening."

Her mother cocked a brow. "Supper?"

Kirsten made an abrupt decision. "Don't wait for me. If I'm not here by six, go ahead without me."

"Be careful, *Datter*," she warned and turned back to her book.

Kirsten checked her appearance in a mirror before retrieving her fur-lined cloak and calfskin gloves. She went out the front door and climbed into her waiting carriage.

The ride to the Heinrich Hotel was only a mile-and-a-half long and was accomplished in a mere ten minutes, even with streets full of carriages. Kirsten told her man to wait, assuming she would need to provide transportation for the Colonel and his mysterious contact. The bank was a good two miles further and, despite his declamations to the contrary, Kirsten didn't believe Reid would want to walk so far.

"The cold has to stiffen his leg," she muttered. "Stubborn Norseman."

Inside the hotel she asked the clerk to let Colonel Hansen know that she had arrived, and took a seat in the small lobby to wait for him. She didn't have to wait long.

"Miss Sven!" Reid's voice filled the lobby. He beamed at her as he approached. "Your prompt response is quite impressive."

Kirsten glanced at the very attractive man following Reid and of a sudden didn't wish to sound overly eager. "I had already made plans to come this way. Your message, Colonel, was a happy coincidence."

Reid held out a hand toward his dark-haired companion. "May I present Major Thomas Campbell, adjunct to General Washington? Major, this is Miss Kirsten Sven, the woman I told you about."

The major gave Kirsten a formal bow.

"Miss Sven? How is it that a woman as lovely as yourself has not yet been drawn to the altar?" he asked with a smile which guaranteed to melt any woman's resolve.

Almost any woman.

"Unfortunately, there seems to have been some sort of war, Major," Kirsten gave her standard answer to the query she heard countless times. "All the best men have run off to fight in it."

Campbell's laugh was rich and smooth. Kirsten didn't imagine many women turned him down for anything.

"I shall let my wife know," he quipped, grinning. "She doesn't always see beyond my abundant faults."

That was surprising. "You are married, Major?"

"Sixteen years," he replied. "And five children."

"Congratulations," Kirsten complimented.

The major made a dismissive gesture. "I believe the congratulations are yours, Miss Sven. Colonel Hansen has told me a bit about the work you have done. I'm quite impressed."

"Shall we discuss it along the way?" Reid suggested.

"My carriage is outside," Kirsten said. "It's too far to walk."

"May I?" Major Campbell offered his arm.

Kirsten smiled and glanced at Reid. He seemed a little put out. She hooked her hand through Campbell's elbow. "Of course, Major."

Kirsten took her accustomed seat in the carriage and waited to see how the two men would sort themselves. Reid deferred to his superior officer, who entered first and sat facing Kirsten. She wondered if Reid would sit beside her, thus displaying their friendship, or take the seat opposite her and set the tone as strictly business.

Business won out. Kirsten was neither surprised nor disappointed; gazing at the two uniformed officers across from her, she figured she had the most beautiful view in the city.

"Tell me, Miss Sven, how you came about raising these funds?" Major Campbell asked once the carriage was in motion.

"I became aware of the need after Captain—I'm sorry—

Colonel Hansen was injured," she began. "He explained that he hadn't received any pay for the past couple of years, so when he needed to replace his destroyed uniform and supplies he had no way to pay for them."

Major Campbell's eyes narrowed thoughtfully. "I see."

"As I thought more about it, I realized that the families of soldiers who were injured or killed were in a very bad state if their provider wasn't receiving the monies owed." Kirsten shrugged. "Someone needed to do something. So I took it on."

"Miss Sven also began two groups who sew clothing for soldiers," Reid injected. "Major McIntyre has taken charge of their disbursement."

Major Campbell's countenance eased. "You have been busy."

"Yes, sir," Kirsten admitted.

"And the fund-raising?" he prompted.

"Charity balls and auctions," she replied. "People love to be entertained. And they love to feel as if they have done good in the process."

"How much have you raised?" Campbell asked.

Kirsten's brows pulled together. "There should be some interest accrued, so we'll learn the actual total at the bank. But at last count the amount exceeded five thousand dollars."

The major whistled his surprise. "That's quite impressive, Miss Sven."

"Thank you, sir." Kirsten slid her glance to Reid. He grinned his pleasure at her, his eyes looking a bit bluer than gray at the moment.

The carriage slowed to a stop.

Reid climbed out first and helped her down. She took his arm before he offered it and smiled up at him. He winked at her and waited for Major Campbell to join them. The trio entered the bank.

Reid sat quietly as Kirsten and Major Campbell signed papers giving the major equal access to her special account. The plan, as discussed with the banker, was for Kirsten to continue to add funds as they were raised, and for Campbell to withdraw them as needed.

"Do you want to set limits on the amounts withdrawn? Or who receives the monies?" the banker asked the pair.

Kirsten looked to Reid for confirmation. "If Major Campbell has earned General Washington's trust, I believe he deserves mine."

Reid nodded his agreement. "I wouldn't have asked him otherwise."

"I assure you, Miss Sven, all of the money will go to toward your expressed purpose. You have my word," Major Campbell promised.

Kirsten returned her regard to the banker. "No limits. No conditions."

Another half hour dragged by with more documents written and signed. A clock chimed half-past eleven.

"May I suggest luncheon?" Reid said as the last paper was complete. "I'm rather faint with hunger."

"You're always hungry," Kirsten teased without thinking.

Reid cringed.

Major Campbell's brows lifted. "You and the Colonel are well acquainted, then?"

"He lived in my home for three weeks during his recovery," Kirsten hastened to explain. "I noticed his healthy appetite back then."

"Ah." Major Campbell did not appear entirely convinced.

She jumped to her feet, causing the three men in attendance to scramble to theirs. "Shall we?"

✷ ✷ ✷

Reid kept an eye on the clock. Kirsten noticed.

"Do you have other business pressing?" she asked. Reid thought he detected an encouraging note of disappointment.

"I have to testify at half-past two," he explained.

Kirsten and Campbell both looked at the clock, which had chimed half-past one ten minutes earlier.

"We should leave." Kirsten turned her attention to Campbell. "Where might I drop you off, Major?"

"I'll attend the trial for a bit," he said. "You can leave us both at the hall."

"I'm happy to."

She didn't appear in the least bit happy to, making Reid certain of her disappointment. He was disappointed as well. Somehow he must find a way to ask her to please wait in the city and have supper with him later. Alone.

The little group settled their bill with Major Campbell refusing to let Kirsten pay any part of it. Reid sat silent, his strapped financial situation already well known by both of his companions. That didn't help his somber mood, his thoughts already on his coming testimony. The man he knew only as one-o-seven had given him a very important document—which was tucked inside his jacket since the moment he received it.

Today, he would place that document and further information at the feet of the court. What they did with it was up to them; his part of the trial should be finished.

"Colonel?"

Reid's attention wrenched back to Campbell, who was already on his feet. "Yes, sir."

The major flashed a crooked grin. "Are you coming?"

Reid stood slowly, stretching his right leg. "Yes, sir."

Seating in the carriage mimicked their first ride, though this time conversation was lacking. Each of the three seemed to have something private occupying their thoughts. The major watched the passing city view. Every time Reid looked at Kirsten, her eyes were on the floor. He patted his jacket and felt the reassuring stiffness of the parchment.

The carriage stopped. Reid descended first. Major Campbell said something apparently polite to Kirsten in a warm tone that masked his words before he exited the coach and closed the door. Reid took three steps toward the hall alongside Major Campbell, then stopped.

"Go ahead. I forgot something."

He spun and loped back toward the carriage which was rolling away. The driver reined in the horses when Reid barked, "Hold!"

He flung the door open.

Kirsten was on the edge of her seat, her eyes wide. "What's amiss?"

"Stay. Have supper with me."

Her mouth curved. "Yes."

He nodded, closed the door, and pounded permission for the driver to continue on his way.

Reid strode back toward the visibly bemused major. "Let's go."

As it turned out, Reid wasn't called to testify until nearly four o'clock. He sat, fidgeting, and tried to listen to a Lieutenant drone on about the list of munitions which were stockpiled in anticipation of the French army's arrival.

"...thirteen casks of black gunpowder...forty-one canon balls...twenty-two muskets..."

Reid's head jerked up when his chin hit his chest. He glanced around to ascertain if anyone noticed.

"Was I snoring?" he whispered to Campbell.

The man looked startled. "No. Was I?"

Reid shook his head and chuckled. "I don't know why they have to write down everything the man says," he complained. "Can't he just hand them the list?"

"Colonel Reidar Hansen." His name echoed off the bare walls.

Reid elbowed Campbell and stood. "Here, sir."

"Come forward. We'll hear your testimony now."

Reid walked to the front of the room and took his seat.

The man he affectionately designated Paper-shuffler peered at him. "You indicated to the court that you have additional information?"

"I do." Reid pulled the documents from his jacket's inside pocket. "This is the birth record of Johan Symington of Westminster, London, England."

"Who is he?" the man demanded.

"According to this signed and sworn testimony by a customs agent in Baltimore, he and Jack Smith are one and the same."

"Hmph. Let us see that."

Reid regained his feet and walked forward, handing the parchment and the letter to two different men.

"When did he arrive on the continent?" another man asked.

"A mere six months ago. And he immediately volunteered for the Continental Army," Reid answered.

Paper-shuffler's full hands dropped to the tabletop. "How did you come by all of this, might I ask?"

"You said you weren't a spy!" declared the man who asked him if he was.

Reid gave the panel a patient smile. "I am both noticeable and well known. I have served in the Continental army since before its official inception and was elevated to the rank of colonel after being nearly killed in this specific incident being investigated. If anyone wished to pass information anonymously, they would certainly be able to find me."

"Was this information anonymous?" spy-man clarified.

Reid gave him a cool gaze. "Not to me. I am acquainted with the source."

"Who is he?"

"He wishes to remain anonymous." Reid offered a mirthless smile. "He fears for his life."

The men huddled together, passing the information back and forth between them. Reid waited for them all to come to the same conclusion the Culpers had: the Englishman Johan/Jack set the blaze, which in turn exploded the munitions, preventing General Rochambeau's forces from restocking their weaponry. And he killed the five card-playing foot soldiers when he did so.

Too bad they couldn't hang the bastard five times.

I'd still like to try.

A gavel hit the table, stilling the mumbles of conversation which had bubbled throughout the room.

"Thank you, Colonel Hansen, for this invaluable evidence. We shall finish our investigation, come to our final verdict, and pass all necessary sentences. Once our verdict is made public, if you are not named, you will be free to return to your regiment. That is all."

Reid spun on his heel and walked toward Major Campbell. He knew the words *if you are not named* were stated as a matter of course, but hearing them still clenched his belly.

"Buck up, Colonel," Campbell said. "You weren't on trial."

Reid donned his cloak and focused on the Major's words. "That's true."

As they exited the hall and stepped into the gray light of evening, Campbell stopped him. "Where did you get those documents, by the way?"

Reid considered the man who had General Washington's close confidence. "One-o-seven."

The major nodded. "Good man. One of the best."

He slapped Reid on the shoulder and tipped his head toward the street.

"Your carriage awaits. Have a good evening, Hansen."

CHAPTER EIGHTEEN

Reid climbed into the carriage and closed the door. He took the seat facing Kirsten, though for a moment he thought about sitting next to her.

After supper.

"Thank you for waiting for me," he said as the carriage began to roll forward.

Kirsten shrugged. "I had some errands to attend to in the meantime."

"I'm glad you didn't just sit here." Reid shifted in his seat, realizing his legs were closer to Kirsten's than was proper. "It was almost four when they finally asked to hear what I had to say."

She leaned forward, put her elbow on one crossed knee and rested her chin in her palm. "And what *did* you have to say?"

"I had evidence that the man who is charged with setting off the blast had recently emigrated from London." Reid felt he could say that much without jeopardizing the trial. After all, Kirsten wasn't about to run off and tell anyone what he said.

"How did you procure that?" Her eyes widened beautifully. "Your spy contacts?"

"I never said I was a spy," he objected.

"No—you said that you would deny it, whether you were, or were not." The foot at the end of her crossed knee began to wiggle. "So what evidence did your spy friends give you?"

Reid rolled his eyes. "Someone who knew the man brought a letter from the customs office in Baltimore that stated the man entered the country only six months previous to the incident."

Her forehead wrinkled in consideration. "There has to be more than that. What else?"

Reid bit back his smile. "He volunteered for the Continental Army immediately."

"That's easy information to discover I would imagine, for a spy who is also a Colonel." She tapped a finger against her lips. "But something kept it from being obvious."

Reid folded his arms across his chest. "What would that be?"

"Something simple, I would think. Such as he changed his name," she posited.

Reid allowed one side of his mouth to curve upward.

Kirsten sat up straight. "That's it? I solved it?"

"He did change his name, yes."

Kirsten clapped her hands, the calfskin of her gloves muffling the sound. "So he set off the explosion to keep the supplies out of French hands."

Reid tipped his head in acknowledgement.

She smiled. "This spy business is fascinating."

"I'm not a spy," Reid said.

Kirsten ignored him. "It's like a big puzzle, isn't it? Only the pieces are hidden."

Reid leaned toward her. "This is war, *Prinsesse*. Not a game. Five soldiers died and three officers were injured."

That dampened her spirit some. "I'm aware, Reid... But you and your spy friends caught him. And he'll be punished."

"I'm not a spy."

"How will he be punished?" she asked, pushing past his declaration.

Clearly he wasn't making headway in his denial. "He'll hang," he said. "Unfortunately he only has one neck to break."

Kirsten nodded slowly. "You've done well, Reid."

"No soldier fights alone," he reminded her.

She narrowed her eyes. "Can women be spies?"

He stuck a finger in her face. "Do not even *begin* to consider attempting such a course!"

She batted his hand away. "Are there no female spies at all? I find that rather hard to fathom."

"It's a dangerous commission, Kirsten," he warned.

She gave him an exasperated look. "So is childbirth. But we do it every day. So are there?"

"One," he allowed. "I have heard rumors of one."

Kirsten gasped. "Do you know her name?"

"I wouldn't tell you even if I did," he blustered.

"Then how do you know she exists?" she challenged. "It's probably just a fabrication."

Reid huffed his frustration. "Three-fifty-five."

"No, I believe it's already past five," Kirsten looked out the carriage window. "You came out of the hall sometime after the four-thirty bell."

"No," Reid explained slowly. "Culpers use numbers. No names. And she, number three-fifty-five, is the only one arrested by the British and hanged as a spy. So far."

The color disappeared from Kirsten's cheeks. "They hanged a woman?"

"It's not a game," he repeated.

"What are Culpers?" she ventured.

"A ring of American spies commissioned by General Washington."

She pointed a finger at him this time. "How do you know so much about them, if you aren't one of them?"

Reid laughed. "Everyone in the army knows about them. Not everyone is recruited to join them."

"But you were," she stated in a very self-satisfied manner.

Reid threw up his hands. "Believe what you will. But I'll say this until they put me in the ground: I am not a spy."

And then he winked.

***

In retrospect, the wink was probably a bad idea.

Reid knew how badly he felt when he learned Kirsten was royalty. He didn't feel it was right for him to hold out information, which he hoped someday soon would be important in her life as well as his.

In spite of how vehemently she protested, Reid felt he could lay siege to her objections to marriage and wear them down. No matter how long that might take.

He looked up from his soup. "I'm sorry, my mind was occupied. What did you say?"

"I said," she gave him a chiding look, "you never told me if the trial was over."

"Oh." He shook his head. "No not yet. Another day or two I imagine. They seemed to have all they needed."

"Then what?" she pressed.

"Then they hang the bast—the culprit," he responded.

Kirsten breathed a quiet giggle at his self-correction. "No, I meant for you, Reid. What will you do?"

About to declare his intentions out loud for the first time, he pulled a steadying breath. The decision was so fresh in his mind that he couldn't look at her when he spoke it.

He tapped the swirled silver handle of his soup spoon against the rim of his bowl, the *ching* of the china dulled by the creamy liquid inside.

"I have decided to leave the army."

Kirsten said nothing.

Reid lifted his eyes.

Her soup spoon hung suspended and dripping over her bowl. Her drawn cheeks made her eyes appear huge, like two perfect discs cut from a summer sky.

"Why?" The one syllable spilled from her lips while the rest of the world seemed to freeze in place.

"I need to ask you a question," he stalled. Once he listed his reasons, she might think differently of him, and he needed to know what she thought of him at this moment. "What do you see when you look at me?"

The suspended spoon plunged into the bowl. "What do you mean?"

He wasn't going to let her avoid his query. "It's a simple question. Look at me. Tell me what you see."

Kirsten sat back in her chair, chewing her lower lip. Her brow lowered. Her gaze moved over the parts of his frame that were visible over the table's edge.

"I see an army officer. A capable soldier with obvious physical strength and mental acuity," she began. "I also see an unusually handsome man, one with dark blond hair and gray eyes rimmed in blue."

"Is that all?" he challenged.

"No."

"Tell me."

She shifted in her chair and leaned forward again. "I see kindness in the lift of your mouth. I see a sense of humor in the web of lines around your eyes. And I see resolution in the set of your jaw."

"What else?"

She hesitated. "I see... I see a man who intends to find contentment, even if it doesn't look like what he expected it to."

"You are an optimist," he observed.

Kirsten withdrew and looked at her unfinished soup. "I used to be. Not anymore, I'm afraid."

Reid reached for her hand. "Why not?"

Her lips formed a tremulous smile. "Life got in the way."

"And yet you see nothing but good when you look at me?" he pressed. "Let me tell you why I'm leaving the army."

Her eyes flicked back to his.

"I'm so damnably tired. Tired of the whole thing. I cannot imagine forcing myself to go back no matter how strongly I believe in our cause. I'm worn thin. I don't believe I'd survive."

Kirsten began to rub his hand the way she had the day he woke up to her. He watched her smooth fingers move over his rough skin.

"My leg is weak. The muscle pulls sometimes, and the bone aches. I can't run as nimbly as I could before I was hurt."

She gave a tiny nod. "I noticed that you limp a little sometimes."

"And yet you called me strong," he said. "Don't dismiss that optimism so readily."

She wrinkled her nose at him. "Those are the reasons why you decided?"

"And my eyes," he added. "I still need the tinted glasses if there is a lot of glare. My ability to shoot straight has been affected."

"I didn't know that," she murmured. She turned his hand over and began to massage his palm. Gooseflesh tingled up his arm.

"There wasn't a reason to tell you."

Kirsten continued her ministrations but didn't meet his eyes. "So a soldier who can't run fast or shoot straight has lost his value."

"As a soldier, yes," Reid stated. "But not as a man."

She did look at him then, her expression still resembling a wild creature caught unaware.

"I am still strong. My mind is still sharp. I like to believe that I am kind, and have a sense of humor," he said. "And you were right when you said I still intend to find contentment in my life, even if it doesn't look like what I expected it to."

Kirsten let go of his hand and plunged hers into her lap. "You're courting me again."

"No, I'm not," he said truthfully. "I asked you as a friend to tell me what you see in me. I sincerely wanted to know."

She frowned. "For what purpose, then?"

Reid leaned back in his chair. "I've never spoken to any woman, at any time in my life, as honestly as I have spoken with you."

"And?"

"And I trusted you to tell me the truth. You did so."

Kirsten flinched a little. "I'm sorry about the royalty."

Reid waved a hand in dismissal. "Unimportant. Don't give it another thought."

He smiled at Kirsten and leaned forward, speaking in a conspiratorial tone. "I'm encouraged to hear that I'm not perceived as a hopeless case."

"Not at all, Reid," she assured him, though she didn't return his smile.

At the pause in their conversation, their waiter stepped forward and cleared away the reminder of their soup; a moment later their main course took its place. They ate in silence.

★ ★ ★

"I'm sorry I wasn't good company tonight," Kirsten apologized.

"Nonsense," Reid objected. "Friends don't need to jabber nonstop like mockingbirds to enjoy being together."

He offered his hand to steady her as she climbed into the carriage. She was about to insist that he accept a ride to his hotel when he climbed in after her.

"Do you mind?" he asked.

"No, I was going to offer," she replied.

Then he did what she hoped he would do, but refused to allow that hope to mature.

He sat next to her.

"I thought we could share our warmth," he said. He threw an arm around her shoulders and tucked her close. "Better?"

The driver appeared at the door. "To the Colonel's hotel, Miss?"

"Yes, thank you."

The door clicked shut and the carriage shook as the man climbed to his seat. The conveyance began to roll.

"You'll be gone soon, won't you?" she murmured.

"Perhaps. Perhaps not," he replied.

She looked up at him. "I hate when you say that."

He only smiled.

Kirsten realized with a shock that she had made a grave tactical error. She knew it the moment his lips touched hers. Her defenses were not only down, they were blasted away by the delicious taste of him.

Reid turned toward her. One large hand slid behind her head, holding her gently in place. His mouth played with hers. Teasing, exploring, possessing. When his tongue slipped into her mouth she moaned her surprise—and her delight.

She gripped his cloak in an attempt to anchor herself in a suddenly spinning world. She made no attempt to pull away and wondered if that made her a harlot in his eyes.

I don't care.

No man had ever kissed her like this before. There was nothing halting, sloppy, or aggressive in the way Reid's lips seduced hers.

And it was a seduction. His kisses made her wish he would keep kissing her forever.

When he did pull away, she struggled to open her eyes.

"My hotel," he whispered.

She looked out the window and breathed, "Philadelphia."

Reid turned her face back to his. "What?"

"Nothing. Never mind," she mumbled, embarrassed to have said their location aloud. She leaned away from him but was still caught under his arm.

"May I call on you tomorrow?" he asked as he smoothed her hair behind her ear.

"I—I have my sewing ladies," she stammered. "And you

already said your stitches are uneven."

Reid chuckled. "I'll come by later. Around three?"

Kirsten nodded. "I may have supper plans after that," she lied.

Reid withdrew his arm and touched his forehead in salute. "Until tomorrow, *Prinsesse*."

He opened the door and exited the coach without looking back.

CHAPTER NINETEEN

February 20, 1782

Kirsten waited to make her announcement until all the ladies who were expected had arrived. Her sewing circles had long outgrown the parlor, and today seventeen women sat in every available seat in the drawing room. Tea and sweet biscuits were served, as was her custom as hostess, before they spent the next three hours sewing.

"Ladies, may I have your attention?" Kirsten began.

Conversations dwindled. Cups drifted into laps. Eyes turned toward her, expectant.

"Most of you know the story of the injured army captain who recuperated in my home last September, and that his misfortune—sadly shared by all of our Continental Army soldiers—is the reason this circle was formed."

Heads nodded. A few whispers were exchanged.

"That officer is now a colonel and he has returned to Philadelphia for only a brief period of time." Kirsten ignored her heart's painful thump. "And through him, I was able to make a connection with a major who will disperse the fruit of our labor to our very deserving men at arms."

Happy gasps and smiles bounced around the room.

"Not only that," Kirsten offered. Curiosity shushed the room. "But together with the Tuesday group, we sewed a total of sixty complete sets of clothing in our five months together!"

She started the applause, exclaiming, "Ladies, you are to be congratulated for your service!"

Everyone in the room joined in, beaming. These women had all shared the exhaustion of war and the loss of husbands, fathers and sons. To be able to accomplish something—which was of actual worth to their soldiers—lifted their collective spirits.

"Thank you so much, Kirsten, for organizing this," one woman said, her worn expression sincere. "I know my son would appreciate it if he was still with us. To be able to comfort another mother's boy helps ease my grief."

Murmurs of empathy and agreement circled the drawing room.

Kirsten crossed the space between them and took the woman's hands. "God bless you, Jane-Ann. And may He bless all that you have done."

The older woman gave her a shy smile and nodded in return.

Once the tea and biscuit celebration was cleared away, the ladies of Philadelphia pulled out their needles, thread, yarn, and fabric with animated conversation and renewed determination.

"Gud forbannet det!"

Reid swore as he read the missive summoning him back to the trial at two o'clock that same afternoon. Judging from yesterday's experience, he would be occupied until it was too late for him to make his three o'clock appointment with Kirsten.

"Skitt!"

He needed to send her a note. The question was what to say.

Reid suspected that Kirsten's claim to have supper plans was an attempt to throw him off. In all the time he spent around her, she only had the one awkward suppertime attempt by her parents to match her with a hapless suitor. Reid suspected her fabricated deflection was based in how he made her feel.

Kirsten's surprising reaction to yester evening's kisses displayed none of her declared disinterest in him; in fact, she exhibited quite the opposite. Pliable in his embrace, her eager response heated him so thoroughly that he feared losing control. He hadn't kissed a woman for such a long time. And he hadn't cared for any woman the way he cared for Kirsten in his entire life.

Aware that he trod a precarious path, Reid planned his

continued assault strategy. If Kirsten truly did have a supper engagement, he couldn't see her today in any case. If she did not, then she had the option of inviting him to join her later, though to do so she would need to claim her plans had changed. That might make her appear abandoned or desperate; Reid didn't believe she would choose that.

Better to say:

My dearest K ~

I deeply regret to inform you that my presence has been demanded once more at the trial this afternoon, so I will be unable to keep our appointment. I understand that you are engaged for the rest of the day, so please let me know when you are available to reschedule.

As always,
R

PS ~ try adding "—vald" or "—tor" to the end of his name.

As he folded the note, Reid smiled. If his instincts were right, Kirsten would be left by herself until she summoned him to join her. A little assumption of another man's motives combined with his unexpected absence might carry him a long way toward his goal.

Kirsten was happy to see Reid's handwriting, but his words doused her mood as effectively as tying it to a rock and tossing it into the freezing Delaware River. And though his teasing reference in the postscript was at odds with his stated purpose of courting her, his apparent lack of jealousy stung.

Or possibly it was his confidence in his superior qualities that knocked her sideways.

In any case, she was not going to see him today, and the realization of how deeply she desired to disturbed her mood even further. Kirsten stuffed the note in her pocket and picked up her needle and pretended to listen to the conversation closest to her.

If she thought about it, she could still feel the heat of Reid's mouth against hers and the scratch of his stubble on her chin. The way his breath huffed on her cheek. His strong embrace. His long fingers buried in her hair. He made her feel things she didn't understand. He made her want things that terrified her.

"I'm sorry," she said to the woman who spoke to her. "What did you say?"

"I hope that wasn't bad news," she replied.

Kirsten blinked. "The note? Oh. No. Only an appointment I need to reschedule."

"That's a relief," another woman said. "I always worry when a letter arrives, I must admit."

Kirsten flashed a reassuring smile. "It's really nothing."

"Do you need to take a moment to answer it?" a third woman offered.

"No, I don't." Kirsten glanced at the clock; just under two hours remained in their sewing session. A long afternoon and uneventful evening extended after that. "I'll answer it after we finish here. Now, tell me about that new grandson of yours."

February 21, 1782

Reid walked to the Sven's home. Kirsten neglected to offer him a carriage ride to luncheon, but he was unconcerned about that. He enjoyed the physical activity after so many days spent in his hotel, or the hall where the trial was being held, and he knew the exercise was good for his leg.

Today was overcast, but he kept the tinted spectacles in his pocket in the event the sun made an appearance later. As he walked the familiar route, he kept his eyes lowered and focused on what he planned to say to Kirsten.

His hand was being forced by the imminent end of the trail. Once judgment was passed on the morrow, Johan would either be set free immediately, or hung the next day—the outcome which Reid bet on. His own testimony had been compelling enough that he was reexamined at length yesterday afternoon. If the panel didn't convict the bastard now, Reid wondered if the man would even survive a single day before some American soldier took justice into his own hands.

I doubt it.

The army would pay Reid's hotel bill for the day the verdict was announced. If found guilty, they would pay for Reid to stay on an additional day to see justice done, before releasing him to return to his regiment on his own. He hadn't yet resigned; he was waiting until the last opportunity to be certain of his status.

After that, Reid had no money to pay for lodging to remain in Philadelphia. He could probably secure a couple nights with the Pennsylvania regiment by the docks, but once he resigned his commission he had no right to army-supplied room and board. That meant his culminating battle for Kirsten's hand needed to be launched soon.

Today.

He wasn't certain enough time had passed between them, but if she didn't refuse him outright he would give her time to think while he traveled to Boston and his family. If she gave him any encouragement at all, he would return to Philadelphia and camp on her lawn if necessary.

Reid was not about to surrender this campaign without giving it his best effort. He was setting the direction for the rest of his life, after all. A goal like this deserved his full attention and commitment. A good soldier would never enter battle armed with anything less.

Kirsten was dressed in one of her favorite gowns. The dining room table was set, and her requested menu was being currently prepared if her nose was to be trusted. She checked the clock again to find it had moved a mere three ticks since the last time she looked. Reid wasn't expected for another half an hour.

He would be walking. Perhaps he would arrive earlier. *Or later*, the unhappy thought surfaced.

She hadn't sent the carriage for him because Henrik and Marit required the transportation for that day. Some city official was sponsoring some sort of gathering for some reason Kirsten hadn't listened to because she realized that meant she would be alone in the house with Reid. With a dozen servants, of course. Still, she was as nervous as a cat in a roomful of hounds.

She paced to the front windows and peered down the drive. Nothing.

She decided on impulse to change her necklace. Climbing the stairs to the second floor, she walked to her room. Pulling out her box of jewelry, she held several options against her throat and considered each one's effect in her dressing mirror. Deciding on a simple strand of pearls, she put the rest of the jewels away.

Kirsten re-pinned a loose curl, stood, and smoothed her green silk gown. She left her room, drifted down the stairs, and strolled into the parlor.

Exactly eleven minutes had passed.

She sighed. Her nervous boredom made her stomach clench. Kirsten walked back to the tall windows beside the front door and looked down the drive again. Then she smiled.

Reid's hat was just visible, bobbing with his stride as he approached the house.

Kirsten watched the vision enlarge until she saw the whole man. He walked with energy. Determination.

She pulled away from the window, lest he look up and see her. She moved to the drawing room and sat on one end of the settee, leaving room for him to join her. Licking her lips, she wondered if he would kiss her again.

And she wondered if she would let him. She had been clear in her stance on marriage, but that didn't mean she couldn't kiss him. Even so, men did take kisses as indications of feelings that were not necessarily present.

Reid's knock at the door was answered by the butler, who in turn accepted his cloak and hat before escorting him into the drawing room. Colonel Hansen's expression proved that her attention to appearances this morning did not waste a moment of her time.

"You are stunning today, your highness," Reid said. He gave the back of her hand a lingering kiss. "I am but a poor, battered soldier by comparison."

Kirsten giggled. "You were already a poor, battered soldier before you arrived."

Reid's gray eyes twinkled. "A fact which was confirmed the moment I stood next to you."

"Will you sit? I'm not certain our meal is ready," she demurred.

Reid claimed the other side of the settee. "I assume Henrik and Marit are joining us for luncheon?"

Kirsten shook her head. "No, they took the carriage and are spending the day at some event," was her embarrassingly vague explanation.

"So it's only you and I, alone?" Reid probed.

For some reason that made Kirsten very uncomfortable. "You and I and fourteen servants," she clarified.

"Of course." Reid laughed and teased, "Will they be enjoying the meal with us?"

She poked his arm; his solid muscle didn't give way. "Stop."

Reid dipped his chin. "I apologize. My mood is giddy with both the end of the trial, and seeing you again."

Bubbles of pleasure suffused her chest at his words and she beamed at him. "How did it end?"

"Seeing you? Or the trial?" he replied with a grin.

"Reid, you are impossible!" she chastised.

He gestured widely. "I don't wish to answer the wrong question and be misunderstood."

Kirsten rolled her eyes, her exasperation good-natured. "Let's begin with the trial, shall we?"

Reid nodded. "Testimony concluded yesterday. Today was set aside for debate, and the verdict will be announced tomorrow."

"Then what happens?" she asked, sincerely interested.

"If the man accused is found guilty of the charges, he will swing from the gallows the next day," he said, all jocularity gone. "The day after that, I leave."

A jolt of shock heated Kirsten's core. Reid. *Gone.* "And if he is acquitted?"

"Then he is set free on the morrow, and I am cut loose the day after that," he replied.

Kirsten clenched her fists to keep her hands from shaking. "What do you believe will be the outcome?"

"He'll hang," Reid stated, his gray eyes gone cold as granite. "Or he'll be shot soon afterward."

"And you?" she pressed.

"I'll go to Boston and visit my family after I officially resign my commission. I haven't seen them in years. And besides..."

Some of the light returned to his eyes. "They won't charge me rent."

"Can you not stay a little while longer?" she asked, knowing the answer.

He leaned closer. "Where would I stay, *Prinsesse*? Here?"

She was trapped. To answer in the affirmative would mean she accepted his courtship. "I suppose not," she conceded.

He fell back as if wounded.

The butler appeared at the door. "Luncheon is served."

Reid stood and offered his hand to Kirsten. "We discussed how the trial ended. Shall we discuss how seeing you again will end over our meal?"

"If that's what you wish." She forced a smile and accompanied him to the dining room.

"The food smells delicious," he complimented.

She couldn't tolerate the aromas any longer. His suggested topic had eliminated every trace of her appetite.

CHAPTER TWENTY

Reid found some encouragement in Kirsten's desire for him to stay in Philadelphia, though when pushed, she backed off from inviting him to stay in her home. He wasn't surprised really, and yet he couldn't help but be just a little disappointed.

He held her chair as she sat, and took the chair to her right. Their meal was served in courses and was every bit as delicious as it smelled. While they ate, Kirsten didn't ask what he wanted to say about her, and he didn't offer. Reid knew that once the conversation began, it could escalate rapidly and he hated to waste fine food when emotions prevented him from tasting it.

For that reason, he made certain their conversation hovered over safe topics such as her charity work on behalf of soldiers and the ins and outs of the trial. Kirsten even asked about Boston and what he expected to find when he got there.

In time, however, dessert was a crumbled memory and their coffee had grown cold. The moment for truth had arrived.

"Shall we talk here?" he asked. "Or in the parlor?"

Kirsten frowned a little. "Not the drawing room?"

"For what I want to tell you, I think the room where we first met and shared secrets is more appropriate." He rose and stepped behind her chair, making the preferred decision for her. "Shall we?"

Kirsten stood and faced him. "Don't be foolish, Reid."

"Foolishness is furthest from my mind," he assured her.

They walked in silence to the parlor. Reid closed the door behind them.

"My reputation will be ruined if word of this closeting gets out," she warned.

Reid pinned her gaze with his. "Do you care?"

"No," she admitted.

She sat in a chair, her back straight and her fingers laced in her lap. Reid pulled a chair close to hers and sat. His heart marched to a silent cadence in his chest and blood thrummed in his ears. All the time he spent thinking about what to say was, apparently, fruitless as his mind went completely blank.

Kirsten tilted her head. "Did you have something to say?"

"I did," he admitted. "But the 'how to say it' part has escaped me."

Her eyes shifted to regard her tangled hands. "Just say it. Be honest. Get it over with."

Reid's resolve solidified as the most obvious explanation fountained from his lips. "Kirsten Sven, I am hopelessly in love with you. I want to marry you."

She didn't look up. "I told you not to be foolish," she whispered.

"Foolish would have been to *choose* such a path. I, on the other hand, had no choice," he said. "I didn't want to love you."

"What changed your mind?" she murmured. "Tell me so I may change it back."

"Ah, therein lies the problem. I tried for five months to change it back, but my mind—or rather my heart—refuses to budge." Reid stared at her twisted fingers as well. "My mind knows the obstacles, I assure you."

She did look at him then. "List the obstacles."

"Finances, to begin with." He waved a hand around the room. "I cannot provide for you like this."

Her character was obviously stung. "If I ever chose to marry, all of 'this' would not be my concern," she snapped. "What else?"

"Your parents don't want me as your husband. Your father clearly said so," he reminded her.

Her brow twitched. "They would come around in time. I'm their only child and my father truly likes you. What else?"

Reid thought for a moment. "I suppose the last obstacle would be you."

Her eyes narrowed. "How, exactly?"

He decided to take a risk; the tone of their conversation warranted it. Reid leaned forward and kissed her.

She didn't push him away, neither did she reach out for him. She whimpered her resistance but her body ignored her and her mouth opened. Reid fell to his knees in front of her and pulled her close, claiming her as his own. Her hands broke apart and grabbed his waist. He poured his love and respect for her into his demonstration, praying she would understand.

When he broke away from her, she was breathing hard. Her lips were swollen and their deepened color blurred. She looked up, her turquoise eyes brimming, her hands fisted at his sides.

"Tell me why I'm an obstacle, Reid," she croaked past her tears.

"Because you won't admit that you love me," he murmured.

She closed her eyes and the poised drops spilled down her cheeks. "It doesn't matter if I love you. I will not marry you."

Reid rested his forehead against hers. "I don't understand, Kirsten."

"It's not you, Reid." She sniffed. "I won't marry anyone."

The suspicion Reid had been silently carrying in his heart for several days sat up and took notice. "Tell me what happened to you," he asked her for the second time.

"No." Her forehead rubbed against his.

"Something did happen," he prodded.

"Please, I beg you, Reid. Leave me my dignity," she pleaded.

He pushed her back so he could look into her eyes. "How can you think so little of me?"

She coughed her disbelief. "Of you? How is this about you?"

He still held her arms. "You do love me. And if you do love me, you should trust me to be worthy of that love."

"You *are* worthy," she declared. One hand swiped at the tears which streamed, unstopped.

"Then tell me, *Prinsesse*," he said softly.

"If I tell you, then you won't love me anymore." She ran the back of her hand under her nose.

Reid fished out his only handkerchief and wordlessly gave it to her.

She wiped her nose. "And if you stopped loving me, I think I'd die."

"So you would rather send me away forever, with no explanation, and spend the rest of your lonely life knowing that one worthy man loved you but nothing came of it?" he exclaimed.

"That's better than ruining everything!" she cried.

Frustrated, Reid gave her a little shake. "There is nothing you could say that would make me stop loving you. Trust me—I have imagined every possibility," he argued.

Her gaze narrowed angrily. "Trust *me*. There is indeed one which you haven't considered."

Reid let go of her and sat back in his chair. He was getting nowhere in this skirmish. He needed to pull out his canon.

"I don't care if you are not a virgin," he stated. "Neither am I. It doesn't matter."

Kirsten's eyes rounded. "How dare you!"

"That's it, isn't it?" he shot again. "You are afraid your husband will find out on your wedding night that you succumbed to a rake during a youthful affair and you are ruined."

He saw the slap coming and braced for it. Even so his head jerked to the side. The princess had a fine, strong arm.

"You have no idea what you are talking about!" she screamed.

"Careful. The servants will hear you," he warned.

Kirsten's regard leapt to the closed parlor door. The color drained from her cheeks enhancing the red rims around her eyes. She stood and stalked to the door, throwing it open and leaving the room.

Reid followed. Kirsten paced in jerky circles without looking at him or saying a word, until the butler appeared with both of their cloaks and his hat. She put hers on, accepted her gloves, and hurried out the front door.

Again, Reid followed, jamming his hat on his head and tossing his cloak around his shoulders as he did.

Kirsten strode down the drive, keeping to the wheel ruts and out of the snow drifts. He noticed she had the wrong sort of slippers on and they would be ruined by the slush. He thought to pick her up and carry her but discarded that idea immediately. He didn't wish to wrestle with her—and besides, she could afford another pair.

"Are we walking into town?" he asked when he reached her side.

"No," she grunted.

He peered up at the low-hanging clouds. "Enjoying the weather?"

"Stop it," she growled.

"What are we attempting to accomplish, then?" he demanded.

Kirsten halted. She looked back at the house, a good fifty yards away. "We are accomplishing uncompromised privacy."

Reid nodded. "Everyone can see us, but no one can hear us."

"Exactly."

"I'm listening when you are ready to speak, Kirsten. Take your time." He settled in and waited.

Her sobs intensified. He wanted to hold her but sensed her repelling tension. She soaked his handkerchief, but he didn't have another one to offer.

"Are your feet cold?" he asked finally.

She looked down. She nodded mutely.

He swooped her up, then, in one seamless motion. He backed away from the wet carriage tracks and lowered himself to the snowy ground, his right thigh burning with the extra weight. He sat on his cloak and fumbled for her slippers.

"Don't," she rasped.

"You'll get frostbite," he responded and pulled the ruined footwear off. With one hand he massaged her toes before he tucked her cloak around her feet, and then his cloak around them both. "That should help. I'll carry you back to the house when we are finished."

His act of kindness set her off again.

"I don't deserve a man like you Reid," she wailed. "And you deserve a much better woman than me."

He chucked a knuckle under her chin. "Will you let me decide for myself, *for Guds skyld?*"

Kirsten shuddered. It was the sort of shiver caused by crying too hard. "I will tell you. But when you finally see my point, don't feel obligated to start lying to me about how you feel."

Reid put up one bladed hand. "I promise I will never lie to you."

She bounced a little nod. "And you can never tell anyone. Ever. Even my parents don't know."

Reid found that easy to understand. Single children carried the burden of both their parents' dreams on their shoulders. Hiding perceived disappointments became second nature. "I promise."

Her lips quavered again. "I have never said any of this aloud."

"I'm warm and comfortable," he assured her. "There is no rush."

Kirsten stared off in the distance. "My parents always wanted to send me to visit my mother's family, but I kept putting it off. First, I needed to practice the language. Later, I wanted to complete my education."

She pulled an uneven sigh. "When the Declaration was signed, they gave me no choice. They wanted me safe, they said. Away from the fighting. I was gone within the month."

Reid shifted her weight and tightened his arms around her.

"Obviously, everyone hoped I would find a suitable husband while I was there," she continued. "And I wasn't opposed—as long as he was willing to come to America. After being raised here I found the strictures of court too confining, and the attitude of the royal family too... elitist."

"My guess is that none of the men you met wanted to risk living in this raw and uncivilized land," Reid offered.

She allowed a sardonic huff. "No, they did not. Every proposal I was offered involved me remaining in Denmark and having my parents sail over for the wedding. I wasn't to be allowed to leave court before the ceremony, lest I be somehow sullied in the process."

Kirsten's shoulders began to shake anew. Her eyes squeezed closed and she pressed the handkerchief to her nose.

"I turned them all down," she moaned from under the cloth. "I only wanted to come home."

"And you did," Reid said.

Her head shook side to side. "Not until... it was too late."

A chill flowed through Reid's veins, one that had nothing to do with his snowy throne. "Tell me."

"Two of my cousins didn't care for having their proposals rejected. They saw me as a second-class option, after all, and felt they were doing me a favor..."

Reid's arms tightened again. His pulse surged.

"One night, they trapped me in a room. They locked the door."

"Å min Gud," Reid moaned.

"They took turns with me, Reid. Not one man, but two."

Rage reddened Reid's vision. "Kirsten..."

"It hurt so much. I screamed as hard as I could but they stuffed a rag in my mouth."

Reid felt his own throat thicken with her grief.

"They kept violating me, Reid. Cocks and hands, over and over. I think I fainted because one of them slapped me."

"How did you get away?" he whispered.

"I didn't. Don't you understand? They kept at it for hours. When they finally tired of me, they shoved me out into the hallway and left me there."

Reid pulled his own shuddering sigh.

"Somehow my maid found me and helped me to my room. I bled for three days. I—I couldn't defecate for four. Pissing set my quim on fire."

"You don't need to say more," Reid offered.

She shook her head determinedly, still staring at nothing. "Yes I do. You have to understand everything."

Reid clenched his jaw and tried not to commence his own enraged screaming.

"I was seriously injured, Reid. I don't know if I can ever have normal marital relations. Or if I even want to. And there is a chance I cannot bear children because of what they did to me."

"Were you examined by a doctor?" he croaked the obvious question.

"No. Only by my maid. But she was experienced with women and birthing, and told me what damage she saw." Kirsten's breath came in spastic gasps. "We never told anyone. And as soon as I was able to walk I snuck away from the palace, boarded a ship, and sailed for America."

Reid rested his cheek against her hair. He began to rock her slowly, side to side. His heart broke for her.

"I still love you," he whispered.

"And I love you," she whispered back. "But now you see how impossible marriage is."

Reid wanted to argue with her, but in all honesty he didn't know where to begin.

He shouldn't tell her that what happened to her didn't matter, because it did. Just as much as his war experiences shaped him, this horrific attack shaped her.

He couldn't claim to be satisfied with a marriage that didn't include normal bedroom activities because he ached to share that with her.

And he wouldn't lie and say children didn't matter. Having sons of his own was one future goal he expected was still within his reach, no matter where he landed.

Stunned to his core, all he could do was try to comfort her.

"We can't make that decision at this moment," he mumbled. "We need some time."

Kirsten pushed herself away from him and reached for her ruined slippers. She struggled to put them on while he watched, silenced by the trauma she described. She climbed off his lap and began a wobbling, slipping course toward the house.

Reid clambered to his feet and hurried to lift her out of the ice and snow. He carried her to the house, not looking at her, his mind reeling and disoriented.

He set her down in front of her door and reached to unlatch it.

"Kirsten," he began.

She pressed her fingers to his lips. "Nothing you can say will change my mind. Please don't ever mention it again."

She stepped through the door and closed it, gently, in his face.

CHAPTER TWENTY ONE

February 23, 1782

Kirsten couldn't stop crying. After she sent Reid away yesterday afternoon, she ran up to her bedchamber, latched the door, and sobbed.

Saying the words aloud brought back every bit of the shock and pain which she had been so studiously shoving out of her consciousness for the past two-and-a-half years. When she closed her eyes she saw the leering, drunken gazes of her cousins, their trousers open and their cocks engorged. She felt the rope around her wrists cutting her skin, the linen handkerchief gagging her, and the light-headed desperation of trying to pull air through her nostrils as her chest heaved and her pulse raced with terror.

It was a horrific nightmare played out while she was fully awake. Her muffled screams, ineffectual. Her bound limbs, immovable. Her fury at being abused, impotent.

As she truly faced what happened to her for the first time, her body revolted. She shook uncontrollably. Her breath came in spastic gasps. Unstoppable tears burned her eyes. Grief at all she lost that night engulfed her, pulling her into a dark, hopeless void. She saw no way out.

Ruined for marriage. Probably unable to bear children. All her intelligence, spark, and beauty wasted. And she was only twenty-four when her future was so violently and vindictively stolen from her.

The only reason Kirsten was able to speak of the attack

yesterday was because Reid held her so tightly when she did. Cocooned in her cloak and his, alone in the open air with no chance of anyone else hearing, his arms like ropes of steel binding her close. Protecting her. Keeping the world at bay.

Fresh tears streamed from her eyes, their sting prompting yet another salty wash in the cycle holding her captive. Her head pounded and her throat burned.

Curled in a ball on her bed she ached for those arms around her again. She would give up everything she owned in this world if that one thing could be possible. If Reid could lie beside her, hold her and stroke her hair, and tell her he loved her.

One precious, impossible moment in time where her life wasn't ruined.

Kirsten finally rang for her maid sometime after dark last night. Willow bark for her throbbing head, eucalyptus for her stuffed nose, snow packs for her swollen and burning eyes. Oat porridge with honey for supper; food her stomach wouldn't reject. Her hair brushed while she sat in her nightgown by the fire. No explanations expected or offered. She climbed under her blankets before her parents returned.

Reid would probably say goodbye when he left this time. Make some conciliatory gesture. Say he would write to her.

She would tell him not to.

Maintaining a friendship between them had no point. Reid needed to move forward in his life. Find an appropriate wife. Because of the war, there was an over-abundance of single and widowed women in the country. If he chose well, he would have both land and sons. He had a future full of possibilities.

Kirsten rose early, though she wasn't certain she ever slept. The reflection in her mirror was rather disturbing. She rang for more willow bark tea and applied another round of snow packs to her puffy eyes.

Too bad I don't have tinted glasses.

The prompted thought of Reid rested like a stone against her chest. At the least there was one last thing she could do for him. She needed to accomplish the task today; in the event the man on trial was set free, Reid would leave Philadelphia on the morrow.

Snow made the swelling in her eyes recede a little. Powder helped disguise her reddened nose. The tea took the edge off her headache, though the core of her pain still remained.

Even so, the mirror presented a faint resemblance to the woman who usually stared back at her. A shift had occurred, and Kirsten knew it. That woman was gone forever.

She climbed into the carriage, angry to see the sun shining brightly on the snowy landscape. For the world to appear so cheery felt like a personal insult added to her multiple injuries. Though her physical ones had healed within a month of the abuse, the injuries to her soul left harsh and immutable scars.

When the carriage stopped in front of the bank, Kirsten straightened her shoulders and stiffened her resolve. She dismounted with her driver's help and strode toward the door.

Reid paced the streets of Philadelphia, his exhalations of breath resembling a vigorous stallion. He tossed in his bed all last night, furiously plotting ways to extract painful revenge on Kirsten's royal jackass cousins. Slow, torturous, and disfiguring revenge. Revenge which left them alive, yet physically unmanned.

The way they left her.

That's not entirely true.

Kirsten's spirit remained. And her intelligence and her beauty. Other than the horrific and unconscionable way it was taken, Reid honestly didn't care about her virginity.

Thank you, God, that there was no child from those fucking bastards.

Reid did care about the attack, however, and the resultant pain Kirsten lived with now. Between his escalating plans for retribution, he deeply ached with it. Sorrow filled his chest and spilled silent down his cheeks. She carried a frightful burden and had done so alone, too ashamed to share it.

Until yesterday when she laid it on his shoulders.

He wanted to pick it up and carry it for her; he just wasn't certain the war had left him man enough to do so.

Through the last nine years, almost every one of Reid's hopes had dissipated. Not one of them died a heroic death, making a last stand for purchase. Instead they dimmed, like light at the end of a day, until night owned the sky. There was no real delineation. They simply disappeared.

No occupation, other than soldiering.

No home of his own. No wife or children.

No way to support them even if he had them.

How, then, could he accept Kirsten's weighty situation? What valuable thing would he offer her in exchange for it? And what sort of marriage could they have if he did?

Reid looked up and saw the river. He turned right and kept walking.

In spite of her fears, Reid was fairly certain he could woo Kirsten to the marriage bed. Time, gentleness, and loving her in increments would most likely breach that wall. That wasn't a concern to him.

What about children?

Yes. What about children.

Reid always imagined that he would be a father. Passing on wisdom to his sons, outrageously spoiling his daughters, spending his old age surrounded by grandchildren—perhaps even great-grandchildren. At nearly thirty-two years of age now, the prospect of great-grandchildren was unlikely. And if he fathered a son who took as long at Reid had thus far to get around to the task, even grandchildren were not assured before he died.

Perhaps that doesn't matter after all.

In truth, Kirsten was merely afraid she couldn't conceive. She had no way of knowing for certain until she tried. Reid believed that if any couple went into marriage with the expectation—the *sincere* expectation—of a childless union, then they would not be disappointed when that eventuality played itself out.

The problem with Kirsten was the uncertainty. Hope would remain, unquenchable, until the possibility of conception no longer existed. If expectations and continued disappointment grew to bitterness, it would become a wasting disease in the marriage.

Reid turned another corner and kept walking.

The other side of the mental path which he trod led away from Kirsten. While consideration of how he might manage with her as his wife had occupied his thoughts thus far, he had not yet regarded a life without her.

His gut clenched.

During the five months before he returned to Philadelphia, he thought of her daily. Hourly, at times. Holding out a snippet of hope that he might see her again, he knew he would court her if he did. If he walked away from her now, as she claimed she wanted him to, how would he cope?

The exasperating princess held his hopeless heart in her hands. The thought of even *trying* to find another woman to give it to made his bones tired. He had never loved before. He knew he would never love again. If only she hadn't waited so long to appear, his happiness might have had a chance to grow.

What sprouted now was withering before his eyes. He didn't know if he could save it.

A memory niggled at his thoughts. He stopped walking, closed his eyes behind the tinted spectacles, and waited for it to come into focus.

One time, when he was about twenty, his father said something about—what was it?—stepping out, doing the right thing, and trusting that all would be right in the end.

Reid asked him what he meant by that.

Martin had laid a hand on Reid's shoulder. "There may be a time in your life when you are faced with a hard decision, son. If that happens, you'll know what the right choice is."

"Then why wouldn't I choose it?" Reid challenged, offended at the implied slight.

"Because," Martin looked hard into his eyes, "the consequences will alter the course of your life."

Reid hadn't understood his father's words at the time, but he noticed how Martin smiled at Dagny after he said them. Reid's mother blushed and smiled back. Reid knew then that his parents shared a secret. Though they never mentioned it, clearly some covert affair cemented their bond as devoted husband and loving wife.

Martin Hansen had always been the quality of man Reid hoped to be someday. His time was running out.

Reid opened his eyes and started walking again. Clearly the right choice in his situation was to marry Kirsten Sven—if he could convince her to have him. What happened in the past was done. How that affected his future was unknown. Here and now, he was in love with her. No other man would ever be right for her because only Reid knew her secret.

She trusted him with her shame. God willing, she would trust him now with her life.

A crowd stood in the deceptively sunny day outside the hall housing the military trial. They parted like ice floes when Reid cut through. His tall stature, clad in his officer's dress uniform, declared his importance. He heard his name murmured in the crowd and knew his involvement in the explosion was recognized.

"Captain?" a soft feminine voice cooed at his elbow.

Reid turned toward the source. "Colonel," he corrected.

A very attractive woman, probably in her mid-thirties, fluttered her lashes in his direction. "I beg your pardon, Colonel."

Reid smiled politely. "May I help you?"

She laid a hand on his arm. "I'm having a dinner party this evening and wondered if you might be free to attend."

"Who, may I ask, extends the invitation?" Obviously she expected him to know.

The hand tightened on his arm. "Madame Janine Chesterley, widow of the late Warren Chesterley," she said.

Reid thought he detected a slight emphasis on the designation of widow. "This may be my last night in Philadelphia, Madame," he declined. "I regret that I have preparations to make for my departure."

Her hand began to move up his arm. "Under the circumstances, and if you don't mind my asking, might you be convinced to remain in our city?"

Reid was rescued from answering by the appearance of a young clerk with a roll of paper in one hand. He stood at the top of the steps and unrolled the document.

"The court martial of Private Johan Symington, also known as Jack Smith, has reached its decision," he called out in a voice freshly cut from puberty. "The accused has been found guilty of malicious destructive intent and the murder of five Continental Army soldiers."

Reid heaved a sigh, blowing out the breath he didn't realized he was holding, and nodded. Approving rumbles shook through the gathering.

"Symington is sentenced to be hung by the neck until dead," the man continued without any display of emotion. "The sentence will be carried out at the Pennsylvania Regimental Quarters at ten o'clock tomorrow morning, February the twenty-fourth, in the year seventeen hundred and eighty-two."

Without pause, the clerk turned on his heel and walked back inside the building.

Reid looked down at Madame Chesterley and wondered if there was any reason at all to accept her invitation now that he had two more nights in Philadelphia. The movement of a carriage a little way down the street drew his gaze and answered that question for him.

"I'm so very sorry, Madame Chesterley," he said as he began to move away. "I'm afraid I cannot. Will you excuse me?"

Reid pushed through the crowd in the direction of Kirsten's carriage, willing her to stay in place until he reached her. He saw her pale face in the window before she sat back out of sight. Once free of the crowd, he loped the final distance and pulled the door open.

Kirsten huddled in the far corner of the coach. "What was the verdict? I couldn't hear."

"Guilty," Reid answered. "He'll hang tomorrow morning at ten."

Her gaze fell and she gave a little nod. "Justice has been served."

He pulled off the tinted glasses and peered into the shadows of the carriage. "Forgive me for saying so, sweetheart, but you don't look well."

Her eyes flicked up to his. "Neither do you."

"I didn't sleep much last night," he confessed. "I had a lot to think about."

Her consideration dropped away for the second time. "I didn't sleep either."

She appeared fragile as a baby bird kicked from its nest too soon. Reid wanted to climb into the carriage and hold her in his arms, but was afraid that such forward behavior might further distress her. So soon after her shocking confession, he thought it best for Kirsten to set the tone for their interaction.

"I'll be in Philadelphia for two more nights," he offered.

She didn't look up. "Yes, I know. Because of the hanging."

He forced his tone to sound kind, not desperate. "When may I see you?"

Her chin lifted. Her eyes followed. "I really don't feel at all well today, Reid. Will you come tomorrow?"

"Yes. Of course." He knew by the look of her that she told him the truth. "I'll come mid-day, after the sentence is carried out."

"Thank you." If she tried to smile, she failed. "I'll see you then."

"I love you, Kirsten." The words would not be held back.

She didn't reply. A single tear rolled down each cheek.

Reid stepped back and shut the door. He pounded the side of the carriage and the horses stepped into action.

CHAPTER TWENTY TWO

February 24, 1782

Reid was at the docks by nine. He claimed a spot where his back faced the morning sun; he wanted to watch Johan die without any painful glare in his eyes.

The Pennsylvania Regiment soldiers built the scaffold yesterday after the verdict was read. In his march around the city to clear his head, Reid passed them by. The celebratory tone of their efforts didn't surprise him in the least, considering that five of their friends had fallen in the man's scheme.

"Morning, Colonel," a young soldier offered as he approached. "Here for the hanging?"

"I am," Reid answered.

"You're the one what was hurt bad, ain't you?" he ventured.

Reid looked down at the earnest young man. At first glance he appeared to be just a teen, but closer inspection clarified the lines around his eyes and mouth.

"Yes," Reid said. "I spent three weeks recuperating before I was able to return to my unit."

The soldier nodded. "And you testified, didn't you? You helped get the bastard."

"He is indeed, a bastard," Reid agreed. On a hunch, he asked, "Did you know the men who died?"

The soldier nodded solemnly. "I was supposed to join them when my shift as guard was over."

Reid clapped his hand on the man's bony shoulder. "God was

watching out for you."

He gave a crooked smile. "That's what my wife says."

Reid was surprised to hear the man had a wife, yet marriages often happened before the couple reached twenty years of age. "She's a wise woman. You are blessed."

He laughed. "She says that, too."

A shout from the barracks pulled their attention.

"That's for me." He saluted Reid before he loped away. "Have a pleasant day, sir."

Reid watched his back and thought about the man's words. *A pleasant day*. Was that possible?

First, he was going to watch a man die. A rope would be snugged around his neck and—if Johan was lucky—his neck would be snapped when he dropped to the end of the rope's length.

Reid did a mental calculation and thought the scaffold might be a bit short. He hoped the Pennsylvanians hadn't made mischief to extend Johan's dying. If the neck wasn't broken, the hung man would slowly strangle, bucking and panicking as his body fought for air.

Not that he didn't deserve it.

Afterwards, he would plead his case with Kirsten and try to convince her to accept a husband—him. Reid held no assurances that he would succeed, but he intended to give it his very best effort.

By the time Johan was brought out to the scaffold, a large crowd had gathered. They howled as he appeared. If this was summer, Reid would have expected rotten fruits to be lobbed in the convicted killer's direction. As it was, a few eggs hit the mark.

Reid watched as the rope was looped into place around the man's neck and tightened. He couldn't hear the exchange between the preacher and the killer, but Johan spit on the scaffold in punctuation, drawing another round of angry howls. Everyone on the platform stepped back.

A major extended an arm, his sword glinting in the sun. When his arm dropped, so did the hinged floor of the scaffold. Reid winced to see he was right.

It took Johan seven minutes to die.

✯ ✯ ✯

Kirsten sat in the drawing room, the pouch of money on the table beside the settee. She had determined the purpose of this interview was to say their final goodbyes; Reid's purpose was irrelevant. Her decision was made and would not be unmade.

She slept yesterday afternoon, at last. Her nap was mercifully dreamless, unlike her night. Twice she awoke, panicked and fighting off her attackers.

Kirsten knew that she must stop ignoring what happened to her. She must allow the grief and fear to rise up, and then stare them fully in the face. Only then would they fade into the background of her life. They would never be gone; but they might at the least be quieted.

Marit babbled on at breakfast about the previous day spent with Henrik and the city official named Marcus Whitehead, or Matthew Whitfield, or some such name. Kirsten smiled and made the requisite sounds of interest and approval—and thought she had effectively hidden her troubles from her mother.

"What's happened, *Datter*, to make you so sad?" Marit asked of a sudden. The question incongruously followed a litany of yester eve's sumptuous dessert offerings.

The easiest lie was closest to the truth. "Reid is coming over to say his goodbyes later."

"He's returning to his duties, then?" Her mother tried to appear sympathetic, but her relief at getting the colonel away from her only child was clear as the crystal water goblet in her hand.

"No, he's resigning," Kirsten sighed. "He's going home to Boston."

Marit's brows lifted. "How did the trial turn out?"

"I'm surprised you didn't hear," she said truthfully. "That man was found guilty. He's to be hung in an hour."

"Such a tone," Marit scolded. "A man is about to die."

"Three men were injured and five men died because of what he did. Not to mention the destruction of supplies." Kirsten stood. "I'm going to read in the drawing room until Reid arrives."

Now Kirsten looked down at the novel which lay unopened in her lap. Unable to bring her thoughts around to any subject other than the conversation she was about to have, she simply listened to the clock ticking the seconds away and waited for Reid's knock on the door.

When it came, she nearly jumped out of her dress.

Kirsten stood, set the book beside the little pouch and faced the drawing room door. Her mind was made up, she thought again. *Nothing he can say will change it.*

Reid walked in and smiled at her.

Her resolve took a direct hit.

He approached and held out his hands. "Sweetheart, I'm so glad to see you are much improved."

Kirsten laid her hands in his without thinking about it—and immediately regretted it. His large hands were warm and strong, like the arms he held her with. "I—I am, yes. Thank you."

Reid pulled her close and his mouth took hers.

A last kiss.

She didn't stop him. She didn't have the heart to.

When the tender moment passed, he gestured for her to sit. "I have something I need to tell you. Shall we close the door?"

Kirsten's glance slid to the portal. Was it preferable to risk her parents' overhearing their possibly revealing conversation, or risk their indignation at the closed door closeting her alone with Reid, unchaperoned. The closeting won out.

"Yes, please." When he sat beside her she added, "We still need to keep our voices low."

"I understand," he said.

"I won't marry you," she blurted.

"Hear me out," Reid countered.

"No, you need to listen to *me*, Reid," she pressed. "I will not marry you—or anyone."

He shrugged. "Why not?"

She gaped at him. "What is this game?"

"It's not a game," he stated.

"Well, whatever you choose to call it, I am not amused," she snapped.

Reid took her hand and began to massage it the way she had his. "Let's back up a bit. I know what happened to you, and you know my circumstances."

"Yes," she hissed.

"Now—why won't you marry me?"

His fingers felt so good on her hand she forgot to be angry. "Are you asking for a list of reasons? Again?"

He nodded. "I am."

"I'm not a virgin," she whispered, her face heating at the admission.

"Neither am I," he whispered his response.

"Don't mock me," she warned and tried to pull her hand from his.

He held on and flipped it over to massage her palm. "I'm not mocking you. I respect you as a fellow human. Why should we have different expectations based on our genders?"

Kirsten glared at him. "Because men are—they can't be expected to—it's not healthy."

Reid huffed a chuckle. "Who told you that? Let me guess. A man trying to win sexual favors from you."

Kirsten's face flamed as she considered the question she was about to ask. "Yes. Why? Are you telling me it's not true?"

Reid stopped rubbing her hand and looked her intently in the eye. The blue rim around his gray irises darkened. "I haven't had a woman for four years. Do I appear in any way diminished to you?"

"No," she admitted. *Not in the least.*

His ministrations resumed. His fingers began to move languidly up her arm, touching her lightly and raising gooseflesh. "Your next objection?"

Her heart kept a strong yet increasing cadence in her chest. "I—I don't believe I'll ever be able to let a man touch me... the way..." her voice hitched, catching in her throat. She couldn't say the words with Reid so close, stroking her forearm so sensuously.

"The way." He repeated and kissed her wrist.

"A husband..."

Reid tasted her skin, his tongue tracing a narrow trail upward from her wrist to her elbow.

"Touches his wife?" He asked before placing a lingering kiss in the sensitive crook of her arm.

"Yes," she breathed.

He lifted his head. His mouth was inches from hers. "Is this pleasant for you?"

She couldn't lie to him. "Yes..."

He kissed the spot behind her jaw just below her ear. She shivered as a delightful shock snaked from her neck to her belly.

"Imagine what I could do, *Prinsesse*," he whispered in her ear.

"If I had freedom with your naked body."

Kirsten gasped. She leapt from the settee, more embarrassed at her own response than angry at his suggestion. "How dare you!" she yelped.

Reid leaned back, his expression bemused. "I apologize. I only intended to disarm your objection. Forgive me if I overstepped."

She paced several steps to the right, then back to the left. She gripped her hands in front of her waist and refused to think about how Reid's touch made her feel.

"I believe that all you'll need is a gentle approach," he continued softly. "And if that doesn't work, there are other things which can be done."

Kirsten stopped pacing and stared at him. She almost asked him what sort of things before she remembered that her goal was to *dis*courage, not *en*courage the man. She moved behind a chair, placing the barrier between herself and the compelling colonel.

"That well may be, Reid. But there is still the question of whether or not I can ever bear children," she stated with quiet determination.

His gaze faltered and she marked it. Any hope that may have sparked inside her died.

"I don't care," he said.

"And you are lying," she replied.

Reid shook his head. "Of course I hope for children, Kirsten. But if none ever come, I would rather have a childless marriage with you, than spend my life without you."

Kirsten closed her eyes, unable to bear the pleading look in his. "No. I cannot do that to you. It isn't fair."

"*Prinsesse...*"

"No. No!" She opened her eyes. "My reasons remain intact, and my answer is no."

An expression of horrified understanding washed over Reid's face. "I've been a fool."

That statement surprised her. "What?"

Reid's head fell forward until his chin nearly hit his chest. "*Å min Gud*, I was so blind."

Kirsten came around the chair. "What are you talking about?"

Reid slapped his palms on his thighs and pushed himself to his feet. He looked down at her, his gray eyes gone cold as tombstones.

Trepidation tangled in her chest, choking her like an overgrown weed.

"This isn't about you, is it?" he growled. "This is about me."

She frowned. "What about you?"

Reid threw his arms wide. "I should have listened to your father. He warned me. But like a fool, I believed your love for me would triumph."

Kirsten grabbed his shirt, desperate to make him understand. "It's not like that."

"No? Convince me," he challenged.

"I'm the one who is not marriageable!" she cried.

"So you say," Reid growled. "But I am willing to marry you anyway!"

Kirsten let go of his shirt and fell backward into the chair she had taken refuge behind. She should have stayed there.

"Anyway?" she rasped. "*Anyway?*"

"Yes!" Reid yelped. "In spite of all your objections, I am quite willing to take you to wife!"

Kirsten shot up from the chair and pushed her face into his. "I may be ruined, but I don't need your pity," she growled.

He glared down at her. "What are you talking about?"

"*I* am *not* a charity case!" she hissed.

"But I *am,* am I right?" Reid spun away from her and strode around the room in angry circles. "I am a damned fool."

Kirsten grabbed the pouch of coins from the table and held it as far in front of her as her arm would reach.

When Reid saw it, he stopped as if hitting a wall. His eyes narrowed. "What is that?"

Kirsten straightened her shoulders and refused to sound weak. "Your back pay."

"My—*what?*" he roared.

"Don't be an ass. Take it. You earned it," she spat.

He jabbed a finger from across the room that she swore she could feel hitting her chest. "Is that from your money?"

She gave him the coldest look she could muster. "It is the *army's* money. And now it's yours. Take it."

Reid waved his hands in front of his chest. "Hell, no!"

"It's been signed off as yours," she informed him with far less satisfaction that she expected. The bag still dangled from her outstretched hand. "The army considers your account settled, and no more payments will be forthcoming, Colonel."

His jaw fell open. His steely eyes shot blue-edged arrows at her. "So if I don't take this money here, now, I get nothing? Ever?"

Kirsten pressed her lips together so hard they shook. She gave him a tense nod.

"*Gud forbannet det til helvete!*" he swore.

She held her ground, her arm twitching with each beat of her pounding heart.

Reid stormed toward her. Kirsten flinched. He ripped the pouch from her hand.

"You have made your point, *Princesse*."

Reid strode to the drawing room doors and flung them open. He bellowed into the entry hall, "My cloak, please!"

The butler scurried over with his cloak and hat.

Reid turned to look at her. He stood tall, proud, more of a man than any man she had ever known. *Or may ever know*. His intense stare set every nerve in her body on fire.

"I love you with all of my heart, Kirsten Sven," he said, his tone defeated. "And I will do so for as long as I live."

Kirsten found her voice buried in Reid's imminent departure from her life. "Let me call the carriage."

He gave a quick shake of his head. "Don't bother."

And he was gone.

CHAPTER TWENTY THREE

Kirsten stood at the window and watched Reid disappear. She felt thin, torn, and hollowed out.

"I heard shouting." Her father's soft, deep voice dribbled over her shoulder. "What have you done, *Datter?*"

Kirsten heaved a sigh, unable to draw enough breath to move the stone in her chest. "I told him I wouldn't marry him."

He rested a hand in the small of her back. "Is that all?"

"No. I gave him his back pay. From the charity money." She looked at Henrik. "The charity money I raised for that purpose."

His brows lifted. "Did he take it?"

Kirsten nodded.

"He's a proud man and rightfully so. I understand his anger," her father said.

"You like him, don't you?" Kirsten asked, needing the answer to be yes.

"Reid Hansen is a man to be both respected and liked," Henrik stated. "Even if he doesn't have royal blood."

Kirsten turned back to the window; nothing in the snowy landscape moved. "I couldn't marry him," she said softly, trying to convince herself.

"No." Henrik kissed her temple. "I don't believe you would have been happy with him."

Kirsten stood at the window, staring after Reid, and wondered what in God's name she was going to do with her life now.

February 25, 1782

Reid dressed in his battle clothes and stuffed everything else he owned into his leather pack. He had a map in his coat pocket and his coins inside his shirt. Kirsten had given him two hundred dollars—enough to pay him for five years of soldiering.

If he had bothered to count it before he left Kirsten yesterday, he would have given half of it back. As it was, he had no desire to return to the Sven home. And going there just to throw money back at the princess seemed rather petty.

So Reid decided to keep it. At least he would gain something from the destructive debacle that was Kirsten Sven.

He ate a hearty breakfast and packed the leftover food in his satchel. As long as the weather held, he would walk. He could cover thirty miles a day by walking ten or so hours at a steady pace. Boston was only ten days away at that rate.

And if the weather turned, he could either wait it out in an inn or pay for a carriage ride.

Reid rubbed his thigh. The constant motion would be good for it. Keep it warmed and stretched.

Walking would also keep his mind focused. Off of Kirsten.

When Reid walked away from her yesterday he couldn't look back at her. He couldn't let her see his grief streaming down his cheeks. For the second time in three days that confounded woman had brought him to tears. Once in pained empathy for her situation, and again because she was too damnably stubborn to accept the man who loved her and stripped his soul bare for her.

Ten days. Reid ached to be home. He hadn't seen his parents for years. As silly as it sounded for a man of his age and position, he wanted his mother's company. He knew that Dagny would listen to his disappointments and comfort him. She was a wise woman. Perhaps she could tell him what to do with the rest of his life.

Reid stepped out of the hotel onto the busy street and began his journey. Tonight's destination was Trenton in New Jersey. Reid hooked his tinted spectacles over his ears. He wore his pack on his shoulders and carried his rifle.

One foot in front of the other. Get started. Keep moving.

Don't look back.

March 10, 1782
Ten miles west of Boston

Reid was exhausted. Home was only two hours away, but he wouldn't make it today. Over the last fourteen days he had trudged along rutted, muddy roads on one day, tripped over frozen ridges the next. He spent two extra days in Hartford when a storm blew through. On five occasions his soldier's uniform caught a driver's attention, and his limping gait won him a seat in a coach or on the back of a wagon.

Other days, however, he only managed part of his goal, held back by a late start or an early end. When his strength was about to give way, he either made a fire and slept under the protection of a rock, or he knocked on a farmer's door and asked for a spot in their barn. He hunted along the way, or bought food from taverns and housewives.

One rainy night near New York he even treated himself to dinner, wine, and a room at an inn.

The sun was lowering and Reid didn't trust himself to find his way in the dark. He saw lights in a house and stumbled toward it. He brushed himself off, ran his hands through his hair, and stood up straight. He knocked on the door.

A man answered. His narrowed eyes swept over Reid. "Can I help you?"

"I'm a soldier on my way home to Boston. The light's failing and I won't make it in time. I'm wondering if I might shelter with you for the night," Reid said.

"I'm not sure," he replied.

"I can pay something for your trouble, if that's a concern," Reid offered. The aroma of freshly baked bread wafted over him and made his mouth water.

"Sean, who is it?" a woman's voice asked.

Sean spoke over his shoulder. "He says he's a soldier on his way to Boston."

A blonde woman pulled the door wider. She was tall and held a toddler on her hip. "I'm certain we could—oh, my God!"

Reid stared at the woman whose face had familiar features, but somehow wasn't quite recognizable. "Do you know me?"

"Reid!" she cried. "Don't you know your own sister?"

"Anna? Oh, Anna!" Reid began to laugh. "How old are you now?"

"Twenty, thank you very much," she said with a giggle. "This is my husband, Sean MacIntyre. And our daughter, Sophie. Come in!"

Reid staggered through the door and dropped his pack on the floor. He leaned his rifle against the wall and stuck out his hand toward Sean. "Reidar Hansen. Firstborn of Martin and Dagny Hansen."

"Ah, yes. The one conceived on the ship," Sean said as he gripped Reid's hand.

Reid looked at his youngest sister. "Does everyone know that story?"

She shrugged, grinning. "It's a great story."

"Take a seat, Reid," Sean urged. "We were about to have supper."

Reid claimed a chair and watched Anna settle Sophie into another before setting a plate and silverware in front of him.

· "I hope you like chicken," she said.

"I do. It smells wonderful," Reid answered. He didn't believe the truth was polite—that a soldier who had walked from Philadelphia would eat just about anything set in front of him.

Sean sat across from Reid. "You're in the army?"

"Yes. I'm a Colonel—well, I was before I resigned."

"Resigned?" Anna asked as she set small platters of food on the table. "Why?"

The realization that he must become accustomed to answering this question smacked Reid in the chest. "I was injured in an explosion. It was time."

His baby sister's eyes rounded. "Are you recovered?"

"Scarred but healthy," he assured her.

Anna sank into the chair to his left. "Do you know about Olav?"

Reid closed his eyes, the weight of his assumption pressing him down. "Where? When?"

"Johnstown. In October," she said softly. "He wasn't killed, Reid. But he lost an arm."

At least his brother was alive; that was a relief. "Where is he now?"

"He's with *Mamma* and *Pappa*. You'll see him tomorrow." Anna began to heap food on his plate. "They've found some work he can manage."

"Is there anything else I should know?" he asked. His belly rumbled and his mouth watered, but he waited for Sean to be served before picking up his fork.

"We haven't heard from Nils for five months," she said.

"You didn't hear from me for longer than that in seventy-nine," he reminded her. "He never was much for writing anyway."

"Eat, Reid. Don't wait for me," Sean urged.

Reid picked up his fork and began to do justice to the victuals. He listened while Sean and Anna described their wedding two years ago. Sean had returned after five years of soldiering to claim the farm when both of his parents succumbed to smallpox. He was twenty-one at the time. Little Sophie made her appearance ten months after the wedding.

"And her brother or sister will be here in August," Anna said shyly.

Sean beamed at his wife.

Reid considered the somber toddler who chewed on a spoon and regarded him with wide green eyes and tousled blonde curls.

He wasn't certain how he truly felt about babies. Perhaps if the child was his, he would feel more affinity for it. Or perhaps pondering the possibility that he would never be a father had shown his true colors.

"Congratulations," he said after a pause. "I'm glad to find you so well, Anna."

She smiled at him. "And I'm glad to find you alive, Reid. But I think if you don't lie down soon, you may fall off that chair."

"I am tired," he admitted. "I've come from Philadelphia and I walked for the most part."

Sean stood. "Come on. We have a bed in the back room."

Reid retrieved his pack and rifle. "Thank you."

Half an hour later, Reid was lying at an angle on the bed, stripped to his shirt and covered with a blanket he remembered from childhood. He smiled. Obviously Anna absconded with it when she married.

A small fire rounded off the edges of the room's chill. It felt like luxury to him after so many nights spent sleeping rough. Reid closed his eyes and—as he had for every night since Philadelphia—said a prayer for Kirsten to find her peace.

March 11, 1782

Reid walked up to the front door of his parents' three-story home in the heart of Boston and opened the door.

"Martin?" his mother called from deep in the house. "Have you come for lunch?"

Reid's throat clutched at hearing his mother's voice. He paused before answering, hoping he didn't crumble to soggy bits in front of her.

"It's Reid, *Mamma*," he managed.

A scramble of footsteps preceded his mother swirling around the back of the staircase and into the hallway. She stopped in a whoosh of skirts as if confronting a ghost. Her pale gaze covered him from hat to boot.

Reid closed the door behind him and yanked the hat from his head. "I've come home."

Her chest began to heave. She stumbled toward him, arms outstretched. "Reid! Oh, Reid!"

Reid gathered his mother into his arms and held her as if he would never let go. Only two inches shy of six feet in her youth, he noticed she had compressed a little since he saw her last.

"I am so glad to have you back safely," she cried, holding him close as well. "My prayers have been answered."

"And I have missed you and *Pappa* greatly all these years," he croaked. "But I'm done with war."

Dagny pushed away from him, a different gaze evaluating him now. "Are you injured?"

"I was," he began. "Didn't you receive my letter?"

His mother's eyes widened. "No! How badly?"

"That's a long story for later. But I have recovered."

The door opened behind him and Reid turned to see who had entered. Though the face was recognizable, the pinned-up empty sleeve would have identified his brother instantly. "Olav!"

Olav stepped back, shocked. "Reid?"

Reid grabbed Olav in a brotherly hug, avoiding pressure where his left arm abruptly ended. Olav pounded Reid's back in return.

"It's good to see you again, *bror*," Olav mumbled.

Reid pulled back and pointed at the missing limb. "I was sorry to hear."

Dagny slipped her arm around Reid's waist and looked up at him, brow wrinkled. "How did you know?"

"As Providence would have it, I asked to shelter at a farmhouse yester eve." He allowed an impish grin. "And do you know who answered the door? Anna."

Dagny's face brightened. "How is she?"

"She's fine. Sean is fine. Sophie is fine." Reid pointed at his pack on the floor. "I have a letter and a jar of honey for you."

Dagny squeezed his waist again, and then addressed his brother. "Olav, will you please go over to the offices and ask you father to come home as soon as he is able?"

"Shall I tell him why?" Olav asked.

"Hell, yes!" Reid answered for his mother. "I don't want to give the man apoplexy on my first day home!"

Dagny pinched his side. "Such language."

"I'm sorry. Mamma," Reid said, grinning down at her. "I should say I don't want to give *my father* apoplexy on my first day home."

His mother gave him a playful shove. "I see soldiering hasn't repaired your impertinent tongue."

Reid winced the tiniest bit when his right thigh twisted. Dagny gasped.

"You are still injured!" she accused.

"No, I'm healed," he insisted. "Only the scar pulls at times."

"I'll go after *Pappa*," Olav stated grimly. He disappeared out the door which closed heavily behind him.

"He's having a hard time," Dagny said.

Reid picked up his pack and rifle. "It's only been four months. I imagine it still pains him."

Dagny nodded and took his arm giving it a tight squeeze. "Come upstairs and we'll get you settled in."

CHAPTER TWENTY FOUR

Martin Hansen stood eye-to-eye with Reid, joy splitting his face in halves. "I cannot believe you are finally here, son. Standing right in front of me. After all these years!"

Martin's receding hair held more silver than any other color. He wore a pair of magnifying spectacles perched on the end of his nose. His grip was strong, however, and his voice displayed the vigor of a younger man. Reid realized with a shock that his father's sixty-first birthday was the next day.

"Consider me a birthday gift," he teased. "Because I don't have another to give you, *Pappa*."

Martin clapped him on the shoulders. "I couldn't ask for a better gift. It's so good to have you home."

Home. Reid expected that word to fill him with peace, not the roiling discomfort that stirred his chest. He would need to think more about that.

Supper was chaotic. Reid's sister Karan joined them with her unruly brood of three—her husband Arthur was on guard duty. Tobias, Reid's youngest brother, brought a sweet young woman named Caroline to the gathering and declared that she might soon become a permanent part of their future family occasions.

"We are waiting for her father to return from Williamsburg to ask permission," he explained. Caroline blushed and smiled.

Liv, the one born after Reid, had her two sons aged thirteen and eleven in tow. Their interest in *Onkel* Reidar's war experiences clearly had her on edge.

"Where is Alex?" Reid asked her.

"New York. He's due to come home any day," she said. The set of her mouth and the dart of her eyes displayed her unspoken concern.

"I just came through there. It's quiet now, I'm certain he's fine," he assured her.

"End this quickly, Colonel Hansen. I've risked a husband. I'll not risk my sons," she grumbled.

Reid put up his hands. "That is no longer up to me."

"Have you left the army, son?" Martin asked.

"Yes I have, *Pappa*," he replied.

"What will you do?" Dagny asked. "Will you stay in Boston?"

Reid hesitated. "I haven't decided yet."

"Where would you go?" Tobias asked.

Reid shrugged. "I haven't the faintest idea. I'm completely at loose ends right now."

His revelation prompted a round of suggestions from his siblings—most of them impossible. One or two held merit, but only if they held any of Reid's interest. Olav sat quietly at the end of the table, seeming to have nothing to say.

Reid watched his brother and saw the clear signs of a man who held no hope. It was like looking in a mirror.

Granted, all Reid was missing was his heart. His bodily parts, though scarred, were all still attached and functioning. And even though Reid had no expectation of future entanglements, he was otherwise whole.

Olav clearly needed a good woman. There were plenty of war widows who would take a one-armed man over no man at all. He wondered if Olav had made any attempts.

Those who loved once knew love was possible. Reid chuckled inwardly at this ironic trail of thought. *I'll never love again, but you, brother, should apply yourself diligently to the possibility.*

Reid looked around the crowded, noisy supper table at his mother, his father, two of his sisters, two of his brothers, and five assorted children.

He never felt so lonely in his entire life.

★ ★ ★

Reid sat in the kitchen sipping tea heavily fortified with brandy. He should have been exhausted, but the disquiet which plagued him from the moment he walked into Boston was now stealing his rest.

He didn't understand why this place, his home since his birth, had ceased to be a refuge. It wasn't as if he had left behind some unresolved relationship. Nor had any trauma befallen him here—other than the advent of war. Reid had always thought of Boston as where he belonged.

Tonight he was not so assured.

Footsteps on the wooden staircase announced that he would soon have a visitor. The easy creak on the steps told Reid it was not his father. He stood and procured a second cup, then poured water in the tea to steep.

He was glad that his mother was awake. He loved and respected his father, but at times when he was troubled he found his mother's presence soothing. She was a shrewd woman and he admired her quiet strength.

When his mother appeared in the doorway, he held up the brandy bottle in question.

"Just a little," she said with a crooked smile.

Reid obliged her before reclaiming his seat.

Dagny sat next to him, tucking her robe around her legs. "Can you not sleep?"

Reid shook his head. "No. And I don't know why."

Dagny picked up her cup and stirred it absently. "When were you injured?"

"September second," he said.

"How did it happen?" Her voice was soft and she didn't look at him.

So many times in his life she had asked him questions in this same manner. Her calm expression, displaying neither assumptions nor judgment, encouraged confidences. Reid gave his mother a sideways glance.

"Why do women always want to talk to me in the middle of the night?" He chuckled before realizing with horror what he had just confessed.

"Talking in the dark, when no one else is around, feels very safe," Dagny replied, apparently missing what he just revealed. "Was it a bad injury?"

"A British sympathizer exploded a stockpile of guns and ammunition in Philadelphia," Reid began. "I was close enough to the blast to stumble backward and fall. I hit my head—hard. My eyes were burned. And I had a chunk of metal in my thigh which left a six-inch scar."

Dagny leaned closer and peered into his eyes. "You said you were recovered?"

"Yes, *Mamma*. Your little boy is worse for wear, but overall I'm fine," he teased.

Dagny gave him a chastising slap on the knee. "Just wait until you have children, Reid. Then you'll understand how it feels."

Reid twisted his lips. "That may never happen."

"Why do you say that?" Her voice was soft again.

"I don't know." He shrugged. "I'm just so disoriented by being here, I suppose nothing makes sense to me right now."

Dagny sipped her tea, now that it was ready. She stared into the fire and didn't say anything.

Reid finished his tea and refilled his cup with straight brandy. "Why do you think that is, *Mamma*? Why do I feel like a stranger in my own home?"

"Because it's not your own home," she whispered.

Reid stared at her. "I don't understand."

Dagny faced him again. "When you left, Reid, you were still a young man. You hadn't yet found your path."

"Are you saying I'm an old man now?" he bristled.

She smiled. "No. I'm saying that you are in your prime now. This is the time for you to establish yourself, your home, and your place in this world."

"How do I do that when all I've known for the last nine years is war?" he asked, desperate for the answer.

Dagny laid her hand on his arm. "What women talk to you in the middle of the night?"

Of a sudden, Reid understood how his own shifts in conversation had knocked Kirsten off balance. Now he realized where that habit originated. He also realized that nothing snuck past his mother.

Reid sighed. "Her name was Kirsten. After I was injured I was taken to her parents' home to recover."

"How long were you there?"

"Three weeks."

"And she visited you in the night?" Dagny probed.

Reid grinned, in spite of himself. "It wasn't like that. My eyes were bandaged and I was laid out. I couldn't even stand up."

Dagny held out her cup; Reid poured her a dollop of brandy.

"She was disquieted as well," she observed.

"She was," he admitted.

"How did things end between you?" Dagny looked toward the floor and sipped her brandy.

"The first time, her parents made it clear that I wasn't an acceptable choice for her." Reid mentally kicked himself for adding the designation *first time*. There was no way his mother would let that pass.

She didn't. "When was the second time?"

"There was a court-martial for the man who set off the explosion. I returned to Philadelphia to testify," Reid said, adding, "I was there for two weeks that time. I resigned from the army after the man was hung. And then I came here."

Dagny looked into his eyes, her expression kind. "What happened, son?"

Reid's throat thickened in a very unmanly way. "She refused me," he managed.

Dagny leaned back in her seat and sipped from her cup. Reid couldn't explain why, but having said the words aloud seemed to ease his pain a little.

"Do you love her?" his mother murmured.

Reid wanted to say no. "Yes, *Mamma*. I do."

"Then you have two choices, Reid. Only two," she offered. "The first is to go back to her and convince her to change her mind. Make her love you."

"She already loves me. She just doesn't want to marry me," he admitted.

"Explain that," Dagny prodded.

Reid didn't want to betray Kirsten's confidence. Even if he never saw her again and she never knew about it, he was determined to protect her.

He settled on, "She had a bad experience and she doesn't trust men. She intends to remain unmarried for her lifetime."

"Even though she is in love with you?" Dagny asked, clearly

puzzled.

Reid lifted one shoulder. "I could not sway her, *Mamma*. I did try. Hard."

Dagny sighed softly and shook her head. "Then your only other choice is to forget her."

Reid pressed the heels of his hands against his eyes. "I'm trying. But she haunts my every waking thought and half my sleeping ones."

"You need some occupation, son. What will you do?"

His hands fell to his lap. "What is there to do?"

"*Pappa* doesn't have enough business to hire you, I'm afraid. Tobias has been working there all along, and now Olav..." She let the sentence die.

"I don't want to burden *Pappa*," Reid assured her. "I suppose I'll start looking for a position tomorrow."

Dagny stood and Reid followed her example. He set his cup down and wrapped his arms around his mother. She hugged him back and they stood, unmoving, for a long time.

"I love you, *Mamma*," he said.

"You'll find your way, son," she said against his shoulder. "You are too much like me *not* to."

March 19, 1782

Nine days. Nine long, fruitless days, pacing the streets and docks of Boston. Nine days searching for just one position that Reid could see spending six days a week working at without wishing he had died in the explosion. Or setting another one to accomplish the deed.

Reid was tired. Not in his body as much as in his character. The way things ended with Kirsten, coupled with the attempt to find a decent way to support himself now that he was done with the army, exhausted what little emotional strength he held in reserve. He learned one thing from the bustle and busyness of Boston, however.

He ached for peace and quiet and a new beginning away from war and strife. Simple as that.

Reid snorted. *Not so simple*.

He had money, now. Enough to get something started. The

problem was he had no idea what that something was.

The door to his father's architectural office opened and a stylishly dressed couple walked out. Reid smiled to himself—hopefully his father had been contracted to design their house. He stepped aside to allow them passage before he strode inside with more energy than he felt.

"Hello, *Pappa*," he said. "Did you sell them plans for a mansion?"

"Two," Martin said without looking up. "One on top of the other."

Reid laughed. "May I take you to lunch?"

Martin looked up. "Is the day not treating you well?"

"Perhaps. Perhaps not."

His father grinned. "I hate when you say that."

"I know," Reid countered. *You aren't the only one.* "I'm hoping you'll become angry enough to jump out of that chair and chase me into Roberson's Tavern."

Martin's gaze fell back to his notes. "I'll be done in a minute."

Twenty minutes later, Reid faced his father over a bowl of fish chowder. "I don't believe Boston is the right place for me anymore," he confessed.

"I'm not surprised," Martin admitted. "I have never seen you so restless."

Reid pinned his father with his stare. "When you decided to leave Norway, what was the pivotal reason?"

Martin set his spoon down. "I wanted to follow my passion for building. Norway wasn't the place to do that."

"Was there anything else?" Reid asked.

"There was a family situation," Martin said carefully.

Reid gave him an expectant look.

"My grandfather made my father promise to make me the next Hansen heir, bypassing your Uncle Gustav." Martin complied. "I didn't want to usurp my brother."

"Oh..." Reid frowned. "You never told me that."

"You never asked." Martin picked up his spoon again. "So why are you asking now?"

"I am at loose ends," Reid admitted. "I'm not Colonel Hansen anymore."

"Who are you?" his father asked.

Reid's shoulders slumped. "I'm not certain."

"Let me ask you this, son. What is your passion?"

Kirsten. Reid stared at his chowder bowl, silent. He needed to find a different place to lay his heart. Someplace far enough away to forget her.

"Reid?" Martin prompted.

"I want peace and quiet. Land. My own home," he blurted. "But I have no means to procure them."

A shadow passed through Martin's expression. "Have you finished your soup? I need to make a stop at the post office on the way back."

"Yes." Reid pushed his bowl away, his appetite eaten by his foul mood. He stood and paid for the meal from his carefully parsed funds.

Father and son donned their cloaks and stepped into the cold drizzle of an early spring day. They didn't converse as they made their way along the streets toward the post office. Inside the brick building, Reid followed Martin to a board with multiple notices tacked on it and pamphlets spread on a counter in front of it.

Martin began to peruse the leaflets, obviously in search of something. Reid waited patiently, lost in his own melancholy.

"Ah—here it is!" Martin waved a printed sheet over his head. "Take a look."

March 1, 1782
Five Hundred Acre Land Grants in the Missouri Territory
Available for White Men aged Eighteen to Thirty-Eight.
Must apply at the Saint Louis Land Grant Office in Person.

Reid read the notice twice. "They are giving land away?"

"So it says." Martin looked him in the eye. "Interested?"

Was he? Reasons not to go abounded. The distance, for one. If he arrived too late to claim a parcel, he would have spent time and money for nothing. The fact that he would be living in the wilderness by himself for another.

Of course, he could hunt. Skin the animals and either use or sell the pelts. He could certainly build himself a cabin before winter. Maybe take seeds with him and plant a small garden.

His heart began to pound. He could do this. He could go to

Missouri, claim the land, and set up his own kingdom. Be sovereign over his own property, as he had mentioned to—*never mind*. Perhaps somewhere along the way, he would find a new passion.

One could always hope.

Reid nodded soberly. "This is what I need to do, *Pappa*. I need to start a new life as Reidar Hansen, far away from war and unhappy memories."

Martin suddenly looked older. A little sad—as if the inevitable happened and he was already prepared. He threw an arm around Reid's shoulders.

"I believe you're right, son," he said. "But let me be the one to tell your mother."

PART THREE:
SOVEREIGNTY

CHAPTER TWENTY FIVE

May 14, 1782
St. Louis
Missouri Territory

Reid tied his pair of draft horses to the railing and, dusting himself off, climbed the wooden steps and opened the door of the St. Louis Land Grant Office.

"Is this where I apply for the land?" he asked the clerk behind a desk.

The thin, balding man looked up. "It is."

"Is there land still available?" Reid prodded.

The man nodded. "There is."

Reid glanced around the room. Flattened maps littered the one large table, and rolled ones filled a bank of cubbyholes. There was no posted indication as to what his next action should be.

He faced the man again. "Will you give me five hundred acres please?"

The clerk lifted a sheet of printed paper from a neat stack, retrieved a quill pen, sharpened the point, and looked up at Reid. "Name?"

"Reidar Magnus Hansen," Reid answered and spelled out his names.

"Wife?"

"No."

"Children?"

"No."

"Born?"

"Boston. Seventeen-fifty."

"Age today?"

"Thirty-two."

The clerk squinted at the paper. "Raise your right hand."

Reid did so.

"Do you swear that you will occupy and settle the land you receive, are of sound mental and physical condition, upstanding in character, and will behave in a lawful and upright manner for as long as the land is in your possession?"

The door to the office swung open. A tall man—nearly as tall as Reid—stuck his head in. "Is this the land grant office?"

"I do!" Reid shouted, unsure of how many grants were still to be awarded.

"Sign here," the clerk handed Reid the quill. He faced the newcomer. "It is."

The man glanced at Reid, then back at the clerk as he stepped inside the office. "Is there land still available?"

"There is," he answered.

The man grinned. "I'd like to apply."

"Be with you shortly."

Reid bent over and scratched his signature at the bottom of the document, solidifying his prior claim to whatever tracts were being released. He handed the paper back to the clerk.

"Over there on the table are the plots. Yours is number fifty-seven," the clerk said. He lifted another printed sheet and looked at the next man. "Name?"

Reid crossed to the table, listening with half-an-ear to the answers.

"James Rikard Atherton."

"Wife?"

"Beatrice."

"Children?"

"No."

"Born?"

"Raleigh, North Carolina."

"Year?"

"Seventeen-fifty-two."

"Age today?"

"Twenty-nine."

The clerk squinted at the paper. "Raise your right hand."

Reid looked at the topographical map for plot fifty-seven. He also perused the one for plot fifty-eight, making an assumption which quickly proved correct. James joined him at the table, and Reid laid the maps side-by-side.

"So we shall be neighbors." Reid offered his hand. "Reidar Hansen. Call me Reid."

James shook Reid's hand. "James Atherton. Call me James."

The men bent over the maps.

"Will you be farming, James?" Reid asked.

"That is my plan. I'll grow tobacco, wheat, and corn to sell," he replied.

Reid raised his brow. "That's ambitious."

James' smile was confident. "I've got slaves coming from North Carolina with my wife."

Reid hadn't thought much about slaves, other than to know that owning them wasn't a path he would ever choose. But then, he wasn't a farmer. He tilted his head, considering the layout of the two grants.

"You have quite a bit of forested hills in this section," Reid pointed at the map. "That will be tough to farm."

James nodded. "True... You have some nice land in this part, however. What will you grow?"

Reid shook his head. "I'm not much for farming. I'm more of a hunter. I understand there are plenty of beaver, fox, wolf, and bear in the woods. Their pelts fetch a nice price back east."

"So you won't plant this land?" James sounded disappointed.

"I don't plan to." Reid straightened as did James, until the two men met eye-to-eye. "I do have an idea, however."

"I'm listening," James said.

"What if we redrew the boundary between the plots," Reid suggested.

"I get your flat land and you get my hills?" James clarified.

"Exactly." Reid turned to the clerk who sat silently at his desk writing up their deeds. "May we do that?"

The clerk scratched his head. "As long as none of the outer borders are affected, I don't suppose it matters what you two do a'tween yourselves."

Reid and James grinned at each other. They spent the next hour with graphite pencils, trying to evenly apportion the land according to the topography. They were not successful; there was simply more arable land than hills.

"There is one last option," Reid posited, stroking his two-month beard.

James stretched and rubbed his lower back. "What?"

Reid ran his finger over their most recent re-written border. "We split the land as we have it drawn here, then I lease these two hundred acres to you to farm."

James tapped his chin thoughtfully. "What terms?"

"A percentage of the profits seems fair," Reid offered.

"Ten percent?" James asked.

"Thirty," Reid countered.

James scoffed. "Fifteen."

Reid wagged his head back and forth, his lips pressed together. "Twenty-five. After all, the land will lay fallow otherwise," he bartered.

"I can't afford that. I have costs, you know," James objected. "Shall we simply settle on the twenty percent we are both heading toward and go have luncheon together?"

Reid laughed. He shook James' hand again, this time sealing their bargain. "I think you and I are going to get along very well."

After explaining to the clerk exactly where they wanted their shared border to be drawn, the two men stepped out into the balmy spring air and hazy sunshine of the spring day.

"Are those your horses?" James asked nodding toward the big pair Reid had tied to the rail.

"They are," Reid answered. "They're Vermont Drafters."

"I'm not familiar with the breed," James said as he walked up to the saddled stallion. "He's, what, seventeen hands?"

"Roughly." Reid patted the animal on the neck. "He wasn't saddle broke when I bought him, so the ride was interesting."

James chuckled. "You'll breed him to the mare, of course."

"Might be able to sell a few foals if they prove fertile enough," Reid replied. The big animal nuzzled his shoulder, his tail busily whisking away flies.

"When did you arrive in St. Louis?" James asked.

Reid grinned. "An hour ago."

James looked surprised. "Where are you staying?"

Reid shrugged. "I don't know."

James clapped him on the shoulder. "In that event, let's go to my hotel to eat and get you sorted for the night."

"I am guarding my funds rather tightly," Reid explained, determined not to be embarrassed by his situation. "I'll find a spot out-of-doors."

"Nonsense!" James objected. "I want to begin laying plans with you, neighbor, and I can't do that if you are off in some hidey hole somewhere. Besides," he clapped Reid on the shoulder, "I'll pay for it. After all, I might have agreed to twenty-five percent."

Reid laughed at that. "Then I accept. Because, I might have agreed to fifteen!"

✯ ✯ ✯

At the Saint Louis Auberge, James arranged for Reid's room while he took care of his horses. Their comfort was more important than his own, in truth. Without their assistance he could not carve out his home in the wilderness. He paid a little extra to see them both well fed and his pack of supplies well guarded.

"I ordered you a bath and a shave," James said once Reid joined him in the dining room. "I hope that's acceptable."

Reid's first response was to be offended. Who was this man to pass judgment on his condition? Thankfully, his good sense kicked in before he said anything rude—as did his desire for both of those luxuries. God only knew when he would have the chance to enjoy either again.

"Thank you, James. I appreciate it," he said.

James waived a dismissive hand. "What's the point of having money if you can't spread it around?"

Reid peered at his new acquaintance. "If you have money, what are you doing out here?"

James' lips curved. "Now that's a story."

"I have time," Reid prodded.

"I'll tell you mine, then you tell me yours. Agreed?" James said as their server approached the table.

"Agreed."

"We have smoked meat and fish," the man stated without

ceremony. "Which'll it be?"

"What sort of meat?" Reid asked. He'd had enough rabbit and squirrel during the past long weeks of travel to last him a lifetime or two.

"Bison."

"And the fish?" James asked.

"Bass."

"I'll have the bison," Reid decided. His mouth was already watering.

"And I'll have the same," James said. "And a pitcher of beer."

The man walked away as abruptly as he arrived. He returned immediately with a foaming pitcher and two tall crockery mugs. He set everything on the table with a resounding thunk.

"Food'll be here presently," he mumbled before lumbering off.

"Charming fellow," James quipped.

Reid poured the beer. "Your story?"

"Ah yes." James lifted his mug and leaned back. He stretched his long legs under the table, careful not to hit Reid's. "My wife is a beautiful woman who comes from a wealthy family," he began. "I have money of my own, mind you, but her family has been in America longer."

"Do I detect an accent?" Reid asked.

"My parents were from Sussex. I've been told I speak a sort of southern English, English, if you understand what I mean?" James said with a quirk of his mouth.

Reid chuckled. "I do. Go on."

"Her family owns a tobacco plantation in North Carolina. Very large, very lucrative." James sipped his beer. "And while Beatrice is the darling of the family, she does have an older brother."

"Who will inherit the plantation," Reid finished the thought.

"Precisely."

Reid drank his beer as well, finding it surprisingly good. "So you came here to establish yourself?"

"That, and to escape the fighting. You know that most of the battles have now moved south?" James asked.

Reid nodded. "I was a colonel in the Continental Army until a few months ago."

"Were you?" James leaned forward. "Why did you leave?"

Reid shook his head. "Finish your story first."

"Fair enough. " James leaned back again. "We married a year ago. No children as yet. When I decided to come for the land grant, she stayed behind. I'll send word that we are all set and she'll come by boat with everything we own."

"And everyone," Reid added.

James' brow lifted. "Pardon?"

"Your slaves," Reid clarified, careful not to allow judgment to seep into his tone.

"Oh! Right." James bounced a nod. "I'll probably settle her here in Saint Louis until I can get enough of our house built to live in comfortably."

"What sort of structure will you build?" Reid asked of a sudden. He hadn't thought much about his own home beyond the log cabin he must finish before winter set in. Now that he was a landowner, he needed to consider these things.

I'm a landowner. He smiled into his beer.

"Something quite solid. Stone and brick, I imagine. You know about the tornadoes, don't you?" James queried.

Reid frowned. "No. What are they?"

James' arms whirled in the air. "Massively strong, sudden, circular winds. They can tear a tree out by its roots and leave the house standing next to it untouched. And vice versa."

In spite of the violent storms he experienced on his journey, Reid found that description a bit ludicrous. "Are you joking?"

James' eyes pinned his. "Not in the least. You'll see."

Their plates of smoked bison meat were plopped in front of them, along with a loaf of hot bread and a crock of butter. The food smelled so good that Reid's stomach rumbled audibly. He grabbed his fork.

"So you'll build of brick and stone, then," he said before taking his first bite.

James nodded and stuck his fork into the tender meat heaped on his plate. "I will. I have the plans with me. I'll begin modestly and add on as each part is completed."

Reid broke a chunk of bread from the loaf. "That seems wise. Perhaps I'll do the same."

"Do you have plans with you as well?" James asked.

Reid shook his head. "I wasn't certain I would get the land. I'll come up with something."

James rested his elbows on either side of his plate and tore a piece of bread into chunks, popping each piece into his mouth. "So what about you, Reid? What's your story?"

CHAPTER TWENTY SIX

Reid blew a breath out loose lips. "I was born in Boston to a pair of Norwegian immigrants who met on the ship coming over. My father studied engineering and architecture at Oxford before deciding to come to this continent."

"Well that explains your coloring and your size," James chortled. "I so seldom meet a man whom I can look in the eye, not in the scalp."

Reid rolled his eyes. "I know what you mean. I get a crick in my neck at times."

James laughed. "Did you go to university?"

Reid nodded. "Harvard. I studied engineering and architecture like my father."

"So designing your own house won't be a problem," James observed, still forking meat into his mouth.

"I don't believe so, though I never was able to put my education to use," he admitted.

James' brow furrowed. "Why not?"

"War. It came to Boston first," Reid answered.

"Right! The 'tea party'!" James exclaimed.

"That was December of seventy-three. I was twenty-three at the time. Fights erupted everywhere and full on battles began in seventy-five. I've been fighting ever since," Reid said.

James grunted. "Nine years."

He nodded, speaking around a mouthful of bison. "Indeed."

"Why did you resign?" James asked.

Reid pulled a heavy sigh and gulped the rest of his beer. He refilled his stein and then James' as he spoke.

"I was injured in a blast in Philadelphia, set by a British sympathizer I was tracking who had volunteered in the Continental Army. As a result, I have a large scar in my thigh which limits me some, plus my eyes were burnt and I'm still sensitive to too much light. But I did receive the promotion to colonel for my efforts."

James threw up his hands. "You were tracking? What does that mean?"

Reid allowed a crooked smile. Admitting a little truth here in this remote wilderness was probably safe. "I was a type of spy. For the Americans."

The other man's jaw dropped. "You were?"

Reid merely smiled and swallowed a mouthful of meat and beer.

"Did you at least catch the man?" James pressed.

"Oh, yes. He swung quite nicely." Reid winked at James. "For about seven minutes, as I recall."

A laugh burst upward from James' chest. "He deserved that. I'll wager."

Reid's mood sobered. "He killed five men, and injured three others. Not to mention the loss of munitions. I would say he deserved even more."

The men ate in silence for a few minutes before James prodded Reid to continue. "What brought you here, then?"

"I had no prospects in Boston, and only my soldier's back pay. When I saw the advertisement for the grants I had nothing to lose. Besides," Reid wiped the last bit of meat from his plate with a chunk of bread, "I'm ready for some peace and quiet—and some honest labor building things up, not blowing them up."

James nodded. "I certainly understand that after this past year." He swiped up the last bit of his meal as well. "So, are you married?"

Reid's heart lurched. *Skitt*. "No."

"You're not?" James' appeared sincerely surprised. "Forgive me for asking, but why not?"

If he was going to live the rest of his life as this man's neighbor, there was no reason to begin that relationship with a lie. "She wouldn't have me."

"Was she blind?" James blurted. "Or merely a fool?"

Reid coughed a rough laugh. "*Å min Gud*. If only she was."

James reached into his pocket and pulled out a few coins. He set them on the table and drained his beer. Then he stood and pointed at Reid.

"First, I assume that was Norse, so you need to teach me some. Secondly, let's go procure our land deeds and make certain they are correct."

Reid rose to his feet and rubbed his stiffened right thigh. "Agreed."

The pointing continued. "And third, when we have supper tonight I'm ordering a bottle of whiskey and you are telling me about this woman."

Reid made a face. "Is that necessary?"

"The whiskey? Yes." James grinned. "The story? Perhaps not. But I'm interested."

"We shall see," Reid gave a little ground. "But I will require quite a *lot* of whiskey."

✫ ✫ ✫

"Cheltenham?" Reid looked at the clerk. "Where is that?"

"About ten miles southwest of where we are standing," he said. "Your plot is south of the town center, and yours," he pointed to James, "is south of his."

James peered at the map of his plot. "This appears to be drawn correctly. Reid?"

Reid examined his own map. "Yes. Yes, it does. We'll have to amend the documents ourselves afterwards to map out the lease."

"And write up the terms," James added.

Reid looked at James. "We should do that while we are here in town so the signatures can be witnessed."

"Might you do that for us?" James asked the clerk.

"I suppose," he agreed.

"Shall we do it now? Finish our business?" Reid suggested.

James nodded and crossed to the big table. "Let's do."

The men spent the next hour-and-a-half writing and copying their contract, and signing all legal documents related to both the lands grants and their lease agreement. When they finished, and all signatures were in place along with the official stamps, Reid straightened and allowed the reality to wash over him.

"By, God. I own five hundred acres of land," he said to James, awestruck. "And just over a year from now, I will begin receiving an income off your efforts."

"It won't be much to begin with," James warned.

"My salary as an army officer was only forty dollars a year," he admitted. "And I wasn't always paid."

"In that case, you'll feel like royalty!" James teased, grinning.

Reid's heart gave another lurch. *Skitt skitt skitt.* He rolled up his papers. "Let's go. I'm ready for that bath."

★ ★ ★

Reid soaked in the hot water until his fingers and toes turned to pale pink prunes. He rubbed his rubbery fingers over his cleanly shaved jaw and wondered when he might be cleanly shaven again. Once he went to his property, his attention would be consumed with finding the right spot for his house, and then building a cabin to live in until he could afford something else.

But if I have no family, what's the point?

His thoughts needed to be reined in; they could not trot down that path right now. Somehow, he would manage. He would look for a woman to join him, and not worry about love. They might even have a child or two. And if that failed, he would invite one of his nephews to join him and take over the land when he passed.

Above all, he needed to plan only one step ahead. His first priority after surviving the coming winter was to create the home he would live in for the rest of his life. Later he would think about who might share it with him.

For all he knew, Beatrice Atherton might have a sister.

Reid couldn't keep himself from wondering how Kirsten fared these past three months. Was she still doing her charity work? Did her sewing circles still thrive now that the clothes were being sent to their intended recipients? He was glad he was able to help direct the clothing and the funds. Truly both were sorely needed.

Reid's head fell back against the tall tin tub. The water was cooling, but getting out of the tub meant stepping into his new life. A life without Kirsten.

That wasn't right.

A life without the *hope* of Kirsten was more accurate. She would be with him always.

How did he fall for her so quickly and so hard? Perhaps it was because he was vulnerable when he met her. Injured and blinded, his defenses were smashed to kindling and he was flailing for solid ground to stand on. Kirsten met him in the midst of his fears. She calmed them without thinking him any less of a man for his temporary weaknesses.

Or perhaps it was because, on the first night he was aware after the explosion, he heard her deliberately sink her suitor's hopes in such a clever—and frankly hilarious—manner. She certainly knew her own mind and was confident enough not to be pushed into a situation not of her own choosing.

Most likely, he realized with a jolt, it was because he somehow recognized the wariness in her gaze, the fear in her declamations against marriage, and the protective way she held herself aloof. His instincts told him she was hurt, even if he didn't consciously realize it. All he knew was that he was overwhelmed with the desire to protect her.

Yet in the nights when she snuck into his room, she showed him her true character. That must be when he fell. In the intimacy of the darkness, and the uninhibited way they talked. He saw her for who she was, and she was more attractive to him than any woman ever had been. Reid wanted her even before he laid eyes on her.

Why in hell did she have to tell me she loved me?

He heaved an uneven sigh.

It was bad enough that he had to walk away from her knowing he loved her. If his feelings had not been reciprocated, however, he could convince himself of a mere infatuation. A boyish dream, though he was far from being a boy. Unrequited love was easier forgotten.

But to know—to *know*—that she loved him in return was like carrying a firebrand inside his chest. Her stubbornness and her fears and her distrust of all men were barricades she refused to let him breach. His canons were useless.

He had no choice but to leave her for a second time.

The water was cold. Reid was beginning to shiver. He levered his hands on the rim of the tub and pushed himself up. He grabbed the linen towels and scrubbed himself warm and dry. By the angle of the sun he knew James would be expecting him in the dining room soon.

As he dressed in clean clothes he tried to steel his heart for an evening of James' questions. Copious amounts of whiskey would definitely be required.

May 15, 1782
Cheltenham
Missouri Territory

The men followed the road toward Cheltenham—if two wheel ruts through weeds and grass could be called a road. At least the trees had been removed. The day was sunny; Reid wore his gray-tinted spectacles. While he told James the bright light was the reason, in truth it was as much his pounding head from yester eve's libations.

Somehow, James had gotten Reid to drink more whiskey than he intended, and tell more about Kirsten than he cared to. He hoped James had enough to drink to forget most of what Reid confessed.

Because Reid had.

James drove his wagon in front. Reid followed astride the stallion with the pack mare in tow. All of his worldly goods and purchased supplies for his new life rested on these two animals' backs. For twelve-hundred miles these horses faithfully carried him to a new life.

Reid purchased his tools in Boston, not knowing what opportunities would lay along his path. Sledge hammer, pick, axe and hatchet, saw, hammer, hand drill and bits, a level, twine and rope, shovels and spades. A frying pan and a covered iron pot. Tin plates and utensils. A mattress to stuff with meadow grass. Blankets. Knives of all sorts.

If he forgot anything, he hoped to purchase it in St. Louis. Judging by his brief stay in the city, that seemed a likely hope.

The ten miles took almost three hours at their lumbering pace through this newly carved wilderness. When they reached the town of Cheltenham, they found only a tavern and a church, both constructed of wood.

"Life's most basic needs, I suppose," Reid mused.

James pulled to a stop in front of the tavern and climbed from his wagon. "I'm going in to check our directions."

Reid laughed and swung down from the stallion. "Good. I'm thirsty, too."

☆ ☆ ☆

They were almost a mile south of the tiny town when James waved a hand over his head and whooped. "There's the marker! That's your land!"

Reid saw it; a red-painted stake by the trail.

My land.

He rode ahead of James to be the first to set foot on the property. After dismounting in a smooth whirl, he stilled. The knowledge that the dirt under his feet was *his* dirt overwhelmed him. Hope bubbled in his chest for the first time in months.

James pulled forward and halted the wagon behind him.

"Too bad she can't see this," he said softly.

Reid didn't need clarification as to whom James meant. "Let's follow the map to the property line on the south side," he replied, choosing to ignore his friend's comment. "So you might stand on your land as well."

He lifted himself back into the saddle and consulted his compass. "Shall I lead now?"

"Please do," James answered, grinning widely enough to break his face to two. "I'm actually giddy."

Reid kicked his horse into motion, tugging at the mare's tether. He managed a bit of a trot until James whistled at him to slow down. Apparently James wasn't the only one who was giddy.

"There it is," Reid called over his shoulder. He reined in the horses when he reached the next stake and waited for James to catch up.

James hopped from the wagon when it was still moving. He threw himself on the ground, face first and limbs flung wide.

"I'm here!" he shouted into the ground. "I'm finally here!"

"Ha! Are you going to swive it?" Reid scoffed, laughing.

James shot him a look over his shoulder. "I might. Will you look away?"

"No. I want to watch," Reid countered. "I've been alone quite a bit lately."

Both men burst into loud, uncontrolled guffaws, shared glee spilling from them like water from a crumbling dam. Reid even did a little dance while James rolled in the grass.

"Oh, God! This feels even better than I thought it would!" James climbed to his feet and brushed bits of grass and leaves from his clothes. "Shall we ride on?"

Reid faced James. "Not yet. Here is our plan. We'll set up camp here, on the border between our properties. In the next couple of days we'll remark the new border so it matches what we drew. After that, we'll mark out the leased land."

James nodded. "That sounds fine."

"No matter what we are doing in the days to follow, we will both return here, to our camp, before sunset every day to share our evening meal," Reid continued. "This way we will know if one of us has met with any mischief."

"And if one of us has?" James queried.

"Two shots, with a count of three between them," Reid answered. "That way it won't be mistaken for hunting."

"That makes sense," James agreed. "Now I have a plan as well."

Reid lifted his brow. "And that is?"

"Every seventh day, we'll take my wagon into St. Louis," James said. "We'll get supplies, post letters, eat a real meal, and sleep in a real bed."

"I don't need to go," Reid demurred.

"Yes, you do," James declared. "We are going to take turns driving the wagon, you'll help me load and unload supplies, and you'll keep me company. For those favors, I'll pay for your hotel room."

Reid cocked his head and considered his new friend. "I don't suppose I might dissuade you."

James leveled his gaze. "No."

"Are you always this stubborn?" Reid groused.

James rolled his eyes. "Me, stubborn? Seen a mirror, Norseman?"

Reid made a *tsking* sound and shook his head. "Let's get our camp set up."

CHAPTER TWENTY SEVEN

May 22, 1782

The first seven days flew by faster than Reid thought possible. He and James spent two days with their compasses and maps, lugging around a bucket of red paint, and marking on trees the redrawn border between them, the leased land, and finally the perimeter of their grants. Once that task was accomplished the men spent their days apart, but always met back at their campsite in the evening.

Reid brought small game every day; until he had a place to hang and smoke or dry larger animals, such as the abundant deer, he didn't want to risk drawing predators by having raw meat and blood nearby. So he and James dined on rabbit, grouse, pheasant, or even fish from the wide creek that flowed through Reid's forest.

Reid made the decision to build his cabin nearest to what would eventually become the road from James' estate, past his, and north into Cheltenham. Now it was only a trail, one which barely accommodated James' wagon. The more they drove it, however, the clearer the way would become. Reid decided to make the removal of saplings and large rocks part of their weekly trip. He told James so.

"I think that is a fine idea," James agreed. He tossed his axe into the back of the wagon. Reid did the same and added his pick.

"The road from Cheltenham to St. Louis wasn't so bad," Reid observed. "But you and I will need a decent path if we are to be bringing in building supplies and carrying our produce to market."

James nodded. "True. Are you ready?"

Reid pulled himself onto the seat of the wagon. "Let's go."

The single mile into Cheltenham required an hour-and-a-half to traverse with their new objective. Reid and James stopped trying to ride in the wagon and simply walked in front of the horses, clearing as they went.

"Such exertion requires a bit of refreshment, don't you think?" James asked once they reached the tiny town center.

Reid wiped his brow on his sleeve. "I do indeed."

The men entered the tavern. Two of the three men they encountered on their arrival were there. They were hunched over a packet of papers.

"Hello," James called out. "Tom? Frank? Good to see you again."

"And you as well," Frank answered. "How are you faring?"

"We are doing well." James said. "We are on our way to St. Louis for supplies."

The tavern's owner, Isaiah Freeman, appeared through a door behind the bar. "St. Louis, did ya say? Will you carry something for me?"

"What is it?" Reid asked before James could answer. His soldiering background made him wary of delivering unknown packages from unknown persons.

"Mail. Letters." Isaiah pointed at the packet. "We got this yesterday and some of it'd been waiting more'n a week in the post office there."

James looked quizzically at Reid. "I believe that would be fine. I have business at the post office myself. Do you agree?"

Reid nodded. "If it's only a matter of letters, I don't see that as a problem."

"In fact, we plan to make the trip weekly for a while," James offered. "Once my wife arrives, she'll be staying in the city until I can get enough of the house built for us to winter in."

"So you'd be willing to carry our mail?" Tom brightened. "That'd be a fine help, sir."

"Reid?" James faced him.

Reid looked around at the men's earnest faces. They were living out here in the Missouri Territory, so far from the war and the fighting and the intrigue that his suspicions seemed ridiculous. He needed to relax his wariness, and begin to trust the men who would surround him for the rest of his life.

"I think that's a fine plan," he conceded.

Isaiah reached under the bar and lifted a small stack of folded and sealed papers. "Here you are. And thank you kindly."

"You are quite welcome." Reid took the letters and tucked them in the pocket of his jacket.

"Do you need anything else?" James offered. "We'll be back tomorrow."

Isaiah shook his head. "Not that I've had time to think about," he said. "Perhaps next time."

"We'll carry what we have room for," Reid cautioned.

"Understood," Isaiah replied. "I do have a larger wagon if you ever need it."

Reid was struck by the trusting offer. "Thank you. I—I might, actually."

"For what?" James asked.

"I'm planning to order some milled lumber for next week. I want a planked floor in my cabin," he explained. "I've spent enough years living and sleeping on dirt."

"How's that?" Tom asked.

"I was in the Continental Army for nine years. I resigned as a colonel in February," Reid explained.

"Did we win yet?" Frank barked.

Reid grinned. "Not yet. But we will."

"Better hurry up," he groused.

"Two beers!" James said to Isaiah. "Then we're on our way."

Isaiah set the large mugs of brew in front of Reid and James. Reid was so thirsty he downed his in one long pull.

"What do I owe you?" he asked, setting the mug on the smooth wooden bar.

"A packet of mail," the tavern owner replied with a wink.

Reid smiled and slapped James on the shoulder. "I do believe we are going to be quite happy here!"

May 30, 1782

Reid hauled another of the milled planks in place. He had built a twelve foot by eighteen foot rectangle foundation of notched tree trunks, two high, and today he was pegging the floor boards to them. Sweat ran off him in rivers in the humid weather; he stopped often to gulp a tin cup of the clear creek water he hauled up by the bucket.

Digging a well would be his next big project.

And then he'd dig a privy and build a shed over it.

"Such luxury," he chuckled.

His hobbled draft horses grazed nearby, ready to be pressed into service when needed. He already used them to drag the trunks into place after he leveled the ground where his cabin would stand. As he built, he would use the horses to pull the heavy notched logs up slanted planks into position, until the walls stood eight feet above the floor.

For his roof, Reid decided to follow the old Norse traditions. When his father built a hunting shed in the forests of Massachusetts, he taught Reid how to make a sod roof. It required birch bark— seven layers—and Reid saw a stand of birch in one corner of his new land. His old-world roof would be solid, weatherproof, and durable.

The creek would provide an abundance of rocks for his fireplace. All he needed was cement, which he would buy on his next trip to the city. As his walls grew, so would his hearth and chimney. At this rate, his cabin should be finished by the end of June.

Reid squinted at the sky. The day was heavy and humid. A layer of angry clouds had crawled through the blue canopy, and now they began to wrestle in a way Reid had never seen before. He sat back on his heels and watched, fascinated by the building storm.

"REID!" James bellowed. "REID!"

Reid stood and turned toward his friend's voice.

James galloped toward him astride one of his wagon horses, bareback and tearing up the ground between them. "It's a tornado! Get under your floor!"

"What?" Reid cocked his head. Did James say *under his floor?*

James yanked at his mount's head to slow the frantic animal before he threw himself from its back. He stumbled but regained his balance as he ran toward Reid. "Don't you hear it?"

A sound which had been growing around them broke into

Reid's awareness. Wind roared through the trees, seeming to come from all directions at the same time, as though an army of forest-shattering trolls surrounded him. Thunder came from nowhere and shook the ground beneath his feet. The horses whinnied their fear.

James grabbed his arm and pulled him off the planks and to the ground. "Get underneath—quickly!" he commanded, and did as he bid Reid to do.

Reid had the unreal sensation of being in a dream. Nothing around him made sense.

The hairs on his arms stood up.

The air suddenly felt thin, as though its soul was sucked away.

He looked to the southwest and saw a shape like a pewter funnel extending downward from the tarnished clouds swirling above it.

"What the hell—" His words were cut off by James jerking his left leg out from under him. His right leg buckled painfully and he fell to all fours in the dirt.

James grabbed his shirt and pulled him into the crawlspace under his newly pegged floor.

"I am not playing a game here, Reid!" he shouted. "Move to safety!"

James rolled further under the floor and Reid followed suit. He faced the opening and tried to discern what was happening.

The trees he could see began to bend in unison, changing directions as one. Some leaned impossibly, others snapped like twigs with deafening cracks.

Hail bounced off the packed dirt beyond their shelter and pelted the floor boards above them so loudly that Reid covered his ears tightly with both palms. Though he expected rain to follow the hail, none fell as yet.

A booming wind shook the boards above him for several long minutes, until Reid feared that all of his hard work might take wing and fly away.

Finally, with a final whoosh, the world calmed.

The hail stopped. The wind settled. The trees halted their frantic dance.

Reid rolled over and looked at James. "What in *helvete* was that?"

"Tornado," he replied. "Go on, we can get out now."

Reid turned back and shimmied his way out from under the floor. The world he faced was drastically changed from the one he left behind less than half an hour ago. He twirled in a slow circle, taking stock.

The three horses cowered on the ground, snorting and tossing their manes in angry protest. Thank God they were alive and appeared unhurt.

His stack of floorboards had been upended, but none were broken that he could see. Thank God again.

The forest around his clearing was littered with downed trees.

"You can use them for your walls," James suggested as he stood next to Reid. "If they broke off long enough.

Reid nodded, still stunned. "And the dead wood I'll chop for firewood…"

James climbed over the foundation's rectangle barricade. "I'll go see how I fared."

Reid stumbled after his friend and grabbed his arm. "Is this what all tornadoes are like?"

James gave a little shrug. "Some never touch the ground, so they are no more than extremely strong winds. When they do touch the ground, they can destroy anything in their way."

Reid looked around him again, searching for clues he must learn to recognize. "And this one?"

James pointed to a newly cleared patch of forest about twenty-five yards to the southwest of Reid's house. "Touched there."

He turned toward the road and another downed grove. "Maybe there. Or that may have been a stand of dying trees that succumbed on their own."

"*Skitt*." Reid muttered. "*Skitt skitt skitt.*"

"Shite, indeed," James agreed having successfully understood the word. "*Now* do you believe me?"

Reid nodded slowly, his gaze still moving with disbelief over the devastation. "How often do these storms occur?"

"It's hard to predict," James admitted. "And they come on so fast. But in my experience they occur mostly in the spring and mostly in the late afternoon."

That answer was only marginally helpful. "But how often should I expect this sort of thing?" Reid pressed.

James looked him in the eye. "Perhaps four or five times a

season? I cannot be certain, but that seemed the average in North Carolina."

Reid snorted. "Well I, for one, have made a decision."

"What is that?" James asked.

Reid raked his fingers through his disheveled hair. "My house shall be built of quarried stone. With a heavy slate roof."

"As will mine," James concurred. "As will mine."

June 19, 1782

James' knees bounced the whole way to St. Louis as he fidgeted on the wagon seat and drove Reid batty.

"What if she's not there?" Reid asked. "Will we wait for her?"

James turned rounded eyes and a lifted brow toward him. "Would you mind?"

Reid wanted to say *yes, I would mind*. The walls of his house were up and the slanted roof in place. He just laid the last of the sod on it yesterday afternoon. But he had no door as yet. Nor a well dug. Nor a corral or shelter for his horses.

Nor a privy.

And yet, James had become a very good friend. Kind and generous and very good company. If the tables were turned, Reid would certainly wish to wait for his own wife to arrive.

"No, not at all," he said. "If need be, I can always walk back."

James relaxed a bit. "I appreciate it, Reid. Thank you."

Reid smiled, though the emptiness in his heart echoed with every steady beat.

God, bless Kirsten. Give her peace.

In an occurrence which Reid felt was a blessing to himself as much as James, the men discovered upon their arrival that Beatrice and the entire Atherton household had arrived in St. Louis two days earlier.

A keelboat loaded with furniture and household goods had been unloaded into a warehouse to be stored until James' new house reached a sufficient level of construction to make the final transfer. His slaves still waited aboard a second boat until he would lead them to the property. Reid tried his best not to make any telling faces or disparaging comments. He would, after all, reap a twenty-percent benefit from the darkies' labors.

Beatrice and one of her maids were ensconced in the hotel.

"Darling!" James enthused when he saw her.

Beatrice was a curvy woman with rich, auburn hair. Her eyes were a clear blue to James' warm brown. Her head tucked neatly under James' chin when he embraced her.

Reid stayed back, not wanting to intrude on the couple's reunion.

When James seemed to remember his presence, he turned happy eyes to Reid. "Dearest, may I introduce our neighbor, and my friend, Reidar Hansen?"

Beatrice extended a gloved hand as her slow gaze covered Reid tip to toe. "It is quite a pleasure, Mister Hansen."

"Please call me Reid, madam, as we are to be neighbors for life," Reid said. He accepted her hand and pressed it to his lips.

"A gentleman!" she approved, looking at James with a bit of surprise in her expression. "And here I thought we'd be among scoundrels and natives."

One corner of Reid's mouth curved. "You don't know me as yet, madam. Perhaps you should withhold judgment," he quipped.

James laughed.

When he did, Beatrice's initial shock at Reid's words dissipated. She withdrew her hand.

"Mister Hansen—*Reid*—I see you will keep us all on our toes." She gave him an impish grin and tapped his arm with her folded fan. "Until I decide otherwise, you may call me Beatrice."

Reid bowed at the waist. "Welcome to the Missouri Territory, Beatrice. This land is most certainly enhanced by your bountiful beauty."

James chuckled at Reid's playfulness and smacked his shoulder. "Get your own wife, Hansen. This one's mine."

CHAPTER TWENTY EIGHT

June 20, 1782
Philadelphia

Kirsten slammed the door to her room. Yet another suitor was invited for dinner.

Since she sent Reid away four months ago, the invitations and paraded possibilities had increased in frequency. Some of the men came from New York or New Jersey as her mother cast an ever-widening net.

Most of them were perfectly fine gentlemen; it wasn't their fault that Kirsten had no interest. Yet as willful and outspoken as she was about not marrying, her protestations fell on deaf ears where her mother was concerned. Continuing the royal line meant everything to Marit. And Kirsten's stubbornness had met both its source and its counterpart in her mother's.

Kirsten sank into a chair. She pulled an embroidered linen handkerchief from her pocket and began to mop the tears that flooded her eyes. For the last four months she quite often burst into tears for insignificant reasons such as this one. Carrying the handkerchiefs became a habit as a result.

More and more, however, she knew that her battle was a futile one.

No man was ever likely to win her heart, now that it was completely claimed and broken. Kirsten had locked that door when she sent Reid away, and she knew the key could never be found by another.

Oddly, that fact made the prospect of marriage a bit less abhorrent. Perhaps she should set her fears aside and truly consider the options which lay before her.

Because Kirsten was completely exhausted, both in her heart and in her soul. Looking ahead to another half-a-decade or more of her mother's matchmaking attempts made her want to saw her wrists open with a dull knife. She simply did not have the strength to withstand such an assault for much longer.

So—what is actually at stake here?

All she it would take to make her mother truly happy was a child. If she didn't love the man who bedded her, she needed only to close her eyes, grab the mattress, and let him try to impregnate her once a month.

She could give him a length of time, say twelve months, to accomplish the deed before she shunned him from her bed. If she didn't conceive, at least she could truthfully tell her parents she tried.

After that, her husband could take a mistress and Kirsten would live in peace. Perhaps they would be lucky after all, and she would birth a child to spoil and coddle and give her life some purpose. Miracles did happen.

Kirsten's handkerchief was soaked and her eyes began to ache. There was no snow to pack against them this time of year, only a cloth with cool water. She rang for her maid and ordered willowbark tea. In one hour she must dress for dinner, until then she would remain alone with her new thoughts.

★ ★ ★

Emil Helland waited with her parents in the drawing room. He came to supper alone. Kirsten judged him to be past forty by the grayed edges of his light brown hair, but thought his age sat well on him. He was fastidiously clean and tidily dressed, though Kirsten noticed frayed edges on the cuffs of his frockcoat and a faint stain on the lace ruff of his shirt.

"I'm pleased to meet you, Mister Helland," she said with a small dip of her chin.

"Lord Helland," he said in a smooth tenor tone. "My father was the Baron of Odense."

Kirsten's eyes flicked to her mother who stood beaming beside Emil. "So you are Danish?" she asked, regarding him once again.

He bent slightly at the waist. "I am, my lady."

"Lord Helland's father was a second cousin to my brother's first wife." Marit offered the pedigree as if it were the wax seal on a marriage contract.

Kirsten cocked a brow. "Danish and with royal connections? Why have we not met sooner, I wonder?"

"Lord Helland is a widower, Kirsten." Marit gave the man a sympathetic smile. "His wife passed away three years ago."

"I'm so sorry, Lord Helland. Do you have children?" Kirsten asked.

"No, sad to say," Emil replied. "My wife was a few years older than I and unable to produce any offspring as it turned out."

"I certainly hope I would have better luck," Kirsten blurted before adding, "But that's in God's hands."

Her face heated at her blatant honesty. If she was to finally accept a man as her husband, then his virility was a factor. Twelve months. That was all she was willing to give.

Emil Helland smiled wistfully. "I would hope so as well."

Henrik cleared his throat. "Shall we move to the dining room?"

Emil offered his arm. Kirsten accepted. He wasn't as tall or as muscled as Reid was, but his frame was trim and not flabby. That was helpful.

Comparing every man she met to Reid Hansen, however, was not. If she made her parents' dreams come true and accepted Emil Helland, that was a habit she needed to break immediately—or she might truly go insane.

The small party of four moved to the table. Emil held her chair and then took the seat across from her. He smiled at her with an odd glint in his eye. If she read it right, he seemed to indicate a shared understanding of what was really going on here. Kirsten was intrigued.

"*Hvor lenge har du vært i Amerika?*" she asked. How long have you been in America?

"*Mesteparten av livet mitt. Jeg ble født her,*" he answered without pause. Most of my life. I was born here.

"Have you visited Denmark, then?" she continued in English.

Emil nodded. "When I was in my early twenties I lived with

one of my cousins there for several years while I attended university."

"Why did you return?"

A shadow flicked over Emil's brow. "He died."

"And so you came home," Kirsten posited. "And then you married."

"Exactly," he concurred. "My wife and I enjoyed ten companionable years together before the smallpox took her from me."

"And now Lord Helland is looking to make another happy connection," Marit stated.

Kirsten considered the man across her table. There was nothing objectionable about his person. He certainly wasn't leering at her salaciously as some of the prospective suitors had, and yet his attention was focused solely on her. Those were both positive marks on his side.

She made a decision. "I have organized a charity ball for tomorrow evening, Lord Helland. I do not as yet have an escort."

"I would be honored to accompany you, Lady Sven," he replied.

Kirsten nodded. "Thank you, lord Helland. Under the circumstance that we are, in all probability, some sort of distant relation, you may call me Kirsten."

The man gave her a genuine smile. "Please, call me Emil."

Kirsten sipped her wine and glanced at her mother.

Marit was so puffed up and ruddy with glee, Kirsten was afraid the woman would explode.

At least one of us is happy.

June 21, 1782

Kirsten refused to admit it to herself, but once Reid was gone from her life some of her enthusiasm for her charities on behalf of the Continental Army soldiers had dimmed. Reid was right when he told her she was doing it for him, but that only spurred her to keep up her efforts. She hated to believe she could be so self-absorbed and shallow in her philanthropic pursuits.

Even so, this might be the last ball she arranged. The amount of work which went into them was overwhelming her now. If she married Emil Helland then no point remained for continuing.

Marit fluttered around her, making certain her dark blue gown was smoothed to perfection, and her hair pinned as high as it could be made to go. All the while, chattering happily about what a nice man Emil was.

Kirsten finally grabbed her mother's hands and stilled them. "*Mamma*, please calm down. You are driving me to distraction!"

Marit's shoulders relaxed. "I only want you to be happy, *Datter*. This may be your chance."

Kirsten appreciated that her mother didn't say it may be her last chance, though Kirsten knew the woman was thinking it.

"I shall give him the opportunity to win me over, *Mamma*. The rest is up to him," she cautioned.

✷ ✷ ✷

Kirsten noticed the ball's attendees noticing her. For the first time at any of her events she arrived on the arm of a gentleman, one who was clearly contending for her attentions. She watched other people's reactions, using them as a barometer for her own judgments.

Curiosity was a clear winner, as she expected it to be, but that was a neutral response and had nothing to do with the man himself. What she watched for was any sort of revulsion, disgust, or disdain. Any reluctance to interact with Lord Helland, or telling glances once someone did. No matter what her situation, Kirsten would not align herself with someone whom her society spurned.

Thus far, all was well.

She also evaluated women's responses to Emil as a man. Did they flirt a little? Were they attracted to him? Kirsten encouraged him to dance with other women, claiming that as the hostess's counterpart it was his duty to assure no woman was left without gaining attention at some point in the evening.

Emil complied with her request without complaint. In fact, he sought out the homeliest of the single women and begged them to partner with him for the next song. He was smooth, genteel, engaging, and kind. The man was making points, there was no doubt about it.

Kirsten tried to shift the direction of her thoughts to a more personal one. She regarded Emil and wondered if he might ever win her love.

A stab of physical pain accompanied that consideration as her heart thumped its objection. There was only room for Reid, and the soldier filled every corner of her affections. The best any man could ever hope to gain from her was companionable friendship.

My wife and I enjoyed ten companionable years together...

The sudden realization that perhaps Emil expected nothing more from marriage than that lit her mood like a lamp turned to its highest flame. If that expectation proved true, then Kirsten might be able to tolerate matrimony with the man.

She glanced over the dance floor until she saw him, smiling down into a dowager's eyes as he led her through the dance steps without visible effort. The woman was clearly smitten in a way Kirsten never could be. Perhaps that wasn't going to be a problem after all.

***

Kirsten had picked Emil up from his hotel in her own carriage and now, at the end of the evening, she dropped him off there. It was certainly unconventional, yet consummately practical. The man didn't seem to mind.

He sat on the seat across from her during the short ride, appearing relaxed and comfortable. He complimented her on the exquisite decorations, fabulous food, and talented musicians.

"And your gown is breathtaking, I must say," he added. "Where did you have it made?"

"Celeste's," she answered, surprised to be asked. "Do you know it?"

Emil chuckled. "No. But if I ever live in Philadelphia for any reason, I'll want to be familiar with the most competent seamstresses and tailors."

Kirsten pondered the way he phrased that statement. "How have you found Philadelphia thus far?" she probed.

He tilted his head and gazed at her in the dim light. "I see possibilities, most definitely. I am encouraged."

Kirsten narrowed her eyes. "And yet?"

Emil laughed again. "You are a most astute young woman."

"Thank you. Now answer the question," she challenged.

He hesitated, obviously gathering his words. "I'm not certain that a man of my particular temperament will be a satisfactory choice for a vibrant young woman such as yourself."

Now it was Kirsten's turn to gather her words. She contemplated how much to say at this juncture, and how much to hold back, in the event Emil came forward with his intentions at a later date.

"I am of the opinion, Emil, that we should continue to know each other better before any choices are made," she said carefully. "If we do decide we might suit, a frank conversation of expectations would be warranted at that time."

Emil bounced a series of small nods. "I see the wisdom in that approach. But you will consider my words, will you not?"

Kirsten gave him a soft, reassuring smile. "I do believe you might be surprised to learn more of my 'particular temperament' as well," she offered.

Emil gave her a startled look. "Really? I wouldn't have guessed it."

Kirsten realized with a jolt that there was more to their cloaked conversation than she understood. Yet she didn't feel comfortable asking Emil for an explanation here in the carriage. Instead, she offered him her hand.

"I look forward to seeing you again," she murmured.

Emil kissed the back of her glove. "My lady, it was a pleasure."

He disembarked without trying to kiss her.

* * *

Marit was waiting up for her return. Kirsten had no objections—but she did have questions.

"How was your evening?" her mother asked before Kirsten could open her mouth.

"Quite a success. We raised several hundreds of dollars," Kirsten answered just to be contrary.

"You know what I mean," Marit scolded, adding, "But well done."

"Thank you, *Mamma*." Kirsten settled in a chair and removed her gloves. "These events are so exhausting. I'm not certain when I'll host another, if ever."

"Perhaps you will have other things to occupy your time," Marit suggested with no attempt to hide what things she referred to.

"How did you come across Lord Helland?" Kirsten asked of a sudden. She sipped the cup of chamomile tea her mother offered, curious as to the answer.

"He sent a letter of introduction, listing his lineage and royal connections," Marit responded. "I sent a letter to Denmark concerning his claims, and then invited him to Philadelphia straightaway when they were confirmed."

Kirsten nodded her understanding. "He is actually quite charming."

"Will you see him again?" Marit's voiced quivered with hope.

"I believe so. I wouldn't be surprised if he called on me," Kirsten admitted. "But he is rather poor, isn't he?"

Marit made a dismissive gesture. "He fell on hard times when the war began. His business dealt with imported goods."

"And he ran afoul of the English, I'll wager?" Kirsten opined.

Marit gave an apologetic shrug and a beguiling smile. "This war has been a trial for us all."

Kirsten's gaze moved around their richly appointed drawing room. *Perhaps not for all.*

"So by marrying me, he would regain his lost wealth," she stated the obvious.

"And you, *Datter*, would gain a husband with the correct background for your station," Marit concluded the thought.

Kirsten gave her mother a wan smile. "Everyone wins their objective."

"Yes," Marit patted Kirsten's knee the way she had when Kirsten was a child. "Everyone wins."

CHAPTER TWENTY NINE

June 26, 1782
Cheltenham

Reid was astounded by how much work a hundred bodies could accomplish in less than a week. James' slaves followed his wagon on foot from St. Louis to his land grant in Cheltenham the day after Reid met Beatrice. Once there, they set up a city of tents and stone-edged fire circles. Some of the women cooked while the majority set to clearing the land.

During a trip to St. Louis a couple weeks earlier, James ordered stone and brick to be delivered. Now that he had the labor, his house was beginning to take solid shape. James moved his camp away from Reid's to oversee every aspect of its construction.

The spot James chose for his house was a mile-and-a-half from where Reid's house would stand. Only a twenty-five minute walk through the forest, following the creek. Still, Reid missed their nightly conversations and shared meals. His loneliness deepened as he contemplated that this was the way his life would progress now that Beatrice was in Missouri.

"Will you be able to plant anything this summer, do you believe?" Reid asked as the men drove to St. Louis. Each week that they did so, the road became more established.

James nodded. "Root vegetables like turnips or beets should do fine, if I plant next month. Some greens as well, though they won't sustain us over the winter."

"I'll be hunting, remember," Reid said. "I can't eat an entire elk or bison by myself."

James grinned at him. "That's generous of you, Reid. Thank you."

Reid huffed a laugh. "After all these trips to St. Louis, complete with room and board, I owe you a debt."

"I told you, you are doing me a favor!" James countered. "Especially now that I have to leave my wife behind and ride back with you."

"Don't get any ideas. I'll not sleep in your camp," Reid joked.

James punched him in the arm.

Once they reached St. Louis, Reid left James at the hotel and drove the wagon to the hardware and tack store to buy hinges for his door and shutters, plus another bag of cement for the stone edging of his well. Eventually he would dig deep enough for a pump, but for now he was simply tired of hauling water from the creek. Plus, he needed a water supply that reached below the freeze line for the coming winter.

James was a lucky fellow, Reid mused as he traversed the streets of St. Louis alone. In fact, the man was probably swiving his wife right now.

Reid pushed Kirsten from his thoughts and considered the brothel which he was unintentionally driving the wagon towards. Would he ever seek comfort in such a place?

Perhaps.

There was no 'perhaps not' that followed the thought.

"Not today," he muttered. "Not until I come to the city alone."

Not that he thought James would chastise him for making such a choice, but because James would probably tease him mercilessly if he knew. Admittedly, Reid would do the same if the situation was switched, so he couldn't blame his friend. Life would be easier without that added harassment was all.

Reid turned the wagon toward the hotel. After weeks of washing in the creek, he felt like a hot bath on this trip. And a shave. His spirits needed the boost if he was to refrain from sinking into a morbid mood at supper with James and the lovely Beatrice.

✶ ✶ ✶

James' wife's wide eyes looked like dinner plates when Reid

walked into the dining room. Reid looked over his shoulder, expecting to see some ten-foot-tall monstrosity following him. When he found nothing out of the ordinary, he faced Beatrice again.

"What's amiss?" he demanded, his brow wrinkling in confusion.

Beatrice fanned herself. "Good Lord, is *that* what you look like?"

Reid shifted his gaze to James. "What is she talking about?"

James rubbed his chin. "I believe what my wife is trying to say is, that once the fur and filth of our rough life is removed, you cut a very respectable figure."

"Oh!" Reid felt his face catch fire. He gave Beatrice a stiffly embarrassed bow. "Thank you, madam."

Beatrice continued to fan herself. "It's warm in here, don't you think?"

"Very," Reid grumbled as he took his seat.

James was the only one of the trio who appeared unconcerned. "I was telling Beatrice about our house this afternoon," he began a new subject.

Reid nodded and signaled to the waiter. "A pitcher of beer, please."

"Yes, sir," he answered and hurried to the task.

Reid looked at Beatrice who stared at him quite openly. "The house is coming along quite impressively," he concurred. "Of course, your *husband* chose the perfect spot and had already begun digging out the foundation."

"I look forward to seeing it," she replied with a crooked grin, obviously marking his emphasis.

When the pitcher arrived, Reid poured mugs for himself and James while James selected a wine for Beatrice. Food choices were agreed on and their supper order placed.

Beatrice leaned on her elbows and pinned Reid with a different sort of gaze than when he first entered the room. "You are not married."

"No," he rumbled.

"What have you been doing with your life?" she asked.

Reid shot a glance at James. "Did you tell her nothing about me?"

James grinned at him. "You have not come up in our

'conversations' thus far."

"Besides," Beatrice interjected, taking her husband's hand, "I'd rather hear it from you."

Reid drained half of his mug and wiped his mouth on a napkin. "I was in the Continental Army for nine years."

"No time for a wife. I suppose that makes sense," Beatrice allowed. "But what about now?"

Reid's brow lowered. "What *about* now?"

"Is there no one you wish to share your new life with?" she dug.

Reid's glance shot to James. During their campfire talks his friend had heard plenty about Kirsten and the heartbreak of leaving her behind. How he wished James would jump into the conversation now and spare Reid the pain of having to tell the story again.

But he didn't.

"There was someone," Reid admitted.

Beatrice leaned closer, her voice low. "What happened?"

"She wouldn't have me," he said quietly.

Beatrice gave Reid a puzzled frown. "May I ask you a personal question?"

Reid shrugged. "You already have. One more doesn't matter."

She pinned his gaze with hers. "What did you do wrong?"

"What? Nothing!" he blustered.

Beatrice wagged a finger in front of his face. "You are wrong, Reid."

"How can you say such a thing?" he demanded. "You cannot know that."

Beatrice turned to her husband. "May I speak honestly?"

James waved a hand in permission, the amusement in his expression infuriating. Beatrice regarded Reid again. His jaw jutted; he was ready to fight.

"You are a very, very handsome man, now that you are cleaned up and we can see your face," she began. "You are intelligent, educated, experienced, hard-working, honest, and loyal."

Reid glared at James.

His friend made an apologetic face. "Fine, I'll admit it. Perhaps you did come up in one conversation."

Reid pulled a calming breath. His jaw relaxed as he tried to think of an objection to Beatrice's compliments, though that pursuit felt ingenuous and, quite frankly, stupid. Who in their right mind would object to such a glowing description?

"What is your point?" he growled.

"My point is, any woman would be honored to walk down the street on your arm," she said. "So what did you do wrong that sent her away?"

"It wasn't because of me," he insisted.

"Did she love you?"

He nodded. "She said she did."

"Then what was it, Reid?" Beatrice pressed.

He glared at her, trying to find the words that would explain Kirsten's situation while protecting her private shame.

"She has a mistrust of men," he managed. "Some distant family members were cruel to her."

Beatrice's demeanor softened in an instant. "Did she tell you about it?"

"Yes."

"All of it?"

His eyes narrowed. "Yes."

"And what did you say?" she whispered.

"I said—" Reid's voice cracked as memories flushed his body and stole his strength. He cleared his throat. "I said that I was willing to marry her anyway."

Beatrice' eyes rounded with none of the flattering admiration they held earlier. This time, she appeared utterly horrified.

"Was she a charity case?" she yelped.

"That's what she said!" he shouted. "No! Why would anyone say such a thing?"

Reid looked at James hoping his friend would second Reid's outrage. Instead, James gave him a pained expression. Confused, true, yet still pained.

"Willing?" Beatrice repeated. "*Anyway?*"

Reid's mouth flapped open then snapped shut. Something wasn't right, but he couldn't yet define what that something was.

Beatrice stared at him, hard. "What would you think if she said those same words to you?"

A jolt zinged through Reid's awareness and nailed him to his chair. Beatrice hit her point straight on and Reid wondered how he could have been so consummately stupid.

"Oh, God," he groaned.

She nodded. "Oh, God, indeed."

Reid looked at James and wondered if his own expression had gone as pale and pained as his friend's had.

"I should have said nothing mattered but how much I loved her," he said, stunned. "I should have begged her to marry me for that reason and that reason alone. Nothing else held any weight."

Beatrice laid a hand over his. "Yes."

The room started to waver as if he was looking through glass during a driving rainstorm. Reid dropped his head to his folded arms resting on the tabletop. He closed his eyes and concentrated on taking slow, even breaths.

Skitt.

Skitt skitt skitt skitt skitt skitt skitt skitt skitt skitt skitt.

Gud forbanner all denne til helvete.

"I cannot believe I didn't realize," he croaked. "How could I have misspoken so badly?"

Beatrice patted his elbow. "You are a man, Reid. And you spent nine years in the company of other men. The finer points of language were not part of your military career, I'll wager."

Reid lifted his head and looked at the couple sitting at his table as if seeing them for the first time. "It's my fault," he said, still shaky with shock.

"What will you do?" James asked, his concern clear.

Reid stared at him. "What can I do? Do you know how far it is to Philadelphia? Nine hundred miles!"

James said nothing. Beatrice sat up straight. Their food arrived and the plates were set in front of them. No one lifted a fork.

"I can't go back," Reid stated. "Six weeks to get there, six weeks to return…"

James and Beatrice exchanged worried looks.

"I wouldn't be back until the end of September or early October," he continued his own objections.

"Your cabin is built," James said. "You would still have time to chop your firewood and dig your well before the weather turns too cold."

Reid stared at James. His pulse began to surge. "No, it's not possible."

James shrugged. "I am not going to encourage you either way.

This is a decision you must make for yourself."

"And live with the consequences yourself," Beatrice murmured. Her gaze fell to her plate.

"What if she still said no?" Reid argued. "I will have lost all that time."

"You are right, Reid," James stated and picked up his fork. "You are a land owner now. You have a house to build and a lease to be concerned with. You don't have three months to waste running across the country."

"The leased land is your concern, not mine," Reid countered, confounded by that statement.

"Oh, yes. That's correct." James met his gaze again. "You only have to manage the steady income."

Reid's heart pounded so hard that the blood rushing in his ears made it hard for him to hear. He stared at the plate of food in front of him and wondered what he was supposed to do with it.

"Did you find your hinges?" James asked.

Reid looked up. "What?"

"The hinges. For your doors. Did you find them?" James repeated.

"Yes," Reid grunted.

"And the cement?" he asked.

Reid nodded. At least he believed he did.

James shifted in his seat and gestured with his fork. "Try the venison. It's excellent."

CHAPTER THIRTY

June 28, 1782

Kirsten spent an entire week of days with Emil Helland. She didn't intend to do so, but that was how persistent the man proved to be. What surprised her was how little she minded the attention.

She held no illusions that he was falling in love with her, nor she with him. What grew between them were an easy friendship, a peaceful camaraderie, and an increasing sense of honesty. In spite of that, Kirsten had no intention of ever telling Emil about what happened to her in Denmark. She saw no reason to.

One thing was quite clear, however. The time for her to make a decision which would shape the rest of her life was here. She was twenty-seven years old; soon she would be considered unmarriageable. While she told herself that remaining unattached for life would never bother her, she discovered of late that the idea had started to niggle at her in an unpleasant way.

Loneliness crept into her room at night and wrapped its dark hands around her heart. If there had not been a handsome Norse soldier who loved her, she might never have known what she was missing. But there was. And she did. For that reason alone she might consider Emil's suit.

Then there were her parents. Kirsten had never seen them so happy.

Her father seemed to relax, as if worry for his only child had been perched on his shoulders like an ugly bird of prey, ready to devour all hope that Kirsten would have companionship when he was gone. Until now, she never realized how worried he was for her.

Obviously, her mother was thrilled. Marit walked around the house smiling and humming to herself. She hadn't snapped at anyone all week.

For the first time in her existence, Kirsten understood that she was not an independent entity, one whose choices and paths affected no one but herself. She was part of a family, albeit a small one. Perhaps she did owe her parents some sort of repayment for all they had done for her throughout her life.

It wasn't their fault that her snobbish royal cousins in Denmark turned out to be such corrupted, cruel, and pathetic excuses for men. As horrific and painful as their abuse was, what happened to her simply happened. Though she was burdened with the repercussions, only her attackers were to blame, not *Pappa* and *Mamma*.

Beside all of this, Kirsten grew so weary of the constant stream of parental pressure and hopeful husbands. She didn't enjoy turning them away, one after another. She considered herself to be a kind person for the most part. She hated hurting their feelings. Most of them, anyway.

She heaved a heavy sigh.

When Emil arrived today, she needed to speak with him about his intentions. And his expectations. And hers. There was no reason to wait—once she stated her matrimonial conditions, he would either prove amenable or he would not. Kirsten would begin to make her future plans after she received his answer.

✫✫✫

"Let's take a walk, shall we?" Kirsten suggested. She looped her arm through Emil's and led him back out the door before he could object.

"Where shall we go?' he asked, matching her slightly-more-than-strolling pace.

"I find that halfway down the drive is a lovely spot," she answered without looking at him.

"Ah. The time for a serious talk has come," he observed.

She did look at him then. "How did you know?"

Emil tipped his head toward the large house looming behind

them. "We are in plain sight but cannot be heard."

Reid figured that out, too.

Her heart lurched at the memory. Her impending betrayal of its feelings did not help.

"I do want to speak openly with you, Emil. But what I have to say would upset my parents if they were to overhear," Kirsten confessed.

"Will I be upset?" he asked.

Kirsten peered up at him. "Perhaps. But I don't believe so."

"I'm intrigued, my lady," he quipped.

Kirsten stopped their forward progress and handed Emil the blanket that was draped over her other arm. He unfolded it and flipped it open on the grass in the shade of a lone tree. He offered his hand and she settled on one half of the blanket.

He joined her, half sitting, half lounging, and waited for her to speak. Though he might appear relaxed at first look, Kirsten saw his nervousness in the clench of his fingers and the lines around his mouth.

"Let me begin by stating that I am going to be brutally honest, Emil. If we are going to entertain any sort of future together, I believe that to be utterly necessary. Do you agree?" she asked.

His expression was a comical combination of relief and fear. "Yes. I do."

"Very well." She shifted her position slightly, steeling herself for what was to come. "I never intended to marry. Unlike many young women, I have lost my attraction to men."

"You hinted at that before," he said carefully.

Kirsten was surprised. "Did I?"

Emil nodded. "When we compared our 'temperaments' at the charity ball. Do you recall the conversation?"

"Oh. Yes." Kirsten pulled her thoughts back to her planned path. "The point I was trying to make was this: in all the time we have spent together, you haven't tried to kiss me, nor have you made any physical advances of any kind which extended beyond social conventions."

Emil stared at her, unmoving.

"I take that to mean that you are not physically attracted to me," she continued.

He gave his head a tiny shake. "Kirsten, you are a stunningly beautiful woman, and—"

"Stop!" She put up a hand. "What I want you to understand is that I am not physically attracted to you either."

His eyes narrowed. "And?"

"And..." She lost her nerve. Kirsten closed her eyes, pressed her lips together, and waited for her heart to stop punishing her ribs.

"Kirsten?" he murmured.

She put up her hand to stop him again. She forced her eyes open, moving her gaze up slowly from the blanket, to his torso, and finally his eyes.

"In my opinion," she said quietly, "there is more to a marriage than the bedding."

Emil relaxed a bit, though his gaze was still wary. "I agree."

"I believe we can be fast friends."

His chin dipped. "Again, I agree."

"You want financial security," she posited. "Marriage to me would provide you with that."

Emil's face flushed with embarrassment. "Not *only* that."

Kirsten's shoulders slumped. "Please, let's not play games with each other, Emil. If we are to enter into marriage together, we must be clear about what each of us gains."

He gave a little shrug. "I understand. Yes." He tipped his head. "What do you expect to gain?"

"First of all, it will make my parents very happy. They have been trying to marry me to a suitable husband for almost a decade," she admitted.

"Based on what I've observed, you are absolutely correct there," he agreed.

"They worry about me. I am their only child," she explained.

"And secondly?" he probed.

Kirsten felt her face flush with her own embarrassment. She had never discussed the sex act with any man—even Reid—and she was unsure if she planned the correct words to explain her proposition.

"My parents want an heir." Emil recoiled the tiniest bit, but Kirsten marked it. "We would need to um, engage, to make that happen."

"That is how procreation works," he said.

Kirsten pulled a deep breath. "But since neither of us would be entering this agreement as a typical husband and wife, I suggest a time limit."

Emil's brow crinkled. "A time limit?"

She nodded. "We will attempt to conceive a child for the period of one year. Once a month during the twelve months following our nuptials."

His expression didn't change. "And then?"

"And then we stop."

"Stop engaging in sexual relations?" he clarified. "Forever?"

Her face heated again. "Yes."

Emil shifted his stance, his expression grown pensive. "We might succeed, you realize."

Kirsten gave him a small smile. "And if so, we'll have a little son or daughter to spoil and fuss over."

"And if we do not, what will you tell your parents?" he pressed.

"I'll tell them that God has not seen fit to bless our marriage any more than he saw fit to bless your first one," she answered. "Then I will tell them that we are quite happy together—and remind them to be glad you are not a second-time widower."

Emil laughed. "That ought to satisfy them."

"They are the ones pressing us together," Kirsten pointed out. "If we prove infertile, they cannot blame either one of us."

"Especially if we present a loving front," he added. "Which we shall."

Kirsten's mood sobered. "There is one other condition I need to mention."

Emil's guard came up again. "And that is?"

"I understand that men have a greater need for the physical pleasure of sex than women do."

Emil's gaze faltered. "Some say that's true."

Kirsten laid a hand over his. "After our first year is up, I have no objections to you taking a lover."

He stared at her, hard. "Are you certain?"

"I am."

"That's very generous of you…" he said softly.

"I don't want to deprive you, or make you miserable because of my own unfortunate proclivities," she replied. "All that I ask is that you are discreet."

"Of course!" he declared.

"Because if anyone *ever* discovered anything regarding you and your infidelity, I would divorce you immediately and leave you penniless," she warned.

"I understand perfectly." He squeezed her hand. "I still say you are being unexpectedly generous."

Kirsten gave him another small smile. "If we enter into this pact together, Emil, we must be generous to each other."

He appeared to have understood something anew. "So you might take a lover as well?"

Kirsten frowned. "No. I'm not attracted to men. Did you misunderstand me?"

Emil blinked and his mouth hung open a few moments before any words exited his lips. "Oh. Yes. I believe I did misunderstand. But I have grasped your meaning now."

Her eyes pinned his. "And are you still in agreement with all I have said?"

He nodded reassuringly. "I am. Yes."

"Fine, then." Kirsten stuck out her hand. "None of this will be in writing, but we shall have a gentleman's agreement."

Flashing a crooked smile, Emil shook her hand. "This discussion has been surprising, I must admit."

Kirsten chuckled and rearranged her skirts. "You may proceed, if you are so inclined."

"Proceed?" he asked.

"In order to make our arrangement official, I believe you need to ask me a question," she clarified. "Do you wish to make our arrangement official? Or do you need more time?"

Emil smacked his forehead. "Of course! Give me a minute."

He climbed to his feet and took a few steps away from the blanket. He shook out his clothes, brushed bits of grass from his stockings, and straightened his shoulders. Then he turned to face her. "Miss Sven, might I ask you a question?"

She smiled sweetly. "Yes, Lord Helland."

He approached the blanket and knelt in front of her. "Might you do me the honor of becoming my wife?"

Panic surged through Kirsten's veins, turning them to fire and then ice. Until this moment, all of her conditions and arrangements and conversations felt like a stage play. Now this man—this kind, thoughtful, sweet man—was asking her to make good on her words.

"Kirsten?" he whispered. "Have you an answer?"

Her mouth went as dry as dirt on a hot summer's day. She tried to swallow and coughed. She covered her lips and waved a hand in front of her face in kinetic apology.

She nodded, then, unable to say the word at first.

"Is that a yes?" Emil asked.

"Yes," she croaked. "Sorry. Yes."

★ ★ ★

Kirsten and Emil walked back to the house in silence, her arm looped through his. This time he carried the blanket. Kirsten thought of it as a shroud—because despite all of her bravado, she was terrified over what she had just done.

There was no reason for that, she chided herself. Emil was a fine man. Because he was essentially penniless, they would be living in her home. In fact, he would probably move into their house fairly soon, and then join her after the ceremony.

We shall have separate bedrooms. Connected by a doorway.

That custom was more European than American, but she would say he insisted on it.

All she needed to do was let him use her body a couple times a month or so for his own sexual release. That shouldn't take him long. Then in a year she would be free to return to her own interests. Emil and she would become fast friends, and the world would believe they were happily married.

He opened the front door to her home and she walked in first.

"Could you summon my parents?" she asked the butler.

"They are in the drawing room, Miss," he responded.

Emil handed him the blanket. "Shall we share our good news?" he asked with a grin.

Kirsten plastered a happy smile across her cheeks. "There is no reason to delay."

Emil led her into the drawing room. Henrik and Marit looked up from their newspaper and book, respectively. Their shared expression of anticipation twisted her gut with last ditch trepidation.

Forgive me, Reid.

"*Mamma? Pappa?* We have news," she stated in a tone she prayed reflected obvious joy. "Emil has asked for my hand in marriage, and I have accepted him."

CHAPTER THIRTY ONE

June 28, 1782

Reid didn't sleep much during the night he spent in St. Louis, nor did he sleep well last night back in his Cheltenham cabin. The understanding of how his words sounded to Kirsten tormented him without relief, until the resultant anguish stole all hope of rest. Worse than that, however, was the endless looping debate within himself over what he should do about it.

His first thought was that Kirsten was nine-hundred miles away. If he pushed himself and his horse to cover thirty miles a day, the journey would require a full month of constant travel. At twenty-five miles a day, five weeks would be eaten up—assuming the weather cooperated and never washed him out or blew him away.

Six weeks was a logical expectation.

Besides the lost time, there was no way to know if he would be welcomed in Philadelphia. Kirsten was furious when he left her last. For all he knew, she had moved on in her life and had no further interest in him.

If only he could believe that.

Reid swung the pick. Though dawn was half an hour away yet, this day was already hot and damp. Accomplishing a task before the sun pounded down on him made more sense than lying on his mattress and trying to force himself to sleep. The lure of water within reach outside his door made digging the well a productive way to work out his frustration.

He wasn't a wagering fellow, but if he was, he would bet on Kirsten's heart. She had not allowed herself to care for any man in the last six years—nor in the years before she went to Norway and Denmark, apparently.

When she admitted that she loved him, Reid knew he was her first love as clearly as she was his. First loves were powerful things, he'd always been told. Now he believed it.

"Even if she loves me, she's likely to turn me away again," he told the draft mare who nuzzled his shoulder. The horse was coming into season and the stallion grew increasingly restless around her. He'd have to remove the fetters or the big animal was likely to hurt both himself and the mare in his eagerness to breed.

"Perhaps I should build the corral first instead of the well," Reid mused.

He mopped sweat from his brow and considered the dozens of haphazard trees felled by the tornado. Their tumbled chaos matched the wreck of his emotions. Lying where they were tossed, thrown in all different directions, there was no obvious indication of the wind's path which had destroyed them.

And yet, damaged as they are, they are still quite valuable.

That was the crux of the situation which he failed to convey to Kirsten.

Both of us are damaged, but we found value in each other.

Reid dropped the pick and sought sanctuary inside his cabin. He intended to work on the hinges for the door and window coverings later, when the shade inside the thick log walls would be welcomed. Instead, he began to drill the necessary holes now.

As he worked, those words circled in his thoughts, pressing him toward movement. The pain in his right thigh, however, begged not to be pushed into the journey. It was clear, either his heart or his body would pay a price for his choice of course in the coming months. Reid wondered which would kill him faster.

He sat back on his heels and looked around the bare room. He had never lived alone during any period of his thirty-two years. First off, he had six rambunctious siblings. Next came his years of university schooling. Last were the endless days as a soldier in the close company of other men. He had lived out his existence in the center of a crowd.

Here, on his five-hundred acres, he was absolutely alone.

Though their properties aligned side-by-side, James' house was being constructed a mile and a half away. He hadn't met any other neighbors—nor was he aware whether other neighbors existed. Reid's hours were so consumed by his tasks and his nightly suppers with James, that he hadn't noticed his solitude.

Until now.

Reid stood. He walked outside and began to pace.

I need companionship. A partner.

The easy answer was to ride into St. Louis, seek out hardy women who wanted marriage, and pick one whose conversation entertained and whose body allured. As a man, Reid did have quite a bit to offer, as Beatrice so succinctly pointed out. Plus there was the land and the lease income. He had become an excellent prospect for a husband.

The problem with that solution was Reid's knowledge that every woman he met would be held up to Kirsten as the standard for what he sought. *Skitt.*

"Nine. *Hundred.* Miles!" he bellowed at the rising sun. "Do you know how *far* that is?"

He kicked a fallen branch which hit the closest tree. A flock of startled birds burst forth in a flurry of feathers and indignant squawks. Reid dragged his hands through his hair.

He tried again to convince himself that to return to Philadelphia was a fool's journey. That he should stay, finish what he needed to accomplish before winter, and find a wife in St. Louis. Settle for what was here, now, and forget what might have been if he hadn't spoken like an ass.

He failed.

Reid fell to his knees, overwhelmed by what lay before him but unable to choose otherwise. There remained no doubt; this was a battle he needed to fight. If he surrendered now, he was forever lost. He wouldn't be able to look himself in the mirror—whenever he procured one—and call himself a true man of character. So how could he ask any woman to see him as one?

Going back to Philadelphia and Kirsten, he might well fight hard and still be defeated. Yet he would fight without ceasing until the death of hope, and an immovable enemy, turned him away. Subsequently he could hold his head high, knowing he didn't simply give up.

He would lay down his life in offering, and gather up its tattered shreds if his offering was refused. After that, his wounded heart would be cauterized.

Scars felt nothing. He would choose any amenable female to assuage his loneliness and warm his bed. And he would move ahead with what remained of his life without looking back.

★ ★ ★

Reid expected James to be more surprised when he rode his draft horses up to the man's house. Instead, James grinned so widely that his scruffy cheeks furrowed like a newly sprouted field.

"You're going, then," he said without preamble.

"I am." Reid dismounted. "I've come to ask a favor first."

James nodded. "What do you need?"

Reid held out the reins. "The mare's coming into season and I'll want him to breed with her," he began. "Might I leave them with you until I return?"

James accepted the leather straps. "Of course. But do you plan to walk the whole way?"

Reid smiled a little. "I was hoping you might loan me a saddle horse for the journey, in exchange for putting these two to work for you."

"I can do that," James said. "I am getting the better end of it, you know."

Reid chuckled. "Not if I ride your horse to death, you're not."

James shrugged. "Then I'll take the foal as repayment."

"I always forget what a shrewd bargainer you are," Reid groused good-naturedly. "But I'll bring you a horse back. My wife will be riding it."

James led Reid and the draft horses to his corral. "I recommend the black one. He's young and feisty, and he loves long journeys."

"My thanks." Reid moved his tack and pack to James' horse.

After Reid mounted the prancing steed, James grinned again and stuck out his hand. "God speed, Reid."

Reid shook his friend's hand, gripping it strongly. "I'll see you at the end of September."

July 4, 1782
Philadelphia

"One month from today," Kirsten declared. "I don't wish to wait any longer." *Hell doesn't get cooler because one postpones entry.*

Marit's shocked gaze shifted from Kirsten to Emil. "Is that enough time?"

Emil set his soup spoon next to his bowl. "I'll need to go to Baltimore and retrieve my things," he said. "It's a three day journey in either direction. Plus I'll need to settle my accounts."

Kirsten considered her fiancé. "Do you have enough money?"

"Kirsten," her father growled. "That is none of your concern."

She pressed her lips together, clenched her jaw, and nodded demurely. Anything to get this ordeal over with.

Henrik shifted his attention to Emil. "We'll discuss your move to Philadelphia in my office after luncheon."

Emil bounced a nod. "Yes, sir."

"I'll take charge of preparing his new room—the one which will adjoin mine," Kirsten volunteered. "In the meanwhile he can sleep in the green room. Do you agree, *Mamma?*"

Marit still appeared stunned. "What? Oh, yes. The green room. Of course." She looked at her husband. "Henrik, how many guests do you think we might serve if we have the wedding on the lawn?"

Henrik appeared to be thinking about his answer but Kirsten would be surprised if he was. "Two hundred," he replied.

Marit's expression plummeted. "We'll need to seat at least three hundred. Don't you believe we can?"

Henrik gave his wife a tender smile. "Did I say two hundred? I meant three hundred. Perhaps three hundred and fifty."

"Oh, thank goodness!" Marit exclaimed. "I'll need to get to the printer today to order the invitations."

Kirsten shot a surreptitious glance at Emil. The man showed no signs of distress.

"You have been through this before," Kirsten observed.

"I have," he chuckled. "And I found that keeping quiet, and doing as I was told, proved to be the best path."

"The Swedes Church is Lutheran, but isn't large enough. We'll have to use Christ Church in spite of its ties to the Church of

England," Marit continued. "I will visit there first."

"Shall I come with you, *Mamma?*" Kirsten asked. "It is my wedding, after all."

Marit gave her daughter a genuine smile, her eyes crinkling at the corners. "Yes, of course. We'll have such fun!"

★ ★ ★

Fun may not be the word Kirsten would have chosen for the afternoon, but she did find herself caught up somewhat in her mother's glee. Marit babbled happily all the way to the church and, now that the wedding date and time were written into Christ Church's ledgers, they were off to the printer.

"I believe I'll have two hundred invitations printed," Marit planned aloud. "That would be four hundred guests, but at least a quarter of them won't attend."

Kirsten knew that to be true. Her experiences with her charity balls had the same sort of response. "I believe *Pappa* was right," she said. "Three hundred people are only forty tables. The lawn is plenty large to accommodate that number."

"We'll put up a tent for the food to keep it protected," her mother continued. "And have the musicians playing under the portico."

"That sounds lovely, *Mamma.*" Kirsten leaned forward. "What if it rains?"

Marit paled. "Awnings. We'll need enough to cover all the tables."

Kirsten patted her hand. "Don't fret. You are going to make everything beautiful. I trust you." *And planning this wedding myself is the* last *thing I want to do.*

Marit grasped Kirsten's fingers. "I cannot begin to tell you how happy your father and I are."

That was my hope. She smiled at Marit. "I'm so glad, *Mamma.*"

Marit's eyes moistened. "I must be honest with you, Kirsten. We despaired that you would ever choose someone suitable."

Kirsten throat tightened. "Oh, *Mamma*…"

"You were so stubborn," she replied. "We were worried you would be left completely alone in the world when your father and I passed."

"I'll be fine, truly. Please don't worry any further," Kirsten urged.

"We won't, now that you've chosen Lord Helland." Marit's expression shifted. "I was quite concerned, however, when you spent so much time with that soldier. I feared you might do something foolish."

Her heart lurched, shouting that it had not forgotten. Kirsten needed to avoid that subject at all cost. "Why do you believe Emil Helland is suitable?"

Marit leaned back, obviously surprised by the question. "For all the reasons which you are aware of."

"Tell me. I want to hear what you and *Pappa* see in him," Kirsten pleaded.

She wanted—needed—to compile a mental list of Emil's attributes, meant to counterbalance Reid's. She had determinedly shoved the soldier from her life, and the gaping hole he left must be filled with something if she was to survive the rest of her years.

"Well, to begin with, he is of the correct bloodline for a princess. Your inheritance will never be in jeopardy," Marit said.

Kirsten frowned. "Why would my choice of husband imperil my inheritance?"

"Because the bulk of your property is in Norway. The king would never allow anyone from a different country to claim the land. If you died before your husband, the lands could be confiscated if your children haven't yet reached the age of majority." Marit waved a hand. "Even then, they would only be half Danish or Norse, so who knows."

"But if my husband was pure Norse, all would be well?" Kirsten couldn't stop herself from asking. "Or Danish?" she added when her mother's glance jumped back to hers.

"Yes," she stated. "And Emil Helland is of pure Danish heritage, so that makes him an excellent candidate."

"What else?" Kirsten probed. "Besides having the correct parents?"

Marit shrugged. "He's educated. Intelligent. Mature. And he treats you with more respect than anyone I have ever seen."

"What sort of respect?" she asked, curious what her mother meant.

"Well…" Marit's cheeks pinkened. "He doesn't slaver over you like a dog in heat."

"*Mamma!*" Kirsten giggled at her mother's blunt words.

Marit flashed an irritated yet amused expression. "It's true, *Datter*. You are so very beautiful. The younger men who came before didn't seem able to see beyond that."

Except for the blinded soldier, of course. He saw straight into her core. And he loved her for who she was inside.

Stop it.

Once he knew what happened to her, he saw her as less. There was nothing to be done about that.

Kirsten forced a soft smile. "You are right. Emil has enormous respect for me. As I do for him."

"That is the beginning of a truly strong marriage, Kirsten. You have chosen well," her mother complimented.

The carriage stopped in front of Fraser's Print Shop. Kirsten let her mother disembark the carriage first, and then followed her from the stifling carriage into the nebulous waft of a breeze. July in Philadelphia was usually hot, and always humid. On this oppressively warm day Kirsten was taking the first tangible step into her marriage.

From the frying pan, into the flames.

CHAPTER THIRTY TWO

August 1, 1782
Forty miles west of Philadelphia

Reid hobbled his exhausted horse, removed the saddle and pack, and made preparations for sleeping out-of-doors for yet another night. After these five weeks of travel, his beard was long, his hair tangled, and his clothes smelled strongly of horse and sweat. Fighting the looks of tavern-owners when he asked for lodging was no longer worth the effort. He was so close to his goal that the easiest choice was the preferable one.

The question he faced tonight was, should he try to cover the remaining miles in one day?

Reid pulled dried venison and biscuits from his satchel and sat on a fallen log to eat. He washed the simple meal down his parched throat with water from a tin canteen. His belly still rumbled when he finished the victuals, but he had no desire to hunt, skin, and cook any game.

The black stallion grazed hungrily nearby. James warned him of the animal's temperament, but by now the journey had worn away all his rough edges. Reid and the horse formed a bond of sorts. There were times when Reid swore his mount could read his mind.

Reid stretched out on the ground and stared at the darkening sky. Stars pushed their way through the veil, the strongest ones first, the shy ones lagging. Every night of his travels, Reid fell asleep thinking about what he would say to Kirsten when he appeared at her door.

And every night, he planned a different speech.

The truth was, until he stood in front of her, there was no way to know what words would come from his mouth. An apology was called for, that was certain. But to start with that felt weak. He needed to go into this battle with guns firing.

The biggest gun he owned was that he still loved her. The next salvo should be that he was the perfect husband for her, for so many reasons.

Name them, she would say.

I know the truth, he would answer. I know who you are. I know about your pain. And I want to spend the rest of my life washing it away. I love you that much.

Only after declaring the intentions of his heart would he confess to being a badly-spoken ass and ask her forgiveness.

Reid pulled a deep breath and shifted his position, searching for a modicum of comfort on the ground. At least the summer was in full force and the ground wasn't frozen. So many of his military nights were spent with half his body warmed by a fire, the other half chilled by winter air. His hips and shoulders would ache from the cold which seeped into his bones from the hard earth. Compared to those days, this journey was filled with luxury.

Reid rubbed his right thigh.

Forty miles was too much for one day.

If he covered twenty-five or thirty on the morrow, he would arrive in Philadelphia before noon the next day. He would stable his horse, find lodging in a hotel, and order a bath and a shave. Pay someone to launder his clothes. Trim his hair. Polish his boots.

When he knocked on Kirsten's door, he intended to present the most decent picture of a man that he could conjure at this point. If she still had any objections to accepting him, they would not be based in his appearance. He would make absolutely certain of that, even if doing so required an additional day's delay.

This battle was worth it.

August 2, 1782
Philadelphia

A layer of heavy clouds gathered and cooled the afternoon.

Even so, Kirsten fanned herself continuously as she and Emil walked through the rehearsal for their wedding. In two days, she would become Lady Kirsten Helland. She had already been practicing her new signature.

The month since announcing her intention to accept Emil had been the oddest one of her life. On one hand, the days dragged by. Now that her decision was made, Kirsten wanted to move forward with its course as quickly as possible. The sooner she was married, the better.

No more uncomfortable suppers with suitors. No more pressure from her parents. No more questions about what her life would be like when she was thirty and beyond. When the deed was done, she could shift her focus and settle into her arrangement with Emil, a man whom she genuinely liked.

Not loved, liked. Yet who knew how she might feel in the future?

On the other hand, the thought of bedding him frightened her so, that the days of this past month flew screaming by. She thankfully bled last week so that bit of disgusting awkwardness wouldn't play a role in their wedding night. All she needed to be concerned with was tamping down her terror. Wine was definitely going to be called for, and plenty of it. If she drank enough, maybe she wouldn't cry.

"Kirsten?" Emil said.

She swung her face toward him. "Yes, dearest?"

"Father Mark asked if you have any questions," he replied, squeezing her hand.

Her mind was utterly blank.

She offered the pastor an embarrassed smile. "Might we walk through it all one more time? I confess to being a bit distracted."

The cleric chuckled. "Most brides are, truth be told. Yes, of course, we can walk through the ceremony once more."

Kirsten let go of Emil's hand and walked to the back of the church. She waited for her father to join her, then hooked her arm through his. He patted her hand.

"It's all going to be fine, *Datter*," Henrik murmured.

"Is it, *Pappa?*" She looked up into his eyes. "Do you truly believe so?"

"I would not have given my blessing if I didn't," he replied.

"Emil has a kind and solid character. He will be devoted to you."

Kirsten looked forward and considered the many faces at the front of the church, heavy with expectation. "What about love?" she whispered.

Henrik reached over and turned her countenance back toward his. "Love will come. In time."

She wagged her head slowly. "I'm not certain of that, *Pappa*. I am afraid my only chance at love went back to Boston months ago."

Henrik's expression darkened, mimicking the gathering storm outside. "He wasn't right for you, Kirsten. You need to push him from your thoughts, now and forever. You owe that much to the man waiting up there by the altar."

"You are right, *Pappa*," she conceded. Kirsten went up on her toes and kissed her father's cheek. "I trust you. You wouldn't agree to something if it wasn't good for me, would you?"

"Never," he assured her. "You are the light of my life, and I only want to see you happy and settled."

Kirsten drew a deep calming breath and lifted her chin. "We're ready now," she called out.

A flash of lightning lit the whitewashed interior of the church. Everyone present stilled for the several seconds required before the trailing thunder arrived. When the sharp rumble reached the building, it rattled the windows.

"At least it won't be raining in two days," Henrik observed. "This is a very positive development."

Kirsten watched the rain begin to fall, the heavy drops reminding her of tears as they washed away the traces of her former life.

August 3, 1782

Reid was spattered with mud and wet all the way though to his very bones, he was certain. There was no way to disguise the fact that he had been traveling rough for some time and was subsequently caught in yester eve's downpour. So he didn't even attempt to.

He stood in the entry of the same hotel where the army had put him up, and asked for a room, a shave, a bath, and a maid to wash his clothes. When he flashed a gold coin, all of his requests were met with courteous acceptance.

"May I stable your horse for you?" the clerk offered.

Reid shook his head. "He has faithfully carried me nine hundred miles, thus far. I'll see that he's well settled on my own. When I return, the cleaning-up shall begin." He glanced down at his mud-caked boots. "I'll need my boots shined as well."

The clerk grinned. "Of course!"

When Reid returned to the hotel, a barber followed him up the staircase, and a tub of steaming water waited in his room. Reid sat in a wooden chair—so his filth wouldn't ruin the upholstered one—and submitted to the man's ministrations.

"Shall I cut your hair as well?" he asked.

"Yes, I believe so. About to here. No shorter." Reid pointed to an inch below his ear lobe. Tying his hair out of his eyes was critical when he was at war. That habit wasn't about to die now that he lived in the wilderness.

The barber proved swift and skilled. Reid gave him several copper coins for his efforts. Next he peeled off his clothes, creating a careful pile of flaking mud and sodden linsey-woolsey. He left the aromatic hill of garments beside the door for the laundress.

Naked, he stepped to the tub and submerged himself in the hot liquid.

Some folks claimed bathing was unhealthy, but Reid could not understand how something that felt so good could be thought harmful. He much preferred the company of clean people and strove to wash his important parts daily, even if that meant availing himself of cold creeks or melted snow. After weeks of travel, it was the lack of laundry that set him to reeking, though he relished the chance to wash the dust of the road from every inch of his skin.

He felt odd being back in Philadelphia. His first trip here was extended by unplanned devastation. His second visitation was for the trial and subsequent hanging of the sympathizer-turned-assassin. Neither visit was particularly pleasant.

Yet through those situations, he met Kirsten. Reid believed in God strongly enough to think that He might have orchestrated events to turn out as they had. And if Reid hadn't been such a fool, his words would have won the girl, not repulsed her. Even so, he had faithfully returned to repair things between them.

Please, Father, grant me the right words.

Reid soaped his shortened hair feeling bits of sand rinse loose from his scalp. He had saved one clean shirt and one pair of trousers throughout his travels, knowing he couldn't appear at the Sven mansion looking and smelling as he did today. In addition, he needed his coat brushed and spotted, and his boots polished before he could visit.

His belly rumbled. He looked at the clock. The hour of four past noon was rather early for supper, but Reid only had the last bit of venison and one biscuit for breakfast. There was no midday meal for him.

He stood in the tub, water splashing from his pinkened skin, and reached for the linen towels. He blotted himself dry, enjoying the cool evaporation on this warm August afternoon. He stepped from the tub and dried his lower legs and feet. Being clean and unclothed felt good on this hot day.

Reid caught a glimpse of himself in the mirror. He frowned and twisted to get a better look.

"I thought I was in fine shape when I was a soldier," he muttered. "Apparently I was mistaken."

The weeks of heavy labor spent building his cabin had sharpened his musculature. He was leaner than before, with both the construction work and the deprivation of traveling trimming fat from his body.

Not that I was ever soft, of course.

He rummaged in his pack for a comb and straightened his wet hair. The new length was good, he thought. Long enough to tie back, yet short enough to let the locks hang free without looking derelict.

Someone knocked at his door.

Reid wrapped a towel around his hips and cracked the door open.

"You have laundry, sir?" a plump and rosy-cheeked matron asked.

"Yes, here it is. Thank you." Reid opened the door further, using it as a shield against his state of undress.

As the woman gathered up his clothes, he said, "I'll need my boots later. Possibly my jacket as well."

She made a *tsking* sound. "I can get them boots back to ye in a couple hours, but I'm afeared this coat's goin' to need a mite more work."

Reid considered which might prove the better choice: to make his visit in his shirtsleeves today and blame it on the weather, or to wait until the morrow when he could appear in proper attire.

I'll decide that on a full stomach.

"Very well. Please get the boots back to me as quickly as possible. I can wait until the morrow for the jacket."

"Very good, sir." She turned and left, holding the garments far away from her body.

Reid shut the door, combed his hair one more time, and dressed in his last clean ensemble. Without his boots, he would wear a pair of Indian slippers to supper, ones he traded for on his journey. They were exceedingly comfortable and he wore them indoors whenever he sought shelter in farmhouses or inns along his way. He just hadn't worn them to dinner as yet.

"There's always the first time for everything," he murmured, slipping them over his bare feet.

He stood, checked inside his shirt for his money pouch, and made his way to the dining room.

★ ★ ★

The meal was delicious. The wine was excellent. Reid felt so physically satisfied, he was in danger of falling asleep in his chair.

The clock chimed half past five. His boots were supposed to be back in his room by six or so. Reid decided that a short nap was in order. The Svens never dined before seven in the evening, sometimes as late as eight. He could nod off until his boots were returned, and then—should he awaken refreshed enough to visit tonight—he could walk to their estate as quickly as retrieving and saddling his horse.

"Let the poor fellow rest," he said to himself as he climbed the stairs. The sun wouldn't set until eight or so, anyway. He left his curtains open and stretched out on his bed fully-clothed.

Reid was startled awake by a pounding on his door. He looked at the clock as he stumbled to his feet, though its face was hard to read in the dimming light. He squinted. Half past seven? Had he slept for two hours?

A young boy with a grimy face held up Reid's boots. "Here ye be, sir. I done 'em meself." He appeared quite pleased.

Reid accepted the boots and carried them into the room, the boy following close on his slippered heels. He turned up the lamp.

"You've done a good job, son," he complimented. "Is that why it took so long?"

He nodded unabashedly. "Ma said I had to do it right or I weren't getting the coins."

Reid fished for his pouch. "Do you get to keep the money?"

"Half!" he exclaimed with a grin. He held out a hand, his fingers blackened by the polish.

Reid dropped the coppers into the boy's palm.

His eyes rounded. "Thank ye, sir!" The little fellow spun and bolted from the room lest Reid ask for any of the riches back.

Reid chuckled as he closed the door. He crossed to the washstand and splashed cold water over his face, washing away his sleepiness. The bath, meal, and nap had done him wonders and he felt reborn.

He looked out the window at the lowering sun and tried to decide what to do. If he left now, he would reach the Sven's house before the sun's light disappeared.

Reid stepped in front of the mirror and regarded his reflection with a critical eye. His hair was neat and clean, as was his jaw. If he waited until tomorrow to make his visit, he would be sporting a fresh batch of stubble. Either that, or be forced to pay for another shave.

Going to their home tonight without his gentleman's jacket, he would appear unsuitably casual. Yet when he was a guest in their home during his recuperation, he was dressed far worse than this. In addition, when he was in Philadelphia in February, he always dressed in a manner which was socially acceptable. His reputation should be secured in that arena.

"So, what am I waiting for?" he challenged himself. "Why pay for one more night in this hotel than I absolutely must?"

Reid sat on the bed and pulled off the slippers. His decision was made.

CHAPTER THIRTY THREE

Kirsten pushed her beets around her plate trying to make it look as if she had eaten more than she had. Her appetite grew less every day as her future galloped toward her without restraint.

She told herself time and again that once the ceremony was over, and she let Emil bed her, the worst part would be past. She was certainly strong enough to survive repeated swivings for the next twelve months. After her agreement with Emil was finished, her life would be returned to her. She must remind herself again of the reasons she was doing this: to be free of parental pressures, and sexual pressures, and perhaps gain a child out of the bargain.

Kirsten heard her name. "Yes, *Mamma?*"

"You look tired. Are you feeling well?" her mother asked.

"I'm afraid I am tired. All the wedding preparations took a greater toll than I expected." She sculpted her features into what she hoped was a convincing smile. "Other than that, I'm quite fine."

"Perhaps you should go to bed early," Emil suggested.

Kirsten nodded. "I believe I will. I have to rise early on the morrow to be ready in time."

She leaned back as her plate was removed. As she watched the servants carry away the uneaten remainders of their meal, she wondered what it would be like to be truly hungry. Not the sort of hunger caused by a troublesome heart or ridiculous pettiness, but the sort that saw no ending. No relief.

She told herself that was why her father and mother warned her away from Reid—he had no prospects which assured that hunger would be forever banished from his doorstep. Even so, she couldn't imagine him going hungry tonight, wherever he was. He was resourceful. Intelligent. A hunter. He would always have food.

"Coffee, Miss?" a servant asked, a gleaming silver pot held in white-glove-protected hands.

"Yes, thank you," Kirsten murmured. "What's for dessert?"

"Apple crumble, Miss," he replied as he filled her cup. "With rhubarb."

"That sounds delicious." Kirsten reached for the little pitcher of cream.

Cream. Without a cow, there would be no cream. Without cream, she didn't care for coffee. A life with no coffee was not anything to cry about. There was always tea.

Kirsten fingered the elaborate silver handle on the spoon with which she stirred her coffee and cream. Embellishments made the implement more pleasing, not more efficient. Either way, someone had to wash it—and the delicate porcelain cup with its matching saucer as well.

Sturdy crockery would be less bother.

Why was she even thinking this way? After the wedding she and Emil would still be living in this house, though he was changing to the newly refurbished room adjoining hers. The servants and china would still be in place tomorrow, and the day after that, and the day after that.

Her parents would still sit across the table from her at meals. The carriage would still be at her disposal. Her gowns still made by the same tailor. Kirsten would enjoy every comfort which her parents' wealth provided, and inherit that wealth when they passed.

There was no reason to consider what her life would be like under different circumstances, other than to be grateful that she was marrying such a perfect candidate. One whose disruption of her privileged existence would be minimal.

So why did she feel like her life was ending, not beginning?

Kirsten stood, drawing the others' attention. "I am more tired than I realized. I'm going to retire to my room and read a little until I fall asleep."

Henrik stood as well, and moved to give Kirsten a hug. He kissed her forehead. "Good evening, my darling *datter*. Sleep well. Tomorrow is a big day."

Marit smiled up at her. "I shall see that you are not disturbed. Shall I send up chamomile tea? Or willowbark?"

Kirsten shook her head. "No thank you, *Mamma*."

Emil rose and walked around the table. "I'll escort you to your room."

Kirsten wanted to scream at everyone to please just leave her alone, but she didn't. She took Emil's arm and walked by his side out into the hallway and to the bottom of the stairs.

"You don't have to come up," she said quietly.

He rounded to face her, his expression somber. "Are you certain you wish to do this?" he asked.

No.

"Yes. Of course. Why wouldn't I be?" she asked, though her chest ached. Inhaling was difficult.

"We do have an unusual agreement," he pointed out without need. "I would understand if you had second thoughts."

Her eyes widened. "Don't you want to marry me?" she whispered, aware that her parents were in the next room, albeit several yards distant.

Emil smiled, almost shyly. "I do, yes. I believe we are perfect for each other, considering our personal inclinations. Not everyone is so honestly matched."

Kirsten nodded. "That is true. Thank you, Emil."

He kissed her forehead the same way her father always did. "Sleep well, my love. Tomorrow you are not only the princess, but you are the queen."

⋆ ⋆ ⋆

Reid walked the familiar mile-and-a-half path north and west to the Sven's home. His mood was mixed, part excitement and part dread. He was excited to see Kirsten again, and hoped his surprise appearance on her doorstep might stun her enough that she could move beyond her objections to marrying him.

If she still loved him, of course. Which he believed she did.

The dread was that she would remain obstinate and refuse him yet again.

If she did, Reid decided he would give her three days. Just as Christ rose from the dead on the third day, Reid might be able to raise Kirsten from her emotional tomb. Love was a powerful force, especially when it was shared.

There were, of course, Henrik and Marit's objections to be dealt with.

The last time they saw Reid he was no longer a colonel in the army, but a homeless man with no expectations. Henrik's generosity saw him clothed. Their daughter's charity work paid his salary.

Now he was a landowner. Five hundred acres, with a guaranteed income. True, his land was undeveloped and thus far wasn't part of the United States of America. But the way this fledgling country was flexing its muscles, he imagined the Missouri territory would be absorbed at some point. The march west hadn't yet found its boundary; from what he was told, St. Louis was less than halfway across the continent.

In light of this change of his circumstances, Kirsten's parents would have far less to object to. And he was a full-blooded Norseman, for God's sake. Not only were there darn few of them to be found in this country, but he haled from an old and established Norwegian dynasty. That was another strong point in his favor. He was of the correct heritage to marry their royal daughter.

If they still objected, but Kirsten was amenable to his proposal, Reid would simply tell Henrik what he told him before—he was a grown man, Kirsten was a grown woman, and they didn't need Henrik and Marit's permission to marry.

The sun had already tucked itself behind forested hills when he approached the Sven estate's long driveway. In the dusky light ahead Reid saw large ghostly shapes he didn't understand. When he got closer he realized they were awnings with tables and chairs under them. Off to the right was a tent with flaps hanging to the ground on three sides.

Kirsten must be having one of her charity events.

This one was going to be rather impressive, he thought. Though how she could raise any money with the expense of renting all those coverings, plus the settings for the guests, was a mystery to him. Reid had confidence that Kirsten would be one to succeed, if anyone could. She hadn't failed at any of her endeavors thus far.

Reid's pace slowed as he walked under the portico. He smoothed his hair behind his ears, straightened his shirt, and tucked it into his trousers. With a determined breath, he climbed the steps and knocked on the door, wondering if the pounding of his heart might have already alerted the household to his presence.

Horace opened the door. His expression was comically blank for a moment, until he recognized Reid.

"Colonel Hansen, welcome," he said. His initial grin quickly disappeared. "What are you doing here?"

Every nerve in Reid's body went on alert. He didn't bother to correct the man's greeting, nor ask why the butler didn't answer the door. "I've come to speak with Miss Sven, Horace."

The valet's uncertainty at his expressed intent hit Reid like a cannonball. Something was definitely amiss.

"Who is it?" Henrik's voice came from the other side of the door.

Horace's voice lowered. "It's Colonel Hansen, sir."

Henrik stepped into the doorway. "Thank you, Horace. That will be all."

The valet backed away and dissolved into the house.

Henrik's expression was not friendly. "It's nice to see you again, sir. How may I help you?"

Reid steeled his resolve. "I've come to speak with Kirsten."

Henrik shook his head. "I'm afraid she's not available."

"Is she at home?" Reid clarified.

"She is," Henrik said before he thought better of it. "However she has retired for the night."

Reid believed he was being put off and that thought angered him, though he tried to remain civil. "In that case, I can return tomorrow. What time is best?"

"My daughter is busy tomorrow," Henrik responded. "I'm afraid she won't have time to speak to you, I'm sorry. But I will let her know you came by."

Henrik closed the door in his face.

Reid stood on the stoop, flushed and vibrating with fury. He had severely misjudged his rapport with Kirsten's father, that much was clear. His fists clenched.

He had two options: come back tomorrow and politely try again, or open the door and walk into the house, skirting around all polite conventions.

Reid grabbed the door handle, squeezed the latch, and pushed the door.

Henrik and Marit stood in the entryway, obviously discussing the wrinkle which his sudden and unexpected appearance had created in their otherwise smooth lives. They turned toward him, dually horrified by his behavior if their matched expressions could be trusted.

Reid threw his hands up in a gesture of surrender. "Forgive me Henrik, Marit, for bursting in like this, but I have come nine hundred miles to speak with Kirsten," he said, his tone gathering volume and authority as he continued. "The very *least* I deserve is for you to give Kirsten the chance to ignore me herself!"

"Lower your voice, sir," Henrik growled. Marit cast an anxious glance up the stairs. A man Reid didn't recognize appeared in the dining room doorway.

Probably another forced suitor.

The Sven's were proving as stubborn as, well, Norsemen.

"What do you mean you've come nine hundred miles?" Henrik demanded. "Boston is only three hundred miles from Philadelphia!"

"I didn't come from Boston," Reid declared. "I came from St. Louis!"

"Where on God's earth is that?" Marit demanded.

Her curiosity bought him time, so Reid didn't care how many questions they put to him. He kept his voice as strong as he dared in the hopes of rousing Kirsten himself.

"The Missouri territory," he stated. "That is where I live."

Henrik's expression warred between interest and concern. Concern won. "I'm sorry, Reid, but you are going to have to leave."

Reid stood his ground. "I'm sorry as well, Henrik. I respectfully ask, again, that you allow Kirsten to be the one to send me away."

"I cannot do that," he responded. "You will simply have to accept my answer."

"No, I don't." Reid clasped his hands behind his back. "If you continue to refuse me, you will have two choices."

"How dare you?" Marit gasped.

Reid ignored her. Soldiers didn't win battles by backing down. "The first choice is that you throw me bodily from your home."

"I never!" Marit's outrage cut off her words. "Henrik!"

Henrik's face was now a blotched shade of burgundy. "See, here!"

"The second choice," Reid tipped his head toward the stairs, "is that I storm your castle and find her on my own."

"That won't be necessary."

All eyes turned toward the staircase. Kirsten stood on the landing clad in her dressing gown and with bare feet. Her pale eyes were open so wide they dominated her features. She clutched the top of her gown closed but Reid could see her hands shaking from his vantage point. Her cheeks were drained of color until their eyes met, and then they ruddied violently.

The initial battle was won.

Now the war would begin.

Kirsten thought she might be dreaming, though she was still awake. Whoever arrived at this odd hour sounded exactly like Reid. She obviously had that man on her mind on the eve of her wedding, a situation which was disconcerting to state it in the least of terms. She opened her bedroom door so she might understand the words being spoken.

Consuming disbelief held her motionless for several moments. Her surging pulse made it hard for her to comprehend that Reid was really here. What was he saying about nine hundred miles?

Kirsten grabbed her dressing gown from her bed. She jammed her arms into the sleeves as she hurried to the top of the stairs. She barely had the garment tied around her waist when she reached the landing and she held the top closed with a trembling fist.

Reid looked up when she spoke. Her cheeks grew painfully hot.

His blue eyes were clear, his gaze strong and steady. His hair was shorter, his body thicker—but with muscle, not fat. Whatever he was doing nine hundred miles from here was certainly building him up.

His stance was changed as well. In spite of her father's blustering, the erstwhile colonel appeared calm, not intimidated, when delivering his ultimatums. A powerful determination and confidence emanated from him with such strength that it inexplicably frightened her.

"Reid, what are you doing here?" she managed.

He moved to the bottom of the stairs. "I have come to apologize."

"For—for what?" she stammered.

"I clearly misspoke when last we met," he said evenly.

Kirsten frowned a warning. "Reid…"

He raised a hand to shush her.

"What I *should* have said on that day was this…" He hesitated and cleared his throat. Her parents stared, as if transfixed.

"I love *you*, Kirsten. I love the very same woman who stood before me that day, and who stands before me now, with my entire being."

He dropped his hand and pinned her gaze intently with his. Each of his next words was its own sentence, heavy with a meaning which only she and he understood.

"Nothing. Else. Matters."

A sob whooshed from her chest as though he had punched her in the gut.

"Reid," she rasped. "I'm getting married tomorrow."

Surprised understanding washed over his face, robbing it of color. He stepped back as if he, too, had been punched. His jaw fell open as he turned toward the dining room. Kirsten realized with a jolt that Emil must be standing there, listening to everything that transpired.

For a moment, the entry hall was filled with living statues.

The Reid slowly tilted his head and slid his intent gaze back up to hers. "It would appear that the question is, *who* will you marry?"

"There *is* no question!" Marit shouted at him. "Are you delusional?"

Reid ignored her mother's outburst and returned to the foot of the stairs. He stared up at her with no pretense, and no readable expression on his face other than naked hope. Kirsten let go of her dressing gown and gripped the railing with both hands.

"Please, Reid. Don't…" she whispered. She drew a ragged breath, her heart and mind warring on opposite fronts, her trembling frame their bloody battleground. There could be no victor here, only casualties.

"I've come for you twice, *Prinsesse*. But I'll not come again," he said softly. "Get dressed. We need to talk."

CHAPTER THIRTY FOUR

Kirsten whirled and ran up the stairs out of his sight. Reid turned to face her enraged parents, choosing to ignore the fiancé standing silent in the dining room doorway.

"My circumstances have changed," he began.

"I don't care," Marit declaimed. "You are not a suitable match for our daughter!"

"And he is?" Reid tossed a thumb over his shoulder. "He's twice her age!"

"I'm hardly fifty-four!" the man objected indignantly as he stepped forward. "I'm only forty-three."

Reid spun and faced him, glaring his challenge.

"We haven't met," he barked. "My name is Reidar Magnus Hansen. I resigned as a colonel with the continental army after nine years of war. And you?"

The man's chin drifted upward while the corners of his mouth pulled down. "Lord Emil Helland. My father was a second cousin to King Frederick's first wife," he stated haughtily.

"King Frederick is my brother," Marit answered.

"I am aware," Reid growled at her. He faced Emil again. "How much land have you?"

"More than you, I'll wager," Henrik huffed.

"How much?" Reid pressed.

"Well, none now. I lost it to the British," Emil sneered.

"And did you fight them to get it back?" Reid demanded.

Emil's disdain was clear. "No! I'm a gentleman, not a soldier."

One corner of Reid's mouth twitched. "Nothing *but* men in the army, Emil."

"What?" he exploded. His face was so red, Reid was afraid he might suffer an apoplexy.

"What is your meaning, Hansen?" Henrik snarled.

"Pay me no mind," Reid waved his hand and gave Emil his solid back. "Henrik, what you and Marit need to know is that I own five-hundred acres free and clear in the Missouri territory. Two-hundred acres are being leased, and will provide me with an annual income in addition to my own industry."

The older couple exchanged startled glances.

"Furthermore, *jeg er fullblods norsk*," he reminded them. "Though that was always the case."

Henrik gaped at him. "Are you seriously suggesting that we allow you to replace Lord Helland as groom in tomorrow's wedding?"

"See here, sir!" Emil yelped. "We have an agreement."

Reid ignored him and flashed a nervous smile at Henrik. "That is up to your daughter, isn't it?"

★ ★ ★

"What is up to me?" Kirsten quipped as she hurried down the stairs. With her maid's help she slithered into a summer gown and soft slippers. Her hair was tied back from her face but hung scandalously loose down her back.

Reid turned around to face her.

"Don't answer that!" she commanded, hoping to assure his silence. She hooked her arm through his. "Let's go."

As she pulled him toward the door, Emil called out, "Where do you think you are going?"

"Kirsten!" Marit shrieked. "What are you doing?"

Kirsten stopped and stared up at Reid. Thankfully, he did not appear smug. Nor did he evince any trepidation. He simply expected her to do what she must.

"We do need to talk," she repeated his claim. "And privately."

"Alone? In the dark?" Emil cried. "I cannot allow that!"

Kirsten shot him an incredulous glare over her shoulder. "We are not yet married, Emil. You have no say. Unless you wish to cancel the wedding over it."

The man's mouth moved soundlessly.

Reid grabbed the handle and pulled the front door open. Kirsten tightened her grip on his arm and the two of them stepped into the night.

They walked down the drive without speaking. Once they were several yards from the house, Reid stopped. Lamplight glowed from the house as well as from the city, dimly washing them in amber. Blue light from the rising moon cast their shadows on the drive. A cooling breeze blew loose strands of hair into Kirsten's face, tickling her cheeks.

"Tell me again why you are here," she began.

"I came back to apologize and marry you," he answered.

Kirsten stared up at him. "Did you believe my answer would be changed?"

"I did, yes. Once you heard me out." Reid waved a hand at the ghostly awnings and uninhabited tables. "Clearly your stand against the institution itself has fallen."

Kirsten frowned. "This is different."

"How?" he challenged.

She tucked the errant wisps of hair behind her ears. "Emil and I have an understanding."

Reid's head tilted. "What sort of understanding?"

Kirsten hesitated; it was none of Reid's business. Yet if she told him, he would see how unsuitable a wife she was for any man. "I only have to bed him for a year, and then only for the purpose of trying to get his child on me. Whether he succeeds or not, I'm freed from his physical affections after twelve months."

"So he agreed to sleep chastely beside you for the rest of your lives?" Reid asked.

"Separate bedrooms," she admitted.

Reid huffed a laugh. "I'm not surprised."

Kirsten was. "Why do you say that?"

Reid seemed to be reconsidering his response. He hung his hands on his hips and shifted his weight to his left leg. "I don't wish to discuss Emil. That's a waste of my time. I want to talk about you and me."

"You and—we aren't engaged," Kirsten objected, ignoring the stone gathering weight in her chest.

Reid ignored her words. "There are two things you need to know. Two things you must thoroughly understand."

Kirsten shook her head. "How can I make *you* understand? My path is set."

"The vows are not yet spoken. I arrived in time." His glance moved over her head and swept across the array of tables, chairs, and canvas. "Barely, but still in time."

"You came back from Boston for nothing, Reid," she said softly. "I'm not the wife you deserve."

His brow lowered and even in the twilight his eyes pinned hers. "I didn't come from Boston!" he barked, startling her. "I came from St. Louis!"

Kirsten backed away from his anger. "Where is that?"

"Missouri territory." He stepped forward, his expression unchanged. "Nine hundred miles to the west."

"You came nine hundred miles just to talk to me?" she clarified, stunned by the magnitude of his journey.

"No," he said slowly. "I came nine hundred miles to *marry* you."

She refused to acknowledge his declaration. "What were you doing in St. Louis?" she deflected.

Reid raised a fist with one stiff finger jutting skyward. "That's the first thing you must know. I am now a land owner. I own— without lien or prior claim—five hundred very fertile acres in Cheltenham."

Five hundred acres was a figure even her parents would be impressed by. "Cheltenham?" she squeaked.

"Ten miles southwest of the city of St. Louis," he stated. "Furthermore, I leased two hundred of those acres to the gentleman farmer, whose property adjoins mine, for twenty percent of all profits from that land. In perpetuity."

Comprehension enhanced Kirsten's rapidly recalibrating estimation of the man standing in front of her. "Now you'll have an income."

Reid nodded. "Plus whatever industry I choose to engage in."

"What will that be?" She was sincerely curious. "What might you do in the wilderness?"

Reid's frame seemed to release a bit of tension at her response. "I'll hunt, of course. Sell the pelts," he began. "Raise some sheep for their wool and meat, I think. Perhaps a bison or two. Of course, once I build our own quarried stone house I can design homes for others who come. If they're interested."

When he referred to his house as *ours*, Kirsten's belly did annoying little flip-flops. "Where will you live until your house is built?" she asked, ignoring them.

Reid's lips curved. "We'll live in the log cabin I built before I came to fetch you. It's quite sturdy and has a solid wood floor. It's not so grand as this," he nodded toward her mansion, "but you won't live in filth. You'll be quite snug."

"Stop doing that," she whispered.

He leaned closer. "Doing what?"

"Calling everything ours and talking as if I will be there with you," she answered, holding her ground.

"It's the truth," he murmured. "Emil is not the man for you, whatever ridiculous arrangement you believe you want."

She lifted her chin. "And you *are* the man?"

"I am."

Tears stung her eyelids. "I cannot be the sort of wife you want. You know that."

Reid smiled softly. "You don't know yourself, Kirsten. You have quite a bit of passion locked away in here." The tip of his finger landed just above the valley between her breasts.

She wondered if he felt the lurch in her heartbeat. "I don't want to—I'm not inclined to—I can't—" she stammered her objections, not able to complete any of her statements.

Reid's finger traveled upward. His hand unfurled and slid behind her neck, under her hair. His soft, warm touch sent shivers skating up and down her spine. Shivers of pleasure, not fear, she realized with a start.

"You were badly abused, it's true. There is nothing to be done about that." Reid's tone was low and soothing. So very confident. So very reassuring. "You are like a spirited young filly, whipped for no reason by a cruel owner. All you need is skillful gentling to move you past your fears."

Reid's mouth hovered over hers. "Trust me," he whispered.

Kirsten eyes drifted shut. Reid's smooth skin smelled of soap. Her hand moved up into his shortened hair and her fingers slid against his scalp. His lips played over hers, teasing with promise, until she leaned into the kiss demanding more. Reid obliged. His mouth opened and his tongue slid against hers.

A little moan escaped Kirsten, pushed up from her chest by startling sensations she didn't recognize or understand. Reid's hands slid down her back. One pressed her chest to his, the other rested just below her waist. His tender possession of her body wasn't frightening; instead she felt like a precious jewel in his grip. Something to be treasured and revered.

Could it be he's right?

Their embrace lasted several minutes. With each passing second, Kirsten felt a piece of her fear fall away, like old paint peeling from a plank of wood, revealing the naked grain beneath. When Reid ended the kiss she leaned against him. She had no strength left to push him away.

"Don't marry me out of pity," she pleaded.

Reid grabbed her shoulders and held her back so she could see his face. "Good God, woman. I wouldn't make an eighteen-hundred-mile journey for the sake of *pity!*"

Kirsten gasped. Her eyes rounded in the face of his frustration. "Then—"

Reid gave his head a brisk shake, silencing her. "With every tree I felled, every log I hauled, and every milled plank I pegged into place, you were there with me. Concern for your comfort was foremost in my mind. I couldn't make you leave. And I couldn't forget you."

Some perverse trait in her character made her ask, "Did you try?"

"Hell, yes, I tried." His admission threw some paint back on the wooden wall she hid behind. "It wasn't until my conversation with James' wife that I understood how my ill-chosen words made you feel."

Her brow wrinkled. "James' wife?"

"The gentleman farmer. Our neighbors," he stated.

"You talked to her about me?" Kirsten wasn't certain how she felt about that.

"I did—after she asked me what I did wrong," he admitted. "And then I knew why you sent me away."

"You said *our* again," she whispered.

Reid tightened his fingers. "And I'll not stop saying it. My home is your home. My heart is your heart. I cannot live my life without you beside me, Kirsten."

Tears blurred her vision. "I'll always believe you feel sorry for me. I'm damaged goods, Reid."

"Not in my eyes." Reid loosened his grip and his hands dropped away. "I don't feel sorry for you."

Kirsten stared hard into his eyes, trying in the darkness to discern the truth.

He raised one hand. "No, that's not entirely correct."

Her belly clutched. *No. Oh no. No no no.*

"I feel sorry for what happened to you. If I could take that away from you I would," he began. "But it doesn't diminish your worth one whit in my estimation."

Kirsten waited. She needed to hear something more, though she wasn't certain what that something was.

Reid spread his arms. "Love isn't about finding someone who is already perfect. It's about loving someone with all of their imperfections in place."

Her throat tightened. Almost...

"None of us is perfect, Kirsten. Quite obviously I am not. Do you love me in spite of that?" he asked.

All she could do was nod. She swiped away the tears rolling down her cheeks.

His brow twitched. He swallowed heavily. He dropped to his knees in front of her, his arms still wide. "Then why can you not believe that I love you in the same way?"

There it was.

With a cry and a sob, Kirsten fell against him. Reid's arms wrapped around her hips, his face was pressed against her bosom.

"I'm sorry, Reid. I'm sorry," she said, weeping without restraint. "Please forgive me."

"There is nothing to forgive," he replied, his voice hoarse. "We both made the path difficult."

"Then we must forgive each other," she insisted.

Reid let go of her and climbed to his feet. "We have. And now, there is one more thing which needs to be said."

Kirsten's emotions were too raw for her to anticipate what that last thing might entail. Fear surged through her again. "What?"

Reid took both her hands between his work-roughened palms.

"Kirsten Sven, will you do me the honor of becoming my wife on the morrow?"

A relieved laugh burst from her. It was followed by another, and another, until she was giggling uncontrollably.

Reid leaned down to meet her eyes. "Is that a yes?"

"Yes!" she yelped.

Reid lifted her in a tight bear hug and spun her around in giddy circles. "Thank God!" he shouted. When he set her down, he added, "My journey back to Missouri was going to be indescribably dismal if you refused me still!"

He kissed her again. Though less lengthy, this kiss was no less intense.

"I love you, Kirsten," he whispered against her mouth, his forehead pressed to hers.

"And I love you Reid," she answered in kind.

They stood still, leaning on each other, sharing the quiet peace of the moonlit evening for several long moments, before the reality of their agreement forced Kirsten to move away.

"I suppose we should inform my parents," she said quietly.

Reid gave her an amused smile. "And your displaced fiancé."

Her mouth rounded with a sudden and unpleasant realization. "I'm breeching our promise! They will have to give him what they agreed to when he married me!"

"What is that?" Reid asked. "Your inheritance?"

She nodded, horrified. "Half, anyway."

He shrugged. "I don't care. I will take care of you."

"But—it's—a lot of money!" she sputtered.

Reid chuckled. "It's not important. All I care about is taking you to wife. Unless..." His expression darkened.

"Unless what?" she demanded.

He glanced at the mansion. "Unless you aren't willing to live under less luxurious circumstances."

For the split of a second Kirsten wondered if Reid could have somehow heard her earlier thoughts. "No! I mean no, that's not a concern. I am willing to live with less."

He looked down at her. "Washing our dishes? And our clothes? Sweeping our floor?"

Kirsten looked over her shoulder at the huge house and its gleaming windows.

"This house has held my secrets for long enough. It's time for me to come out from under its protection." She faced Reid again. "Tomorrow I'll become a new person—your wife. I'll happily begin my new life with you. And I'll embrace everything which that new life entails."

He grinned. "I guarantee this will be an adventure like none you ever imagined."

"I'm frightened enough as it is," she chided him. "Don't make it worse!"

Reid pulled her close again. "I will protect you always, Kirsten. Never forget that."

She shook her head against his chest, unable to find her voice.

CHAPTER THIRTY FIVE

Reid let Kirsten enter the house first. He saw her shoulders straighten when she did so.

The coming scene was not going to be a pleasant one. Not only was Kirsten's fresh decision at odds with her parents' wishes, but Reid—her newly intended husband—had argued with them quite vehemently just before Kirsten reappeared.

"They are all in the drawing room," she murmured, looking up at him. Her light blue eyes were hard as glaciers.

All Reid could do was pull her close for a quick, quiet kiss. "*Jeg elsker deg.* I love you so much that I crossed a continent to marry you. Remember that."

Kirsten smiled and her cheeks pinkened. "*Jeg elsker deg, også.*"

"So go tell them," he whispered.

His soon-to-be wife nodded and strode purposefully toward the drawing room door. He followed close behind and, though his longer strides felt less urgent, his heart was marching in pace with her.

"*Mamma, Pappa.*" She greeted her parents before turning to the room's third occupant. "Lord Helland."

Three pair of eyes lifted their regard over her head and slammed into Reid. He gazed blandly back at them, not allowing any clues to show in his expression.

Kirsten waited for her silence to draw the curious attention back to her. "I want to assure you all that I am still getting married tomorrow."

"Thank the Lord!" Marit exclaimed.

Emil looked suspicious.

Henrik clearly wasn't convinced of her meaning. "Are you certain, *Datter?*"

She nodded. "I am *Pappa*. But there is one detail I need to clarify."

Reid almost laughed at the drawn out manner in which way Kirsten was presenting her news. Either she was thoroughly enjoying the moment, or she was terrified to state her recent decision aloud. Even so, the confused looks of concern which each of the three fixed on her were quite amusing.

"What detail?" Marit snapped.

Kirsten faced her mother. "I shall stand at the altar with Reid. Not Emil."

The room exploded, reminiscent in Reid's mind of the impact which brought him to Kirsten in the first place.

"No!" Marit cried. "I'll not allow it!"

Emil jumped to his feet, looking stricken. "Are you breaking our agreement?"

Kirsten stared at him. "Don't worry. You will still be paid. That's why you wanted to marry in the first place, was it not?"

"Kirsten!" Henrik bellowed, obviously appalled.

"Give him the money, Pappa," she said in a kinder tone as she turned to face her father. "I don't need it."

Marit rose to her feet, glaring at her daughter. "You were gently raised, Kirsten. You are not prepared to live the life of a pauper!"

"I'm not a pauper," Reid growled.

"You are not nobility, either!" she snapped.

"I am better suited to care for your daughter than any man she has ever met," Reid countered. "Why do you think she has never agreed to marriage before?"

"She agreed to marry me," Emil declared.

"Only to satisfy her parents," Reid stated. "She told me about your arrangement."

Emil paled and sank back into his chair.

Kirsten's alarmed gaze bounced to Reid's.

"What arrangement?" Henrik queried, looking from one man to the other.

Reid waved his hand dismissively. "It doesn't matter. The point is moot now."

"He is right, *Pappa*," Kirsten interjected. "Reid is the only man I ever truly wanted to marry."

"But he walked out on you!" Marit's outrage flowed in waves off her trembling frame. "And he did so twice! What's to stop him from abandoning you again?"

Kirsten rounded on her. "You sent him away the first time, *Mamma*. You cannot deny that."

Marit's chin lifted. "Not the second time. He did that on his own."

"No. He did not." Kirsten's voice dropped so low that the room's inhabitants stilled in order to hear her words. "That time *I* sent him away."

"Why?" Henrik asked gently.

Kirsten looked up at Reid, her regret shining in her eyes. "In my own pride, and my own stubbornness, I mistook the words of his proposal."

"He proposed?" Henrik frowned at Reid. "I forbade you from courting her."

"And I told you I would court her anyway, don't you recall?" Reid asked, his tone blunt. "I was a colonel in the army. I didn't take orders, I *gave* them."

"Such insolence," Marit grumbled. "It's unthinkable."

"*Mamma*, I'm twenty-seven. Reid is thirty-two. We are hardly errant children to be ordered around," Kirsten pointed out.

Henrik shook his head and ran his hands over his thinning hair. "I have my reservations, *Datter*, and so many of them," he said. "Are you very certain?"

Kirsten gave her father a tender look. "I am, Pappa. I love him very much."

Reid stepped behind Kirsten and rested his palms on her shoulders. "And I love Kirsten. Beneath all the wealth, the title, and her royal status, lies an intelligent woman of strong and resilient character, independent thought, and with a fine sense of humor."

Marit shot one last volley. "And she's beautiful. Don't forget that."

Reid chuckled at the memory of how that played out between him and Kirsten. "If you will recall, Madame Sven, I was blinded when I became acquainted with her."

"Even so, her appearance must influence your affections," Marit pushed.

Reid felt Kirsten stiffen under his hands. He shot the woman with a sharp gaze. Anger fizzed through his veins.

"I didn't cross a continent for just a pretty face, I'll guarantee you that," he warned. "And for you to suggest such a thing is an insult to your daughter. I suggest you apologize."

Marit gaped at him. "What?"

"Darling, that was a bit harsh," Henrik agreed.

Marit glared at him. "I apologize—but only for trying to ferret out the truth of this man's motives."

Kirsten looked at Reid over her shoulder and winked. Her meaning was clear; that was the best apology her mother would give. The clock chimed ten times.

"The hour grows late, *Mamma*. I'll send Reid back to his hotel in our carriage," she stated. "First, we need to discuss some of the details for tomorrow."

Marit paled. "What will we tell the guests?"

"The truth. That I am marrying Colonel Reidar Magnus Hansen, retired veteran of the Continental Army, and landed estate owner in the Missouri territory." Kirsten shrugged. "That should make them sit up and take notice."

"Are you suggesting that we move forward as if nothing has happened?" Marit's incredulity almost made Reid laugh again.

"As the sister to the king of Denmark and Norway," Reid posited, "I am certain you may call upon your upbringing and experience to smooth over this diplomatic situation."

Marit gave him a narrowed stare. Obviously she understood the double edges of his pointed statement.

"Of course I shall," she responded, choosing the higher road as Reid assumed she would.

Reid considered Kirsten. "What were your plans for tomorrow night?"

Her face reddened and she bit her lower lip before she answered. "We were staying here. Emil was to move into the room adjoining mine."

Reid turned toward the silent man he forgot was even in the room. "That won't do. We'll return to my hotel and reside there until we depart."

"I'll pack a small trunk tonight," Kirsten said. "Then I'll need to return here during the days to pack up the remainder of my things."

Marit lowered to the settee, her expression somber as fresh realization sculpted it. "You'll be leaving us."

Kirsten gave a tiny nod. "Yes."

She lifted teary eyes to Reid. "When?"

"We can stay a week," he offered. "I've decided to sail back, rather than drag my wife across the rough countryside. We'll take a ship from here to New Orleans, then a keelboat up the Mississippi River to St. Louis."

"Can you afford that?" Kirsten murmured.

Reid squeezed her shoulders. "Yes. I received all of my back pay, if you will recall."

Kirsten smiled and patted his hand. Reid noticed that Henrik watched their exchange, his expression pensive.

Reid stepped away from Kirsten and approached her father. "Will you give us your blessing, Henrik?"

"Would it change anything if I said no?" he asked.

Reid shook his head and held out his hand. "But I'd appreciate it, even so."

Henrik's mouth moved as if chewing his thoughts before spitting out his words.

Kirsten came to Reid's side. Her arm rested against his. "*Pappa?*"

Henrik considered his daughter. "You are indeed an exceptional woman, Kirsten. I must respect your decision. And yet I pray you will never come to regret it."

"Thank you, *Pappa*," she whispered.

Henrik grasped Reid's hand firmly. "Don't keep her away from us."

"I won't," Reid promised. "We'll come back to visit every couple of years, as long as our situation allows it."

"Thank you." Henrik looked at his wife. "It's done, Marit."

Emil cleared his throat. "About *my* situation…"

Henrik faced the man, his expression compassionate. "I'll have your money the day after tomorrow. You may remain here as our guest for the week, if you care to."

Emil nodded, looking relieved. "Yes, sir."

Kirsten slipped her hand into Reid's. "Will you please summon the carriage, *Pappa?* Reid and I will wait outside."

Reid's fingers tightened over hers. They felt so soft and small in his hand that for a moment he wondered if he was making a mistake by taking her away from the easy life she was accustomed to.

I'll make it up to her, he vowed.

Bowing politely to Henrik and Marit, Reid led Kirsten to the front door. They stepped out into the balmy night, now brightly lit by the risen moon.

"Crockery," Kirsten said. "And pewter."

"I beg your pardon?" Reid responded.

She looked up at him, half of her face in shadow and the other half blued by the moonlight. "China and silver are too fragile and require too much care. I'll buy a set of crockery dishes and pewter tableware for our cabin."

Reid blinked at her. "You have already decided?"

She nodded. "And my dresses will be cotton, linsey-woolsey, and wool. Satin and silk aren't washable."

"Won't you miss them?" he asked, examining her reaction.

Kirsten's brow wrinkled. "Are there balls for us to attend?"

Reid coughed a laugh. "Not unless we host one!"

"Then, no." She grinned at him. "I am very much looking forward to wearing comfortable dresses and simple hairstyles."

The thought of Kirsten's body being freed from such tight restraints sent a different sort of fizz through his veins. Now that their marriage was imminent, he must plan how best to bring her happily into his bed.

"I don't expect to consummate our marriage tomorrow night," he said softly. "In case that was a concern of yours."

Her mood shifted and she pulled back. "You will have the right."

"Yes, I will. But I promised to protect you, as you might recall." He leaned over to whisper in her ear. "And that means I'll take my time. Having you experiencing your full pleasure in my bed is definitely worth waiting for."

"Oh," she breathed.

He took her in his arms and kissed her very well.

This is just the beginning.

CHAPTER THIRTY SIX

August 4, 1782

T hankfully, Reid's frock coat was cleaned, and he had a lace stock in his bag. He wore the same trousers and shirt as yesterday because the rest of his clothes hung dripping on the line behind the hotel. He did pay for another shave, however.

When he traveled to Philadelphia he had no assurance that Kirsten would agree to marry him, so it never occurred to him that his wedding could happen less than twenty-four hours after his arrival. Though he wished he could present a more elegant figure, at the least he was neat and clean.

The Sven's carriage met him at the hotel and transported him to Christ's Church. The red brick building stood over three stories tall, with a thick, square tower rising a full story over its pitched copper roof. An elaborate whitewashed wooden steeple doubled the height of the tower and was visible for miles.

Reid climbed the front steps and walked inside. The ceremony was nearly an hour distant, but a few guests were beginning to gather inside the bright, white sanctuary. Dust motes danced in the sun which spilled through the windows as if to celebrate his coming nuptials. Reid smiled.

Thank you, Lord.

A cleric in black robe and white stole approached. "May I help you, sir?"

"Yes, thank you," Reid answered. "I am the groom."

The cleric gave him a kind look. "Perhaps you have the wrong church. Today's wedding is between Kirsten Sven and Emil Helland."

"Not anymore, I'm afraid." Reid offered his hand. "My name is Reidar Magnus Hansen. As of yester eve, I am the man marrying Kirsten Sven today."

"Father Mark." The man shook Reid's hand mechanically, one of his eyebrows lifted while the other fell. "I was not informed."

"The decision was made around the hour of ten last night," Reid explained. "When Henrik arrives, he can confirm the change."

Father Mark stepped back and his gaze measured Reid from the hair tucked behind his ears to his tall polished boots. "If what you are telling me is true, I must confess you appear a more suitable candidate for the princess."

Does everyone know?

Reid dipped his chin. "Thank you, again."

Father Mark beckoned Reid. "Come with me. I'll need your information for the new documents."

"Of course." Reid followed the cleric into a small room off the narthex.

✲ ✲ ✲

Kirsten paced in the entry hall of her home until the carriage returned from transporting Reid. She climbed inside with her father's help and took her seat. He handed her mother in next. Marit sat across from her and Henrik sat beside her.

"You'll wear yourself out before the day has begun," Marit chided.

Kirsten smiled cheerfully. "I'll be fine."

"I'm glad to see you happy, *Datter*," Henrik said as the carriage turned from their long drive onto the road. "I was worried about you."

"I was worried about myself, *Pappa*," she replied honestly.

"Your life will be vastly different, married to the soldier," he observed. "But you know that your mother and I are always willing to help you in any way we can."

Kirsten leaned against his shoulder. "Thank you."

She reached for her mother's hand and gripped her father's. "I love you both so much. You have always done what you believed was best for me, and I appreciate that more than I can say." She squeezed their hands. "I promise you, Reid is the perfect man for me. I shall be happy, as long as I am with him."

When the carriage stopped in front of the church, Henrik helped his wife disembark first. Kirsten's pulse pounded with anticipation as she laid her gloved hand in her father's. She stepped to the ground, held his arm, climbed the steps, and walked inside.

Reid stood at the front of the church, his tall frame erect and proud. He turned to look at her and a thrill flittered through her core. His dark blue coat made his eyes look more blue than gray, and the white lace stock at his throat contrasted nicely with his sun-darkened skin. Kirsten decided she liked his shortened hair, its color shot with golden sunlight.

Father Mark hurried up the aisle. "Ah, good, you have arrived. Please come with me."

Kirsten wanted to speak with Reid but was dragged away by her parents. She looked back at him over her shoulder. He grinned his understanding. Her heart did a cartwheel.

Ensconced in the little office, Henrik confirmed the change of groom. Father Mark was clearly relieved that the story the impressive man conveyed was the truth and not the ravings of a lunatic who must be bodily removed from the premises. Kirsten imagined the eleventh-hour switch of spouse was not the way the cleric's business normally transpired.

Kirsten applied her signature to the new set of wedding documents, right below Reid's strong hand. She recalled the dread and resignation she felt just two days ago, signing the same agreements beneath Emil Helland's name. Today she felt as if a two-hundred pound boulder was lifted from her back, and it made her giddy and grateful.

Thank you, Lord.

"May I speak with Reid now?" she asked.

Father Mark blew on her signature to dry the ink. "I can ask him to come back here," he offered between puffs. "I don't believe you'll want the guests to see you, do you?"

"Are there guests here?" Kirsten asked, looking at her father.

He chuckled. "The church is already half full."

Kirsten's cheeks warmed. "I only noticed Reid."

Marit sighed and patted her arm. "In spite of my many

misgivings, I suppose that is a good sign."

"I shall escort my lovely wife to her seat and ask your groom to come give you a word. A very *brief* word." Henrik winked and rested his hand in the small of Marit's back. "And just before the ceremony I shall announce the change of participant."

"Thank you, *Pappa*." Kirsten watched her parents walk away together. Her mother leaned against her father, and his palm slid around her waist.

For the first time Kirsten understood how much they truly loved each other. She hoped she and Reid would still feel like that once they had been married for thirty years.

Father Mark remained with her in the office as a chaperone, though Kirsten thought that was silly. In less than half an hour, the man approaching them would be her avowed husband and have all the rights incumbent in that status. Did grooms ever ravish their intended in the backs of churches, then sprint away before the ceremony? She giggled at the idea.

Reid cracked the door and stood in its opening rather than enter the room. Kirsten gazed into his face, disbelieving her good fortune.

"You wanted to see me?" he murmured, his expression tender. "You haven't changed your mind again, have you?"

"No, of course not," she said softly, finding herself shy of a sudden. "I only wished to tell you how handsome you look, and how glad I am that you came back for me one last time."

Reid brushed invisible lint from his jacket. "I thought I would have time to find suitable attire. Thankfully, the hotel valet had already cleaned my coat."

He leaned into the room, then, and looked at Kirsten as if she was a dream which might disappear if he glanced away. "If I had not come back, I would have spent the rest of my life wondering if I had squandered my greatest opportunity for happiness." He blew a sigh through his teeth. "Thank God I arrived in time."

"I do," she whispered, her throat thickening.

Reid grinned. "Remember those two words, *Prinsesse*. They'll come in handy later."

Standing in the front of the church beside Henrik, Reid took a military stance out of habit—back straight, feet apart, and hands clasped behind him—as the father of the bride introduced him to the incredulous crowd.

"Some of you met Colonel Hansen at my daughter's charity ball, when he returned to Philadelphia to testify in the court martial and trial," he explained. "Now he's retired from the army, and a land owner in the Missouri territory. He returned to Philadelphia just yesterday to press his suit with my daughter."

Henrik rubbed his jaw, his eyes twinkling. "As you can see, he was successful in that endeavor."

A tentative chuckle rippled through the visibly shocked guests.

Henrik threw up his hands. "Her mother and I celebrate her sudden happiness, and hope you all will as well."

A smattering of applause echoed off the high walls as heads tipped and comments were murmured to neighbors. The reception after the ceremony should prove interesting.

Reid stepped to the appropriate side of the altar, turned, and waited. Henrik leaned over the front pew to kiss Marit on the cheek before striding toward the back doors of the sanctuary. In the high loft at the back, a quartet resumed their stringed instrumentation. The smooth, melodic sound filled the bright space and Reid wondered if he was glimpsing Heaven itself.

When the song ended, and the next tune began, the back doors opened.

Kirsten stood in the double doorway beside her father, one arm looped through his and the other holding a bouquet of pink roses. Reid noticed earlier how the blue watered silk of her gown matched her eyes, yet he was struck again with her deceptively delicate beauty. Her smallish stature housed a willful nature and a determined strength. Without those qualities, she would not have claimed his heart. Nor would she be walking toward him now, her head high and her face beaming.

When they reached the altar Reid faced Father Mark. The cleric's words sounded like gibberish to him, so consumed was he with the thought that he very nearly missed this chance. Reid moved when told to, answered in the affirmative when spoken to, and kissed Kirsten solidly when finally allowed to do so.

"I love you, wife," he whispered.

Her eyes glittered up at him. "And I love you, husband."

✷ ✷ ✷

Kirsten gazed out at the hundreds of wedding guests on her lawn and was quite certain that more people were here than in the church by half. She suspected that several guests went to gather their friends, regaling them with the scandalous tale of her switching the groom, and urged them to come see for themselves.

She didn't care. With this particular groom at her side, she didn't need to feign her happiness.

Reid leaned toward her and touched her crystal goblet with his. "This wine is excellent."

"No expense was spared, I assure you," she replied.

Her new husband smiled at her. "I want you to thoroughly enjoy yourself this day. Drink the wine, eat the food, dance to the music. Show the world that you are confident in your decision."

"I will, if you will," she challenged.

His smile softened. "Happy?"

"More than you can know," she murmured.

"Good." He planted a lingering kiss on her lips, again stirring up reactions that were foreign to her.

"I want to make a toast," he stated when the kiss ended.

Kirsten swallowed her disappointment with a gulp of wine. "What sort of toast?"

"One which I believe will surprise your mother," he answered.

Kirsten grabbed Reid's arm. "Don't say anything controversial," she begged.

"Of course not," he promised, though his puckish expression belied his words.

"Please, Reid, I mean it," she said.

He laid a hand over his. "Your parents are now my parents. I will never do anything to intentionally upset them."

Kirsten snickered. "Beside marrying their only daughter and spiriting her away to St Louis, that is."

"Cheltenham," he countered before rising to his feet. His baritone voice rose over the noise of the crowd as he lifted his glass. "Might I have everyone's attention?"

Bit by bit, conversation died out and bodies twisted to face Reid.

"First and foremost, I would like to thank Henrik and Marit

Sven for this beautiful feast. I am well aware that this celebration was planned for another, but even so, the food and libations are superb. Don't you all agree?"

Applause broke out in different areas of the lawn. Kirsten felt a blush rise in her cheeks at his blatant acknowledgement of her seemingly fickle nature. Reid took a sip from his glass before he continued, and she followed suit, hiding behind the crystal goblet.

"Secondly, I had quite an opportunity to think recently," he chuckled and rubbed his thigh, "as I traveled on horseback the nine hundred miles from St. Louis to Philadelphia."

Several people smiled and a few laughed.

"I came to convince Miss Sven to marry me." Reid made a show of relief, mopping his brow with his napkin. "Thank goodness I made it in time!"

More laughter tittered through the crowd. Kirsten realized her new husband was winning the guests over by stating the obvious, and doing so in a good-natured manner. She lowered her goblet and smiled her support.

"Somewhere in... Ohio, I believe it was... I came upon a startling realization." Reid flashed her a crooked smile. "So I'm going to tell you all a little story."

Kirsten gasped. There had already been enough startling realizations for one day. She refused to allow her smile to fade, but her eyes tightened in a warning which he ignored.

"I had a great-uncle in Norway who was the Baron of Hamar." Reid turned to Marit and Henrik, who stared at him in surprise. "Don't become overly excited, Marit. He married into the title."

Marit flipped her hand at him and forced a smile, allowing the joke to go unanswered. Kirsten's mother evinced good breeding in awkward circumstances, that was certain.

"My father spent quite a bit of time with this particular uncle before he immigrated to Boston, and he told me more stories than I can count about this man's escapades," Reid continued. "He was quite unique in many ways."

The crowd was silent, enthralled by the prospect of gossip-worthy information.

"As it turns out, my great-uncle was well acquainted with your father, Marit." Reid gestured toward Kirsten. "Who is, of course, your grandfather."

"Christian? The sixth?" Marit yelped, pulling Reid's attention back to her. "How well acquainted?"

Reid grinned. "My uncle, the Baron, provided discreet services for King Christian whenever something of a sensitive nature arose."

Marit's gaze danced between Reid, Henrik, and Kirsten. Obviously this connection both impressed and disconcerted her.

"What was his name?" she demanded.

"My uncle?" Reid clarified, though Kirsten recognized a dramatic pause when she saw one. She bit back her mirth, not wanting to spoil her husband's carefully constructed moment. "His full name was Brander Edvard Hansen, Baron of Hamar."

Marit's mouth and eyes rounded, mimicking each other in shape. "Brander Hansen—the *deaf* man—is your great-uncle?" she cried.

"Did you know him?" Reid asked, surprised.

"Yes!" Marit's gaze moved over the lawn, though Kirsten believed her mother saw nothing but the past. "I remember him coming to the palace several times when I was a girl. I was always so fascinated by his hand motions."

Reid glanced at Kirsten, his triumph cloaked in tenderness. "It would seem our families share a royal connection after all," he said.

He faced the guests and lifted his glass. "To the unexpected twists and turns of life. May all of yours turn out as well as ours!"

Kirsten stood and clinked her glass against Reid's. When he kissed her before they drank their champagne, the cheerful crowd applauded.

CHAPTER THIRTY SEVEN

Reid saw the joy in Kirsten's eyes and felt as if his ribs might actually crack, his chest unable to contain his happiness. His life today was so completely different from eleven months ago, the day of the warehouse explosion. He was amazed by the good which rose from the ashes of that tragedy.

When Marit admitted to knowing his great-uncle Brander, he was shocked. Of course it was possible, he just hadn't considered that it might have happened. If his father and his new mother-in-law ever met, they would have interesting stories to share.

Another pang that his family was not here at his wedding jabbed him. Before going to bed the night before, Reid wrote out a long narrative of what had occurred. In his detailed explanation, he apologized that he was unable to delay the wedding until they could attend.

As he wrote the letter, however, he realized that he and Kirsten could travel to Boston—by coach—and sail from that port to New Orleans. She could meet his family, and they could meet her. He hadn't said anything to Kirsten as yet, intending to surprise her with the journey.

Reid counted his money, then, and made a decision. Their life in Missouri would sustain itself for a large part, so if he spent the equivalent of one year's salary as a soldier on their travels during the next month, he would consider the expenditure worthwhile. He had a wife to woo, after all.

He sat back in his seat and judged the angle of the sun,

wondering how long he and Kirsten were expected to remain at the celebration.

Henrik tapped his shoulder. "Care to take a walk?"

Reid squeezed Kirsten's hand before he stood, curious as to Henrik's purpose. He followed Henrik toward the house and around one corner. They could still see the lawn, but the solid building blocked some of the sound.

"Cigar?" Henrik asked, offering the rolled tobacco to Reid.

"Yes, thank you." He held the cigar to his mouth, drawing air to allow the cheroot to light.

"Marit hates the smell, so I have to smoke out of doors," Henrik explained.

He lit his own cigar. The two men puffed in contemplative silence as Reid waited for Henrik to speak his mind.

"You have married into the royal family, Reid," Henrik stated after a pace. "I'm not certain you understand what that means."

"Tell me," Reid said simply.

Henrik nodded. "First off, she has been gently raised. You'll need to ease her into your rougher life."

"Understood," Reid answered, wondering if Henrik knew how his daughter chafed under the restrictions of that gentle raising.

"Secondly, she is our only heir. As such, your firstborn child will eventually receive all of Marit's holdings in Norway."

That was surprising. "I didn't know Marit had holdings."

"She does," Henrik continued. "About ten thousand acres in Rollag. She receives an annual income from what is produced on that land."

Reid wanted to ask how much that income was, but knew his query might not be taken well. It would be better all around if he waited and found out when the time came. "Is there anything else I need to know?"

Henrik shot him a glance. Obviously he expected the monetary question. "Yes. Marit's brother is king. Kirsten is technically in line for the throne."

Reid stepped back, stunned. "Could that happen?"

Henrik made a face and shook his head. "Probably not. Frederick has had two wives and a mistress. Together they have produced seventeen offspring, and the legitimate ones all have a claim superseding Kirsten's."

Reid heaved a relieved sigh, before taking a steadying puff from the pungent cigar.

"Even so," Henrik continued, "you need to be aware. Your children might face that someday, though the circumstances would necessarily have to be extreme."

"Like a continental war or a devastating plague," Reid offered. "Unlikely."

"Exactly." Henrik drew on his cigar and blew out the smoke. "How's the cigar?"

★ ★ ★

Kirsten wondered what her father said to Reid, but had no chance to ask him until they climbed into her carriage and left the wedding celebration behind.

"Nothing important," he answered with a chuckle and a wave of his hand. "He only wanted me to know about your Norwegian inheritance, and your claim to the throne of Norway and Denmark."

"Oh, that." Kirsten giggled. The afternoon spent drinking champagne made her giddy. "So nothing of importance, then?"

Reid laughed and pulled a folded paper from his pocket. "No. He did give me this note, however, and said we should read it privately."

Kirsten grabbed the missive. "We're private now, aren't we?"

She unfolded it and read the words twice, assuring herself that the inked letters dancing on the page really said what she believed they did. She looked up at Reid, who appeared as surprised as she felt.

"Did you know about this?" she asked, stunned.

He shook his head. "Your father didn't say anything about it."

Dearest Kirsten ~

I struck a bargain with Lord Helland. The majority of your income is safe, as I only gave him thirty-percent. (Why he agreed is between he and I, so don't bother asking.) Once you reach St. Louis, and establish a banking account, forward me the pertinent information. I shall have the funds transferred to your account twice a year, in June and December, beginning this Christmas.

Your loving Pappa.

"I didn't expect this," she whispered.

"How much money are we talking about?" Reid asked, though he appeared uncomfortable doing so.

Kirsten's brow wrinkled as she reckoned the figures. "At seventy percent, the investments should pay nearly two-hundred dollars a year."

Reid's brows flew upward. "This changes our situation, needless to say."

"Yes, it does," Kirsten agreed. "What are you thinking?"

His grin lit up the carriage. "You will have your stone house and your servants much sooner than I thought possible."

"Oh!" She laughed, pleased with his response. "Will you design it?"

Reid winked at her. "I have a surprise of my own."

"What?" She bit her lower lip and waited, tingling with anticipation.

"We are not going to sail from Philadelphia to New Orleans," he began. "We are going to sail from Boston."

Kirsten's champagne-dulled mind required a moment to connect the reasons. "We are going to visit your parents?"

"We are," Reid confirmed. "There was no way to postpone our wedding so they could attend, but at the least they can meet my bride!"

Kirsten leaned toward Reid, inviting his kiss. He obliged, taking his time with her mouth. She wondered if her dizziness was only from the wine.

"You taste like cigar," she breathed when he pulled away.

He gave her an apologetic look. "I'll rinse my mouth before I kiss you again."

"I did not say it was unpleasant," she chided, hoping he would kiss her again.

He did. She sighed her pleasure.

The carriage stopped in front of the hotel. Reid handed her down and escorted her into the lobby. Her footman followed with her small trunk, and trailed behind them up the stairs.

The hotel was one of the nicer ones in Philadelphia, a step above an inn and tavern. Reid opened the door, revealing a tastefully furnished room with upholstered chairs, a writing desk with a wooden chair, and a large fireplace with a carved mantle.

The décor was dominated by a large, four-post bed sans canopy.

Kirsten's heartbeat tripped. Reid said they would not consummate their marriage yet, but clearly she would sleep beside him tonight.

She waited silently while her footman set her trunk against a wall and departed, trying to damp down her nervousness and the sudden twinge of nausea it brought on.

"Are you hungry?" Reid asked softly.

Her discomfort aside, Kirsten felt as if she had done nothing but eat and drink all day. "No."

"Thirsty?"

She shook her head.

"Tired?" he probed.

"Yes, actually," she admitted, meeting his eyes. "I'm exhausted."

"Well then, why don't I leave you alone to make your preparations?" he suggested, much to her relief. "I'll send a maid up to give you a hand. I'll come back up when you're finished."

"Thank you, Reid," she whispered.

He pulled her close and kissed her forehead. "Never be afraid of me, Kirsten. You are in control of what transpires between us, remember that."

She tipped her head back so his next kiss would land on her lips.

☆ ☆ ☆

Reid returned to the room three-quarters of an hour later. The sun was down, though the sky had not yet relinquished all of its light. A cooling breeze walked politely through the open windows of their room, slowly infusing it with a damp freshness. Rain was definitely on its way.

Kirsten sat in the bed, leaning against the headboard. Her pleated-and-laced nightgown was made of fine white cotton, the perfect fabric for warm Philadelphia nights.

The realization that he slept nude, therefore never needing to purchase a nightshirt, slithered through him. Lying naked beside such an exquisite creature stirred him in ways she might not be pleased about.

"I—I don't have a nightshirt," he stammered his warning. "I don't wear anything when I sleep."

Her lips formed an *o* but no sound escaped.

"I felt you should know," he said. "Before I undress."

Kirsten gave a spastic sort of nod. "Thank you."

"I'll go on with my preparations, then." Reid crossed to the washstand and began to undress.

He did so without making conversation, his mind gone blank about every subject save the need to remain calm. He washed his face, armpits, and chest once his shirt and jacket were off. He washed his feet after removing his boots. All that remained on his body were his trousers.

Reid unfastened his flies and pushed his pants and his smallclothes to the floor. He stepped out of them, acting as nonchalant as he was able, and began to wash his private parts.

"I've seen naked men before." Kirsten's words floated through the room's balmy air.

Reid thought she was talking to herself as much as to him. He tossed a small smile over his shoulder and continued his ablutions.

"Your body is beautiful, Reid," she murmured. "I see how well your labors have shaped it."

Reid dried himself, his back to her, irritated that her words caused him to swell. "Are you aware of the effect your compliments have on me?"

Kirsten was quiet. He twisted his neck to see her.

"You said you haven't been with a woman for a long time," she said. "Is that still true?"

He bounced a nod. "It is."

"Under that circumstance, I would be worried if you didn't respond," she said. "But you promised nothing would happen between us without my consent, so I won't be disturbed by it."

"Truly?" he queried.

She flashed a brave smile. "Truly."

Reid set the damp towel aside and turned to face her. "That relieves me more than you know."

He crossed to the bed, watching her gaze fall to his manhood. It stiffened further under her attention. Reid slid onto the mattress and sat facing his wife.

"You are truly beautiful. And I love you so much." His mouth claimed hers, knowing he should taste of the whiskey he drank in an attempt to wash away the cigar.

"Whiskey," she murmured against his lips. "I like that, too."

Reid stretched out on the bed and Kirsten followed suit, her gown hitching high on her thighs when she did so. The room grew darker with the night; neither one of them had lit a lamp.

"May I touch you?" Reid asked.

Kirsten nodded her permission.

"Stop me if you need to," he instructed her.

"I will," she whispered.

Reid trailed his fingertips over her legs, occasionally massaging her skin. He vowed to himself not to go higher than her gown. He felt the chill bumps his ministrations raised.

"That's nice," she sighed.

He leaned over and kissed the skin above the décolletage of her gown, tracing the upper groove between her breasts with the tip of his tongue. She moaned a little. His kisses moved upward, to behind her ear.

"You smell so good," he mouthed against her skin. "I love cloves."

"That's why I still wear them," she confessed, her voice breathy.

Reid kissed her lips again, his palm resting halfway up her thigh. He was hard as a log and he ached to do more with her. Her skin was soft and smooth, and her kisses deceptively inviting. Yet he knew what he must do. A premature assault was never a good idea, no matter which battle was being waged.

"Do you want to touch me?" he ventured.

She didn't answer, but her hand moved downward. He felt her fingers trembling against the sensitive skin of his erection. Her light touch was unbearable; he desperately needed more.

"Grab it firmly," he begged.

Her palm closed around him and she squeezed. "Does that hurt?"

Reid closed his eyes. "God, no."

He laid his hand over hers and showed her how to stroke him. His breath came in sharp gasps.

"I—please—let me—" he grunted the words, unable to complete the request.

To find sexual release with Kirsten as his wife was the stuff of countless dreams, both sleeping and awake. Reid didn't believe he could bear to have reality end less satisfactorily.

"You want to finish," she stated, her tone noncommittal.

"If you..."

He let the words trail off. He bit his lips between his teeth and pressed his eyes more tightly closed. *Please, Kirsten.*

She halted her movements and he knew she was considering his situation, as well as her own. After an eternity of painfully suspended arousal, she whispered in his ear, "Show me how."

Reid clamped his hand over hers again and stroked with the pressure and rhythm guaranteed to complete him. A victim of long deprivation, he was soon overtaken by the rush of exquisite sensations zinging outward through his core, and the momentary disorientation that accompanied his full release.

When it was over, he let out a long, soft groan. He blinked his eyes open, his eyelids being the only muscles he currently had control over. The rest of his body had floated away somewhere.

"Thank you," he rasped.

Kirsten climbed off the bed and returned with one of the damp linens. While Reid cleaned away his emission, a puzzled frown twisted her countenance.

"Why don't women have that?" she asked.

"Semen?" he asked, as confused as she looked.

She made an exasperated face. "No! That, seizure. Or whatever that is."

"Orgasm," he said. "The moment of indescribable pleasure which culminates the marriage act. And of course they do."

Kirsten seemed angry. "Why didn't I when..."

Reid tossed the towel aside and sat up to face her. "Because you were attacked with vicious intent. Those men set out to make the entire experience as horrible and degrading as they could."

A lamp seemed to flicker to life in Kirsten's awareness. "It will be different with you."

Reid took her hands and pulled her back onto the bed. "It will undoubtedly be different. You are my wife and I love you. I will do everything in my power to bring you the same sort of pleasure."

"Orgasm." She said the word as if it were new to her. Perhaps it was.

Kirsten laid down again. Reid rolled her on her side and curled along her back, his knees tucked behind hers.

Her voice was so soft, he almost missed her words.

"I want that."

CHAPTER THIRTY EIGHT

August 14, 1782
Boston

Kirsten watched out the window as the crowded coach jostled its way into Boston. Though Reid held her hand gripped in the security of his, she was still nervous about meeting his family. She hadn't asked Reid what he thought, but she was certain they would know she had not yet allowed her husband to consummate their marriage.

She was close, though.

These last nine nights Reid laid beside her while his hands and mouth roamed over her body, puckering her skin with pleasure and making a tiny ball of excitement grow low in her belly. He grew bolder each night, slipping his fingers into secret places which dampened at his touch.

He had been so patient with her, and so very kind. Kirsten knew without a doubt that Reid would never hurt her. Now her fear was being replaced by burgeoning desire, one deep stroke at a time.

She turned to look at him. Reid's eyes shone with excitement as they flickered over the scenes moving past the carriage. He was such a handsome man when he was somber; lit up with anticipation he was breathtaking.

"Do you think your parents will like me?" she asked for the dozenth time.

Reid chuckled. "As I said, *Prinsesse*. They'll be so relieved that I'm even married, that you only need to be vertical and breathing to fulfill their hopes. Once they meet you, they might actually die of happiness."

She poked his chest. "Don't say such a thing!"

He grabbed her hand and kissed the offending fingertip. "You have nothing to be concerned about, Kirsten. Relax."

Kirsten turned her head and watched the city grow in her window's view, trying to still her apprehension over meeting the Hansens, and her decision to bed Reid fully this very night. The ache in her chest demanded one, and the ache between her thighs demanded the other.

✱ ✱ ✱

The walk to the Hansen home was about half a mile from the coach station. Reid paid to have the trunks delivered, but he wanted to escort Kirsten through Boston and act as a bit of a guide, naming buildings they passed by and describing the role they played in the path toward America's revolt.

"I had no idea," she said. "Now I understand what you told me about going to 'war' earlier than seventeen-seventy-six."

Reid gave a quick nod. "The house is just over here."

He paused in front of the three-storied brick building. Kirsten looked up toward the roof, squinting in the hazy sun. The house was unassuming at first glance, until she noticed the details around the windows and along the eaves.

"Your father had grand ideas," she commented.

"And seven children to provide for," Reid countered. "He was able to work some of his ideas into this building, but time and coin prevented him from doing all that he wanted."

Kirsten lifted one shoulder. "Perhaps he might put some of that creativity into our home."

"Perhaps," Reid agreed. "Are you ready?"

Kirsten gave him the most confident nod she could muster. He took her arm and they climbed the steeps. Before he could lift the latch, the front door flew open. A tall woman with white-blonde hair stood in the opening, her broad smile an obvious echo of her son's.

"*Mamma!*" Reid bellowed happily. He stepped inside and swung his mother around in a spinning bear hug.

"Stop!" she squealed, laughing. "Put me down!"

Reid obliged. He reached for Kirsten's hand and pulled her to his side.

"*Mamma*, this is my wife, Kirsten Sven Hansen." Reid beamed at her and the love in his expression washed away most of Kirsten's worry.

"Kirsten, I would like you to meet Dagny Sivertsen Hansen, the poor woman unfortunate enough to have given birth to me," he teased.

Dagny punched him in the ribs. Kirsten now knew where Reid acquired his unique sense of humor.

She offered her hand to her new mother-in-law. "I'm pleased to meet you, Mrs. Hansen."

Warm hands with pronounced veins and the beginning knobs of arthritis gripped hers. "Please call me Dagny." She glanced at Reid. "So you've been married ten days and you haven't frightened her off yet?"

Kirsten laughed at Reid's comical expression.

"I thought I'd let the family have a shot at her first," he quipped.

"Oh dear." Dagny's eyes widened when they shifted to Kirsten. "Reid said you were your parents' only child. Is that true?"

"Yes, though not for lack of trying was my understanding," she replied. "Why do you ask?"

Dagny looped her arm through Kirsten's. "Let's get you two settled in, shall we?"

Reid chuckled. "What my mother is trying *not* to say is that our family can be a bit... loud."

Kirsten looked quizzically at the woman who stood a full hand taller than she.

"Well, loud. Yes. There were seven of them, you see, and most are married," Dagny began.

"With children" Reid interjected.

"And they do look out for each other..." The woman was obviously dancing around some issue. Kirsten formed a quick opinion of what that issue might be.

"Shall I wear armor and attend the dinner table with a dagger in my boot?" she offered, feigning an innocent moue.

Dagny laughed. "You might want to consider it."

The trio climbed two flights of stairs to the uppermost floor and Kirsten made a discreet evaluation of her surroundings along the way. Though not in any way as grand as her parents' manor, the Hansen house was attractive and clean, and furnished with sturdy, tasteful pieces. Some walls were covered in fabric, some in paper, and two had murals painted on.

"Who is the artist" Kirsten asked.

"That would be Liv, our second child." Dagny tossed a proud look over her shoulder. "She was actually paid to create something similar in one of the houses Martin designed."

"I didn't know that," Reid said.

"You've been gone for years, son," Dagny replied.

"It's lovely," Kirsten complimented. "Your whole house is lovely."

When they reached the third story, Dagny gave the couple a knowing smile. "I'm sorry to put you in a room up so high, but you'll have the most privacy here."

Kirsten swallowed a gasp. Dagny's meaning was clear—a newly wedded husband and wife should be expected to appreciate that privacy.

Reid spoke over Kirsten's shoulder. "Thank you, *Mamma.* Our trunks should be here soon, I believe."

Dagny winked. "They're already here. That's how I knew to watch for you."

She pushed open a door, revealing a large room with a large bed and two small windows. Kirsten's two big trunks and one small one waited in a corner. Reid's pack was draped over a wooden chair.

Dagny gestured toward the open windows. "You should get a cross-breeze up here as well. I believe you will be quite comfortable."

Kirsten smiled at her mother-in-law, wishing they had more than just a few days to become acquainted. "Yes, I'm sure we'll very comfortable, Dagny."

"I'm going to check on our supper preparations and leave you two to settle in." Dagny reached for the door handle. "Come down when you're ready. I'll have coffee waiting."

The door clicked shut.

Reid leaned over and whispered in Kirsten's ear. "Haven't had tea in this house since the incident in the harbor."

Kirsten giggled and turned around to face Reid. She tilted her face upward, inviting a kiss. An invitation he accepted with enthusiasm. The time had come.

"I've made a decision, soldier," she said softly.

"What decision is that?" he asked, his forehead resting against hers.

Her jumping pulse reflected both her eagerness and her apprehension. "We are never going to find a more comfortable and intimate setting than this one until we reach St. Louis. Am I correct?"

Reid pulled back so he could meet her eyes. "Quite, I'm afraid."

"Then tonight I believe we should finish what we started," she stated. "That way, we will have a few more nights to practice before boarding a ship. Even the best ship's cabins are neither spacious, nor soundproof."

"Are you saying that I tonight I may make you *fully* my wife?" Reid murmured.

Kirsten was surprised at the peace which washed through her. This was the right decision and the right time. She laid her palms on Reid's cheeks.

"I am," she whispered, and pulled his face down to hers. This kiss had an entirely different taste. It was flavored with potential, and spiced with urgency.

"I'll make certain to call a reasonable end to our evening," Reid pledged. "Otherwise, my family could keep us entertained until dawn."

Kirsten chuckled. "If I'm going to be entertained until dawn, I want it to be by you."

Grinning, Reid pulled her into his embrace. "I'll do my best."

Supper was even more chaotic than at his last homecoming.

Liv's husband Alex had returned safely from his army post in New York. Her two sons, now fourteen and twelve, seemed to have grown half a foot each in the past five months. Alex queried Reid repeatedly about the explosion, the trial, and his decision to leave the army.

"Might you speak later about that?" Liv interrupted. Her glance jumped to her sons, who devoured their *Onkel* Reid's tales with far more enthusiasm than their meal.

"I believe this war will be over before long before these two can enlist," Reid assured his sister. "It won't last another year."

"I agree with you, Reid," Karan's husband Arthur concurred. He grabbed one of his three children who bolted past the table. "We will be the victors, as well."

Reid watched his brother-in-law pick up the boy and plant him back in a chair, deciding on the spot that his own children would never be allowed to be so unruly.

His consideration moved to his wife. Knowing they might never become parents was a heartache that truly paled when compared to the soul-deep pain of living without her. Kirsten glanced his way and smiled.

Thank you, God.

Reid's youngest brother Tobias tapped his arm. "I wish you could stay for the wedding, Reid."

Tor's fiancée Caroline sat close by his side. "Is there no way?" she pleaded. "It's only two weeks away. Anna and Sean are coming and bringing their new baby girl."

Reid shook his head and gave the young couple an apologetic look. "It will take us three weeks to sail to New Orleans, and another four weeks to travel up the Mississippi River to St. Louis," he explained. "If we can leave by the end of this week, we'll arrive at the beginning of October. Any later than that, and I won't have the cabin ready for winter."

"You do what you must, son," Martin ordered from the head of the table. "We all understand."

"I'm sorry to miss Anna and Sean—and my niece," Reid said truthfully. "But you see our predicament."

A commotion at the front door stilled the crowd around the huge table. Martin stood and Reid followed suit, ready to confront whatever danger might present itself.

A tall, thin, unkempt man strode into the room, rifle at his side. He stopped short, obviously surprised by the nine adults and five children gathered around the meal. His eyes widened along with his grin.

"Nils!" Dagny cried. She leapt up and launched herself at her second son. "*Å min Gud!* I was so afraid..." Her voice was swallowed by her sobbed relief.

Reid set the rifle aside and pumped his brother's freed hand. "Where have you been all this time?"

"Prisoner," he yelped over Dagny's emotional display. "But we got 'em in the end."

If Reid believed the dinner was chaotic before, the explosion of greetings and questions and congratulations which ensued was deafening. He pulled Kirsten to his side and held her close until Nils' attentions landed back on him.

"This is my wife of ten days, Nils," Reid announced. "Kirsten, Nils is my parents' fourth child, and the second son."

Nils' surprise was almost buried under his beard and filth. "Well, will you look at that!" he exclaimed. "How'd this stubborn old man win you?"

Kirsten slid her arm around Reid's waist and tucked herself under his arm. "I married him for his money, of course."

The tiniest moment of silence preceded Reid's explosively raucous response. He laughed so hard his belly hurt and he had tears running down his cheeks.

"There—there is *so* much—so much *more* to that story!" he stammered between guffaws.

"I suppose I'll hear it later," Nils chuckled. His gaze moved to the table. "Is there any food left?"

Martin and Dagny shuffled Nils to the head of the table and pulled a chair next to Martin's. Liv piled a plate precariously high and sat it in front of her brother. Nils patted Olav's shoulder as he passed by the silent brother, obviously noticing the man's missing arm, but not mentioning it.

"Reid was just telling us why he and Kirsten can't stay for my wedding," Tobias announced.

Nils' fork paused briefly in its heavily-laden journey toward his mouth. "You're getting married?"

Tor nodded. "This is my fiancée, Caroline," he continued, pointing a thumb at the blushing girl. "It's in two weeks. Anna and Sean are coming."

Nils turned to Reid and spoke past the shovelful of victuals. "Why can't you stay?"

"We must return to my home near St. Louis in order to be

prepared before the weather turns," he answered.

"Your home?" Nils stopped chewing. One furry cheek bulged with food and he spoke from the other side of his mouth. "When did you move to Missouri?"

"In May." Reid paused. He glanced across the table at his beaming wife, savoring the next bit of information. "I have five hundred acres in Cheltenham."

More chaos erupted as everyone tried to speak at once. Reid gazed at Kirsten, wondering how soon after supper they might be able to make their apologies and go to bed.

To *bed*.

CHAPTER THIRTY NINE

Reid climbed the stairs to their room behind Kirsten as the clock below chimed three-quarters of an hour past eight. He was gratified to see fresh water and linens on the washstand, and the bedclothes folded back in invitation.

"Are you exhausted?" he asked her as he latched the door from the inside.

Her shoulder slumped a little but one side of her lips curved upward. "Perhaps. Perhaps not," she teased.

Reid shook his head. "I have stopped saying that."

Kirsten giggled. "I noticed."

He crossed the room and rested his hands on her narrow waist. "What does that mean?"

"It means," she began as she slid her hands up his arms to loop them around his neck, "that whatever I do next, I want to do lying down."

Reid's body jumped to high alert. "Let me help you with your gown."

Kirsten turned in a slow circle. Reid untied her laces and pushed the dress off her shoulders. Kirsten left off wearing a corset once they were gone from Philadelphia, so when she stepped away from the circular pile of pink cotton fabric at her feet, she was clad only in her chemise. It was the closest to naked she had yet been in his presence.

"I'll wash first," she said. Reid noticed a little tremor in her tone.

"We don't need to do this if you aren't ready," he offered, hating every single word that left his mouth.

"No. I'm ready," she insisted. "See?"

In one swift, smooth motion, Kirsten pulled the chemise over her head and let it float to the floor.

Reid's breath blew out in a whoosh which left him light-headed. For the first time he saw his wife completely unclothed, and the sight was exquisite. She turned and walked to the washstand. Her next words floated back to him, surprising him with their playfulness.

"I hope I'm not going to be the only naked body in this room."

Reid began untying his shirt with one hand and fumbling at his flies with the other. His cock was already stiff, hampering his hurried efforts to free it from restraint. While Kirsten attended to her toilette, Reid hung up their clothes and waited his turn.

When she finished, she tiptoed to the bed and climbed onto the big mattress. Reid moved to the washstand and carefully cleaned the travel dust from his body. He noticed his mother had given them rose-scented soap and smiled. He might smell feminine now, but his wife would feel pampered.

"I wish it was cloves," he said, smiling at Kirsten.

She smiled back. She sat on her knees on the mattress. Her thick blonde hair spread over her shoulders and fell to her waist, bending at angles which reflected the way it had been bound up all day. In the light of the oil lamp, she looked like some ethereal creature too beautiful to be real.

"I know this has been the bane of your existence," Reid began as he approached the bed. "But I cannot spend the rest of our lives pretending you aren't a stunningly attractive woman."

Kirsten's cheeks dimpled. "Now that we are married, you may say that as often as you wish. I won't stop you."

Reid slid onto the bed. He wrapped one hand around the back of Kirsten's neck and pulled her into a teasing kiss. As he brushed his lips over hers, she chased after him, until she grabbed his head and held him still. Her fingers twisted through his hair. Her tongue twisted though his mouth.

"Lie down," he whispered after a pace.

She did so. He lay alongside her. She reached for his erection, but he stopped her.

"This is about you now." His hand skimmed over her belly and moved to her bosom. "I am going to love you well."

He massaged her breasts and teased their tips with his palm before taking one, then the other, in his mouth. Kirsten moaned and buried her fingers in his hair again.

Reid's hand moved downward over her body before settling between her thighs. "If you are readied before I enter," he murmured in her ear. "There is no pain. Only pleasure."

Kirsten's legs parted, giving him room. As he kissed her and fondled her deeply, he felt the readiness in her quim's response. Still, he waited for her to invite him to do more.

She whimpered against his mouth. Her hips pressed against his hand. It was as though she couldn't lie still.

"Please..." she breathed.

Reid shifted his position. "Wrap your legs around me," he instructed.

She did. The tip of his cock rested against its target.

For the first time this evening, Reid allowed himself to consider what he was about to do from his own perspective. The anticipation of loving this woman with his body was many months old, but until this moment, it was nothing but a hope or a fantasy. Now that he was poised to enter her, his arousal vibrated through his body and his cock grew so hard it hurt.

"Do you want to guide me in?" he asked.

The sudden inspiration was grounded as much in his flaming desire to feel her hand on him, as it was in giving her control over this joining. She was not the victim in this bed, she was the instigator. Reid knew instinctively that the distinction was crucial to her response. Kirsten said nothing, but she reached between her legs and gripped him.

"When you're ready," he said softly, then leaned down and kissed her.

He pressed forward a little. She adjusted his aim. He pushed farther. She held him at the right spot. He breached her opening. She let go.

He slowly slid inside, all the way, until no space remained between them.

Reid closed his eyes. He breathed though his mouth. He braced himself, trembling, over Kirsten.

"Ooh..." she sighed.

He opened his eyes a slit. "I'm going to start to move."

She nodded. "Yes..."

He began slowly, keeping as much control as he was able, wanting to give his wife her first peak before claiming his own. As his thrusts gained momentum, Kirsten groaned and twisted under him. Her breath came in spastic gusts, each exhalation a tiny cry of pleasure.

Reid felt himself losing his battle. His hips took over, pushing him deep and fast. His head grew fuzzy. He was almost there.

And then she exploded.

With a loud gasp, her body stiffened. Her fingernails dug into his arm. She tightened and quivered around him, the heightened heat of her quim seared him.

Reid let go, then. He ground against her, pumping himself into her. His release was unlike any he had experienced in his lifetime. Tossed from his body, he literally saw stars arrayed in the black heavens.

As he drifted back into his corporeal existence, he looked down at his wife's awestruck features. Tears rolled from the corners of her eyes. Her legs fell away from him, but she kept her hips close to his and didn't attempt to disengage.

Reid stared into her eyes. His breath still came in short heaves, as did hers. She gave him a tremulous smile.

✳ ✳ ✳

Kirsten wanted to say something to Reid, but her mind refused to cooperate. It was as if every functioning part of her had been sucked into the center of her belly before being flung outward, beyond her existence, with such ecstatic bliss.

She never imagined sex could be like this. No one ever told her. Her experience tonight with her loved and loving husband was the complete antithesis of what happened to her in Denmark. And now she was freed, forever, from those chains.

"Thank you," she whispered.

He smiled and gave her a tender kiss. "I love you so much I can't put it into adequate words."

"I might be wrong," she posited. "But I believe you just told me with your body."

Reid grinned. "You enjoyed that, then, did you not?"

She pulled a shuddering sigh. "*Enjoy* doesn't begin to describe it."

"You had no pain at all?" he probed.

"No. None." She smiled, gratified by his consideration. "Will it always be like this?"

"I have heard it said that it gets better," he replied. "As we learn each other's bodies and know what sort of ministrations we each prefer."

She stared at him, surprised. "There's more?"

He chuckled. "Yes. We haven't used our tongues yet, for example."

Kirsten's mouth fell open. "People do that?"

Reid nodded. "And there are other positions we could try…"

Laughter bubbled up from her chest. A world was opening up in front of her, one she was completely ignorant of, and absolutely interested in exploring—with this particular man.

"I am so thankful you came back for me, Reid." She laid her hand on his short-bearded cheek. "You saved my life, do you know that?"

He kissed her again. His lips held hers for a long moment before he said, "And you saved mine, *Prinsesse*."

Reid eased himself from her body. When the ridge of his softened member left her, she felt another small twinge of arousal.

"How often can we do this?" she asked, curious.

Reid rolled onto his back. "I'm not certain. At least once a day. Perhaps more."

Kirsten grinned. "Every night while we are here. Agreed?"

Reid chuckled. He grabbed her hand and kissed her palm. "Agreed."

He rolled from the bed and turned down the lamp. City lights glowed through the open windows, carried on a soft, salty breeze. Kirsten got up and retrieved her chemise, choosing to sleep in the light garment rather than dig out her nightdress. She washed the stickiness from between her legs in the dim light, wondering if children were in their future.

When she returned to the bed, she snuggled into Reid's embrace. No matter what sort of challenges lay ahead of them in the wilds of Missouri, she knew she was safe in his care.

She fell asleep, contented and fulfilled for the first time in her life.

October 8, 1782
St. Louis

Kirsten and Reid stood at the pointed prow of the keelboat which had laboriously carried them up the Mississippi River against the current. Once they arrived by tall sailing ship in New Orleans, they spent one night in a hotel before boarding this boat.

The river journey took four weeks and required the use of sails on breezy days, and poles pushed by the keelboatmen in the shallow edgewaters on airless days. The vessel did have cabins for a few passengers and the crew, so the journey wasn't unbearable. And many times they disembarked into small towns along the way for provisions, giving Kirsten and Reid the opportunity to stand on unmoving land for a pace.

Even though the two different voyages were largely boring and uneventful, Reid insisted that their chosen modes of transportation were vastly superior to riding horseback for nine-hundred miles.

"Especially if you want to continue our nighttime activities," he added with a wink.

"Well, there is that, at the least," she replied with a crooked smile. Their nights were certainly *not* boring.

Reid pointed toward a clearing in the forest ahead, and the red brick of buildings rising on the horizon. "There it is."

Kirsten watched the small city of St. Louis grow larger in her view. "How many people live there?"

"About a thousand, I believe," Reid answered.

She looked up at him and wondered why she never asked before. "And Cheltenham?"

Reid shrugged. "Perhaps a hundred, spread over the countryside."

Kirsten turned her regard back to the approaching docks. She was beginning to understand how different her life was truly going to be. There were revelations coming which she could never have imagined, she realized.

She squeezed her husband's hand. "You will teach me what to do, won't you?"

"I will," he assured her. "And James has slaves, if you find you need help."

Her brow furrowed. "You would buy a slave?"

"No!" he declaimed. "I would pay for her services, however."

Kirsten nodded, accepting that compromise. Her sheltered upbringing and staff of servants had left out some of the more basic points of running a household, even if there were only two in the house.

She sighed and tucked away a little bit of regret behind her heart. In spite of frequent and enthusiastic bedding, she had gone two months without conceiving a child. Perhaps she was indeed rendered infertile by the violent rape.

Never mind that, she told herself. Reid knew that was a possibility when he married her, and he said nothing about offspring since. He didn't even appear disappointed when her courses began. Perhaps he wasn't interested in fatherhood after all.

"After we dock, I'll pay to have the trunks delivered and then take you to the hotel." Reid's words interrupted her disheartening thoughts. "Then I'll send a note to James that we have returned and to expect us the day after tomorrow."

"What will we do until then?" Kirsten asked.

Reid combed his fingers through his beard. "Today, a bath for each of us, and a shave for me."

"That sounds nice," Kirsten admitted.

"Tomorrow, I'll buy a wagon, and order the stone for our house. Plus we'll buy anything else we can think of that we'll need." He smiled down at her. "I own two Vermont draft horses who have been boarding at James' estate during my absence, so I'll hire a team and driver to load the wagon and take us to Cheltenham the next day."

"How far is it?" Kirsten asked, feeling she should know.

"About ten miles," Reid answered kindly, as if this was the first time he had imparted that information. "Only two hours."

The bustle at the little dock was miniscule compared to either Boston or New Orleans. Reid walked her to the hotel—which was surprisingly nice—as soon as he made arrangements for their belongings.

He bought her an early dinner in the dining room in the meantime, a simple meal of roasted meat, potatoes, bread, and beans. The wine he selected was also a pleasant surprise. Kirsten drank it faster than she should have, judging by her gently spinning head. She stopped for a moment and thought about where she was. This strange and burgeoning land would be her home for the rest of her life.

Reid refilled her glass, then lifted his in a good-natured toast. "Welcome to Missouri, Your Highness."

"Thank you, sir." She smiled pensively and clinked her glass against his. "I cannot wait to enter my new kingdom."

CHAPTER FORTY

October 9, 1782
Cheltenham

Reid worried about what Kirsten might think about the cabin. Though he built every inch of it with her in mind, he had to leave before he was finished. He explained that to her yester eve, when he offered her the same sort of arrangement which James had with Beatrice.

She staunchly refused.

"I want to sleep with you every night. I want to work beside you every day. I want us to create this life together," she insisted.

"Even so," he said. "Should you change your mind, or need a respite, that is always a possibility. I'll not think less of you for it, I promise you that."

"Thank you." She dipped her chin. "I'll keep that in mind."

As the wagon came around the last bend in the grassy road, his cabin came into distant view. "There it is," he said, watching her reaction.

Kirsten grinned. "You didn't tell me you made a Norwegian roof!"

"They know what they're doing," he admitted. "My father taught me how when he put one on his hunting cabin."

Motion around his home caught Reid's attention. He leaned over and squinted.

"Is something amiss?" Kirsten asked.

"I don't—no! My horses are there," he responded. "James must have brought them over."

Kirsten twisted to get a better view. "Is that a carriage?"

Reid began to grin, joy at his new friend's consideration making this land truly feel like his home. "It is! I bet James is there now." He turned his glee toward his wife. "Now you'll be able to meet him straight away!"

James stepped out of the cabin as the wagon rumbled across the small, grassy patch which acted as a lawn. "Halloo!" he shouted, waving his arms. "Welcome back!"

Reid hopped from the wagon before it stopped rolling and loped to his front stoop. He and James greeted each other with a back-slapping bear hug before Reid noticed Beatrice standing inside the cabin.

"Welcome home, Reid," she said with a smile. "Where is your wife?"

Reid spun and hurried back to the halted wagon. "I'll lift you down," he said to Kirsten before doing exactly that.

She regained her balance, straightened her skirt, and smoothed her hair as James and Beatrice approached. "Please excuse my dishevelment. I wasn't expecting to meet anyone just yet," she apologized.

Beatrice rolled her eyes. "Don't give it a thought. I believe you will find the social standards in this wilderness quite lacking." She stuck out a hand which Kirsten accepted. "I'm Beatrice Atherton, your closest neighbor."

"And this enchanting creature is Kirsten Sven Hansen, my wife," Reid stated and gestured his introductions. "Beatrice and James Atherton.

"Enchanting, indeed," James said as he kissed the back of Kirsten's hand. "Now I understand Reid's willingness to make his journey."

"And we are both thankful it was a fruitful one," Beatrice added. "Or the man's company would be quite unbearable at this point."

"Thank you for bringing the horses," Reid said to James. "How did they fare?"

James winked at him. "She's in foal, as you suspected she might be."

Reid shook his head. "And the foal will be yours in exchange for the horse you lent me, just as *you* suspected it might be."

The young man driving the wagon cleared his throat.

"We must unload!" Reid exclaimed. "The wagon is mine, but the boy needs to return to St. Louis with his team."

"I'll give you a hand," James offered.

✶ ✶ ✶

Beatrice took Kirsten's hand. "Come with me. I've something to show you."

As they walked toward the log cabin, Kirsten noticed how solid it appeared. The shutters over the windows were open, as was the door. The women climbed the three steps to the stoop.

"Reid's message arrived yesterday, so I brought some of my darkies over immediately," Beatrice said. "The cabin has been untouched these last months, so I knew it was in no condition for you to move into."

"What did you do?" Kirsten asked, sincerely moved by the woman's thoughtfulness.

"Swept and washed the floor, dusted away the cobwebs, washed the bed linens, and re-stuffed the mattress with wool. The nights are only getting chillier," she answered.

Kirsten stood in the middle of the cabin, casting an evaluative eye around her new accommodations. The clean scent of pine sap was strong. The wood floor was spotless. The mattress on the big bed which was built into one corner looked very inviting after her weeks of travel.

The fireplace appeared to be scarcely used. One iron pan and one covered pot sat on the floor beside it. Surprisingly, a tin bathing tub claimed a corner.

"That was mine," Beatrice confided. "We got a new one for the house and I thought you might appreciate a little touch of civilization."

Kirsten chuckled. "Thank you for thinking of me."

"We women have to stick together, there are so few of us here." Beatrice sighed and her gaze moved to the open door. "I love James so much. But if anything happened to him, I'm not certain I could survive out here."

"Well I'm glad to have you, and I don't even know you yet!"

Kirsten effused. "I'm afraid I am completely out of my element in these surroundings."

"We'll have you over for supper tonight," Beatrice offered. "I know you'll say yes, because your kitchen isn't set up yet. Come over whenever you are ready."

Reid walked through the door with a trunk on his shoulder. He stopped and stared around the room. "Did you do this?" he asked Beatrice, his tone evincing happy surprise.

"We're invited to the Atherton's for supper this evening," Kirsten said happily. "Once we get a bit settled."

Reid grinned and swung the chest to the floor. "And we thank you again."

James came in with another trunk. "I'm quite excited for you to see the house. It's coming along very satisfactorily."

"You are living there?" Reid asked Beatrice.

"I am," she replied. We have the main wing assembled, though not all the rooms are habitable. We are comfortable enough for now."

"I ordered the stone for our house," Reid commented. "If I can find them in this jumble, I'll bring my plans along."

"I would love to see them." James clapped his hands together. "It's so good to finally have you back!"

Kirsten looked around the little group, standing in the snug little cabin, all smiling and chatting as if they had been lifelong friends. She never imagined that her life might take such a turn, and wondered at the contentment which flooded her chest. She smiled.

I'm home.

Reid turned down the lamp and climbed into bed next to Kirsten. The scents of fresh linen and wool were spiced with Kirsten's cloves. He breathed deeply, feeling as if he lay on a cloud in Heaven itself.

"So here we are," he ventured.

"Here we are indeed," she answered.

"What do you think of the Atherton's?"

She snuggled closer. "James is a doll. A bit of a flirt, but with a loyal heart of pure gold."

"And Beatrice?" Reid asked.

"I believe she has been quite lonely since coming here," Kirsten observed. "I expect we'll see a lot of each other. I do think we'll become fast friends, just as you and James have."

His wife's positive response eased one of Reid's concerns. "And the cabin?"

"It's bigger than I expected from your descriptions," she confessed. "And for Beatrice to bring her slaves over to clean it for us was unbelievably kind."

"Are you comfortable?" he pressed.

She wiggled deeper into the bedclothes. "Very."

"Do you believe you will be able to thrive in these conditions?"

Kirsten paused. "I have to be honest—that's an easy answer because I know it's temporary. By next winter we'll have our stone house with all the amenities."

"True," he admitted.

"So for now, I see it as an adventure for you and I to share." She rested a hand on his thigh.

"Tomorrow we'll begin arranging everything the way you want it," he stated. "And we can go back to St. Louis if we find we forgot anything, now that I have my own wagon."

"Um-hm," she hummed. Her hand moved upward to his hip.

Reid slid his palm over her breast, which pebbled at his touch. "Are you trying to seduce me, *Prinsesse*?"

"You didn't carry me over the threshold," she murmured. "The least you can do is christen our first night together in our new home."

Reid tugged Kirsten's nightdress over her head. "Perhaps you should forgo wearing clothes to bed, as I do," he whispered. "It would save us time."

In spite of his teasing words, Reid determined not to rush their joining. After weeks of trying to achieve silent intercourse, tonight he wanted to fully enjoy their experience. He kissed her lips first, and then moved his mouth slowly all over her body.

Her moans of pleasure and pleas for him to hurry aroused him to an unbearable level. He slid into her, iron-hard and aching, the heat of her quim sending sparks through his veins. After several vigorous thrusts, they peaked at the same time. Their mingled cries of sweet release filled the cabin with a sensuous song which Reid knew he would remember for the rest of his life.

He remembered a conversation he had once with Kirsten. Something about every man hoping to found his own dynasty and to reign as sovereign over his own lands. He held her body against his in panting, post-coital bliss and knew that here, with his very own princess, those hopes would be his future.

We're home.

EPILOGUE

January 2, 1789
The Hansen Estate
Cheltenham

"Nicolas, you need to stay in your bed." Reid lifted the solid little boy and placed him back on the mattress. "It's time for you to go to sleep."

"Want my *mamma!*" he yelled, trying to squirm from his father's grasp.

"I'm afraid he's too stubborn to stay put," Addie warned. Little Nicolas had already kicked his nanny in the shin in his effort to get through Reid and Kirsten's latched bedroom door. "I've carried him to bed four times now, but he keeps running back to your door."

"Want my *Mamma!*" Nicolas wailed, his objections shifting from frustration to tearful devastation. "Want my *Mammaaaaa.*"

Reid sat on the mattress beside his obstinate firstborn. "Nicolas, listen. Remember that *Mamma* has a baby in her belly?"

Nicolas sniffed and wiped his angry eyes with the back of a fist. "Uh huh."

"That baby is coming out of her tonight," Reid explained. "She's very busy right now, helping the baby be born."

"I help *Mamma*," Nicolas insisted.

"Yes, and you are very good helper, son," Reid said. "But this is something neither you nor I can help her do."

Nicolas's chin quavered and huge tears rolled from his dark

blue eyes and down his ruddy cheeks. His blond hair stuck out in all directions, victim of his tantrum.

"Want *Mamma*," he sobbed. "Want *Mamma*."

Reid's heart was breaking for his young son. At less than two years of age, he didn't know how to make Nicky understand childbirth.

"What do you suggest, Addie?" Reid asked, at a loss and distracted by the imminent birth.

Addie shrugged. "If you let him sit on the floor outside the door, he'll probably fall asleep and you can carry him to bed."

Reid lifted Nicolas from the mattress. "Come on. You can sit outside the door and wait for *Mamma* to be done. But you must be quiet and listen for the baby, do you understand?"

Nicolas sniffled and nodded vigorously.

"If you aren't quiet, you will have to stay in your room," Reid warned his son.

"Yes, *Pappa*," he whispered.

Reid sat Nicky in the corner next to the door jamb. He held his finger to his lips. Wide-eyed Nicolas touched his own lips with one chubby finger.

A long, loud groan of effort seeped through the heavy wood portal. Reid watched Nicolas, wondering if the birthing sounds might be too frightening for the child. Nicky's lips pressed together as if ready to release a cry. Reid shook his head and made the shushing gesture again.

"If you want to wait here for *Mamma*, you have to be quiet," he said again. "Do you want to stay or go to bed?"

"Stay," Nicolas murmured. He clapped a hand over his mouth.

Reid nodded. "I'll be back in a little while. Addie will stay here with you."

He turned around and descended the stairs to the bottom floor, retreating into his study and closing the door. He poured himself a glass of brandy and sank into a stuffed leather chair in front of the fire. Unlike his son, Reid knew the perils of birthing and had no desire to listen to his wife's labors.

He and Kirsten had been married for five years before Nicolas came along. Reid had given up hope that she might ever conceive and would have been satisfied with the one big, healthy son. When Kirsten conceived a second time, so quickly after the first, Reid had mixed feelings.

On the one hand, having another child and a playmate for the willful Nicolas was a blessing indeed. Reid wished he and his wife might have had an army of boys, but knew when he married her that was unlikely. He held to no illusions from the start, and yet counted every day spent as her husband as an invaluable gift.

On the other hand, Kirsten was almost thirty-four years of age. He was thirty-nine. This child was coming even later in their lives than their first. Though Kirsten was a sturdy woman, fearless in most arenas, the dangers she faced giving birth at her age were undoubtedly increased.

Reid slid to his knees, rested his head on the seat of his chair, and began to pray fervently for his wife and children.

★ ★ ★

Addie shook Reid's shoulder. "I believe you should come back upstairs."

Reid lifted his head from the leather seat. "What time is it?"

"Six o'clock," she answered. "The baby's almost here."

Reid unfolded his body, stiff from being bent on the cold floor. He pushed to his feet and followed the housekeeper up the stairs.

Nicolas was curled on the floor by the door, covered in a tufted blanket and sucking his thumb.

"I didn't have the heart to move him," Addie confessed. "He stayed awake for almost an hour, poor little fellow."

A groan to end all groans vibrated through the door. Silence followed. Reid held his breath.

A sudden and vigorous cry relieved him of his first worry.

"Thank God," Reid moaned as the infant's cries gained strength and volume.

Nicolas's eyes fluttered and his thumb was released with a soft *pop*. The boy looked up at his father, obviously confused. *"Pappa?"*

The door cracked open and the midwife's assistant stuck her head out. "It's another boy!"

"Kirsten?" Reid asked, trying to see past the woman.

"She's fine. I'll let you in when she's cleaned up." The door clicked shut in his face.

Reid crumpled to the floor and gathered Nicky into his lap,

blanket and all. "The baby came out of *Mamma*. You have a brother, Nicolas."

Nicky yawned. "Wanna see."

"In a little while. Can you hear him cry?"

The youngster nodded and sagged against his father. The pair sat on the floor, waiting and listening to the bustle of activity in the bedroom. Finally, the door opened.

Reid clambered to his feet and carried Nicolas to Kirsten's bedside. She sat against the huge cherrywood headboard, cradling their new son. Reid set Nicolas on the foot of the bed. The boy stared at the baby in his mother's arms as if confounded as to where it came from.

Reid leaned over and kissed his wife as if they had been separated for a year. "You survived," he whispered. "I love you so much."

"We have another boy, soldier." Kirsten beamed up at him, her shining eyes saying much more than words ever could. "Your dynasty is thus ensured."

Following is an excerpt from:

LEAVING
NORWAY

by Kris Tualla

Now Available

CHAPTER ONE

June 2, 1749
Christiania, Norway

Martin Balder Gunnar Hansen had never seen such a beautiful woman in all his twenty-eight years. He watched her through the salt-hazed window of the pier's tavern, where he was nursing what was probably the last glass of akevitt in his life.

She sat on her trunk at the Christiania pier wearing a billowing white blouse tied at the neck and wrists. A turquoise over-bodice and brown skirt accentuated her narrow waist and pleasantly proportioned bosom. Embroidery on the over-bodice shimmered each time scudding clouds allowed a wash of sunshine to grace the docks. Draped across her lap was a forest green cloak.

What drew Martin's attention was the look of expectation that played over what were, in his estimation, perfect features. Her eyes darted, her neck craned, and her lower lip disappeared into her teeth. Obviously, she awaited someone.

"What if it was me?" Martin mused. A slow smile grew as he thought about what he would do. He'd twist those thick blond braids around his hands and pull her face to his, teasing those full pink lips just a little before kissing them very well.

"*Skitt.*" Martin took another sip of the gullet-stripping akevitt and followed it with a soothing swallow of cooled beer. The beginning of a long ocean journey was not the time to be thinking such things.

The tumbling stomp of boots on stairs pulled Martin's attention back inside the tavern. A dark-haired man descended with a woman close behind. He was fastening his flies and he had an aura of sensuality that was obvious, even to another man. At the bottom of the stairs he turned, circled the woman with one arm and pressed his hips against hers. The other hand clamped over her breast and his fingers tightened. His kiss was almost violent.

The woman pulled away, her lips swollen and their color blurred. Red-faced but laughing, she buttoned the last button on his well-tailored trousers. She hurried to get him a mug of some indeterminate beverage, which he downed in one long pull. He wiped his mouth on the back of his hand, gave her the mug and slapped her arse. Only then did he reach inside his frock coat for coins.

Martin felt for his pocket watch and flipped it open, idly wondering if he had time for a tumble himself before boarding the ship. He chuckled at the thought. This was not the day to begin frequenting whores. He should save some new experiences for America.

He looked back out the window to the woman, still waiting, still searching. He guessed her to be a bit younger than he. She wasn't wearing any obvious jewelry, though her clothes bespoke a level of wealth and her trunk was new. He wished he could see the color of her eyes.

Martin sighed and finished the last bit of the akevitt. Closing his eyes he let it burn, savoring the sensation. There would be many things he expected to miss about Norway; akevitt was a memory he anticipated would become more pleasant with distance.

As he counted out coins to pay for his meals and drinks, Martin saw the woman stand from the edge of his eye. He turned and held his breath. First abject relief, then radiant joy suffused her countenance. Her cheeks flushed beautifully and her full pink lips spread in the sort of wide smile that he could only hope someone might give him one day. He stilled, curious to see the recipient of this woman's affections.

Martin's gut twisted and shoved his breath out when the dark-haired man, fresh from whoring, took the woman's hand chastely in his and pressed it to his lips. She lifted her face, and waited. He kissed her cheek, obviously disappointing her, but she smiled adoringly even so.

. "Why did it have to be him," Martin muttered to no one.

When she stood to face her companion, Martin realized she was quite tall. The dark-haired man cleared the tavern doorway easily while Martin had to duck to avoid braining himself upon entry; but then he topped out at nearly six and a half feet. He glanced at down, curious about the woman's shoes. Brocade slippers were all she wore. He thought that in heeled court shoes or winter sabots she might stand six feet.

Martin watched the man point at an adolescent boy, flip him a coin, and gesture at the trunk. He lifted the woman's satchel, wrapped her arm around his, and marched down the pier toward the ocean-going vessels preparing for their departures. The boy hoisted the trunk on his back and staggered after them.

Martin watched her leave, feeling as though he had just lost something incredibly important. Resigned to that inevitable reaction—he didn't even meet her, much less know anything about her—he finished his beer, paid his bill, left the tavern, and followed the same path down the pier.

৯৯৶৶

Martin stood on the pier and stared up at the tall masts and lashed sails. All morning he had watched loads of timber, iron ore and copper be loaded into her belly. Now casks of salted cod were being rolled up the plank. The ship had come from London and—after suitable goods were exchanged here—was on her way to America laden with treasures from far-flung lands.

Again Martin felt the thickness in his chest that signaled a cherished idea. *America!* Land of the new. New property. New bridges. New cities. New buildings. His four years at Oxford studying engineering and architecture would open up a multitude of opportunities, not only ancient obligations.

He was running away from those obligations now, and he fully admitted it. That didn't change his need to leave Norway again, and for good this time.

Martin was the second son and the third child born to his mother and father, but he was the first to be born *after* his parents wed. His father, Jarl, made a deathbed promise to his own father to make the legitimate babe heir to Hansen Hall—and all that the esteemed position held.

The problems with that promise were twofold. First, that meant Martin would displace his older brother whom he deeply loved. Throughout his years, Martin had spent enough time with his *Onkel* Brander to know how badly his ascension would wound Gustav, and he had no intention of doing such a thing.

The second problem was that Martin wanted to build things. And the few new buildings being built in Norway all followed traditional styles. Stoic styles which were meant to fend off the winters, not please the eye.

America was young and growing. Martin had letters from several architectural firms offering the possibility of employment. All he needed to do was decide where on the massive continent he wanted to settle. For a man wishing to make his own destiny, America was the obvious answer.

Of course, everyone he knew tried to convince him otherwise. Norsemen were a fiercely loyal lot, and the thought of leaving their ancestral home was akin to treason.

But he rode out of Arendal before dawn on a foggy morning, with one groom beside him on the cart and all his mortal belongings piled in back, and together they made the four-day journey to Christiania. He sent the groom home to Hansen Hall, carrying a letter to Martin's father that explained the reasons his second son had chosen to leave.

And even though Brander Hansen still had a home in Christiania, Martin decided not to visit with him as he passed through. He supposed he was half afraid Brander would try to talk him out of leaving. His uncle could be a persuasive man; even though Brander was deaf, his words held considerable weight. Even so, Martin knew that of all his family, Brander would be the one to understand.

He prayed his father would somehow understand as well. Even if he didn't, Martin would most likely never see him—or any of his family—again.

Martin bowed his head and closed his eyes. He allowed himself to grieve, though only for a moment. He had wrestled long and hard about this decision before coming to the conclusion that the adventure which lay ahead of him was worth the loss. Through his shirt, he fingered the gold chain that held a simple cross. His older sister gave it to him when he sailed for England to learn their language and study at their university in Oxford. Now it would remind him that at least one of his siblings had faith in him. And in his dreams.

God bless you, Liv.

And thank you.

Martin was jostled from his reverie by a heavy bag, which nearly knocked his feet from under him. A gentleman, whom Martin judged to be in his sixties by his slight stoop and long gray hair, strode past him and ignored the abuse caused by his overburdened porter.

"Hurry up, man! I want to get my pick of the cabins before I get lodged in some rabbit's hole!" the old man bellowed.

He was trailed by a plump woman attired in the most outrageous shade of green satin that Martin had ever seen. Her dignity was somewhat saved by a huge, intricately crocheted white shawl which muted the virulent color where it draped the woman's shoulders and abundant curves. She took rapid small steps to keep up with her—husband?

"If I ever marry, my wife will never wear such a ridiculous color!" Martin vowed. Then he snorted at his own declamation. Marriage was highly undesirable at this point in his life. Finding his way on a new continent and in an English colony was enough of a challenge; he had no need for the demands of a woman.

With an evaluative glance at the angle of the sun, he too began to make his way toward the ship.

❧

Dagny tried not to squeeze her fiancé's arm too hard, and thereby betray her nervousness.

She was quite lucky to have caught the eye of a man like Torvald Heimlich. Worldly, darkly handsome, a little bit too adventuresome to be safe but so thrilling in his danger. Living in the convent and attending school there offered no male companionship at all. So when he first approached her, as she shopped for shoes without a chaperone now that she was twenty-five, she couldn't believe he meant to court her.

He bought her a cup of hot chocolate. They talked for almost an hour. And he asked her to meet him again, week after week, in the same place at the same time. And now, eight weeks later, they would be married.

Married. She smiled.

Finally, she would be free of the convent's restraints. Sent there at the age of nine, when her mother died birthing yet another daughter, Dagny had seen little of her four older sisters in the last twenty years. But she never, ever, considered joining the conclave of women who raised her and spent their lives in solemn ritual. All that held her was the inability to figure out how to get away.

Dagny's glance slid sideways, tracing Torvald's aristocratic profile. She sent a silent prayer of thanksgiving because this man offered her a new life. And not just any new life, but one on another continent. America sounded so exotic. The ocean-crossing sounded so exotic. Being married by a ship's captain was so... unconventional. Her adult life, so long delayed, was finally beginning.

Torvald unwrapped her arm from his. "After you, my love," he said waving one hand toward the ship's ramp and resting the other on the small of her back.

With a quick dip of her chin, Dagny lifted her skirt and climbed the wooden plank. At the top, a sailor grabbed her elbow and steadied her as she stepped aboard the large vessel. Dagny tilted her head back and gazed upwards at the masts while Torvald exchanged a few English words with the deckhand.

"This way," he said, taking her arm.

Torvald led her to a steep set of stairs and he descended them first. At the bottom, he turned around and held up his arms. He flashed a mischievous grin. "Come on, then. I'll catch you if you fall."

Dagny responded to the awkward situation with a polite smile while deciding whether to climb down forward or backward. Reaching a decision, she backed down the precarious steps in spite of Torvald's unmuffled laughter. His mirth was less humiliating than falling would have been—and less dangerous to boot.

Still chuckling, he walked down the passage and stopped at one of the cabin doors as she followed. When she stood beside him he pushed it open. "Here we are."

The cabin was about seven feet wide and maybe nine or ten feet long. A built-in bank of deep drawers edged one wall, occupying half the width of the room and ending three feet from the door. A lumpy mattress covered it. Two feet or so above the shelf bed was another, narrower shelf. The two side walls were solid but the outer wall was pierced by a round of thick glass. The lintel, the top twelve inches of the wall above the door, was open to the hallway for ventilation, but barred with turned-wood spindles placed about every four inches.

Dagny turned to Torvald. "Is this my cabin or yours?"

"It's *our* cabin," he said, his voice oddly cocky-sounding. He dropped her satchel on the floor and the hollow sound slammed with its finality. "Did you believe I would pay for two cabins? Even for part of the journey?"

Dagny pressed down her misgivings, certain she had simply missed some part of their plan. "So the captain will marry us today?"

"I doubt he'll have time, my love. Setting sail on such a journey as ours will require his full attention." Torvald leaned against the bed and smiled his sultry smile, the one that made her belly flutter. "But have no fear, Dagny. As soon as he's able, he'll perform the deed."

"And in the meantime?" Her voice sounded irritatingly thin, verging on shrill. Certainly he did not mean for them to share this cabin before they were husband and wife. She was not raised to do so even before she fell under the nuns' unforgiving constitution. Her gaze swept the small space, evaluating its lack of private refuge.

Torvald took her suddenly cold hands in his large, balmy grip. He waited until her eyes met his before he spoke. His voice was warm and thick as soup, and it poured over her.

"Sweetheart, we are betrothed. We are leaving Norway and will spend the next seven weeks together before we land in Boston. Does it truly matter at what point in that journey our vows are spoken?"

"It does to me!" Dagny blurted. Her heart thumped painfully and she shrugged away his heat. This man was supposed to protect her, not place her in a deliberately compromising position. Suddenly her perfect plan revealed a ragged, ugly tear.

Torvald pulled her forward and wrapped his arms around her.

She tucked her face against his neck. He smelt of unfamiliar perfume and she felt his morning's whiskers on her cheek.

"Don't you trust me Dagny?" he murmured.

"Y-yes," she whispered. "I did..."

"And you still can."

"But, I mean, it's just that—well—we cannot share a bed! Not yet!" The fug of her trapped breath warmed her already hot cheeks. She swallowed her tears, determined not to cry in his presence. She had always been such a weakling. Today, of all the days in her life, she needed to try to be strong.

Torvald's soft chuckle shook his chest in staccato breaths. "Are you afraid of me?"

"No!" she huffed. *Well, maybe a little.*

"Are you afraid of making love with me?" he pressed.

"N-no..." *Well, yes.*

"I love you, my darling."

"I know."

"Do you love me?"

"Of course I do! Would I be leaving Norway for any other reason?" she exclaimed. She leaned back and looked into his eyes, searching for assurances. Searching for truth.

"Then stop worrying, darling girl. It's not my intention to cause you harm."

His lips lowered to hers, soft and teasing, pulling away just enough that she chased them with her own. While the nuns had not told her anything about relations with men, Torvald had taught her to kiss. That pastime was so pleasant, she was eager to learn more despite her embarrassment and uncertainty. When he released her from the kiss, she gazed up at him, a tingle growing deep and low inside her and heating her thighs.

She blinked slowly. "I pray he finds the time soon. I do not wish to wait too long for you to be my husband."

"And I have no more desire to wait than you do, my beautiful Dagny," he replied.

Beautiful? Every time he said that, Dagny cringed inside. Since her birth, she had always been the least attractive of the five living Sivertsen sisters.

She was way too tall to begin with. Just two inches short of six feet, she met most men's gaze evenly. Torvald was just a finger's width over six feet, and Dagny found herself slouching when she stood next to him in her heeled boots.

Then there was the question of her bosoms. Though in proportion to her height, they was still much larger than her shorter, older sisters; a fact that the nuns berated her for as if it was a choice on her part to cultivate them. Her common yellow hair was too straight. Her eyes, too pale. Her lips so pink that the nuns always asked if she rouged them, then scrubbed their fingers over them when she said no.

But Dagny wasn't worldly and had no experience by which to judge Torvald's words. Perhaps what he said was true. Perhaps their promises were enough reason to inhabit the space together, until the vows made them husband and wife by law.

But she would not sleep in his bunk, nor allow him to have her, until they were.

On those points she would remain immobile. "Please remind him as soon as you feel it's proper," she whispered, shushing the tiny voice in her head telling her to flee and quickly, before it was too late.

Torvald gave her a condescending look. His voice singed with sarcasm. "Yes, dear."

Dagny's cheeks stretched hot and tight with her feeble smile. Unable to present an alternative, she had just agreed to share the cabin with him. "I suppose we should get settled, then," she said, her tone more of a question than a statement.

"Why don't you do that, sweetheart? You are so much better at these things than I am. I would probably make a mess of it." Torvald glanced at the door. "I'll go explore the lay of the land—or should I say, the ship—while you do so."

Dagny found herself relieved by the thought of a few minutes alone. Her composure was unraveling like loose yarn under a kitten's frantic assault. "Will you come get me when we set sail?"

"Of course!" He kissed her soundly, ending with a loud smack. Flashing a white, toothy smile, he winked one amber-brown eye and closed the door behind him.

Dagny drew a nervous breath and investigated her tiny domain. At the foot of the bed was a small, simple wooden table and chair. A single wall sconce held a small oil lamp, but there was no flint. And no chamber pot.

"I suppose we might carry a lit candle from another part of the ship," she mused. "But how do we—"

Her thoughts were interrupted when the cabin door swung open, pushed by a man she had never seen before. His jaw dropped and he stared at her as if seeing a startling apparition. For a moment, neither one moved.

"Oh! I b-beg your pardon!" His face flushed, making his blue eyes darken in contrast. The first thing Dagny noticed was that the man had to bend over to come through the door. He had to be well over six feet tall. The second thing she noticed was his handsomely sculpted face.

He flashed her a crooked grin and backed out, pulling the door shut; the barrier again stood solidly between them. Only then did Dagny remind herself to breathe.

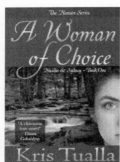

The Hansen Series

A Woman of Choice

Nicolas & Sydney – Book One

"A charming love story!" Diana Gabaldon

Kris Tualla

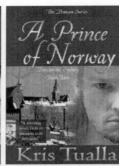

The Hansen Series

A Prince of Norway

Nicolas & Sydney Book Two

A riveting book; rich in passion and intrigue!

Kris Tualla

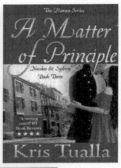

The Hansen Series

A Matter of Principle

Nicolas & Sydney Book Three

A riveting tale!! RT Book Reviews ★★★★

Kris Tualla

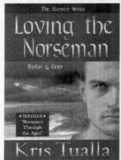

The Hansen Series

Loving the Norseman

Rydar & Grier

★WINNER★ "Romance Through the Ages"

Kris Tualla

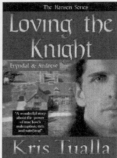

The Hansen Series

Loving the Knight

Eryndal & Andrew Ross

"A wonderful story about the power of true love's redemption; faith and sacrifice!"

Kris Tualla

Desert Breeze Publishing, Inc. Presents

A Discreet Gentleman of Discovery

The Discreet Gentleman Series Book One

Kris Tualla

Desert Breeze Publishing, Inc. Presents

A Discreet Gentleman of Matrimony

The Discreet Gentleman Series Book Two

Kris Tualla

Desert Breeze Publishing, Inc. Presents

A Discreet Gentleman of Consequence

The Discreet Gentleman Series Book Three

Kris Tualla

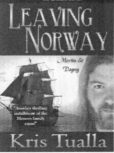

The Hansen Series

LEAVING NORWAY

Martin & Dagny

"Another thrilling installment of the Hansen family saga!"

Kris Tualla

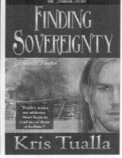

The Hansen Series

FINDING SOVEREIGNTY

Rikhardr Nilsson

"Tualla's stories are addicting. Don't begin to read any of them at bedtime!"

Kris Tualla

Kris Tualla is pursuing her dream of becoming a multi-published author of historical fiction. She started in 2006 with nothing but a nugget of a character in mind and absolutely no idea where to go from there. She has created a dynasty - *The Hansen Series* and its companion series, *A Discreet Gentleman.*

Kris Tualla is an amusing, enthusiastic presenter and available for workshops and speaking engagements. Please contact her at any site listed below.

http://www.KrisTualla.com
http://kristualla.wordpress.com
http://www.facebook.com/KrisTualla
http://www.youtube.com/user/ktualla
http://twitter.com/ktualla

Norway is the New Scotland!

Made in the USA
Charleston, SC
27 January 2013